THE
SPEAKER

RUDY
CAIN

LACEY
DEAVER

Published by
World Video Bible School®
25 Lantana Lane
Maxwell, Texas 78656
www.wvbs.org

ISBN: 978-0-9967003-1-3

Cover art by Aubrie Deaver

Layout by Aubrie Deaver

Cover photo from iStockphoto.com

Serving the Church since 1986

wvbs.org

The Story:
This fictional story was provided to me by my grandfather, Rudy Cain.

May God receive the glory.

Special thanks to:

Orrin Deaver for his work in transcribing the oral story to printed page.

Special thanks to those who proofed this book:

Elizabeth Beall
Loretta Horner
Sharon Cain
Carol Anne Braswell
Lisa Shoptaw

To the American patriot.
Not the "sunshine patriot" who shrinks in the face of adversity, but
the one who won't let fear or seemingly insurmountable obstacles stop
them from rising above, speaking the truth in love, and ultimately
changing the world by doing what they
know to be best for their country.

Lacey Deaver

TABLE OF CONTENTS

CHAPTER 1:

Just north of Miami, under a large sign that pointed toward Orlando and Jacksonville, stood a man. He looked to be in his early thirties, and wore blue jeans, work boots and a white T-shirt. His sandy hair, once combed, was now at the mercy of the warm evening wind. His bright blue eyes were alive and alert, taking in his surroundings with interest. Hoisting a large duffel bag over his shoulder, he stretched out one arm, thumb up as he began to walk slowly along the side of Interstate 95, though none of the passing cars seemed interested in giving the stranger a ride as people made their way home from work in the city.

As the sun was beginning to set, an old white pickup truck suddenly pulled off the interstate onto the shoulder of the road near him. When he saw the pickup stop, the hitchhiker hurried over to the driver's side of the truck.

A weathered Hispanic man, perhaps in his sixties, sat behind the wheel of the pickup. He was accompanied by a woman in the passenger seat. She smiled hesitantly at the young man when he approached the window. Both of them noticed he stopped a few feet from the car.

"Well, young man," the driver said in a gruff but benevolent voice, "where are you going?"

"Hello, sir," the young man answered. "I appreciate you stopping for me. I'm just heading north up toward Jacksonville."

The older couple was impressed by his manner, and the hopeful expression in his eyes made them want to help him. The older man studied him for a moment. The hitchhiker was well built and looked strong. His skin was darkly tanned as though he spent most of his time doing physical labor outdoors. Although he was tall and muscular, he didn't seem intimidating. Perhaps it was the friendly smile on his face. He waited silently through the appraisal, then the old driver waved his hand.

"Hop in the back. I can take you as far as Orlando, if it suits you."

"Oh yes, sir!" the young man's smile grew even wider at his good fortune. "That suits me just fine."

He tossed his bag into the bed of the truck and climbed in after it. The duffel bag made a good backrest against the cab of the pickup. It was a worn old truck and had already seen its best days as a working vehicle, but the hitchhiker wasn't particular about the vehicle. With a contented smile, he leaned back against his duffel bag and gazed up at the sky. He could just see the first stars as dusk fell. The pickup pulled back onto the interstate and merged with the traffic as it continued its journey north.

Across the state in Sarasota, Florida, a large box truck pulled into the parking lot of a business establishment. A large metal building with a sign over the office door said Event and Stage Company. As the old truck came to a stop in front of the building, two men walked out the front door.

The man in front was clearly the elder of the two. Nearly fifty years old, Jack Webb was a seasoned business contractor, very independent and toughened from many years of hard work and an indomitable spirit. His ruffled brown hair was graying at the temples, but otherwise he considered himself to be taking on the years quite well. His thin lips were drawn up in a studious brood, and his arched eyebrows were puckered beneath his tall forehead. The only softness about his face could be seen in his cloudy green eyes, yet those eyes could be as sharp and hard as steel. He was wearing a plaid shirt, dark jeans and heavy boots. His expression was not happy as he advanced toward the old truck that had just driven up.

Behind Jack hurried a husky young man in his early twenties, a tranquil look on his face as if he knew he was alright with the world and the world was alright with him. He was wearing jeans and boots like his boss, but a solid navy T-shirt instead of plaid.

CHAPTER 1:

Jack Webb marched up to the driver's side of the truck before the man inside could get out. The driver quickly spoke through the rolled-down window.

"I know I'm late, boss," he began apologetically, but Jack was not to be appeased so easily.

"Late? Late is twenty minutes! You were supposed to be here four hours ago!" the older man snarled, clearly upset. "I've been calling you for the last three hours, Orville. What's the deal here? What took you so long?"

Orville Glossup climbed out of the truck and stood, chagrined, before his employer.

"I know, I know. But my cell phone went dead and I didn't have my charger in the truck," he said as Jack folded his arms, impatiently awaiting his explanation. "I would have called to tell you, but...no phone."

The feeble attempt Orville made to lighten the mood did not go well with his boss.

"Why weren't you here?" he asked sternly. "Why didn't you get here when you said you would? Three o'clock. That was the time you were supposed to be here. What happened, man?"

"I was on my way, really! My truck stopped running because I blew a radiator hose." Jack threw up his hands and rolled his eyes. Behind him, the younger man snickered, earning a sour look from Orville. "And I had to have it towed to a shop to get a new one put in. They didn't have one, so I had to wait even longer for them to go pick one up. Honest, boss. I got here as quick as I could!"

Jack shook his head in disapproval. His sharp green eyes gave the old truck a once-over, then he rounded on Orville again.

"You told me that you were going to get a new truck for this job, Orville."

"I am–"

"And when exactly is that going to happen? When you break down in the middle of nowhere on another long trip? I can't use junk trucks like this in my line of work," Jack continued.

"I just couldn't swing it with the bank this week," Orville pleaded. "But I'll take care of it next week, I promise."

↑THE SPEAKER

Jack was still frustrated and disappointed that his subcontractor had let him down at such a crucial moment with no time left to do anything but make the best of the circumstances.

"We are so late...we could have been in Jacksonville before midnight. Now it's going to be early morning by the time we get there!" Jack complained. "We better get going right now."

He sighed, took off his hat, and rubbed his head as if he could rub his troubles away. Placing his hat back on his head he turned to the young man beside him.

"You ride with him, Aaron. And you two make sure you get to Jacksonville tonight." he said firmly, pointing a finger at Orville.

Aaron Wright, the young man who had been standing behind Jack, grinning good-naturedly at his fellow employee while Jack was chewing him out, suddenly looked dismayed and began to protest.

"But Jack, I don't want to ride in that old truck!" he cried, despite the warning annoyance in Jack's eyes. "It's hot and there's no AC! And the radio doesn't even work!"

"You get in there," Jack commanded, his tone brooking no further argument. Aaron exhaled grumpily and with slumped shoulders ambled around to the passenger side door. As he reluctantly hopped in beside Orville, Jack put his hands on the window frame and looked in at the two of them.

"I expect you to keep an eye on him," he said to Aaron, nodding toward Orville, who made a face. Aaron softened just a little, accepting the subtle, unspoken respect in return for making him ride in the heat for several hours without air conditioning.

"We have to get there before daylight, so let's get going," Jack continued, slapping the side of the truck as he walked around it and across the parking lot where a similar, but newer box truck waited. On the driver's side door in large letters read Event and Stage Company, with a large American flag painted on the side of the truck. Across the flag, gold letters spelled out 'The American Party'.

Jack got in the new truck, started it up, and pulled out of the parking lot, followed by Orville and Aaron in the other truck. The

4

sun was setting as both trucks left the Event and Stage Company establishment. After driving a few blocks they took the on-ramp onto Interstate 75.

It was late at night when the small white pickup pulled over near a truck stop at the intersection of Interstate 4. As the old pickup came to a halt, the young man lying down in the bed of the truck sat up and rubbed his eyes.

"This is as far as I can take you, amigo!" the old Hispanic driver hollered from inside the truck. The young man looked around, then quickly picked up his duffel bag and jumped over the side of the truck. He walked up to the driver's window, which the old man rolled down.

"You're just south of Orlando," the driver told him. "We go on to Tampa from here."

"This is just fine. Thank you very much sir, I appreciate the ride," the young man thanked him earnestly. The sincerity in his voice impressed the old man so much that he worried about his safety and what would become of him.

"Here now, will you be okay?" the driver asked, and his wife leaned forward to look at the hitchhiker, the same concern on her face. "Do you have a place to stay, somebody you can call to pick you up or anything like that?"

The young man smiled, pulling his duffel bag up onto his shoulder.

"No sir, I don't, but I'll find a hotel when I get into Orlando. I'll be just fine," he said. He seemed so self-assured and confident that the old man and his wife felt better about leaving him. The old driver reached his wrinkled hand through the open window and the hitchhiker gladly shook it. Then he stood back and watched the little white truck pull back onto the interstate and blend into the stream of traffic.

Alone again, the young man shifted the weight of his bag and walked over to the truck stop to freshen up and get something to eat for the road.

When he came out of the convenience restaurant some

minutes later he began walking back across the parking lot in the coolness of the night. He headed back toward the interstate, perhaps to hitch a ride on into Orlando, but a sight on the edge of the parking lot arrested his attention.

Two large box trucks were parked side by side beneath one of the big floodlights that surrounded and lit up the parking lot. One of the trucks was fairly new, but the other looked old and run down. It was the latter truck that had the hood up, and a man had his head inside apparently examining the engine. Two more men stood observing with their backs to the hitchhiker. Seemingly curious, he drew near. As he approached the two trucks he heard the man leaning over the engine saying, "I don't know what's wrong with it, Jack. It just ran out of gas, I guess. My gauge must be broken or something."

One of the men watching folded his arms, clearly frustrated.

"We'll have to push her over to the pump," he said. His voice was gruff and flat. He rubbed his eyes wearily. "I can't believe I have to deal with this," he mumbled to himself.

"Actually Jack, we have a gas can in the back," said the man beside him. "We won't have to push her."

The young hitchhiker came up behind him.

"Excuse me sir, but do you guys need help? I couldn't help but notice you seem to be having some trouble."

All three men turned around at the sound of his voice, the one looking at the engine nearly hitting his head on the raised hood. Three pairs of eyes scrutinized the hitchhiker. He stood calmly under their gazes, waiting for a response whether it be to welcome him or tell him to leave them alone. Jack Webb sized up the young man. He glanced at Orville and Aaron, who shrugged, waiting on his decision.

"If you're a truck mechanic, then yes we do," he said, terse but polite.

"Well, I have done some mechanical work in my day," the young man answered with a small smile. He accepted Jack's answer as permission to assist, and setting down his duffel bag, he approached the truck. Orville stepped back from the hood to let him look in.

"I just ran out of gas when I shouldn't have," he protested, stealing a guilty look at Jack, who rolled his eyes. "My gauge said I still had a quarter of a tank left. But I guess it's not working..."

His voice trailed away as the hitchhiker, after examining under the hood for a few seconds, brought his head back up and turned to Jack.

"Do any of you have a flashlight?" he asked. Jack started to respond but was interrupted by Orville.

"Yeah, I got one in the back," he said nonchalantly. Immediately both Jack and Aaron turned to stare at him.

"Dude," said Aaron, lifting his hands in disbelief. Jack ground his teeth.

"Why on earth didn't you say something before, Orville?" he exclaimed angrily. "We've been standing around here, already behind schedule, and you just now find it convenient to remember you have a flashlight that would speed the process of getting your junky truck fixed? Boy, I oughta..."

"Look, I'm sorry, Jack, OK? I stuck it in the back because I didn't think we were going to need it on this trip and I just now remembered. Besides, we're under those big lights–"

"Go get the flashlight, Orville," said Jack, who looked like he was about to slap him. Orville obediently went and retrieved the flashlight, swatting at Aaron in passing when the younger man made a face at him.

Orville brought the flashlight to the hitchhiker. The young stranger knelt down and looked up underneath the truck. He then climbed onto the front bumper to check the engine area again, holding the flashlight aloft and peering into the mouth of the truck. He spent a couple of minutes moving and working a few things, making a thorough examination. With the aid of the flashlight, he reached down with one hand as though he was testing something. A second later he brought his hand to his face, smelling his fingers.

All this time Jack Webb stood with his arms folded and a brooding expression on his face as he thought of how much time this beat-up vehicle was costing him. He looked one time at his watch, but that raised his blood pressure enough so he decided not to check the clock again until he was back on the road. Orville and Aaron lounged against the side of the truck, talking softly about nothing important. Up on the highway cars sped by, their headlights brightening the dark night.

If we ever do get back on the road tonight we won't be there til 3 a.m. at least, Jack thought glumly. I should have made Orville take a different truck. I should have known we would have more problems with it... He was roused from his frustrated thoughts when the young man spoke again.

"You have a gas leak between the gas tank and the pump," he reported in a professional voice. "The nut is loose. And looking at the radiator hose, have you changed it recently?" he asked. Jack looked pointedly at Orville, who said defensively, "Yes, I had to have a new radiator hose put in earlier today."

"Well," the young hitchhiker hopped down off the front bumper of the truck. "Apparently when they put in the new radiator hose they didn't tighten the gas line back down. It's going to be a real problem unless it's fixed as soon as possible."

Jack groaned. He didn't have time for this. He was late enough as it was.

"Do you have any tools?" the young stranger asked.

The others looked at him in surprise. "Why? Can you fix it?" Orville asked.

The young man smiled. "I think I can if I have some tools to work with."

Jack cocked his head, studying the young man. Maybe he could help them after all and get them off to a quicker start than he was anticipating. He told Aaron to get the tool box from the back of the truck, and the stranger selected a crescent wrench to tighten the loose nut. While he worked, Jack watched him, assessing.

Under the lights of the parking lot, Jack could see the young man had a handsome face, with a very light olive skin tone that made him think perhaps the young man had come from Cuba. But his slight British accent was throwing Jack off. He couldn't quite pin that accent down, and the confusion annoyed him.

After a few more minutes of tinkering, the hitchhiker stepped back from the mouth of truck, his expression satisfied.

"Alright, I think she's okay now," he announced, setting the wrench back in the tool box. "You should put some gas in her and give her a try while I make sure it's good and tight."

Jack told Orville, "Get your gas can and put some in the truck and test it out. Aaron, give him a hand, son."

Aaron picked up the empty five-gallon gas can from the back of the truck and followed Orville to the nearest pump. Jack rubbed the back of his neck, trying not to let his irritation at the inconvenience get the better of him.

"I never should have started on a big project like this with such an old truck," he sighed, more to himself than to anyone else. He turned to the young stranger, who had gone to stand beside his duffel bag. When he saw Jack looking at him, the young man smiled easily.

"Don't worry, sir. I won't go anywhere until we're sure your truck is working." Jack felt his face relax into a slow smile. Then he saw how the young man kept glancing toward the road, almost as if he was expecting someone. A thought occurred to Jack.

"Hey. Are you looking for a ride?" he asked. The young man turned back to him.

"Yes sir, I sure am," he said politely. Jack was impressed with his manners.

"Where are you headed?" he inquired. The idea was forming in his mind that since the young man had so willingly agreed to help him, perhaps he could do something for him in return.

"Well, I was going into Orlando to get a room for tonight, but I'm actually heading on to Jacksonville," the stranger replied. In spite of his reservations, Jack was intrigued by the fellow, enough that he was prompted to do something he had never done before and offer a lift to a total stranger.

"We can drop you off in Orlando, or you could even ride all the way to Jacksonville with us," he offered. The young man smiled gratefully.

"That would be just great, sir. This way I won't have to get another ride tomorrow," he accepted happily. His enthusiasm made Jack smile again, and reminded him a little of Aaron.

Just then, Orville and Aaron returned lugging the gas can. Orville put some fuel into the gas tank and hopped into the truck. The young stranger looked at the fitting once more to make sure it wasn't leaking.

"Everything looks good," he called, closing the hood of the truck. Orville nodded from the driver's seat.

"I'm going to see if she starts!" he called out, and everyone else involuntarily stepped back. It took a few tries, but at last the gasoline reached the engine, and the truck roared back to life. Jack, Aaron and the stranger all whooped and cheered in approval. Then Jack began barking out commands.

"Aaron, get this fellow's bag and put it in the back of the truck," he ordered, his voice rough but also paternal, and he slapped the young man lightly on the back as he walked past him. The hitchhiker picked up his duffel and followed Aaron to the back of the old truck. When Aaron opened the back doors he indicated for the stranger to toss his bag inside. As the two young men walked back over to where Jack and Orville were conversing in front of the hood of the truck, Jack beckoned to them all to follow him. He began walking toward the truck stop convenience store, calling over his shoulder, "All three of you, come on. I'm buying everybody coffee to stay awake."

Returning to the trucks with coffee in hand, Jack told Orville to pull over by the pumps and fill up while he and the young hitchhiker went on ahead of them.

"We're way behind now, guys. We were supposed to be in Jacksonville hours ago. We'll meet you guys at the rest stop just south of Jacksonville, okay?" said Jack, sipping his coffee. He turned to Aaron and again gave him the responsibility of watching over Orville, even though Aaron was the younger of the two by several years.

"I want you to call me if you have any problems," Jack told them seriously. He worried that even though one of the old truck's issues had been dealt with, there might be more to come before they reached Jacksonville. "But mostly what I need you to do," he added to Aaron alone, "is to keep your eye on Orville and make sure he doesn't doze off."

"Hey, I have my coffee and I'm wide awake," Orville protested. "Why does everyone have to pick on me all the time?"

"Dude, it's not you, it's your truck we're worried about here!" Aaron teased him.

Jack and Aaron laughed while Orville rolled his eyes in annoyance, but then Jack's mood grew serious again.

"I'll be just ahead of you two, so again, call me if there are any difficulties. Got it?"

"Yes, boss," they chorused. Jack nodded and walked over to his truck.

"And Orville!" he called loudly, "We better not have any more problems out of that truck of yours!"

Orville saluted theatrically, and Jack cracked a smile. He turned to the young stranger, who was standing near with his coffee in hand, watching the exchange between Jack and his men. Jack felt suddenly in a hurry to be on the road again.

"Get in and we'll get going," he told the young man, who hurried over and jumped in on the passenger side. As the stranger was walking around the truck to get in, Jack opened his door to double check that his .357 magnum revolver was still sitting in the door pocket just in case there was any trouble. Jack was a careful man, and his usual rule was no hitchhikers. He was surprised at himself for letting this young man ride with him, but he just had an inexplicable feeling about him.

They waved as they passed Aaron and Orville on their way back to the main highway. As they came on to Interstate 4, Jack noted the clock on the dash said a quarter to twelve. Another three-and-a-half hours to Jacksonville, he thought ruefully. His brain rebelled in exhaustion against the idea of arriving at their destination at 3 a.m. But it couldn't be helped.

Back at the truck stop, Orville finished filling up the gas tank in the old truck. After he paid for it he told Aaron, "I'm going inside the convenience store and getting another big gas can. I don't want to risk running out again on this trip."

Aaron helped him fill up the new five-gallon gas can when Orville brought it out, and they set it in the back with the other one, so now they had ten extra gallons. When he lifted the full, new can into the back, Aaron shifted the hitchhiker's duffel bag over to make room for the fuel containers. Soon Aaron and Orville were headed out of the truck stop, back on to the interstate in the direction of Jacksonville.

Three minutes into driving down the road with his new passenger in tow, Jack realized he didn't even know the young man's name. He chuckled at his forgetfulness of introductions, and the stranger looked at him quizzically.

"Hey man, I'm sorry, but I just realized I didn't catch your name," he said, shaking his head. The young man smiled warmly.

"My name is David Connally," he answered cheerfully, and Jack stuck out his hand for a firm handshake without taking his eyes off the road. "Jack Webb," he said in return.

"So, David," Jack said after they had ridden along for a few more minutes in silence, "what's in Jacksonville for you? Do you live up there?"

He looked ahead at the road as he spoke. Out of his peripheral vision he saw David taking a long swallow of coffee before answering.

"No, I don't live there," he answered. Jack glanced over at him. The young man was holding his coffee in both hands and looking serenely out the window into the night. He didn't seem to be offering any further explanation, so Jack tried again.

"Well, where are you headed from there, then?" he asked pointedly. David turned his head this time to look at Jack.

"To see America," he said simply. Jack's eyes widened in surprise.

"Uh, where do you think you are now?" he said, trying to hold back a snort of laughter. David smiled at this response but again offered no answer.

"Where are you from, since you're not from Jacksonville?"

Jack inquired. Once again, there was a moment of silence, a moment of guarded hesitation, before David answered.

"No place from around here," he said finally. Jack stared at him thoughtfully for as long as he dared take his eyes off the road in front of him. The cryptic answers the young man gave him seemed to say that clearly, David was not interested in talking about himself. Jack wondered why.

Maybe he's been in prison, and just doesn't want to talk about it, he thought. Jack could live with that. He was laid back and easy-going most of the time, and if this man had done time for something in the past and didn't want to bring it up, that was fine with Jack. He saw the young man's face had closed as though he was retreating into an invisible shell, and Jack needed somebody to talk to so he would stay awake. He quickly changed the subject again.

"David, you awake over there?"

David turned his head at the unexpected question. "Yes sir," he said, a bit curious. "I slept a couple of hours on my last ride, so uh, yes I'm wide awake, Jack."

"Okay, well here's the deal. I've been awake all day and all night, and we have three hours before we get to where we're going," Jack told him. "You're going to have to keep me awake."

"I'll do my best," David said, his cheerful demeanor quick to return.

Jack reached over and fiddled with the radio, trying to tune into a station that wasn't overrun with static or soothing classical music that would put him to sleep in five minutes.

"What kind of music do you like?" he asked David. The young man smiled to himself, saying, "Oh, whatever you like is fine with me, sir, if it keeps you awake. I'm just along for the ride." He took another drink of coffee. As he did, he raised his eyes and noticed for the first time a small photograph clipped to the windshield visor above Jack's head. David's eyes squinted in the dark cab interior as he kept looking up at the picture under the pretense of taking a long sip of coffee. In the dim light he could see the single individual in the photograph was a young man with dark hair about his own age dressed in a military uniform and standing beside a fighter plane.

Jack glanced over and saw David staring upwards. Following the young man's gaze, Jack looked up and his eyes rested on the picture on his visor.

"Oh, yes, that's my son, Ryan," Jack remarked fondly. "He's a pilot. Got into the Air Force about five years ago."

"You must be very proud of him," said David.

"I am, I am," Jack said, looking back up at the picture for a moment. "Ryan's a good kid. One of the most soft-hearted guys you'd ever meet. A fiery patriot, too. That's why he enlisted. He told me he couldn't stand by and do nothing when so many others were helping protect our country."

David looked at the picture of Ryan Webb again. The young man in the photo wore a confident smile.

"I guess you don't get to see him much, since he's in the Air Force?"

Jack took a drink of coffee before answering.

"Eh, no, not as much as I would like."

Jack kept tuning through the radio stations, seeming suddenly reluctant to say any more about his son. He finally settled on country and turned the volume up slightly.

"You like George Strait?" he asked his companion. David grinned apologetically, saying he had never heard of the singer. Jack actually twisted in his seat to stare at David for two seconds before looking back at the road.

"Never heard of George Strait? He's the king of country music! Everybody down south knows who he is! And not the kind of trashy stuff they label as country today. Nah. George only performs real, pure country music, and on top of that, he's from Texas! I can't believe you haven't heard his songs!"

"Sorry," David laughed. "You make him out to be pretty great, though. I wouldn't mind hearing his music if he's as good as you say."

"The best," Jack retorted emphatically, and he turned up the volume a few more notches. Then the two men lapsed into silence.

Jack was the first to break the quiet. "So where are you really headed?" he demanded. If David wasn't going to tell him where he came from he could at least mention where he was going. He hoped David wouldn't hesitate to answer and to his relief the young man didn't.

"I'm just going to see America," he repeated tranquilly. Jack chuckled.

"What do you mean 'see America'?" he asked.

"I just wanted to take off a year, travel around the country, seeing the sights of America, and learning what I can learn from her. I've never really had the opportunity to travel much before."

Yep, definitely an ex-convict, thought Jack, now slightly amused by David's enigmatic manner.

"Well, I've traveled all over America, and it's the greatest nation on earth. I hope you get to see it all." Jack said with a yawn that he thought would surely dislocate his jaw. "I just need to stay awake for the rest of this trip. And we're going to Jacksonville, so if you're keen on seeing America you'll get to see that much of her at least."

"Thanks, that will suit me just fine," David said.

Jack looked over at the young man again, wondering about him and wishing he would explain more about himself. But Jack wasn't about to push him.

"Let me ask you a question now," David said with sudden boldness, making Jack realize he had played the part of the interrogator for the majority of the conversation. He smiled and gestured for the young man to go ahead.

"I noticed on the side of your truck it has a big painted sign saying The American Party with a giant flag. What's that all about?"

Jack shifted his weight in the seat and keeping one hand on the wheel, rested his free arm along the car door. "Well, it's a new organization, or movement if you will, that's moving across the country as another effort to change the political direction of America," he answered.

Appearing interested, David pressed him for more information. "Is it some kind of new political party?" he asked.

"Not exactly..." Jack wracked his already tired brain to think

15

of an adequate way to describe the movement. "The American Party wants to make changes, but they're working within the two parties we presently have. So basically, any political candidate that agrees with and meets their criteria for a seat in government, they will promote, whether the candidate be a Democrat or a Republican." David watched him attentively, waiting, wanting to know more. "They're all about standing for America's foundational principles regardless of the party you belong to," Jack continued. A thoughtful expression spread over his face.

"I believe their true desire is to see this country move back in the direction of what the Founding Fathers envisioned for us in the beginning," he said. "Small government that answers to the people. A genuine respect for the Constitution, putting the people above the agendas of the politicians, you know. That kind of thing."

David sat silently, taking in the information about the organization. His display of genuine curiosity in the political movement surprised Jack. He had not expected that.

"Wow," said David. "That's really very interesting. A unique organization." He bit his lower lip in thought. "How are they doing?"

"Well, our presidential election will be held this coming November," Jack replied, stifling a yawn. "So they will be doing all they can to promote the right candidates to help them get elected this Fall."

"So...is this your party?" David questioned.

Jack chuckled. "No, no, no. My humble part in all of this is my company has a contract with these people to set up staging and audio for their rallies."

"Are you only doing it in Florida?"

"Well, my company's office is in Sarasota, and Jacksonville is our first stop. But after that we will go all over the United States, wherever they ask us to set up for a rally," Jack said, turning on his blinker to take the exit ramp off Interstate 4 and turn onto 95 North toward Jacksonville.

"We're just starting out today," he went on. "Our first one for the year will be in Jacksonville tomorrow. I mean today," he amended, glancing at the dashboard clock, which read one-thirty.

"After that we'll zig-zag across the country setting up for rallies two or three times a week in various places."

"I carry all the staging equipment. The American Party gave me an advance so I could buy this truck and I put their sign on it during the campaign season. My sound guy is carrying all our audio equipment in the other truck that you worked on."

And a beat up piece of junk it is too, he thought in annoyance as he called to mind Orville's declining vehicle. Jack shook his head.

"We should have been in Jacksonville already, but Orville's truck had mechanical problems earlier today so we got started late," he remarked to David. "And then there's all this baloney about the gas gauge not working and running out of gas. It's gonna be daylight before we get there."

A light rain began to fall. Perfect, Jack complained to himself, turning on his windshield wipers. Just what I need right now.

At the mention of the second truck, David asked about the other two men.

"Oh, well, the younger guy is Aaron Wright. He's been working for me personally for a few years now," Jack's voice grew warmer as he spoke of his young assistant. "I knew his parents before his dad died of cancer. His mother is in the nursing home. I sort of took him in and gave him work after an accident blinded his right eye and kept him from joining the military or anything like that. He helps me with loading and unloading, and setting up and breaking down stage equipment. He was having trouble finding other work, so he was pretty happy when I offered him a job."

"He seems like a nice guy," David said, touched by the fatherly tone in Jack's voice when he talked about Aaron.

"Yeah, he's a good kid," Jack agreed, peering ahead through the rain on the windshield.

"Oh, and Orville, now..." Jack shook his head with a sigh of exasperation. "Orville's been under my employment for a few years now. He's my audio guy. He sets up the speaker system at the rallies so the crowds can hear the candidates. Orville operates the sound boards and amplifiers, wires up the microphones, you name it. He's really good at what he does, but he's not always dependable like I need him to be." Jack frowned. "Sometimes he frustrates me to no end, but he gets his work done. He's supposed to travel with us throughout the year, but then, he was also supposed to get a new truck and that didn't happen," he muttered to himself.

"So Jack, how did you get into this stage business?"

"I worked twenty years for the Barnum and Bailey Circus that winters here in Florida," Jack answered proudly, and sat up straighter. "Of course, when you're in the circus business it's always set up and tear down, set up and tear down. And that's what I did for almost half my life, working with the big tops when they were still putting up tents. Even after they moved indoors we were still putting up and taking down. When I finally quit that job about twelve years ago, I started my own business setting up for events, rallies, stages, etc. all around central Florida. But now we're branching out a lot more with this contract with The American Party."

"So, are Aaron and Orville your only two guys or...?"

"Oh no, I have a whole crew in my employ, don't you worry," Jack gestured with his coffee toward David. "They'll be coming along behind us day after tomorrow. Or today, I guess I should say."

David nodded. Sleep was tugging at both men, but as the truck continued down the lonely highway, the coffee, country music and casual conversation kept them awake.

⌠ CHAPTER 2:

At 4:30 a.m., traffic was light and the rain had finally ceased. Jack exited off the highway to a roadside park just south of Jacksonville to wait for the other truck to show up. Jack and David got out of the truck, threw away their trash and stretched their tired muscles. David walked around with his hands behind his head, whistling a tune unfamiliar to Jack. Jack listened for a minute, inhaling the fresh scent of rain-washed air. He kept glancing back down the road and then at the cell phone in his hand. It had been silent for the past couple of hours.

Jack tried dialing both Aaron and Orville, but there was no answer to either call. "Come on, Orville, where are you?" he muttered, pacing back and forth in agitation. He looked up to see David looking at him. "They should have been right behind us," Jack said, looking at his watch. The minutes ticked by. At 5:20 there was still no sign of the second truck. By this time Jack was very irritated and concerned, not to mention mad.

"They couldn't have passed us. I wonder if I should go back and look for them. Maybe they had another problem with the truck and had to stop again. I told them to let me know if anything happened," he said in frustration. He walked around the truck, back and forth, passing David who had sat down on the running board. He couldn't go anywhere; his bag was in the other truck with Orville and Aaron.

Jack rubbed the back of his neck. Worry gnawed at his mind. He raised a hand in the air, made a fist, and then his hand dropped to his side.

"When I get hold of that Orville," he said through gritted teeth.

19

"I bet they're fine, Jack," David tried to soothe the frustrated businessman. "Maybe they stopped to get something to eat."

"I hope you're right." Jack walked over to David and leaned against the side of the truck. "I can't risk being any more late than I am already. I wonder where they are."

At 5:30 Jack's cell phone rang. He flipped it open and held it up to his ear, turning slightly away from David.

"Jack Webb here. The state police?" Jack turned and stared at David, his eyes wide and suspicious. David stood up. Jack tried to keep his voice calm as he spoke into the phone, "Yes, go ahead."

There was a moment of silence.

"A fire?" Jack cried out so suddenly that David jumped. "Destroyed the whole truck? How did that happen?"

David stared at him.

"Where was the accident?" Jack demanded. "Were they hurt? What hospital are they at? But they're both okay, as far as injuries go?" Jack listened a few moments more, then his voice grew hard. "Thank you for letting me know."

Jack slid the cell phone down from his ear. It was clenched so tightly in his hand that his knuckles turned white. For a moment, David was afraid Jack was about to start yelling. His mouth opened in a fury as if to release a flood of irate words, but he managed to get control of himself. He looked over at David as if he couldn't believe himself what he was about to tell him.

"Orville's truck ran off the road and hit a bridge post," he said dully, shaking his head. "The truck flipped over several times and caught fire. Within seconds the whole thing was completely engulfed in flames."

David caught his breath in horror. Jack pressed a hand against the side of his truck and leaned against it, the other hand on his hip as he replayed his conversation with the police in his mind.

"The police said, 'It was like they had extra gasoline stored in the truck,'" Jack laughed softly, but there was no humor in it. "Of course, I was the one who ordered them to have extra gas on hand so they wouldn't run out again. They said the truck blew up in one big fireball and the whole thing is like a burned-out shell."

"Luckily for my men, a number of passing cars stopped and people pulled them out before they were burned," Jack said without expression, though inwardly he couldn't have been more relieved. "I need to call the hospital the police gave me the name of so I can see how they're doing."

He dialed the number for the Daytona Beach Hospital and asked for information regarding two men involved in a fiery truck crash early that morning. He had to wait a few minutes, during which time he resumed pacing back and forth beside the truck while David opened one of the truck doors and perched sideways on the passenger seat. Jack didn't notice how distraught David looked.

Jack supposed it could have been worse. He learned Orville had a badly broken right ankle and very badly broken left leg, and that he was not likely to be walking again for some months with breaks that severe. Aaron was better off than his coworker. He had been knocked out, but after checking him over the doctors thought he was alright except for a bad concussion which would keep him in the hospital for twenty-four hours. The nurse told Jack that Aaron should be released tomorrow afternoon. Jack thanked her and gave her the number to reach him by if they needed to contact him or if anything changed with the conditions of his men.

Closing his phone with a snap, Jack stood silently for a moment. Then he walked slowly, aimlessly over to a nearby picnic table and sat down on the edge of the nearest bench. Leaning his elbows on his knees, Jack put his head in his hands and moaned softly.

"Those guys could have been killed! What am I going to do now?" He rubbed his face dejectedly.

David, seeing his distress, walked slowly over to Jack and sat down next to him, saying nothing. When Jack looked up at David, he detected the concern in the young man's bright blue eyes. Jack had been of help to David. He was his friend now.

"Can I help you, Jack?" he asked kindly, putting a hand on Jack's bowed shoulder. "Can anything be done?"

Jack looked up, but instead of looking at David he stared ahead at nothing, his eyes glassy.

"I've got to be in Jacksonville, setting up and getting ready for The American Party and have everything ready to go by two o'clock today," he mumbled into the morning air. "And now I have no sound man or sound equipment, and no help. My other guys won't get here 'til tomorrow morning..."

David sighed and looked skyward for a moment. Then his eyes widened, and he looked back at Jack.

"I can help," he suggested, his cheerfulness returning in his eagerness to be of help to Jack in a hard spot. Jack turned to look at him. "What?"

"I can certainly help you get set up, but I don't know what to do about the audio equipment. Can we rent or buy some in the city?" David asked, taking charge of the bad situation. Jack shook his head wearily.

"I don't know. I don't know," he mumbled, rubbing his chin. David could easily see Jack was not himself and tried to help him think.

"Why don't we go into town," David told him slowly, "find a phone book and see if someone is renting or selling stage sound gear?"

"Well," Jack said, bringing his head up and folding his arms, "renting it is one thing, but setting it up and operating it properly for this rally is another. I don't know where I'll find a sound man. I'm really between a rock and a hard place."

"I can do that for you," David offered.

Jack stared at him, puzzled. "You can? How do you know how?"

David gave Jack a smile. "Trust me. I can do it with no problem. Let me help you get this done."

Jack studied the young man curiously. Why would David offer to help him, somebody he barely knew, when he could just head on his way without having to worry over what had happened?

But Jack was desperate. Only hours stood between him and The American Party rally in Jacksonville, and he was alone unless he let David show him what he could do.

"You sure you think you can do it?" he demanded.

David nodded.

"Okay then." Jack stood up heavily and jammed his cell phone back in his jeans pocket. He started back toward the truck. "Let's get to town and see if we can find some audio equipment." Jack stopped, looking upward. "Oh great. Just what we need. More rain. Hey, do you have a jacket you can use in that bag of yours...?"

David stopped walking.

"My bag was in the other truck," he said quietly.

Ahead of him, Jack stopped walking. He closed his eyes and exhaled sharply. Slowly he turned to face David, who stood behind him with a sad half-smile. Jack had not known.

"But I thought I told Aaron to put your bag in my truck. Why did he...oh, perfect."

Jack didn't know what to say. Since David was a hitchhiker, Jack knew he must have had most of his personal possessions in that duffel bag. Now it was all lost, gone up in flames. Jack felt terrible, and personally responsible for David's loss. Determined to make it up to the young man, Jack walked up to him and put a rough hand on his shoulder. David looked up at him.

"David, I'm sorry. And I'll tell you this, if you help me out today, I'll do what I can to help you restore what you lost as much as I can so you can go on your way," Jack said sincerely. "But the thing is, I can't get my hands on any cash until after the rally. So let's help each other out today, okay?"

David thought about it for a moment, then nodded in agreement. Jack smiled, relieved. He clapped David on the shoulder and the two men got back into the truck and drove away under the newly-falling rain.

As Jack and David entered Jacksonville, they followed the directions they found in a phone book ad, which led them to the J-Mar Audio/Visual Equipment Rental and Supply establishment. As Jack parked the truck and the two men walked across the parking lot, Jack glanced sideways at David.

"I hope this is your lucky day," he said warily. "Because this is the only place in town, and they better have some equipment available for us to buy, rent or steal."

The corners of David's mouth tipped up just a little. "Oh, I think they will." He pulled open the front door and gestured for Jack to walk on in.

A short, thin man with glasses that Jack privately thought were almost bigger than his head led them to the sales and rental department, showing them all the equipment that was on hand to rent or sell. Jack considered what was needed for his rally setup while David examined the audio systems and sound speakers. He conferred with Jack when he was satisfied.

"This is good equipment, Jack. It's just what we need. I know how to set it up and operate it," he promised. Jack added up the cost in his head. The resulting figure made him bite his lip, but he knew he was stuck under the circumstances. There was no use worrying over it.

At least I'll be compensated, he thought as he and David made the deal.

Leaving J-Mar's business, they traveled through the city and arrived at a spacious park. Jack stopped the truck and consulted his map, studying it with a frown of concentration.

"Yes...yes, I think this is it. Yep." He stuffed the map back in the glove compartment, opened his door, and stepped out. David followed suit and the two men stood looking at the open area of the tree-enclosed park. It was situated in one of the busiest parts of Jacksonville, so as to draw a bigger crowd, Jack guessed.

He began looking around, as though waiting for someone. He saw David looking at him. "This is where I'm supposed to meet Michael Farris, at nine o'clock," he explained. "He'll have all the permits. We can't unload and set up without a permit from the city." He checked his watch. "We have a few minutes."

Jack walked over and folding his arms, leaned back against the side of the truck. David joined him, bracing himself with one foot against the truck while he rested his body against it.

"Does this Michael Farris work for you?" David asked. Jack shook his head.

"Oh, no. He's the manager in charge of organizing the rallies.

Farris is the one in charge of getting the permits for us to set up at each location he's found for us. I work for him," he replied with a short laugh. Checking his watch again, Jack paced a few steps, his rough hands on his hips as he glanced up and down the road.

"Nine o'clock." he muttered impatiently.

He had hardly finished speaking when a shiny silver Lexus pulled up beside Jack's truck. As David and Jack turned, the driver's door opened. A man stepped out, took off a pair of sunglasses and walked toward them.

It was easy to see this newcomer was somebody in charge. His demeanor and bearing spoke authority before he opened his mouth. He was a well-built man, not very tall, but what he lacked in height he made up for in responsibility. His light brown hair, which was somewhat receding, was parted down the side and gelled to stiff perfection under a Stetson hat. He wore a brown leather jacket, slacks and a white button-down polo shirt. As he walked, his black boots thumped smartly on the hard ground. He walked purposefully, as if he were on a mission. The first thing David noticed about this man was the cool but friendly smile that made deep creases in his handsome, tanned face. He had a cleft in his chin, and his eyes were a warm amber. He looked to be in his late thirties.

David and Jack waited until the man was a few steps from them, then Jack walked forward to meet him, David beside him.

Jack stretched out his hand.

"Michael Farris," Jack had a familiar grin on his face.

The man nodded and gripped Jack's hand firmly with an equal smile. "Jack Webb, it's always great to see you."

The man's voice was melodious and soothing, putting the hearer at ease with him. It wasn't low-pitched, but his voice drew one's trust like a magnet. He radiated confidence, but was not at all condescending.

"Same to you, Michael," Jack responded, and released the manager's hand. "And this is David...?" He hesitated, suddenly drawing a blank on the young man's last name.

"David Connally, sir," David stepped forward to shake hands. Mr. Farris nodded to him and said it was nice to meet him.

"Well, Mr. Webb, are you all ready to set up today?" he asked, turning to Jack.

"Yes sir, Mr. Farris," Jack said. "Did you get us a permit?"

"I did," Mr. Farris answered with a smile, reaching into an inside pocket in his leather jacket. He pulled out a folded paper and handed it to Jack. "Here it is. I got it a couple of days ago. Be sure to place it where any police can see it if they chance to come by."

Jack unfolded the thick document and studied it briefly.

"If any of them come by and see you setting up, we want them to see we have a permit to do so," Mr. Farris finished.

"Will do," Jack said. "Now, do you and I need to go see about placement settings?"

"Absolutely."

While David waited by the truck, Jack and the American Party manager began walking around in the park, pointing out different areas where they could locate the rally. They needed a place for the crowd, the stage, and all the audio and sound equipment that went along with it. Jack stood at one end of the park while Mr. Farris stood in the center, trying to size up the approximate dimensions for the rally. David watched them in the distance until Jack and Michael Farris came back toward the truck. As they approached, Mr. Farris suddenly stopped, his mouth drawn up in a puzzled expression.

"Jack, I may be mistaken, but I thought you had two trucks."

"Oh, well..." Jack glanced at David. "About that..."

Jack explained the accident of the other truck to Mr. Farris. The rally manager folded his arms, concerned. "Were your men hurt?"

"One of them has broken bones in both legs, while the other man has a concussion. But he should be out of the hospital tomorrow," he finished.

"So you lost your sound man and you don't have any of your audio equipment with you."

"Well, no. But we rented some here in town, and David here says he can set it all up and operate it," Jack amended, though little doubts began nagging in his mind. He could feel his confidence starting to evaporate at the dubious look on the manager's face.

CHAPTER 2:

Mr. Farris shook his head. Taking a deep breath, he asked, "Will you be able to handle this, Jack? Without your men and using only rented sound equipment you aren't familiar with? We have almost a year's work ahead of us till election day."

"Everything is going to be done right, Mike, don't worry," Jack quickly assured him. "I've contacted my insurance company and they are going to cover the purchase of new sound equipment that we will pick up tonight or tomorrow."

Mr. Farris remained motionless, his eyes doubtful.

"And more of my men will be on their way tonight. They should arrive tomorrow morning, and then we won't want for working hands. I can promise you that we will be ready at the next stop," Jack held his hands up in a final gesture of compliance.

Still dubious, Mr. Farris uncrossed his arms and straightened his jacket. "Jack, we're counting on you, now. You need to be in Macon, Georgia in three days."

"No problem. We're going to get new equipment and another truck, and we'll be there to meet you," Jack promised quickly.

Mr. Farris lowered his head and studied Jack from beneath his eyebrows. "As planned."

"As planned," Jack agreed.

"Alright, then," Mr. Farris said, finally persuaded Jack could do the job as promised. "I will email you the directions and location information for next week's rally. I have to head out today right after the rally and I'll let you know where to meet us."

"Well then, we need to get to work," Jack said briskly. He checked his watch again and his eyes widened. Frustration flickered in his eyes, and Mr. Farris saw it.

"Yes, you two better start setting up ASAP," he agreed. "I'll get out of your hair now, but I'll be back around twelve thirty."

"Great," Jack said simply, and he and Mr. Farris shook hands once more. Then after offering his hand to David, Mr. Farris went back to his car and drove away. Jack didn't stop to watch. He had barely released the party manager's hand before turning to start unloading his truck. David hurried to be of assistance.

"We have only a few hours to get all this unloaded and set up correctly," Jack said. His words came out jerkily as he lifted a heavy box with staging equipment in it to David, who was standing on the ground at the open end of the truck. David took the box from Jack and set it down beside the truck.

"Plenty of time, then," David said, his eyes twinkling. Jack grunted in response.

When they had emptied the truck of everything they needed to set up, Jack and David carried all of the equipment over to the designated spot for the stage. As he put down the last box, Jack turned to David.

"I need to go back and pick up the audio equipment. If you'll stay here and keep an eye on things, I'll just be a few," he said. David agreed to wait, and soon he found himself alone in the park, watching Jack drive away. While waiting for Jack, he began rifling through some of the stage equipment.

Jack returned with the sound system, and the two men began setting up the stage and speakers. David was mostly occupied with unwinding and connecting the many different coils of wire that plugged into the microphone and audio set, while Jack worked on the stage. The men didn't talk much while they worked, but the silence was companionable and suited them both. Occasionally David would hum or sing a snatch of song under his breath, while Jack whistled along with him or to a tune of his own. The time passed by easily.

After a while, David glanced up at Jack, who was rolling out lighting cables. David looked down at the pliers in his hand, then back at his new employer.

"Hey Jack," he called.

"Yeah?"

"Are you very familiar with any of the candidates The American Party is endorsing?" David asked.

Jack stopped working and supported his weight against a chair with his hand resting on the back of it, his eyes turned upwards as he thought for a few seconds.

"I can't say I am, David," he replied, his brow wrinkled. "The party doesn't fill me in on all the details, they just need me to set up the rallies for them, though Michael Farris does bring me in the know from time to time, because he and I go back a way. I do know the name of one man, Joseph Cane, because he ran for Senate and won a few years ago. To my understanding he is a very conservative man."

"Do you think he'll be here today?" David asked.

"I don't know...maybe."

With that, Jack slipped neatly out of the conversation and began whistling under his breath as he continued setting up. He didn't want David to see the frustrated expression cross his face.

There are so many dishonest politicians in government these days, he thought ruefully. It's about time we elected some people with integrity and high moral standing. I hope this Cane fellow and whoever else this group is advocating are good, honest men who won't shortchange the ones who voted for them if they do happen to get elected.

With both Jack and David working so quickly together, the stage and sound equipment were set up by twelve-thirty. The men stepped back to survey their work. Jack's expression was pleased.

"Yes sir," he announced as he looked around, admiring the stage. "We're all set and ready to roll now!"

The stage was thirty feet wide and stood about four feet off the ground, with steps at both ends for entering and exiting the stage. A large cloth banner twelve feet high stretched across the back of the stage, bearing an American flag subdued in the background with the words The American Party in spacious lettering on it. On either end of the stage stood a tall American flag with gold tassels. Standing along the back of the platform beneath the flag banner was a line of folding chairs. The slogan for the rally was printed on a long skirt hanging along the edge of the stage on which was printed in red letters, "Rebuilding The Nation On Its Foundation."

Jack nodded with satisfaction as he looked at their handiwork. With the accident of his subcontractors, the loss of his sound system, and the hassle of trying to find new equipment, he hadn't been sure they would be able to get everything set up in time. Now, he could breathe easy again.

"Everything looks good," he said to David. David let his little half-smile slip across his face. The American flags on the stage lifted and swung gently in the soft breeze.

"But," Jack added, and David turned his head, "how good is our sound?"

"I'll go up and turn it on," David said. "You stand out here and listen to see how it sounds."

David hurried around to the back of the stage platform and turned on the sound amplifiers and speakers. Jack turned around and walked to the very back of the rally area. When David came around to the front, swung himself up onto the stage and looked out, Jack looked pretty far away. Jack gave David a wave. David nodded and walked over to the two microphones standing a few feet apart on the stage.

"Testing, one, two three...can you hear me okay, Jack?" he spoke into the first microphone in voice much deeper than he usually used. "This is a sound test for microphone one...give me a signal if you can hear me."

Jack smiled and waved his hands, calling out, "Great! Sounds good!"

David moved to the second microphone and spoke into it.

"Good afternoon, ladies and gentlemen. We are gathered here today because this country is at a crisis. There are many issues at hand that need to be addressed. For one thing, we must debate the question of solving world hunger. I don't know the state of all the rest of the world, but as for me, I don't think I can live much longer without eating lunch. This is a serious problem and requires immediate attention. Thank you."

Jack chuckled and, clapping his hands, began walking back toward the stage. David grinned and sat down on the edge of the stage with one knee up and his elbow resting on it. As Jack approached, he smiled approvingly at the younger man.

"Oh yes, we're definitely ready to go," he said, leaning against the stage next to David. "It sounds great, David. And about your speech..." Jack grinned, "I could do with some food as well. I didn't realize how hungry I am until just now."

"I thought I might drop a hint," David laughed.

"Why don't I go get us some lunch while you stay here and keep an eye on things?" Jack offered. David fervently agreed, and Jack pulled away from the stage.

"I saw a Whataburger on the way back from J-Mars. Does a hamburger sound good to you? With fries and a drink?" he asked.

In response, David's stomach growled loudly as the young man grinned down at Jack from his seat on the stage.

"Yes, that sounds great!" he exclaimed, and Jack nodded in affirmation.

"Okay then. I'll be back before long. We still have some time before the rally. I think Mr. Farris will be here soon, so you won't be by yourself," he said.

David chuckled. "You already left me alone once before. Are you afraid I'm going someplace?"

"Hey, the first time we were in a crunch to get everything ready. Now this is a leisure trip!" Jack protested. "And I sure hope you don't go anywhere. I wouldn't want to lose my new sound man!"

"Don't worry," David answered. "I'm not going anywhere."

Jack studied the young man sitting peacefully on the edge of the stage with his one knee up and the other leg dangling idly. Once again, questions flooded his mind. Who is this kid?

But Jack didn't have time to pepper David with more questions right now, questions he was almost certain the young man would evade as he had before. So Jack gave David a nod and strode back to the truck.

David lay down on his back on the stage and, putting his hands behind his head, gazed up at the bright blue sky. Lazily his eyes followed the ever-shifting clouds as they passed overhead. He shut his eyes, letting the sunshine soak through his T-shirt and warm his whole body. He had almost slipped into sleep when he heard approaching footsteps. Thinking it was Jack, he sat up and blinked.

Michael Farris was walking toward him. David quickly stood up and jumped down from the stage. Mr. Farris looked around at the platform and banners, and nodded approvingly. When he saw

David, he walked up to him.

"Good work, gentlemen. I'm impressed," he said. Then he seemed to notice Jack was gone. "Where's Jack?"

"He left to get lunch. I'm just waiting for him to get back," David answered, sitting down on the steps of the stage. He watched the rally manager walk around, closely inspecting their work. Finding no fault with it, he came back over to David.

"Yes, you fellows did well. I'll have to tell Jack when he gets back. Now who are you again, young man?"

"David Connally, sir," David said, standing up to shake Mr. Farris's hand again. Mr. Farris eyed him up and down. "And where did Jack Webb find you? Or did you already work for him?"

David hesitated. If Mr. Farris knew the truth: that Jack had found the young man hitchhiking along the road, both of them could get in trouble.

But then David squared his shoulders and said, "No, I just started working with Jack as of today. We haven't known each other very long, but Jack seems like a good guy, and I appreciate the opportunity to work with him."

David's answer satisfied Mr. Farris's curiosity. He walked up on the stage, testing the boards under his smart black boots. Then he called to David,

"Have you tested the microphones yet?"

"Yes, sir. Would you like to hear them?"

"Yes, I would. Hop up here and give me a one-two-three test, will you? But just wait a minute till I get to the back." Mr. Farris hurried down the steps while David ascended them at the other end of the stage. He stood in front of the first microphone and waited until he saw Mr. Farris stop and signal him from the far end of the site. David tested the microphones again until Mr. Farris was satisfied they were working perfectly.

About that time, people began to arrive. As David stepped down from the stage, he could see cars pulling into the area around the park. A few cars with the different state candidates running for various offices in them arrived, and Mr. Farris went over to greet the men and their families as he began taking charge of the rally.

David stood by the stage, watching as more and more people showed up. Already the rally area was rapidly filling, and Jack had still not returned with lunch. David pressed a hand against his empty stomach and tried to focus on the event that was soon to take place. He began studying the faces in the crowd. He looked for Mr. Farris and saw him talking with a dark-haired man dressed in an immaculate gray suit. David also noticed that two men in black suits with earpieces and dark glasses stood beside the gray-suited man. Doubtless, this must be one of the more important candidates. David kept watching him with interest.

From this distance, the man appeared to be older than David, but younger than Jack; perhaps in his early forties. His subdued but sharp clothing, and the way he carried himself while he walked and talked with Mr. Farris, indicated a determined firmness of character. Though they were too far away from him to be clearly heard, David could see the way both men conversed courteously with each other.

As other candidates arrived and spoke with Mr. Farris, he directed them toward their seats until the rally began, and informed them of the schedule details. David silently counted five men who walked around followed closely by security guards. Some of the candidates had their families with them, and all dressed very nicely.

David decided to adjust one of the big speakers while he was waiting. He let his eyes wander over the gathering crowd, then idly back to the large banner, the flags, and the microphones, his gaze following the microphone cords down to the stage and across to around the back where the sound equipment was.

Then David suddenly noticed one of the cables connected to the microphones lay loose on the platform. He went around behind the stage and picked up a roll of gaffer tape. Humming to himself, he walked up onto the stage and kneeling down, began peeling the tape off the roll and firmly pressing it down against the cable so it wouldn't move when people walked around onstage.

Almost unaware he was doing so he began to hum while he worked. A few seconds later he was singing softly to himself.

David didn't notice his singing had caught the attention of some of the people closest to the stage. They smiled at each other and a few began humming along. Some of the more excited audience members cried, "Hey, use the microphone so we can all hear you sing!"

David stopped singing and stood up quickly, taken aback, but the crowd kept urging him to lead the song for everyone. To help him out, several people near the front started singing "America the Beautiful," encouraging those around them to sing along to the song David had started by himself. Soon a great many of the crowd were singing loudly and enthusiastically.

Mr. Farris turned his head mid-conversation with one of the candidates and looked around, surprised. He glimpsed David standing on the stage, a roll of gaffer tape in his hand, looking very out of place up there in his jeans and T-shirt. The manager's eyes narrowed, puzzled. What was happening?

David stood still, staring around at the singing group of people. The flags waved in the wind, adding to the patriotic atmosphere. The sound of voices blending together in praise for America seemed to lift David's spirit and without pausing to put down the gaffer tape in his hand, the young man walked up to one of the microphones and began leading the crowd in the "Star-Spangled Banner." People cheered and clapped when he started to sing into the microphone, keeping the time by waving his roll of gaffer tape. More and more people joined in until nearly everyone was singing. The sound was overwhelming.

Mr. Farris stood off to the side with his arms folded, filled with amazement as he watched David leading singing onstage. The young man had a strong voice and sang with passion, his face lighting up with a grand smile as he sang. Despite his casual dress, he made an inspiring sight standing up there, with the wind blowing his hair and the smile on his face.

Mr. Farris shook his head and turned around to see Jack coming toward him, carrying a large paper bag that smelled like French fries and hamburgers. Jack wore the same expression of wonder on his face as Mr. Farris.

"What's going on...is that David up there?" His first question of curiosity suddenly transitioned into the second question of astonishment. Coming to stand beside Mr. Farris, Jack stared at the stage and his eyes narrowed. "What is he doing?"

Mr. Farris chuckled in spite of his own amazement.

"It appears your new hired hand is also a performer, Jack."

Jack shook his head, lips parted in protest.

"He's not supposed to be up there."

"Well, you'll have to make sure he knows that. But right now it almost looks like that's where he needs to be," Mr. Farris said thoughtfully.

"You're not going to let him stay up there, are you?" Jack said.

"He's not hurting anyone. You want to be the one to drag him off that stage? Just wait it out, Jack. We have a little time."

"Yeah, fine," Jack mumbled. He stuck a French fry between his teeth, only to realize that his appetite had mysteriously seemed to vanish.

THE SPEAKER

CHAPTER 3:

"Jack, what are we going to do about the equipment? Don't we have to take it back to J-Mars today?" David asked that evening as he and Jack walked across the parking lot to Jack's truck after dinner at a local diner.

"I talked to Michael Farris before making arrangements at the motel," he said without looking at David. He seemed put out about something. "He's giving me an advance to purchase the sound equipment so we can keep it for the other rallies," he said after they had gotten settled in the truck.

"Well, that's good to hear," said David. He looked at Jack, his expression puzzled, as if he couldn't figure out why Jack didn't seem open for conversation.

"You alright?" he asked kindly. Jack exhaled sharply as he turned the steering wheel a little harder than necessary. "I'm fine," he grunted. David recoiled slightly, then rested his arm on the car door against the window and said nothing more. A minute later he started whistling softly. Jack couldn't help but recognize the tune, and his ears perked up in spite of his irritation.

"George Strait?" he asked. David smiled.

"I think he's growing on me. You keep playing him on the radio, and I'll keep listening," he said.

Jack released a brief smile as he steered the truck into the parking lot of the rally site.

While Jack and David were preparing to take down the stage and pack up the equipment, two large pickup trucks arrived. Jack grinned and waved his arm in greeting as they pulled up, saying to David on the side, "I called in some of my other employees. We're gonna need some extra help around here without Orville and Aaron, especially since they were the best I had."

Jack's words trailed off, and he couldn't help letting a sigh escape. Then he turned to face the men clamoring out of the new trucks. They had driven through most of the day and into the night to reach Jacksonville in time to help break down the stage and pack up all the equipment. Jack was relieved to see them.

"I can't tell you how great it is to see you all," he exclaimed, vigorously shaking hands with his crew. Each of them knew Jack well, most of them having worked with him for several years, which also meant they knew exactly what to expect out of Jack as soon as he greeted them. After a flurry of directions, they all set to work.

True to custom, Jack was everywhere at once, lifting, pushing and directing. He barely paused to draw breath between shouting orders.

"Alright, boys, we're on a very tight timetable here, so let's get a move on and get everything packed up pronto! We need to be on the road by nine o'clock sharp tomorrow morning! Eric, don't put that in that truck, put it in the other one with the stage set..."

David buckled down to work and didn't take the time to speak to anyone if it caused him to stop doing his job. One of the younger crewmen, an outgoing fellow named Eric Dodge, attempted to engage him in conversation a couple of times, but soon realized that David's work ethic wouldn't allow him to stand still in conversation. Eric soon left him alone to let him perform his tasks undisturbed.

Jack, still trying to do everything at once, could not stand still to watch a task being done in a different way than what he thought it should be, and interrupted Eric and a couple of other crew members who were trying to wedge one of the large speakers into one of the trucks. The truck was nearly full already and much twisting and relocation of equipment pieces was taking place in order to make it all fit. Jack watched the fellows strain and shove for a few seconds before shaking his head and coming over to help them.

"How would you guys possibly get anything done around here without me?" he grunted, his words jerky as he and Eric forced the obstinate speaker between two boxes of cables and other sound equipment.

CHAPTER 3:

"What, without you bossing us around?" Eric wiped an arm across his forehead. "My guess is...faster." Jack aimed a punch at Eric's shoulder, which the young man dodged, and they both laughed. From across the way David heard their laughter, looked up, and smiled briefly before lowering his head and continued winding the cables he had unplugged from the sound system.

Jack noticed David about the same time, and the grin faded from his face. Leaving Eric to finish, he strolled over to David and stood with his arms folded in front of him. David greeted him with a friendly nod, his hands never slowing his work. When Jack said nothing in reply but continued to stand there, David looked up again, a puzzled expression on his face.

"Look, David, I like you. I think you're a great guy, and I'm very impressed with all your hard work."

"Thanks," David responded, a quizzical look on his face.

"But I gotta say, what you did yesterday, well, that's not in the contract. I'm paying you to work, not entertain the crowd."

"I was only singing along with them," David said with a short laugh of disbelief. "Was that wrong?"

"David, you set up the stage, you don't stand on it. You wire the mics, you don't talk into them."

A little smile crept over David's face, almost as if he couldn't help saying, "What about mic testing?"

Jack sighed. "Just don't let it happen again, please. I'm responsible for what you do, so everything reflects back on me, and everything I do reflects back to Michael Farris which, in turn, ultimately reflects on the party itself. We don't want to cause any kind of irritation or disturbance to the big guys. They aren't expecting a side show, especially from somebody they don't even know."

"By 'the big guys' you mean the fellows in charge of the whole party organization?"

"Exactly." Jack watched David's face closely to make sure he was getting his point across. "We do what the big guys say. And I'm pretty sure that you being onstage and cutting into their schedule isn't on their agenda. The people aren't coming here for sing-alongs, David."

39

"I'm sorry," David said quickly, "I didn't mean, I mean, I just thought—"

"It doesn't matter now, what's done is done," said Jack, irritated with himself for even bringing up the subject, though he knew it had to be addressed. "Just do what you're here to do, and leave the microphones to the speakers. OK?"

"Yes sir, I understand," David said softly.

Three nights later opened with the same feverish activity in setting up for the next rally in Jacksonville. Tonight the rally was being held in Macon, Georgia, with large numbers expected. Michael Farris met them at the site with their city permit and was visibly relieved to see the extra men Jack brought with him.

"I feel a whole lot better about this now that you're no longer a two-man show," he joked to Jack, who agreed wholeheartedly with him.

People began arriving at the rally half an hour early. David, who had again been placed in charge of sound because of how well he had done yesterday, was wiring the last speakers by the audio truck when Jack walked over. He wore his usual harried expression he reserved for such occasions.

"Almost ready, David?" he asked, throwing a look over his shoulder at the gathering crowd.

"Just about," David said, then looked up to see Mr. Farris approaching them, wearing his traditional cowboy hat and boots.

"Are we all ready to go, Jack?" he asked briskly.

"Yes sir, everything is ready," Jack answered, shooting David a questioning look, to which the younger man nodded reassuringly. Jack grinned confidently at Mr. Farris, but his boss's next words turned his smile into a frown of surprise.

"Jack, would there be any problem with David going on stage and entertaining the audience with some songs, patriotic ones of course, for about half an hour until we're ready to begin? Not all of the speakers are here yet, and people are still arriving."

Jack bit his lip. He glanced at David and saw the young man's face light up at Mr. Farris's request, but then he looked at

Jack and quickly lowered his eyes. Jack took a deep breath.

"Well," he said slowly, "I guess it's up to him, but...it's just that we aren't paid to be entertainers, Mike."

Mr. Farris's face broke into a smile.

"Is that all you're worried about, Jack? Don't you give it another thought. This is me asking. And we would be more than happy to compensate both of you for your time and trouble." He gripped Jack's shoulder and gave him a friendly shake for emphasis.

"More money, eh?" Jack let out a somewhat forced laugh, but he was beginning to feel a little better. He turned to David.

"It's up to you, then," he said. His tone was flat, but he meant it to be kind. David pursed his lips and rubbed the back of his neck, then rested his hands on his hips and shifted his feet. Finally, he looked up. Mr. Farris suddenly realized how vibrantly blue David's eyes were.

"If it's alright with Jack, I'd be glad to help."

Jack stood in silent thought for a few seconds, then he shook his head. "Go on, get on up there, man," he urged David with a little push. David beamed, all hesitancy gone now, and moved quickly toward the stage.

Mr. Farris turned to Jack. "Look, Jack," he said, "I know how you feel about working the 'one gig for the one job', but I think you letting David go up there is going to be a real help to us all."

"You think so?" Jack ran his tongue over his lower lip. "He's just singing a couple of songs. He's not here to entertain, he's here to work."

"And you think helping me by spiriting up the crowd for the rally isn't work?"

Jack kept his eyes on the stage. "Let's just see how it turns out."

David hit every other step as he made his way up onto the platform and strolled over the microphone. His quiet, mild demeanor seemed to vanish as something else inside him began to emerge. He unhooked the microphone from its stand and, holding it with one hand, waved to the crowd with the other. "How is everybody doing tonight?"

Cheers and scattered applause greeted him from the accepting audience, and David's face broke into a big smile. He chanced a glance over to where Jack and Mr. Farris were standing, and saw Mr. Farris give him an approving nod. Encouraged, David spoke into the microphone again.

"How many of you know the song 'America the Beautiful'?" he asked, and began leading them all in a rousing chorus of "America! America! God shed His grace on thee…"

"He's a natural," Mr. Farris said to Jack, very pleased. He and Jack situated themselves where they could observe the proceedings from out of the way. "Has he done this kind of thing before?"

"Uh, I don't know. I never would have thought so," Jack said, full of wonder as he watched David onstage. The young man seemed transformed, almost ethereal, even, as he stood alone, keeping rhythm with one hand and exuding joy and patriotism with every note he sang.

Jack turned his gaze on the audience, and the expressions on their faces were something else he didn't expect to see. Every pair of eyes, every person's span of attention was focused exclusively on David. Their voices rang out happily, and their faces were lit up with the same fervor of spirit Jack had seen in David. The people all seemed overjoyed to be singing these patriotic songs and it was clear they were enjoying David leading them.

"Seems like he has a real knack for this sort of thing," Jack said, turning back to observe David again. "I've never seen a crowd this stirred up over singing a few songs about America."

"Makes sense. The people of America are in serious need of some real patriots to stand up and show true courage and love for their country. You could say they're starving for some integrity."

Jack mulled over Mr. Farris's words in his mind. "Guess we don't see much of that in today's political arena."

"Integrity? She's as rare as rain in a Texas summer up in D.C. Truth has become a matter of circumstance. And we the people depend upon truth from our leaders, Jack. If we can't trust those in office to be honest with us, yet we allow them to keep on with their sordid agendas, we'll lose our country. Most of these politicians we have sitting high up in government couldn't care less if our Constitution burned before their eyes. Why do they remain in power?"

"Well, the government is growing," said Jack, a troubled frown settling on his brow. "The more we sit back and do nothing, she just keeps getting bigger. And the corruption continues to spread. You heard about that senator down south who got caught in a big scandal and then was blackmailed by some prominent businessman?"

"Yes, I heard that story recently," Mr. Farris replied in disgust. "And what makes my skin really crawl about that whole affair is that I was considering Senator Watson as a potential candidate for The American Party to back in the coming election. He seemed like the epitome of a conservative, moral man who would do most anything for his country. Now look at him. It makes my blood boil. I wonder from time to time if we really do have any men left in this nation who care enough in their heart of hearts to bring us back from the precipice we're dangling over, and will work hard to reinstate what our Founding Fathers established...what's been thrown under the rug for far too long."

"Yes, that's the sort of man we need," Jack said sympathetically. "A leader whose personal agenda lines up with that of the people's welfare, and not just in pretension so he can push his own legislation or fill his pockets with our money. Have you found any other candidates as of yet?"

"We have one or two lined up. You know the name Joseph Cane?"

"Him I've heard of, yes."

"He'll be here tonight. Cane is a state representative from Virginia. He has a fairly solid record of moral stability, and he's a conservative. At least, we know where he stands on the big issues like abortion, homosexual marriage, border defense, etc. He's a pretty decent fellow, seems to have his feet firmly on the ground and knows where he wants to go. I only worry about his ego. He speaks out about what he believes in, and he holds his ground, but he clearly has a very high opinion of himself that transcends the necessary confidence needed."

"Is that a real problem?"

"It could be, if he allows his own vanity to dictate his decisions. But even so, he's one of the best we've found. I like the guy, even if he has flaws. We all do. But The American Party needs somebody she can stand behind all the way with no hesitations, know what I'm saying?"

"Yeah, I guess so," Jack agreed. He and Mr. Farris lapsed into a companionable silence as they both turned to watch David up on the stage, both of them absorbed in similar thoughts.

For the next half hour, as the crowd continued to grow, David included all of them in the singing of famous patriotic songs such as "God Bless America," "The Battle Hymn of the Republic," "My Country Tis of Thee," and several others. The audience joyfully joined in with every song, demanding encores of their favorites. It really was like a giant sing-along as hundreds of voices blended together in singing the beautiful, powerful words.

Before he had been on the stage fifteen minutes, David began adding phrases between songs. "God bless our United States!" he shouted, and the crowd roared with approval and repeated the words. It was as if David couldn't contain the excitement and joy expanding inside him. "Don't we live in the most wonderful nation on earth?" he cried, and a chorus of agreeing shouts answered him.

Jack was inevitably reminded of the Pied Piper story. David seemed to hold the people's attention in the palm of his hand. People began recording him on their cell phones as the event progressed. More and more newcomers were drawn into the crowd and were soon singing as loudly as everyone else. It was as if David had such a presence and mannerism that people really trusted, and they loved participating with him. Jack, in watching the young man in impressed astonishment, thought back over Mr. Farris's words about the people starving for some real integrity and patriotism. In observing the events unfold before him, Jack could see that the people really were hungering for the patriotic songs and words David brought forth. They desperately wanted the message he was bringing just by leading them in singing. Jack could feel the spirit of patriotism flowing strong, and a smile crept over his weathered face.

When the time came, Mr. Farris went up onstage to officially open the rally, and also to thank David and the crowd for their performance. He then excused David so he could begin introducing the candidates.

David willingly surrendered the microphone, but as he left the stage, he turned and waved to the crowd and exclaimed, "God bless America!"

Applause and repetition of his words went on long after David exited the stage.

A week later, Jack and his crew were setting up for a rally in Elizabethton, Tennessee. It seemed that every subsequent rally found people arriving earlier, with the crowds growing bigger. Michael Farris was very happy about this, and said often to Jack that they had David to thank for this. Asking David to go onstage before the rally began to lead the people in a few songs was slowly becoming the regular occurrence.

"People are telling their friends," Mr. Farris exulted as he and Jack sipped black coffee during a rare quiet moment a few hours before the rally was to open. "I've even seen a video somebody recorded of David on their phone posted on YouTube. We have their interest hooked now."

Jack was just as happy as Mr. Farris about the growing audiences and the popularity the rallies had sparked in the cities they visited.

"It's amazing, the response we're getting," he said. "This is the kind of energy that's going to remind the government who's really in charge."

"Well, let's just hope that sentiment stays the same all the way through the primaries coming up," Mr. Farris remarked, taking a swallow of coffee.

"Excuse me," he added a few seconds later, as the cell phone on his belt started frantically buzzing. Mr. Farris downed the rest of his coffee and strode briskly away, holding the phone to his ear. Jack tossed his empty paper cup into the nearest trash bin and walked off to find David.

He found the young man seated on the open end of one of the big trucks, one leg tucked up underneath the other, which was dangling down over the end of the tailgate. He held a book on his lap, and seemed very engrossed in its contents. Jack stood still, aware that David was unaware of his presence, and watched him. David looked very peaceful sitting there, reading with no thought for the world around him. From time to time he nodded, and his lips moved almost imperceptibly, as if he were reading the book in a quiet whisper to himself and agreed with every word. His posture was so easy and carefree, his expression as he bent over the book so intrigued, Jack felt that funny tug inside his chest that was starting to grow familiar to him.

David was always careful regarding anything he said about himself, and Jack was learning not to ask, though his curiosity was bursting every time he looked at David. He still didn't know a thing about him, although, bit by bit, a few things were rising to the otherwise opaque surface of David's shell. Jack tried to put the tiny, shapeless pieces of the puzzle together whenever he thought he knew something else about the mysterious young man.

He seems a pretty staunch patriot, thought Jack, replaying the last couple of rallies in his mind. He also knew David evidently loved to sing, that he liked people, and that people liked him, too. He was a hard worker, and had never been heard to complain, nor did he sweat less than the rest of the crew. Jack had even seen him more than once offer a helping hand to other workers when he wasn't kept busy with his own tasks. And now, he was reading something that looked a lot like the Bible on his lap.

Just who is this guy? Jack wondered, as he had already done before. He also wondered why he wasn't more suspicious and upset about David keeping his life a secret. Surely the young man wasn't telling him about his past because he didn't trust him. But there had to be a reason.

Jack stood in the shade of a tree for a few more seconds, observing David until the calm was interrupted by hurrying footsteps. Jack and David both turned their heads as Mr. Farris hurried round the corner, his cell phone gripped in his hand like a steel trap. He looked a shadow of his usual cool, collected self.

"Hey, Jack!" he called distractedly, "Jack, have you seen David? I need to find David right – oh, there you are!" In mid-sentence, Mr. Farris cut away from Jack and hurried over to David, who was watching them curiously.

"What happened?" Jack called after Mr. Farris, trotting after him, but Mr. Farris ignored his question until he had spoken to David.

"David, we have a real problem," Mr. Farris declared.

"I'm sorry sir, is there something I can do?" David asked, carefully closing his book.

"We have a convoy of vehicles with most of the speakers for tonight on their way, but now they've been delayed on the freeway due to a wreck between two semis," Mr. Farris said, his irritation plainly showing what he thought of the audacity those semi-trucks had dared in making trouble for him. "They may be as much as an hour late, and the rally starts in fifteen minutes!"

Jack felt his hands turning cold as the full weight of the problem sank in. Hundreds of people were already gathered, waiting for the moment when the rally would open with all its fanfare and vibrant speakers, who were currently held up in traffic an hour away. We're done for, he thought gloomily.

"What can I do, sir?" asked David, all ears. Mr. Farris came close and put his hand on David's shoulder.

"David, I need your help." His voice was pleading. "I need you to entertain the crowd until the speakers arrive. I know I'm asking way too much of you," he added as David's eyes widened and he opened his mouth slightly as if to protest. "But at this point my neck is on the line, and I firmly believe you're my best option."

David looked up at the compliment, and a crimson blush spread up the back of his neck. He chewed his lower lip and cast his eyes towards the ground.

"Look," Mr. Farris leaned against the tailgate beside him. "I'm not asking you to give a big speech about the government or anything like that. All I'm asking is that you say a few things to lift the people's spirits. Cheer them on and get them excited about the rally. It doesn't have to be grand or complicated. Man, you could go out there and just lead them in singing again for an hour if you want to!"

The corners of David's mouth twitched up. Encouraged, Mr. Farris put his hand on his shoulder again.

"Please, David," he said softly. "I know I don't have the right to ask. I shouldn't be putting this on you. But you really are all I have. I'm just asking you to do the best you can. Please. For the people."

David's head came up. Mr. Farris's final words seemed to suddenly inspire something inside him.

"I want to help in any way I can," he said passionately. "Is there anything in particular you would like me to say to them?"

Mr. Farris let out a whistle of relief before he could stop himself, and gratefully wrung David's hand. "Just, ah, just talk about America, or our candidates, or whatever you can think of that might spark the patriotic spirit out there. Just hold the audience's attention until the speakers arrive," he said. David nodded thoughtfully. He stood up and walked over to Jack.

"Will you hold onto this for me til I get back?" he asked. Jack nodded and reached for the small book. David hesitated for one brief moment before putting it in Jack's hand. Then he turned to Mr. Farris and gave him a firm handshake, as though reassuring him everything would be fine and not to worry. Then he walked away in the direction of the stage.

"I owe you one, David. I owe you big time!" Mr. Farris called after him. David just waved one arm above his head in nonchalant response, but Jack thought he caught part of a smile on the young man's face as he disappeared around the corner. A few minutes later Jack and Mr. Farris could hear the quieting of the crowd, followed by a raucous cheer. Mr. Farris sagged against the tailgate of the truck where David had been sitting and took out a handkerchief to wipe his forehead.

"I'm telling you, Jack," he said weakly, "if you hadn't found that fellow, I don't know what I'd do. He seems to be a real lucky penny, that one."

"Yeah," Jack mumbled, distracted by David's book in his hands. It was small, leather-bound, and well worn. Jack turned it over and traced the faded gold lettering stamped into the cover with his rough fingertip.

David bounded onto and across the stage, waving to the crowd with both hands. If anyone thought it was odd to see the lone young man standing up there in work jeans and a plaid shirt apparently about to open the rally without any formal introduction, they weren't thinking that when David began speaking.

"Good evening, America! How is everybody tonight?" he said into the microphone, and gave a friendly smile when the usual enthusiastic cheers filled the air. These were people ready for a message to inspire them and fill them with hope for the future. David looked out across the sea of faces for a few short seconds in silence, as if gathering his thoughts. Then he cupped his hand round the mic again and said, "Well, my name is David, and you can think of me as a sort of last-minute addition to the schedule for tonight." There were ripples of laughter, and David chuckled too, and without further ado launched into singing the national anthem. The audience blended their voices with his in glad reception of his infectiously enthusiastic spirit. After singing the national anthem, David quickly started "God Bless America" without more than a few seconds' pause.

But instead of beginning another song after "God Bless America" was finished, David waited for the cheering and clapping to die down into a silence heavy with anticipation. For a few seconds all was remarkably still. Hundreds of pairs of eyes watched David as he moved a few steps back and forth in the center of the stage, the microphone clutched in his hand, his brow furrowed intently. He looked out into the upturned faces, and a quiet smile spread across his face.

Then he began to talk about America.

The audience was so still that it seemed unnatural to hear no

49

THE SPEAKER

other voice than David's in that large area at a time when ordinarily people would be shouting and cheering every few seconds. But tonight, something was different. Tonight, David had the stage.

He spoke of America, her greatness, and how much she was blessed by God in being the wonderful nation that she was. He talked about the freedoms Americans enjoy that no other country and their citizens could boast of, and the riches and beauty of the American land. He spoke of the Founding Fathers, their ideals for their fledgling nation, their sacrifice and the high price they were willing to pay for freedom from tyranny, and the glory of the heritage that only America can call her own. He talked about the Revolutionary War, and the blood so willingly shed on behalf of future descendants so they could be free; when the men of that time so gladly rose up to go to war to defend their land and fight for that which could never be stamped with an estimable value of liberty and justice for all.

When David spoke, it was different than when he sang. In leading the people in song, his voice was loud, strong, passionate, and he was nearly carried away by his own enthusiasm. When he simply talked into the microphone, David's voice was softer, more humble, but no less passionate. He spoke with a reverence and fervor of spirit that no soul in attendance could doubt. His simplicity of speech, his simple gestures, and the way he occasionally stopped speaking for a few seconds to bite his lower lip and gaze upwards at the sky to wink back something in his eyes, though his voice never faltered once, endeared him to the crowd. He held them spellbound as he went on to say how blessed America is and how she was a nation founded on God and His principles, which was the reason why she is so great, and her people so blessed. David's words and voice were so sincere that soon there were few dry eyes in the audience.

David didn't even see Jack, Mr. Farris, and the other members of the crew standing nearby in the wings of the stage, observing in amazed silence as his voice rang out, clear and true, into the approaching night. It was like nothing any of them had ever seen before. Jack had never seen such rapt attention from an audience, never beheld such a large crowd so glued to the speaker's every word as he paced the stage, perfectly at ease with himself and the

50

world, speaking straight from his heart, and only pausing now and then to move the lengthy microphone cord out of his way as it trailed him across the stage. Jack observed how David was expressive, but not overly dramatic, or even charismatic. His speech was not graced with the finest of English vocabulary and yet, the way he presented himself and his message, casual, quiet but passionate, and simple, was wholly satisfying and inspiring. His words were so heavy with meaning, almost pleading, as if he was trying to show the people a word portrait of something very precious to him that he deeply wanted them to understand and love as much as he did. Jack felt moved by the words David said. He had heard them all before, of course, but being reminded of them now, and by such a speaker, it almost brought a mist into Jack's sharp eyes. He remembered the last time he had ever heard such spirited words from a young patriot who wasn't in office. As Jack watched David that night, he could almost see his own son, Ryan, up there in David's place, speaking through David's words.

He cleared his throat quietly and chanced a glance at Mr. Farris, who stood beside him, intently observing David and clearly drinking in every word the young man said. Jack also saw that Mr. Farris looked so pleased with the way everything was going that he couldn't keep a big smile from spreading across his face. Then suddenly, he nudged Jack's arm and pointed towards the back of the crowd. Reporters and a local television crew or two who had arrived to report on the rally were pressing through the audience to record David onstage, what he was saying, and the reactions of the crowd's response to him. There were also many present who were holding up cameras or cellphones to capture the passing minutes of David's speech on video. Mr. Farris and Jack looked at each other, the same wonder, disbelief, and incredulity written on both of their faces. They could see in each other's eyes that they both believed David meant every word he said, and that no man could be more in love with, or dedicated to, his country.

David held the audience for over an hour.

Dusk had fallen by the time Mr. Farris received a call saying the semi accident on the freeway had been finally cleared and the speakers were on their way. The vehicles were arriving when David was still onstage. The first car to pull up contained Senator Joseph Cane and his bodyguards. Mr. Farris hurried over to shake the senator's hand, apologizing profusely for the wreck that had caused the delay.

"The wreck wasn't your fault, Mr. Farris," Senator Cane said graciously. "Accidents happen. Though I thought I might never get off that freeway tonight. Who is that?" he added, staring up at David. Mr. Farris followed his gaze, and a proud smile settled over his features. "That's David Connally. I asked him to get up there and try to entertain the crowd because you guys were stuck in traffic. Although 'entertain' isn't really the right word I would use to describe what he's doing, now that I think about it."

"Huh. Is he any good?" the senator asked, taking in David's working-man appearance and simple demeanor, devoid of any flamboyance.

"Well," Mr. Farris hid another smile. "He sure is something, that's for certain."

Senator Cane gave him a puzzled look. "You said 'entertain.' What's he been doing up there?"

"Oh, don't worry, Senator. Believe me," Mr. Farris looked straight into Joseph Cane's eyes as he said, "you have no idea what he's done for you tonight. I think you'll find the audience is more than ready for you now."

Before the senator could say anything, Mr. Farris skipped up the steps from the side onto the stage. David saw him coming, and turning back to the audience, said loudly, "Hey everyone, let's give a big hand for the man in charge of organizing these rallies, Mr. Michael Farris."

The audience obligingly cheered and clapped raucously as Mr. Farris walked to David's side, smiling and nodding at the crowd. He gave a wave or two, then turned to David.

"The speakers have arrived," he said into his ear. "You've done beautifully," he added with heartfelt gratitude. "Thank you, David."

CHAPTER 3:

And Mr. Farris shook David's hand with a look that said a great deal more than words could. David's clasp was firm and steady as he looked into Mr. Farris's eyes and answered, "It was my absolute privilege, sir."

Mr. Farris nodded gratefully, and gripped David's shoulder. David nodded back. Then he handed Mr. Farris the microphone and, with his hand still on David's shoulder, The American Party manager turned back to the crowd.

"Good evening, everyone! Thank you for coming out tonight. We cannot express how much your presence here means to each of us who have worked for some time now to make these rallies a reality. Now, I know how much you've enjoyed your speaker, David..." More cheers responded to this statement that echoed so loudly, Mr. Farris had to pause. From the side of the stage, Jack, Senator Cane, and the other speakers who had arrived watched in a mixture of fascination and confusion.

"...I know how much you've enjoyed listening to David tonight, and I hate to deprive you of him now, but it is time for our scheduled speakers to come and talk to you about their political beliefs and how they plan to help the nation," said Mr. Farris. Senator Cane folded his arms as he looked at David. Jack saw him, and watched him shift his feet and glance at his bodyguards, biting his lip. He looked utterly discomfited. Jack suddenly choked back a chuckle. Was Senator Cane jealous of the attention David was getting? A young man who was evidently no public figure himself, yet had managed to stir the hearts of the crowd in such a way that when his name was mentioned by Michael Farris, the entire audience couldn't be quiet for at least thirty seconds before he could continue?

"Thank you, David," Mr. Farris said again to the young man, only into the microphone this time. David shook his hand once more, and as the crowd roared, he waved to them as if they were his personal friends, and shouted enthusiastically, "Thank you, everyone! God bless you, and God bless America! Goodnight, all!" David exited the stage to the repetition of those words from the voices of the audience filling his ears.

53

↑THE SPEAKER

David came off the stage on the side where Jack and Senator Cane were standing. He barely glanced at the senator before coming over to Jack, though behind his back, the senator was scrutinizing him carefully.

"David," Jack began as the young man came to his side and Mr. Farris started introducing the other speakers, "that...that was just...man, I can't even find the words. You outdid yourself tonight, son." He kept his arms folded, his tone gruff from trying to conceal his emotions, but his words were full of pride. David grinned sheepishly, his face glowing. He almost seemed bouncy from the rush of being onstage that night. But Jack also noticed he was very sweaty, and his hands were shaking.

"Hey, hey, you better sit down," he exclaimed, his voice taking a sudden paternal edge. He put his hand on David's shoulder and guided him to a nearby seat, slightly away from the stage and the crowd. David sank gratefully into the chair, breathing deeply. Jack grabbed a water bottle from the cooler that was supposed to be for the speakers and unscrewed the cap for David, standing over him in concern as David gulped the water. Then he leaned his head back and closed his eyes.

"Are you OK, David?" Jack questioned. "I hope this wasn't too much of a strain on you. I'm sorry you had to be up there that long..."

"Don't be." David opened his eyes. He seemed to be reviving more quickly than Jack had anticipated. "I'm fine, really, Jack. It's just a very warm night, and I guess all the excitement kinda took it out of me a little. Don't worry about me. And don't worry about tonight. I enjoyed every minute of it. I'd do it again, too. It's the people that are important, not me."

Jack stared at this young man with new respect growing in his eyes. "Well, David," he said, patting David's shoulder, "I can honestly say I don't think I've ever met another person like you. You did something out there tonight, son. And I don't know yet what the aftershock will be, but I think you stirred up something in the hearts of that audience that they really needed to realize was there. You gave them what they were starving to hear. And there isn't a soul present here tonight who won't benefit from what you said."

David looked up at him with a half-grin, as if Jack's unusually warm words were as amusing to him as they were appreciated. "Thank you, Jack," he said, and took another swig of water. "But those weren't my words. I just borrowed 'em."

David flexed his fingers, and the tremors had gone. "I guess I need to get back to the sound equipment now," he said, standing up before Jack could stop him. "Oh!" He suddenly turned to Jack with a question in his eyes.

"Hey Jack, do you still have my..."

"Oh," Jack was slightly disconcerted at the sudden direction David's thoughts had taken. The kid just gets offstage from giving an hour-long speech to an applause like thunder, and he's worried about his Bible. Restraining himself from shaking his head, Jack reached into the inside pocket of his jacket and pulled out David's little black book. Senator Cane, standing a few yards away, craned his neck to see.

Heedless of the senator watching or Jack's bemused expression, David took the book with a "thank you" to Jack for keeping it for him, and caressed it once before slipping it into the pocket of his jeans.

"Hey, David," said Jack uncertainly while trying to sound nonchalant, "You read that often?"

"Every day," David answered, his voice matter-of-fact. "It's the only thing I have that wasn't burned in that truck fire. It goes everywhere I go."

Jack nodded, his eyes on the ground.

"In fact," David paused, a thoughtful expression on his face. "Of all the things I lost, I'm most thankful that I didn't lose this." He patted the pocket where his Bible lay and walked serenely away.

Jack stood there in silence, processing the scene he had just been a part of. As he mulled David's words over in his mind, he suddenly noticed a couple of reporters and a camera man coming around the corner, looking right and left for somebody. Jack didn't have to think twice to guess who they were looking for back here, and hurried after David.

"David! Hey, um," he began, catching up with David and throwing his arm over the younger man's shoulders, "I think you need to get back to the hotel and get some sleep."

"What? No, come on, Jack, I'm perfectly fine, really," David protested in surprise. "Besides, who's going to operate the sound system if I leave?"

Jack kept shooting glances behind them, trying to steer David away from the stage and the reporters. He knew it was a matter of moments before they saw David.

"David, we have other guys here who can turn a few knobs and toggle a switch. We'll get it taken care of. Now you need to go rest. I mean it."

"But, Jack, why..."

"Look, David," and Jack looked him squarely in the eyes. "You're a smart man. You should know when you're exhausted, and truth be told, you may think you feel great, but really you need to sleep this night off. I don't care what you say about being fine," he added, putting his hands up as David tried to speak. "Any other man put on the spot like you were tonight and having to improvise his words to over a thousand people for more than an hour would be sitting down right now having a coffee or something. Men who rehearse and practice their speech for this kind of thing feel tired afterward. So in your case, you have no excuse for not going back to the hotel. Right. Now."

David threw his head back and looked upwards for a moment. Jack had never seen him look so annoyed, but he knew David wasn't angry. Jack looked back and saw the reporters in the distance. It was now or never. The last thing David Connally needed tonight was more public attention. Then Jack saw David's shoulders slump in defeat.

"OK, I'll go back to the hotel," he agreed, and Jack heaved a sigh of relief. He and David walked out to the parking lot, and Jack drove them to the small motel where they were staying. In the truck, David leaned back against the seat, letting his eyelids fall shut again. Jack repressed a tight smile. David was tired, no matter how vehemently he denied it.

"But you wake me up when we need to get everything packed up tomorrow morning," he came awake enough to warn Jack at the door of his motel room.

"Sure, sure. You're still part of my crew," Jack said, with a good-natured slap on the back. David smiled sleepily. "G'night, Jack."

"Night, David. Oh wait, David?"

David turned halfway around, his hand on the doorknob of his motel room.

"Just a thought, but you know, most people don't remember all the words to all the patriotic songs you've been singing. I mean, lots of people are familiar with one or two verses, but they couldn't sing you the entire National Anthem. But you..." and Jack walked closer to David, scrutinizing him thoughtfully. "You can. I guess what I'm curious to know is, how come you know all these American songs so well?"

David looked down at the floor. Jack wondered if he had suddenly driven the young man back into the shell he seemed to be slowly coming out of since the time they had begun working together.

Then David gave Jack one of his square looks and said in a matter-of-fact voice,

"My parents taught me those kinds of songs from when I was really small. I grew up with their words in my head."

"Got it." Jack nodded once and backed away, waving a hand. "See you tomorrow, David."

David raised his hand and then closed the door. Jack hurried back to the truck, his mind whirling.

Later that night, Jack sat in his motel room adjacent to David's, deep in thought. He toyed with a flyer from the rally in one hand, the other hand molded around a paper cup of iced tea. His cell phone rang. It was Michael Farris.

"Hey, Jack, I'm sorry I didn't get a chance to talk to you after the rally tonight. Wow, that was sure something, huh?"

"Yeah." Jack suppressed a huge yawn. "I couldn't believe

57

that turnout. I think it was a real success, Michael. The best we've had yet."

"I gave an interview to one of the reporters there, so that will be good publicity for us," Mr. Farris added.

"Great! We'll take all the outlets we can to get the word out," Jack said.

He then stopped talking and waited, already knowing what Mr. Farris was about to say after he finished clearing his throat.

"Jack...I wanted to thank you for letting your man get up there tonight. I knew David cut a good personality up there and seemed to connect with the audience pretty well before this, but I never could have imagined what happened out there tonight. Did you see their faces?"

"Yeah," Jack said. "Yeah, I did. I haven't seen that kind of emotional current running through a crowd at a political event since the days of Kennedy and Reagan. He did well, David did."

"And you know something, Jack? I believe him. I believe him with all my heart. Every word he spoke out there was the absolute, unvarnished truth. I could see that. You could see that. And the people saw it. They saw his love for America and her people, and they love him for it."

"Well, I think he was glad to have the chance to talk to them," said Jack. "He was a little worn out afterward, but that guy has strength of spirit and positive outlook on life that you just don't see much these days."

"Hmm..." Mr. Farris mused. "It's too bad we don't know more about him. With his personality and evident patriotism, he's just the type of guy The American Party would endorse and support."

"Whoa now," Jack exclaimed, alarmed. "Easy there, Mike. I highly doubt David has any intention of running for a public office of any kind. And I still don't even know where he came from, where he was born, who his family is–"

"Ok, ok, calm down, Jack." Mr. Farris sounded rather irritated. "I never said our party is getting behind David. All I'm saying is that he seems like a really good-hearted, passionate, patriotic man, and that's the kind of man we're looking for to support in the elections.

No one is voting for David Connally."

"I know, Mike, and I'm sorry," Jack sighed. "You just reminded me that I still know hardly a thing about this guy besides his name and that he loves America. He's a hard worker, too, and seems like he gets along well with just about everybody. But other than that...he's a complete mystery to me."

"Well, I like him," Mr. Farris said. "He may be hiding something in his past that he's just trying to forget about and start over. Everyone has secrets. But I wouldn't put a man on the platform who I didn't completely endorse for office, or if I don't know everything about him that I'm satisfied to know. Senator Cane is looking the best out of all the potential candidates we have lined up. He seems to connect with the people fairly well, and I'm impressed with his qualities as a leader. Like I said, he's brimming with confidence in himself."

"But vain," Jack added, thinking of earlier that evening when the senator had been eyeing David like a rival.

"But vain," Mr. Farris agreed. "Still, I would go so far as to say that he'd be a good man to take over the Oval Office, even. I can handle a little vanity from a politician if I know they're working hard to serve the needs of the people in the best way they can. Honesty. Dependability. Decency. That's what I'm looking for in a future president. That's what our country needs."

"And you think Senator Cane carries all those attributes?" Jack asked, draining the last of his iced tea and tossing the paper cup toward the trash can from where he sat.

"To my knowledge, yes. But hey, listen Jack, I'm bushed. I'll talk to you tomorrow before y'all head out again, ok?"

"Sounds good, Mike," Jack answered, bending over with a grunt to pick up his cup that had missed the trash can. "Congratulations on tonight, really. It couldn't have gone better."

"Well, we have your man David to thank for that," Mr. Farris replied with a chuckle, and hung up.

THE SPEAKER

↑ CHAPTER 4:

True to his word, Jack knocked on David's door at seven o'clock the next morning. He wasn't surprised when David answered the third knock appearing fully dressed, as if he had been waiting for Jack to wake up and come get him for some time. The young man did look refreshed, however, and full of energy.

"Morning, Jack!" he addressed his employer, sailing past him toward the truck with a cheerful nonchalance that made Jack shake his head as he closed David's door and followed him out to the parking lot.

"What's on the agenda for today?" David asked as they climbed into the truck and buckled up.

"Besides the usual taking-down and packing up, we're having breakfast with Mr. Farris in town beforehand. I need to make sure we're still all on the same page about a couple of things before we head out."

"Where are we heading out to, anyway?" David questioned. Jack noticed he seemed to be growing bolder in asking questions than he had been before.

"Bowling Green, Kentucky. And it's going to be a big one this time."

"What, the others weren't so big?" David said, clearly puzzled.

Jack suppressed a laugh. "No, David, I wouldn't say a thousand people or so is a really big crowd for this kind of rally we're setting up for. You could ask Farris yourself, but the kind of numbers he and the other heads of The American Party are looking for would probably range in the thousands."

David's eyes widened.

"But that's the kind of number they need to really have an

61

impact before the elections, if they want to make a big difference," Jack went on, fumbling for his phone, which was buzzing persistently on his belt.

"Hey, what do you know," he muttered before placing the phone to his ear and steering the truck with one hand. "Hey, Orville! How you been? Are you doing OK now? Uh-huh, well, I know you're sorry about it, so you can stop apologizing," Jack said. His voice was firm, but not bitter. "How's your ankle and...leg, right? Yeah...Well of course you're going to be out of commission for a while, Orville. That's what happens when people get hurt in an accident. No, I don't want you up here now...oh, come on, Orville! I didn't mean it that way."

Jack glanced at David out of the corner of his eye. The young man sat quietly with his hands in his lap, but he was gazing off into the distance with a strange, almost melancholy expression in his darkened eyes. Jack quickly refocused on his phone conversation.

"Or – Orville, listen to me," he said patiently. "Don't think that because you broke a couple of bones that I'm letting you go, far from it. But you're no use to me in your condition, that's all I'm saying, ok? And when your head's fixed you can join up with us, and I'll welcome my sound man back with open arms. How does that sound to you?"

Jack ran his tongue over his lower lip, then a relieved smile spread over his face with Orville's response.

"Ok then, no problem!" he said. "You just work on getting well, you hear? Ok. Alright, Orville. I'll talk to you later...oh, well, actually, do you know where Aaron is? I thought he'd be on his way up here by now. Hmm...ok, well, hopefully I'll hear from him or see him soon. Take care, Orville."

Jack snapped his phone back onto his belt. He looked at David again, but the young man had ceased to stare out the window, and had pulled out his Bible in which he was now studiously absorbed. Jack tried to crane his neck just a little without appearing to be interested so he could see where David was in his reading, and happened to see the young man had his Bible open to the book of Psalms.

It did not take them long to find the local coffee shop where they were to meet Michael Farris and the rest of the crew for breakfast. Jack did not waste time in getting down to business after they were all seated inside the cozy cafe with their meal and steaming cups of coffee.

"I guess we'll see you tomorrow night in Bowling Green," he told Mr. Farris, taking a careful sip of the hot beverage in his hand. "By the way, when you get there can you send me a map so I can find that place? I almost didn't find this one," he added jokingly. Mr. Farris swallowed a bite of doughnut and nodded briefly as he wiped his mouth with a napkin.

"Sure thing, Jack. I should be there by this evening, and I'll email you extra directions from there," he promised. He then turned to David, who was sitting a little distance from the two of them, quietly eating his meal.

"David," Mr. Farris called, and the young man looked up.

"David, I can't thank you enough for what you did last night," Mr. Farris said. "I personally believe you saved the day, and you got people right in the heart, which is exactly what we're trying to do."

David blushed, and murmured something inaudible before gazing down into his coffee. Jack and Mr. Farris grinned at each other.

"Amazing," Mr. Farris said, low. "He's like our secret weapon, and he doesn't even want any credit."

Jack threw him a warning look. "Careful, Mike. David may be a great people person, but don't expect him to do this every time. That's not what he's here for, remember?"

"You're right, of course," Mr. Farris agreed, though he stole a regretful glance toward the other table where David sat chatting with a few other crew members.

"Oh, Jack, before I forget, as I'm prone to do with all that's going on, I need to tell you that Rick McCoy is coming in for the next rally, in Kentucky," Mr. Farris said, loudly enough for the others to hear. His words produced the same effect on everyone as they noticeably straightened up in their seats and turned their heads at the sound of that name.

"Who's Rick McCoy?" David asked Eric Dodge, who sat beside him.

"Oh, he's the big boss who's really in charge of everything," said Eric, complacently biting into his flaky pastry. "He's the guy Farris answers to. Chairman of The American Party, or something like that. Anyway, I don't think he usually comes down for the rallies. With his job I bet he's unbelievably busy all the time. But Jack said last night that this next rally's supposed to be a really big one, so I guess McCoy thinks it's part of his responsibility to attend, or whatever. I've never met him myself, but from what I heard, he's a real stickler for having things done the right way. And I think he's a cowboy."

"Cowboy?" asked David, who was listening intently to everything Eric said.

"Yeah, he's got a ranch up in Montana, what I hear. So that means he's really tough, doesn't it?"

David stifled a laugh. He looked over where Jack and Mr. Farris were putting their heads together over their coffee, deep in serious conversation.

"Why is he coming? Did he say?" Jack asked.

"He said he needed to be here firsthand to see everything that's happening with the rally. Don't worry, Jack. I'm the one who answers to McCoy."

"Yes, but I answer to you, and we can't risk any more accidents like the one we had on the way up from Florida–"

"Jack, we haven't had any more accidents like that since. We were between a rock and a hard spot last night, but David pulled us out of that one. Don't jinx the next rally," he added laughingly.

"Well, we'll be there by noon tomorrow to set up," Jack said.

"Good," Mr. Farris replied.

Their conversation was interrupted by Eric, who made an excited noise and jumped up with half a doughnut in his mouth, pointing the other half of the pastry at the large TV up on the wall of the cafe.

64

CHAPTER 4:

"Hey! We're on TV!" he exclaimed excitedly.

Jack, Mr. Farris, David, and the others all turned to stare at the screen, which up until then had been showing the local farm and weather reports. The station was interrupted by a news broadcast, with an announcement about The American Party rally last night. As the local newscaster onscreen began speaking, everyone leaned forward to listen.

"Last night the largest political rally this part of Tennessee has ever seen took place here in our charming town of Elizabethton. The American Party, a non-profit, conservative organization, is holding rallies around the country in attempts to reach the public concerning political issues of the day. They stop for a few days in a pre-designated city and hold a rally, then continue on to the next town. The party's manager, Michael Farris, says that, in addition to supporting conservative men who are running for office, The American Party is standing up for the ideals that the Founding Fathers held when they established American government hundreds of years ago."

"What we're really all about is raising awareness in the American people on the state of the nation today," said Mr. Farris as the camera cut to him standing with the rally stage behind him in the setting sun. "Our country is in a bad way these days, and what we want is to remind her citizens that it wasn't always this way. The original system of running the country as laid out by the Founding Fathers is the only true way to run the government, and it's a blueprint for America's people to live their lives."

"Could you explain what you mean by that, Mr. Farris?"

"Absolutely. Take a look around at some of the biggest problems America's facing right now. Abortion. Same-sex marriage. Poor management of the economy because of corruption and dishonesty in Washington. These are just a few, but what do they all have in common? Selfishness. Godlessness. And it seems like there are people on both sides of the line who have problems efficiently handling or even thinking about these issues.

"That's why The American Party doesn't run on a strictly single-party ticket. We support and endorse potential candidates

65

whom we feel carry a strong belief in and respect for the Constitution, as well as a desire and game plan to tackle and really deal with the issues we're facing in our country. These days the administration tends to hide or make only vague statements on where they stand on certain issues, but we need leaders who will succinctly state what they believe about the Constitution and the vital role it plays in the proper functioning of government. We look for men of moral character who want to turn America around, because she's going downhill fast. A couple hundred years ago the American people were more invested in their country, more religious, and more eager to keep the flame of freedom alive."

The on-screen Mr. Farris adjusted his hat, and Jack turned to give him a look. Everyone who knew Michael Farris was well aware of the affinity he carried for his Stetson.

"Nowadays we've become a very selfish, post-modern people, always looking out for number one," his voice on the TV went on. "Common decency seems to have become a thing of the past in many places. The roadblocks to abortion are being struck down by the day, and now you've got homosexuals wanting to get married. Politicians up in Washington are concerned about what they'll get out of the corrupt laws that get passed, and ignore the Constitution every way they can. It's a real mess. All you have to do is read a newspaper or watch the news. But the Founding Fathers stood for something more, something noble. They carried a vision of greatness for the future of their country. They created just the right system of checks and balances so the different parts of the government couldn't override each other. They placed the ultimate accountability of the government in the hands of the people. We, the people, are the ones the government is supposed to answer to. But we don't govern ourselves anymore. We've basically given up on taking responsibility for ourselves as long as the government makes us happy and gives us what we want. People don't care that the government has grown out of control because they just want the government to take care of them. People don't like to hear, 'You need to be responsible, and go get a job,' things like that. They want a babysitter, in so many words. They don't want to work; they just want the benefits from it. They want whatever makes them happy, and they want it immediately. And with that mindset, it's no wonder the government has grown so big and has such terrible leaders. The Constitution gets thrown into the closet and honesty takes a back seat.

"The Founders had the foresight to pen the Constitution in such a way as to make it work for hundreds of years and it hasn't failed us yet. The Founders were always for 'God and country,' and those are the kind of leaders we need today. We want to remind people of that."

"Thank you, Mr. Farris. The American Party reaches out to the people in a rather unique way, leaving its own special mark on the places it leaves behind. In this case, as the candidates who were to speak at the rally in Elizabethton were delayed by traffic, a young man by the name of David Connally entertained the audience like no one we have ever seen before. He sang with and spoke to the audience for at least an hour. I was there reporting on the rally, and I have never seen anything like it. Afterward I was able to interview several people, and all I could hear them talking about was this guy David, and how he had lifted their spirits and made them think about the greatness of America.

"It was quite a turnout, and something of a fluke. We've never seen this kind of attention and praise at a grassroots political rally for somebody who just gets up and starts talking about America. He must really know his history or something. Anyway, the audience was impressed with this David fellow, and it's safe to say he seemed to raise morale at this rally."

The broadcast cut to a commercial, and everyone turned to stare at David. David looked around, wide-eyed and hastily took a long drink of coffee. When he put down his cup, wiped his mouth, and realized everybody was still looking at him, he rubbed his forearm, shrugged and said, "What?"

Mr. Farris leaned back in his chair, poking his tongue into the side of his cheek. He grinned knowingly at Jack.

"I told you so," he said in a low but buoyant voice. Scraping his chair back, he stood up and picked up his Stetson which had been sitting next to him.

"Gentlemen, I need to be on the road as of this moment. I'll expect you to keep up the good work you're doing when we all reach Kentucky. See you there!"

As he spoke, Mr. Farris placed his hat on his head, clapped a rather speechless Jack on the shoulder, and maneuvered between the tables toward the door. When passing by David, Mr. Farris paused a moment, looked down at the young man, and shook his head with a smile of admiration.

"You take care of yourself, David," Jack heard him say. "I don't think you realize how indispensable you are to this cause."

David looked up at Mr. Farris with a small smile and answered, "Oh, I don't know about that, sir. But I will."

"Trust me." Mr. Farris pulled open the cafe door, and the chime of the jingling bell hanging from it accompanied his next words. "You are."

Mr. Farris opened the door to his silver Lexus and stood with one arm propped up on the top of the door, dialing a number on his cell with the other hand. Holding the phone to his ear, he waited.

"Mr. McCoy! How are you?" he said brightly when a voice on the other line picked up. "Yes, I just wanted to touch base with you before I head out. Yes, yes, I'm almost on my way right now... Absolutely sir, will do. There's just something I wanted to speak to you about real quick, um...so I guess you've been watching the news?"

Mr. Farris paused as the voice on the line suddenly grew more animated, and he couldn't get a word in for several seconds.

"David Connally, sir. I really think this guy could be just what the party needs to raise not only our publicity but the excitement and interest of the people. I mean, you saw the news. The crowds love him. And you don't know the half of...."

Again, Mr. Farris took pause as his boss interrupted with a storm of words that caused a small frown to creep gradually over the manager's face, and a small wrinkle formed between his eyebrows.

"But, Mr. McCoy, it isn't like he's trying to run for office or anything, he's just singing! And he's also talking. A little bit. No, we don't know much about him, but…Yes, sir, I understand," he said finally, his voice much more subdued. He slid down sideways into the driver's seat of his Lexus, resting his boots on the pavement. After a few more seconds, he nodded once and said firmly, "Yes sir. I'll arrange a meeting directly after the rally in Bowling Green."

Mr. Farris took a deep breath, then added, "Mr. McCoy, I think you'll be impressed. I really do. There's something about this guy...I think he's good for this party."

The voice on the other end uttered a few quiet words and then the line went dead.

Mr. Farris stuck his phone back on his belt and rubbed a hand across his face. Twisting around so he was facing the steering wheel, he sat up straight and started the engine. As the Lexus hummed to life, Mr. Farris put it in gear and backed out of the parking spot. As he came parallel with the coffee shop, he glanced over and saw David through the window. The young man was laughing heartily with the others. He seemed to fit right in, almost as easily as if he had known these men his whole life. But then, Mr. Farris mused, David seemed to behave that way around anyone. It was no wonder everybody seemed to like him. Mr. Farris smiled as he watched the group inside the coffee house window. Then he set his face toward the highway and drove away.

When Jack and his crew arrived at the rally site in Bowling Green, Kentucky, they were treated to a spectacle. Surrounding the area where Mr. Farris had obtained a permit for the rally were several trucks lined up with satellite TV stations in place. In fact, there were so many trucks they were blocking the entrance to the fairgrounds where the rally was to be held. Jack opened his truck door and got out in a slow daze.

"Wow," he whispered. "How many news trucks do you count?"

David, who had gotten out of the passenger seat and was now standing beside him, whistled softly. "I count more than five," he said, his voice hushed with awe.

"Jack! Jack!"

They both turned around and saw Mr. Farris hurrying toward them, half walking, half running.

"Isn't this great?" he exclaimed when he reached them. He turned to observe the news anchors and cameramen getting their equipment in order in preparation for the events ahead. "I can't believe we already have this much publicity this soon. Mr. McCoy is going to be thrilled!"

Then Mr. Farris bit his lip, and half-turning away from David and Jack, muttered, "If he even knew how to be thrilled."

"What was that?" Jack asked him. Mr. Farris turned quickly back toward him.

"Oh, it's nothing, really! But listen, Jack, I have to tell you, we have people coming in tonight not only from Kentucky and Tennessee, but some are coming from even as far away as Arkansas and Missouri. Can you believe it? We may not have enough room for them all!"

David and Jack looked at each other in wonder, both from the news and Mr. Farris' reaction to it. Jack had not seen the man this worked up in a long time. Mr. Farris was usually very calm and collected with his emotions, and even now in his present state of excitement, he was standing still, but his speech was much quicker, his eyes were sparkling, and he was constantly turning his head every which way to take in all the proceedings around them.

"But, Mike, how did you know who all's coming, when they haven't even gotten here yet?" Jack asked.

"Remember that virtual RSVP invitation we sent out to the surrounding counties before the first rally? Well, we didn't get a lot of responses. Mr. McCoy told me I needed to find a better way of publicizing and getting the word out about our events. But after what David did for us, well, I thought I'd give it another shot. And I was blown away, blown away, I tell you, by the response we got! And the comments that came with the RSVPs. Oh, and listen to this: The American Party is being contacted by nearly every national, conservative, independent, and Republican candidate currently running. They want the chance to speak in our rallies and get our endorsement. I tell you what, Jack, we got ourselves a good thing going here," Mr. Farris said exultantly.

Jack's face broke into a smile, although the sight of all the television trucks and people was still overwhelming. While he was speaking, Mr. Farris walked toward the fairground entrance, and Jack, with a nod to David to follow, hurried alongside him.

Come on, Jack, he told himself. You worked for Barnum & Bailey. A few TV people running around shouldn't be any problem.

But something still nagged at him. The news trucks, all grouped around in a haphazard oval near the rally area, pulled at a memory at the back of his mind. The last time he had seen such a crowd of television vehicles before, complete with their newscasters and camera people walking around, had been back when...

No.

Jack shook his head firmly, the short word almost on his lips that he had to bite in order to keep quiet. Don't think about it, he ordered himself. But against his will, the handsome, boyish face of a young man with dark hair and laughing eyes rose before his vision. It was a face he saw every day. A face that held a look of permanent joy and satisfaction. Eyes that looked back at Jack from a photograph stuck up under the visor in his truck.

"Jack, I need you to help me out in talking to the TV people." Mr. Farris' voice broke into Jack's thoughts, and Jack snapped to attention, banishing the unwelcome images from his mind. "We have to get a space cleared for a helicopter landing, which means a lot of these trucks will need to be moved. Rick McCoy will be flying in from Atlanta in a couple of hours."

"And the rally starts at six, which means we only have a few hours to get everything all set up," Jack commented, glancing over where his crew was unloading and carrying the stage and microphone system over to the center of the otherwise empty fairgrounds.

"So the big boss is coming in, eh?" he said, and Mr. Farris grinned. It didn't touch his eyes. "Yep, he told me he had to come and see this firsthand, what with all the talk on the news about David, and the publicity this party is getting. If I were him, I know I'd want to be up close and personally involved with what's happening, not sitting behind a desk with a phone for my microphone."

"You seem worried."

Mr. Farris' smile dropped. He took off his Stetson, scratched his dark hair, and replaced his hat with a smart tap on the brim. "I spoke with Mr. McCoy yesterday," he said slowly, rubbing his chin. "He wants to speak with David immediately following tonight's rally, so I promised to arrange a meeting for them as soon as David comes offstage. When he's done speaking–"

"Wait, wait," Jack held up his hands in protest. "Speaking? You're going to have David get up there and talk to the audience again? I thought that was a one-time deal. A fluke. A scapegoat to buy you time while your real speakers were stuck in traffic. You already owe the kid one."

"I know, I know!" said Mr. Farris impatiently. "But remember what a great success it was? I was never so happy about a traffic jam in my life. Because of it, we were able to witness something incredible! Don't tell me you didn't listen to what David was saying up there and that it didn't make every bit of sense to you, Jack. We've already notified tonight's speakers, and David has a start time of one hour maximum before the other candidates–"

"David is not a candidate!" Jack shot out, incensed. Mr. Farris looked at him in surprise, and Jack passed his hand over his eyes. He couldn't explain why the idea of David putting himself out there for the world to see bothered him so much, but he had never taken anything out on his friend before.

Mr. Farris scrutinized him for a moment, then said slowly, "Right. You're right. David is not a candidate. He isn't running for any political office. I don't see why such a thought makes you so upset though, Jack."

"I'm sorry, Mike," Jack said wearily, his face turned away from Mr. Farris as he tried to understand the tangle of thoughts coursing through his mind. "I just...he's not here to do that. I know he's talented. I know he's clever with words, and that he's got enough spirit and passion for the whole of America. But, when he gets up there, and he starts saying those things...it just...I guess it just reminds me that we don't have enough men like him, men willing to do or die for what they believe. Men willing to sacrifice wholeheartedly for the good of their country and freedom. And when I think that, I think–"

"That you need to protect him so you don't lose him."

Jack looked up at his boss. Mr. Farris' handsome eyes were shrewd and thoughtful. He looked at Jack as if he could see straight through him, see his every last thought.

"I've watched you and that young man, Jack. I know you're growing to care for him, and I think that's a good thing, especially since he doesn't seem to have a father figure or other family in his life as far as we know. And because he's so good for the party and so good for America, you want to make sure this sudden bright illumination we have doesn't get doused or dimmed. You want to protect this kid, and keep him away from any possible dangers, even the ones you only imagine."

Jack took a step back, as if he could hardly believe that what Mr. Farris was telling him were truths he hadn't even tried to explore within himself, but had subconsciously known they were there all the same. Unsure what to do or say, or even what to do with his hands except cross his arms, he shuffled his feet, gave half of a smirk which signified he could make no denial, and mumbled, "And?"

"And any parent would feel the same way," Mr. Farris said kindly. "Hey, I have three of my own, and I'd do anything in the world to keep them safe. And I know you...with Ryan...no man could be a better father–"

"Don't," Jack's voice was sharp, but also laced with heavy sorrow. Mr. Farris nodded briefly, "Ok, ok, Jack. I won't go there. But Jack..." Mr. Farris moved closer to his old friend. "David Connally is a man, and he isn't your son. It's good you look out for him, but you can't hold him back from an opportunity like this. It would be wrong. With the gifts he has, it's only right that he get up on that stage. When you have something to say to a broken country that desperately needs words of healing, and you know you can give those words, why stay quiet? And if David really loves it up there, then I say let him go."

Jack hung his head. He knew all this. He knew it so well that he hated himself for even thinking about keeping David from

73

speaking to the crowds. But he couldn't help the concern flooding through him, and the fact that he still knew virtually nothing about David and his past only magnified his worry.

"I say we ask David ourselves if he wants to do this," he said finally.

Mr. Farris approved, and they both turned around to where they had left David standing.

"Where is he?"

When Mr. Farris and Jack walked a short distance away to hold their private conversation, David took his time wandering along the fence that surrounded the fairgrounds. Hands in his pockets, he took in with interest the buzzing activity the television reporters were making. Then he saw Jack's crew working on setting up and, looking over at Jack, hesitated, unsure if he should go work on the sound system or stay here with Jack since he had had him come along instead of staying with the crew. But Jack was deep in conversation with Mr. Farris, neither of them paying him any attention now. So David stood a bit awkwardly for a minute, as if waiting to be told what to do before turning to walk back the way he had come. That was when he saw a boy on the other side of the fence near him.

The boy looked to be about twelve years old, with floppy brown hair and a sprinkling of freckles across his nose and cheeks. He clung to the metal fence with his small brown hands, his large eyes following David's every move. As David cocked his head when he looked back at the boy, he noticed the child's eyes were vibrantly green.

David's face broke into an automatic smile of assurance as he approached the boy and stopped a few feet away, the fence between them.

"Hey there," he said, pulling one hand from his pocket to give a small wave. "What's your name, buddy?"

"Robby."

"Well, it's nice to meet you, Robby. My name is David. What are you doing around here?"

"Is there any work over there I could do?" the boy asked

without hesitation. David raised his eyebrows, but his smile grew wider. He glanced back at the trucks and partially-assembled stage area, then turned back and lifted his shoulders apologetically.

"Well, Robby, I don't think we have any jobs for you, but that sure is nice of you to want to help out."

"Oh." A shadow cast over his face, Robby let go of the fence and scuffed his sneaker in the dirt. Then he squinted up at David.

"Aren't you that guy on TV?" he asked, and David chuckled, taken aback by the innocent but direct question.

"I guess I am," he said. "That was my first time, too."

"My dad said you sound a lot different than what the other people say on TV. They don't never talk like you."

David was silent, his eyes thoughtful.

"But I wish they would," Robby added eagerly. "My dad said you said lots of nice things about America. I'm learning history about America in school, and all the stuff you said is right in my book! About the start of America and everything."

David smiled and nodded.

"But my teacher says America's doing everything wrong," Robby continued as if giving a speech. "Well, not everything, but lots of things. And she says America is a...a...oh...oppressor, and she blames America for the bad stuff that's happening in the world, she says."

"Oh, no, no, Robby! That isn't true at all!" said David quickly, his voice filled with concern. "America is not to blame for the rest of the world's problems. America is the greatest nation on earth, and we have freedoms here that no other country has."

Robby nodded slowly, his face awestruck.

"Sometimes," David went on in a patient tone, "bad people become in charge of how things are run, and they throw wrenches in the works, and they want to do things differently than how things should be done. These people say they're going to make everything better, but they really don't. They're only looking out for themselves and what they want. And then they want to blame others for their own mistakes because they're afraid to face the messes they make. This is what some people, like your teacher, don't really understand very well, and then they blame America herself instead of the people who are supposed to be taking care of her, but they aren't doing their job."

David's natural passion was starting to bubble up as he spoke, and Robby was staring at him, open-mouthed.

"My mom said you should be on TV all the time!" he declared.

It was now David's turn to stand open-mouthed, then he laughed and glanced off somewhere over Robby's head before meeting the boy's eyes again.

"Well, thank you very much."

Then his brow furrowed. "Wait, is that your full name? Doesn't Robby stand for something?"

"Yeah," the boy said. "My full name's Robert."

David's head snapped up, and he took a couple of steps back. The friendly smile that had come so easily before now seemed to be struggling to stay in place. His lips tightened, and a heavy line appeared between his eyebrows, almost as though he was experiencing a painful spasm. He felt an aching strain in his hand, and looking down, realized the hand that wasn't in his pocket was clenched in a white-knuckled fist.

The boy was still watching him, but he was a little less sure of the conversation now, and both curiosity and a touch of fear shown out of his eyes. David looked up and saw this. He relaxed himself, took a deep, rather shuddering breath, and the shadow slowly faded from his eyes. He followed that with a new smile, saying,

"That's a good name, Robert. A fine, strong name. Do you know what it means?"

Robby shook his head.

"It means 'bright with glory.' It's a name you'll really want to live up to," said David, his voice more controlled now. He rested his hands against the fence and looked down at the little boy.

"You can do great things with your life, Robby, if you want to. If you let Him, God will do amazing things through you so you can glorify Him. Others will look to you as an example. And if you trust God and live like it, you will be that example."

Robby's eyes were once again filled with wonder as he stared up at David. Then he cocked his head and asked, "Can you talk some more? You sound like those guys my mom watches on BBC."

David threw back his head in earnest laughter this time.

"David! Hey, David!"

David turned around and saw Jack and Mr. Farris walking towards him, Jack beckoning to him. He noticed Jack looked visibly out of countenance.

David turned back to the boy.

"I have to go," he said. "But you remember what I said, ok Robby? You're going to do great things for the Lord someday."

"Bye, David!" Robby called out, dashing off as if he had been sent on a mission of vast importance. David straightened up and watched him go, a far-off look in his eyes.

Jack and Mr. Farris reached him just as Robby scurried away. They both looked at the retreating figure of the boy, then questioningly at David.

"Oh, he said he recognized me from being on TV," David said, pushing his hands back into his pockets.

"So even the kids are paying attention," Mr. Farris remarked jovially. Then in a more serious tone said, "David, I've made some calls, and we would like to give you the opportunity to speak to the audience again tonight, same as before. We can give you an hour before the speakers begin. Of course, the choice is entirely up to you."

Mr. Farris gave Jack a quick sideways glance before adding, "I think, and I know I'm not the only one who does, that you and your words at the last rally were exactly what everyone needed and wanted to hear. You have been such a tremendous help to us, David, and I'm not talking just publicity-wise. You are giving lifeblood to our cause that we didn't even know we needed until you got up on that stage. You really can make a difference, David."

Jack cast an aggravated look in Mr. Farris's direction, who was carefully avoiding eye contact with him. Jack stepped in. "David, you don't have to go up there. Like he said, it's your choice."

He expected David to hesitate, to show a shade of reluctance perhaps. No, it wasn't expectancy. It was hope. He hoped David would refuse. Say no, David. Don't go into the limelight again. It's harder to protect people with rising fame.

But David was smiling and nodding. Jack's heart sank.

"Sure, I'll be glad to speak tonight," he said, and Mr. Farris clasped his hand enthusiastically. Then he gave Jack the I-told-you-so face.

"When you come off the stage tonight, Rick McCoy wants to talk to you," he told David as the three of them walked back toward the rally location.

"Rick McCoy, the man in charge of The American Party?" David asked.

"The one and only," Mr. Farris replied with mock majesty. "Mr. McCoy wants to meet you formally, which only makes sense, seeing as you're sort of becoming a central piece of the party. With all the publicity and popularity you've been drumming up, why wouldn't the head boss want to meet you?"

David glanced hesitantly at Jack, who felt about as nervous as David looked. But when Jack saw the expression in David's eyes, he instinctively stepped forward and said, low, "It'll be fine, David. You'll be fine."

David gave his habitual half-smile. "I know. Thanks, Jack."

"When you finish speaking tonight, Mr. McCoy and I will have a meeting with you in the party's motor home behind the stage, alright?" Mr. Farris said.

David walked a few steps ahead of Jack and Mr. Farris, paused, then turned and fixed his gaze on the stage, which Jack's crew was slowly assembling several yards away. He pursed his lips in thoughtful silence, his hands still in his pockets.

Mr. Farris folded his arms. Jack tried to guess what was passing through David's mind.

"Can I get to work now?" David asked.

"Uh, don't you want some time to prepare what you're going to say tonight?" said Mr. Farris, raising his eyebrows.

"I already know what I'm going to say."

CHAPTER 4:

David turned to Jack, who nodded his assent, and the young man walked away. Jack and Mr. Farris watched him join the work crew and start uncoiling the wires and cords that linked to the audio system.

Mr. Farris rested his hands on his hips, stuck his tongue inside his cheek, and turned to Jack with an amused glint in his eyes.

"Well, he didn't have notes last time," he said. "Now, we better go talk to those reporters about their vehicles. You coming, Jack?"

Jack's eyes were still following David. Without looking at his boss he said softly, "You're right, Mike. David Connally may be the best thing that could happen to this party."

Mr. Farris took a few steps back toward Jack, put his hand on Jack's shoulder, and said, "He may be the best thing that could have happened to all of us. Now, come on. We need to get things moving. Also, one of the Republican primary candidates for president, Joseph Cane, will be here tonight, along with his wife. We'd better get busy."

The air above the fairgrounds was whipped up in a frenzy of dust and grass clippings as the shiny black helicopter slowly descended from the sky. Dusk had only just fallen, with one or two stars already twinkling down. Bright floodlights lit up the area, creating a soft glow in the sky above the site of The American Party's rally. Close to five thousand people were jam-packed before the stage with the large blue-and-gold banner reading "The American Party" across the front. A substantial number of the audience were seated in chairs closer to the stage, but there were many who had to stand much farther away, so that the crowd reached all the way back to the fence surrounding the fairgrounds. A murmur of excitement and expectation rippled through the air, darting in and out amongst the mass of people like an eager spirit, bringing with it the single name that was most often heard on the lips of those attending tonight's rally: David Connally.

Mr. Farris, having just introduced and passed David as he hurried offstage, glanced back once to see that the young man's

79

microphone was working, then headed off to meet the helicopter as it arrived. He stood with his feet apart, clasping his left wrist. His hat was tilted up so the wide, white brim wouldn't throw shadows over his face.

The sound of the helicopter's engine and whirring propeller blades was deafening the closer it came to the earth. When the chopper finally settled on the packed ground, the pilot cut the engine, and Mr. Farris instinctively moved a few steps forward, removing his hat and raising his hand in greeting as the helicopter doors opened and two men stepped out.

The taller of the men was also clearly the elder, though by no means less energetic than his companion. He walked with a spry, almost bouncing step, swinging a leather briefcase in one hand while the other was nestled in the pocket of his slacks below his dark sports jacket. His iron-gray hair was naturally parted in the center, cut shorter toward his face in a soft angle. There were streaks of black still running through the gray. But this man's face did not match the age his hair revealed. In fact, it would appear at first glance as though the face of rather a young man and the hair of a senior citizen had been combined in him. A closer look, however, showed the crow's feet and wrinkles in the delicate skin around his eyes, and the heavy lines in his forehead and between his salt-and-pepper eyebrows. But other than those tell-tale signs of age, he still carried a very youthful countenance with a healthy tan. His lips were firmly drawn across, like the man was in a constant state of hard thinking. His eyes were a stormy blue and set back in his narrow face. These eyes were steady, astute, and quick to detect their surroundings.

The second man was dressed similarly to the first: slacks, a button-down shirt, and a sports jacket. Although he was younger by several years, his solemn expression and wistful hazel eyes whispered hints of a much older soul within. His face was very thin, with sunken cheeks, a large nose, and thick eyebrows that matched his rough black hair. With his slender frame, pursed lips, and slightly pointed ears, he almost resembled a thoughtful elf. He walked with a brisk, heavy stride, and he too carried a briefcase of dark leather.

CHAPTER 4:

As both newcomers saw and approached Mr. Farris, he replaced his hat and stepped forward to shake their hands.

"Mr. McCoy, it is an honor to have you here with us tonight," he said fervently and loudly to be heard over the fading roar of the helicopter, gripping the hand of the gray-haired man.

Rick McCoy's handshake was firm and controlled as he replied, "Thank you, Mr. Farris. I've been looking forward to this, and I'm glad I was able to find time to be away from the office to come down here." His voice was husky, modulated, and low-pitched. He turned and indicated his companion, who was standing behind him.

"My assistant, Jeff Dixon," he introduced the younger man, who stepped up and extended his hand.

"Michael Farris," said Mr. Farris.

"Jefferson Dixon," said the other man with a small smile that looked as though he was sparing of its use. His voice was very deep, with a rich cadence that Mr. Farris did not expect to come out of such a slight figure. He released Jeff Dixon's hand and stepped back.

"Now, gentlemen, we all know why you're here, so please, follow me, and we'll get this evening's business started."

Mr. McCoy gave one terse nod to his assistant, who fell in step on one side of him while Mr. Farris walked on the other side of his boss. Together, the three of them walked away from the helicopter and back toward the fairgrounds.

Mr. Farris promptly escorted Mr. McCoy and Jeff Dixon to an area near the platform where they could observe David in action onstage. The singing was coming to a close when they arrived, and Mr. Farris had his boss and assistant carefully positioned close enough to the stage to see and hear David well, but far enough away so that the angle from which they were standing from the stage was out of David's line of vision.

Mr. Farris had his own reasoning for this that he did not share with Mr. McCoy. He had seen the nervous expression in David's eyes earlier when he had told the young man that the man in charge of The American Party wanted to meet with him personally. Knowing David for the length of time he had, Mr. Farris felt fairly

81

sure that David wasn't really worried, especially since he seemed to make himself agreeable to everyone he met. However, he was not about to let David see him bringing the boss out to actually watch him while he spoke onstage. He knew he had asked a big favor of David, getting up there again in front of thousands of people, and did not want any added pressure on the young man.

Mr. Farris stood beside Mr. McCoy, and kept stealing furtive glances at his boss's face, watching him watch David. Even in the bright floodlights in the fairgrounds, it was hard for him to gauge what Mr. McCoy was thinking. McCoy's face was set like a stone, clean of any expression. After a few minutes of observing David, he crossed his arms and tilted his head to one side. Mr. Farris, now on pins and needles, prayed these movements indicated interest, or at least curiosity, and not displeasure.

Mr. Farris was so involved in observing his boss that he paid hardly any heed to the object of their attention. However, the same could not be said of the audience sitting and standing out in front of David. Their eyes were lit up and their faces rapt, hanging on David's every word. Several phones and cameras were held high in the air, and little red recording lights blinked like Christmas lights. David's passion flowed out of him like water, and it was clear that he spoke straight from the heart. No notes. No pre-written speech. From time to time he would pause, appear to think solemnly for a few seconds, and repeat himself in a way that was swiftly endearing. But nothing was more electrifying than the words he spoke to the crowd of thousands that night.

Mr. Farris was noticing hardly any of this. He was so preoccupied with what Mr. McCoy might be thinking. The next time he looked at his boss, he realized McCoy had turned his gaze from David out over the crowd. McCoy's eyebrows furrowed in an inscrutable way as he observed the cell phones and cameras, the admiring faces, and felt the awed silence of the audience. Once again, Mr. Farris couldn't tell if his boss was pleased, puzzled, or provoked. Then he started worrying over why McCoy would be provoked over what he thought could only be seen as a good thing.

Jeff Dixon stood beside Mr. Farris, and he was observing

David closely as well, though without quite as much scrutiny as McCoy. He now turned and said softly to Mr. Farris, "Is this man a professional speaker?"

"Not that I am aware of, Mr. Dixon," Mr. Farris answered.

"He seems to connect well with the audience," Mr. Dixon said, gazing over the crowd. "And he seems fairly eloquent, if a little rough around the edges. Who writes his speeches?"

Mr. Farris's lips pulled back at the corners, in spite of his anxiety. "No one."

"No one!"

"No. In fact, I don't think David Connally uses notes of any kind when he gets up there," said Mr. Farris. "The man speaks straight from his heart, Mr. Dixon."

Jeff Dixon's brooding countenance took on an expression of incredulity, and his coldly sober eyes widened as he turned to look back at David again. Mr. Farris barely caught the words his boss's assistant muttered under his breath.

"A remarkable ability, the way he speaks."

Mr. McCoy divided his attention between watching David and the audience for about ten more minutes. Then he unfolded his arms, turned to Mr. Farris, and gestured for him and Mr. Dixon to come with him. The three of them convened in The American Party motor home, which was parked a short distance from the stage. The motor home was here for the use of Mr. Farris when traveling for the rallies, but now it was to be the place of an important meeting.

"Let me see if I have this straight," McCoy began as he seated himself at the small table inside the motor home. Mr. Farris stood across from him. "This David Connally, who is onstage right now, is the cause of all this publicity and attention for our rallies?"

"Yes sir," Mr. Farris responded promptly. "You told me so yourself, Mr. McCoy, that you've seen the news. You know he's creating a political stir and drumming up lots of attention for us."

"Tell me everything you know about this guy," said McCoy.

Jeff Dixon walked over to one of the windows facing toward the stage. Pulling back the short curtain with one finger, he continued to observe David in action.

"Well, sir, David's been working for Jack Webb, who's responsible for setting up our stage and sound system for the rallies–"

"And where is he from?" McCoy interrupted Mr. Farris.

Mr. Farris took a deep breath. Here it comes, he thought.

"Well, to be honest, Mr. McCoy, I'm not sure where David Connally is from," he said slowly. McCoy raised an eyebrow and leaned back in his chair, crossing one booted ankle over the opposite knee.

"You don't know where he's from."

His words were more of a disapproving statement than a question. Mr. Dixon turned away from the window towards the other two men as Mr. Farris hurriedly went on.

"Sir, David works for Jack as part of his crew. Jack told me that David had needed a job and so he hired him for the season. We've used Jack for a long time, I've known him for even longer, and I trust him completely. That's why I allowed David to do what he's doing. And after the way he helped us out the first time by keeping the crowd's attention during the traffic jam that made our speakers late, I mean, you saw it for yourself. This guy is a natural with the crowd. And you can see he means every word he says out there. He's got the kind of spirit and patriotism The American Party backs."

Mr. McCoy appeared unmoved. He leaned forward over the table.

"Go get this Jack Webb and bring him in here."

Mr. Farris found Jack backstage, strolling around with his hands in his pockets and looking rather ill at ease. When he looked up and saw Mr. Farris approaching, he quickly lengthened his stride to meet him.

"Hey, Mike, he's really going to town out there. I didn't think he could say anything he hadn't said before, but I tell you, I think he's lighting fireworks tonight," said Jack. He was restless and a bit anxious, but couldn't keep the pride out of his voice. Mr. Farris noticed this, and allowed a smile before putting his hand on Jack's arm and saying, "Well, at this point I wouldn't have expected any less of him. But listen, Jack. Mr. McCoy is in the motor home, and he wants to see you. Now. Come on."

"Is something wrong?" Jack asked, feeling his anxiety kicking up a notch. "That doesn't sound good."

"He wants to know more about David," Mr. Farris answered. "And you're the one who seems to know him best, right? After all, you're the one who found him."

Before Jack knew what was happening, he found himself in the motor home in the presence of his boss's boss, putting himself under subjection for interrogation. Mr. McCoy didn't stand up when Jack entered the motor home, but simply reached out to shake Jack's hand with a chilly politeness that was hard to melt.

Mr. Farris also introduced Jack to Mr. Dixon, whose handshake and greeting were somewhat warmer than his boss's. Then the four men gathered round the table as if they were planning a secret mission.

"How long have you known this David Connally?" McCoy said to Jack.

"About two months now," Jack said. "He was in trouble and needed a job."

"What kind of trouble?" McCoy demanded.

"Well, he'd lost all of his belongings in one of my trucks when it...when it caught fire on our way up to Jacksonville. My driver had an accident," said Jack, feeling more inexperienced and foolish than he had in years. Avoiding McCoy's steady gaze, he continued, "David needed a job since he had no money, and apparently nowhere to go, so I hired him as part of my crew during the rally season."

"So, before that, you had never seen him before? How did he come to be riding in one of your trucks?"

"Well, um..." Jack looked helplessly at Mr. Farris, who answered with a glance of equal uncertainty. If McCoy was already dissatisfied with not knowing anything about the man who was becoming identified (very quickly and publicly so) with his party, he was going to be even displeased to hear the beginning of David and Jack's story.

"I...found David Connally, or actually, he sort of found us, really," said Jack carefully. "My guys and I had a truck problem (it was the same truck that caught fire in the accident) and were pulled over at a truck stop. We were trying to figure out how to resolve the issue, when, David showed up."

"Showed up? You mean he just appeared from the blue?"

"You might say that," said Jack quietly.

"So..." McCoy ran his tongue over his lower lip, scooted his chair back, and looked Jack squarely in the eyes. "He's a hitchhiker."

Jack and Mr. Farris quickly looked at each other, and that didn't escape Mr. McCoy. He rounded on Mr. Farris.

"You knew this, didn't you?" he said coldly. "You let some crazy—"

"Sir—" Mr. Dixon interjected cautiously.

"So where did he come from, then, hmm?" McCoy continued, his eyes kindling quietly. "Did this Connally ever happen to mention where he lives, or where he was going? Or perhaps that just doesn't matter to you gentlemen, because I can see you're already so willing to defend him because he happens to have a good vocabulary and can spout a few patriotic phrases about America!"

"Mr. McCoy, I know it sounds strange, and it is very unique," Jack pleaded. "But he will not talk about his past. I've asked him on several occasions, and he simply refuses to go into it. But whatever you may think, David Connally is not just a common hitchhiker..."

His voice trailed away as Mr. McCoy slowly stood up. He looked around at all of them, then went to the window, jerked back the curtain, and pointing toward the stage outside, said, "So what you're saying is neither of you knows anything about this guy, other than his name and where you found him?"

"He is a nice guy, he minds his own business, he works hard, and he's dependable," said Jack firmly. His blood was beginning to boil as he listened to McCoy talk about David. "I've never even heard him swear. And every weekend he asks me if there's some place in town where he can go worship on Sunday morning, no matter where we are. I've never seen him do anything remotely questionable, Mr. McCoy. David Connally is trustworthy."

McCoy did not appear pacified by this. He let the curtain fall across the window and came close to Jack and Mr. Farris.

"You mean to tell me this thirty-year-old, ax murdering, drug kingpin who just got out of state prison after killing his family is ok to put out there in front of thousands of people with our stamp of approval?"

"Sir!" exclaimed Mr. Farris, stunned. Jack glowered, and felt Mr. Farris put a warning hand on his arm.

"For all we know, that's what he could be," declared McCoy. "This is unprofessional, Mr. Farris. I wouldn't have thought you would let some faceless nobody loose around our rallies without decent background checks and at least some identification.

"Well, sir, he's not a faceless nobody anymore," said Mr. Farris. "The people love him. And he's raising morale."

McCoy sighed and pinched the bridge of his nose, squeezing his eyes shut in an attitude of exasperation and concentration.

"Mr. Farris," he said finally, opening his eyes, "Don't misunderstand me. This guy is impressive."

Jack and Mr. Farris exchanged looks of surprise and excitement.

"But we can't do this," McCoy added. "Without knowing anything about this guy, it's just too much of a risk for us. If the media gets hold of something detrimental about David Connally, we're going to be in trouble up to our necks. And that's assuming there is anything detrimental in his past," he said sharply. "I saw how many TV cameras were out there tonight. I can guarantee you right now that every reporter who's seen this story on the news is trying to figure out everything they can about this guy, and I bet you a dime that they'll come up with more information than, 'I met him at a gas station and he seemed swell, so I hired him.'"

Jack bristled, but before he could reply, Mr. McCoy finished with, "From this point forward, until we figure out what to do with him, neither of you are to talk to anyone in the media about David Connally, or let him talk to anyone himself."

He looked hard at Mr. Farris first, then at Jack. Jack felt relief flowing through him. This wouldn't be difficult, as he was already working to keep David out of the limelight anyway.

↑ THE SPEAKER

But Mr. Farris was perplexed by this negative reaction.

"I understand what you're saying, Mr. McCoy," he said slowly, "but David isn't a candidate. He isn't running for any political office. He's simply entertaining the crowds and getting them excited for our rallies. He's the reason our numbers are this large so early on in the season. Like I told you on the phone, sir," and here Mr. Farris stepped forward, his face and voice in real earnest as he spoke, "David Connally is arguably the best thing that could have happened to rev up attention and publicity for our cause."

Mr. McCoy studied him closely for a minute, putting his hands on his belt. Then he turned to Mr. Dixon.

"Jeff, will you and Jack," nodding to Jack, "leave us alone, please?"

Mr. Dixon picked up his briefcase and gestured for Jack to exit the motor home before him. Mr. Farris tried to give Jack an encouraging look before the door closed after them.

When he and Mr. Farris were alone, McCoy addressed him in a calmer tone than he had used before, though it wasn't his style to speak loudly.

"Look, Michael," his use of Mr. Farris's first name was a sign of their long-standing relationship. "You and I have worked together for a long time now, and I know you're simply doing what you think is right for the party. But I have to tell you, this could potentially be a catastrophic mistake that we couldn't recover from."

Mr. Farris focused his gaze on the floor and said nothing. McCoy sighed again, and came around the table to stand in front of him.

"Look, I know this guy is probably nothing close to an ax murderer, I only say that to make a point–"

"You better not say that in front of Jack again," Mr. Farris interrupted quietly. "He and David have grown close, and I think he looks on David almost like a son."

McCoy drew back, his expression half surprise, half humorous.

"Well, I won't stand in the way of a budding friendship," he said sarcastically. "Like I said, the guy is obviously talented, and if

I got to talking to him personally, I might even come to like him. I know you think highly of him and what he seems to be doing for us. But with the information, or rather lack thereof that we have on him, this is just too big a risk, letting him loose out there."

Mr. Farris swallowed hard, his hand tightening around the back of the chair he stood behind. McCoy watched him, and thought briefly for a moment. Then resignation came over his face, and he came over beside Mr. Farris, put his hand on his shoulder, and said, "I'll tell you what I'll do, Michael. Before tonight is over I'll contact Nathan Blaine. I believe him to be among the top private investigators in the country. He could find a polar bear in hibernation during an Alaskan snowstorm, and what's more, he handles the information he digs up with taste and elegance. If there's anything to be found out about your David Connally, I'd trust Blaine for the job. He won't go off to the media with his findings; he'll report directly to me. We just need to be sure this David isn't hiding any skeletons in the closet that can interfere with his work in the party."

"You're the boss," Mr. Farris responded, putting out his hand. Mr. McCoy shook it heartily and even smiled a little.

"But there is one request I need to make," Mr. Farris added, and McCoy gestured for him to continue.

"We need some security people around here," said Mr. Farris. "Because already the crowds and reporters are trying to get to David before and after the rallies, and Jack and I can't hold them off by ourselves. The more popular David becomes, the harder it will be to keep people away from him. He's going to need some protection."

McCoy knit his brows, deepening the creases between his eyes and on his forehead.

"I believe you're right," he said at last. "I'll be in touch with Blackheart Security. All their guys are ex-special forces from all over. You give them a target to protect, and they'll make access to that target impossible. With them around, you can be sure no one gets to David."

"Excellent!" Mr. Farris exclaimed. Tonight was certainly going better than he had anticipated.

"These guys are not cheap," McCoy added gravely. "But I

know people in high places, and price shouldn't be too much of a problem. The important thing is, we keep David safe and away from people until we know more about him that will convince me he's fit to be doing what he's doing."

"Yes, sir," said Mr. Farris. "But sir," he added hesitantly, "Can he still speak?"

"Speak? I assume he can speak. He's out there speaking right now, isn't he?"

"No, sir, I mean...will he be allowed to be onstage while the P.I. is working behind the scenes?"

McCoy was silent for several seconds. His impassive mask had slipped back onto his face again, making it impossible for Mr. Farris to tell what he was thinking.

"We will see," he said finally.

Mr. Farris thanked his boss, and then noticed the time on the small clock above the door of the motor home. David's time was up. It was time for him to meet the boss.

"If you'll excuse me, I'll go bring David here now," Mr. Farris said, in an effort to appease his boss for being more accommodating than he had hoped he would be, in view of all the circumstances. "It's time for the other candidates to speak."

"Who is up first?" McCoy asked, looking out the window again.

"Joseph Cane, sir. One of our prime endorsements."

"Right. I like Cane. He's got solid ideals and a tough backbone."

"Yes, sir. Shall I go get David now?"

"Yes."

Mr. Farris turned around and walked to the door. As he was turning the doorknob, Mr. McCoy's voice arrested his actions.

"Michael." McCoy's voice was hesitant for the first time that evening, and cleared his throat. "It's not his fault. It's ours, for not checking him out before. I can see you think a lot of him, and I am grateful for all the positive attention our party rallies are getting..."

Mr. Farris stood still, his hand still on the doorknob, waiting.

"What you say may be true. David Connally may be good

for this party," said McCoy. "And if he's clean, we can keep using him."

Mr. Farris slowly turned around.

"You know, Mr. McCoy, I really feel that David is becoming the voice for our cause," he said thoughtfully. McCoy tilted his head to one side.

"By that I mean people are looking to him now, with as much or more attention than our actual endorsed candidates are receiving," Mr. Farris went on. He turned back and opened the door, setting one foot outside. Then he paused and turned around once more.

"I feel like he could be the voice of America herself, sir," he said.

Mr. McCoy nodded once, an acknowledgment of his colleague's words without a promise, and Mr. Farris returned the nod as he exited the motor home.

THE SPEAKER

⌜ CHAPTER 5:

Jack and Mr. Dixon were waiting a few feet from the motor home when Mr. Farris emerged. Jack was standing with arms folded across from Mr. Dixon, whose brooding expression did not invite conversation. Both of them were looking toward the stage area, where David, mindful of his time, was just giving his final farewell to the already-applauding audience. The roar of thousands of hands clapping together was swelling into a tumultuous storm.

When Jack saw Mr. Farris, he hurried towards him, expectant questions hovering on his lips. But Mr. Farris brushed a hand against his shoulder in passing just long enough to convey the silent message that everything was going to be fine, and quickly headed off to get David and introduce the candidates following David's opening.

Joseph Cane was to speak first after David, and the senator was already aware of how unenviable a position was his as he stood waiting for Mr. Farris to come onstage and introduce him. The first speaking slot of the evening was a coveted hour, one that Senator Cane had been almost certain of obtaining. But that was before he had received an unexpected and unwelcome call informing him that he had been, in so many words, bumped to second place to make way for a young civilian who was of no political standing or repute. And what was that young man being given prominence for? Singing and giving some little textbook lecture about America? Senator Cane's feelings had been less than gracious when he heard the news, and these had been his initial thoughts.

"It's been hard enough for me to work my way up, winning votes and loyalty from the people so I could have a seat in the Senate," he complained to his wife, who was listening patiently as they rode that night to the rally in Bowling Green. "I don't have an easy job,

93

and I have a pretty good idea of how this country should be run. I'm the best candidate The American Party has. And who is this David Connally guy? I've never heard of him, and I'm pretty sure I would have if he was anybody. It seems like they're just bringing him on as an entertainer. An opening act. I mean, I've watched this guy. He's nothing special. I don't see why everybody's so mesmerized by him."

"Well, what is he saying to them?" his wife asked calmly, reaching over to straighten her husband's tie. He shifted his weight and moved his head back so she could reach the knot at the center of his collar, his frustrated stare still glued to the back of the headrest of the seat in front of him.

"He's just throwing out a bunch of feel-good stuff about America, how great a country we live in, and how we should be so thankful to God for the freedoms we have, and so on…"

"And what's wrong with that?" his wife interjected. "It sounds to me like he's a very patriotic person. And don't we need more of them?"

Senator Canc moved his head from side to side, heaving an exasperated sigh as if he was at the end of his rope.

"Cassie, all that may sound nice, but we're facing a rather ugly reality in politics these days. I can't afford to give people warm, fuzzy feelings. I need their votes, but I win those votes by telling the truth like it is and promising them a better future. And I work hard to provide that."

"Of course you work hard," Cassie Cane said soothingly, laying a gentle hand on his arm.

"And I guess what irks me about this Connally guy is that he's just killing time out there in front of an audience, when the rest of us, the actual politicians, are the ones who are really doing something to make a better nation for everybody," Senator Cane brooded.

"Oh, I wouldn't say he's just killing time, if The American Party is giving him a full hour to speak to the audience. And if what you said he's saying is true, about being grateful for our freedom, being proud of our history, and so on, I think he must mean it. He's reminding the people about things of value and importance, Joseph. And the American people need to remember how we got here, and remember that things like life, liberty, and the pursuit of happiness aren't just words on paper. They are as real as the men who thought them up and wrote them down. We do live in a great country, dear, and we are blessed to have the freedoms we do. Maybe this Connally fellow is so passionate about those ideas that that's why they let him up there first, to raise morale and get everyone excited about you." And with those words, she leaned over and kissed her husband lightly on the cheek.

He turned his head and looked at her dully.

"You mean they wouldn't already be interested in hearing me speak without Connally up there first?" he demanded, half-playfully, but also half-worriedly.

His wife drew back, affronted. "Of course not, Joseph!"

She sat back in the seat, crossing her arms and shaking her head.

"I'm...joking, dear!" Senator Cane exclaimed, laughing feebly in an attempt to draw her out. She searched his face, and he threw up his hands in defeat.

"Ok! So I wish they'd let me speak first and that they hadn't given a whole hour to some nobody who The American Party isn't even endorsing, and he isn't running for political office either. I mean, who is this guy?" he said petulantly.

"Well, maybe tonight you can find out," she said gently. "But right now, honey, please...can we just enjoy having some time alone together before you have to step out into the public again?"

He sighed, and reached over to entwine his fingers in the hand of his wife.

"Sorry, dear. I'm really, very happy you came along tonight," he smiled at her.

"Me too." She smiled back. "I just never get enough of hearing you speak."

He made a face at her, then squeezed her hand before turning to gaze out the window.

That was all before the evening began. From the time Senator

Cane and his wife were shown to their reserved seats at the rally and David Connally took the stage microphone in his hand, to when the young patriot raised his hand and shouted in closing, "God bless you all, and God bless America!" the senator hardly took his eyes off him.

To a bystander, Joseph Cane might have looked rather stony, or maybe even angry, with his brows drawn together, and his hardened mouth which was partially concealed by his hand. He was a slender man, not very tall, but well built. His eyes were the color of graphite, with surprisingly thin eyebrows brooding just above them. A pucker was drawn between his eyes, as if he spent too much of his time dwelling on challenges he needed to overcome. His heart-shaped face had a high forehead, with his dark hair combed back in careful waves. His small ears stuck out from the sides of his head in a rather undignified way, more noticeable now after his recent haircut. His jaw locked as he stood still, creating a foreboding firmness around his lips. In his navy suit, white tie, and lapel pin of an enamel American flag, Senator Cane looked the picture of a professional U.S. politician, one full of promises, ideas, and personal agendas.

His scrutinizing gaze took in David's clothing, which was nice but still a bit too casual for such an event, the senator decided. He listened to the passionate cadence of David's voice and felt irritated because it seemed as though the young man was trying to stir up emotion on purpose in the audience that really wasn't necessary. And why were so many people taking pictures and videos of him? It wasn't as if he was extraordinarily handsome or possessed some great oratorical gift. He was plain-spoken, a little rough around the edges. Certainly not as articulate or polished as most people would be in his position. And when he started talking about God, the Founding Fathers, and how America was built on principles from the Bible that every American citizen should be proud to remember and uphold, Senator Cane leaned back in his seat with a sound of impatience. This was a waste of time. Everybody already knew all that about the nation's history and what kind of people shaped it so. Was all this really necessary?

The senator's train of thought continued in this manner for

the remainder of David's speech.

David handed over the microphone and strolled cheerfully offstage, waving once or twice before hopping down the side steps and nearly colliding head-on with Joseph Cane. The senator had gone backstage a few minutes before the end of David's hour to be wired for sound (he disliked hand-held microphones) and take his place where he would enter the stage after Mr. Farris introduced him. When David bumped against him, he quickly turned to apologize.

"Wow, you're just...full of energy, aren't you," Senator Cane remarked with a forced laugh, straightening his suit jacket and trying to look unaffected by the encounter.

Seeing the senator appear jovial regarding the incident, David smiled in return, saying, "I guess I feed off the energy in the audience, sir. They've always seemed so nice and receptive to me, and for that I'm grateful."

Senator Cane smiled tightly. "How wonderful for you."

"I'm David Connally," David added, holding out his hand with his friendly smile.

Senator Cane looked down at David's hand, wondering how long he could forgo taking it until he appeared rude, but also not wanting to leave behind a message of invitation. When he looked up and saw David's smile falter, he reached out and shook his hand once, and hard. He released it before David let go.

"Joseph Cane, United States Senator for Virginia," he said impressively, very aware of the importance of his title. He expected David to be impressed, but the young man just nodded and said, "Nice to meet you, Senator. Virginia is one of the places I plan to visit one of these days. I hear she's a beautiful state."

"Yes, she is." Senator Cane stared at David, distracted in his confusion.

"So, Mr. Connally, it appears you're getting quite a bit of publicity for yourself," he remarked, glancing toward the stage where Mr. Farris was still in the midst of his introduction. "Just what is it that draws people to you?" he added, trying to sound cheerful but nonchalant.

97

David shrugged modestly. "I just speak from the heart, sir. I'm not trying to become famous or anything. I tell the people what they need to hear, and as I'm speaking, I'm reminding myself as well."

"Well, you sure make it look easy out there," the senator said with another forced smile. "I guess some people don't have to work as hard as others for the attention they need from the public."

David's countenance fell, and confusion filled his face. "Senator, I–"

Just then the audience broke into applause again, and Mr. Farris suddenly joined the two of them. "They're ready for you, Senator!" he said to Joseph Cane.

Cane nodded. "Thank you. Mr. Farris," he said, and swept past David without another glance.

Mr. Farris turned to David. His buoyant expression changed to concern when he saw David's face.

"Hey, man, what's wrong? You were sensational out there!" he exclaimed, shaking David's shoulder in an effort to knock his usual cheerfulness back into him.

"Thank you," said David softly. He turned back to look at Senator Cane, who was now pacing the stage and speaking in a very expressive manner with the tiny mic clipped to his necktie.

"Hey, David, Mr. McCoy is ready to meet you now," Mr. Farris broke into his thoughts. "You want to come with me and see him?"

"Uh, yeah, sorry. I'm ready," David replied, and turned his back on the stage and audience.

Mr. Farris knocked once on the door of the motor home, just for the sake of politeness, then opened the door and entered with David behind him.

Mr. McCoy was sitting at the table with the small chandelier lamp hanging above it switched on. He sat with one hand on the table while the other rested on the booted ankle of his leg that was crossed over the knee of the other leg. In this position, and with his form partly shrouded in shadows cast from the lone table light, the leader of The American Party presented a formidable image.

Mr. Farris closed the door behind David and himself and reached over to flip the switch beside the door.

"Let's have a little more light in here," he commented, partly to break the silence and partly to make David feel more at ease. As the interior of the motor home was suddenly filled with light, Mr. McCoy stood up.

"David," Mr. Farris said, "I'd like to introduce you to my boss, Rick McCoy, chairman of the party."

David took a few steps forward, and Mr. McCoy met him halfway with his hand extended. After they had shaken hands, Mr. McCoy gestured for David to have a seat, and he followed suit while Mr. Farris also sat down at the table beside his boss.

"Now, Mr. Connally," McCoy began, folding his hands atop the table, "I'm speaking on behalf of The American Party when I say that we appreciate your help in entertaining the people before the rallies. You seem to have a natural ability of communicating with people, and from what I've seen, most people seem to like you pretty well."

"Thank you. I'm glad to help, sir," David responded humbly.

"Have you done this sort of work before?" McCoy questioned.

David seemed to think for a moment before answering.

"No sir, not exactly," he said. "I just love God, and I love America and the American people. If there's anything I can do to help the country and the people who live here, then I'll do whatever I can, as best I can."

His reply, quiet but also bold and ringing with conviction, created a smile on the face of Mr. Farris, who gave his boss a meaningful look.

"Well, that's wonderful, Mr. Connally. This country needs all the patriots she can get," Mr. McCoy said. He was watching David carefully. But David was watching him as well, mild curiosity reflected in his eyes.

"Sir, you don't have to call me 'Mr. Connally'," he said. "I'm fine just being called David. That's my name."

Mr. Farris turned his face away to hide a smile.

↑ THE SPEAKER

McCoy shifted his weight to lean forward in his chair, and with a clearing of his throat switched topics.

"Now, er, David, don't get me wrong. I appreciate all the hard work that you're doing for the party and the candidates. You have provided a great service for us so far. But there's something that we need to talk about. Both Mr. Farris here and Jack Webb have told me that for no apparent reason will you discuss anything about your past. Is that true?"

David nodded slowly.

"I don't want to pry, but can you tell me exactly why that is?"

David looked at his folded hands on the table in front of him. His lips tightened.

"Because, as chairman of The American Party, I'm sure you can appreciate that in my position I can't be too careful with the decisions I have to make in regards to these matters," McCoy said. "I am responsible for the people who work under me, for those who work for The American Party. I can't afford to—"

"I made a promise," David interrupted. His face had gone pale, but his voice was steady, as was his gaze as he looked directly into McCoy's penetrating eyes.

Mr. McCoy stopped and drew back. He exchanged looks with Mr. Farris.

"I made a promise," David repeated stolidly. "And I can assure you, sir, that my past has no bearing on my future."

There was silence for several seconds as McCoy processed what he had just heard. David sat silently, shifting his eyes back down to his hands. Mr. Farris thought he looked as if he was straining to suppress some great emotion inside himself.

"Well, David," said McCoy at last, breaking the heavy silence, "I can respect that. But I really need you to put yourself in my place for a minute. Don't you realize that every newspaper and television reporter is, or will be, out flipping the tiniest rock trying to find out who you are and where you came from? And I can assure you," he added, leaning forward and jabbing the tabletop with his forefinger in making his point, "they will find everything they're

100

looking for. It's what they do best. My question to you, now, is this: are they going to find something about you that will embarrass or harm me, this party, or the people, in any way?"

"No, sir," said David firmly.

McCoy ran his tongue over his lips, looked down as if gathering his words, then leaned both elbows on the table as he fixed his iron gaze on David.

"David, I need you to understand how serious this is for me and the party," he said in a voice that made Mr. Farris glad he wasn't in his boss's line of sight. "Now think carefully, and answer me one more time. Will anyone be able to find anything that will hurt myself or the party?"

David now leaned forward. His eyes were steady as he said, "No sir. They will not."

McCoy, though secretly relieved to hear David's words, nonetheless still had several reservations about the young man. After all, they still knew very little about him. But McCoy's countenance perked up as he stood up from the table following David's last answer. David quickly rose too, and so did Mr. Farris.

Mr. McCoy reached out and shook David's hand, saying, "That's what I needed to know. It's been great meeting you, David, and once again, I appreciate everything you've done to help us. Now, if you could please give Mr. Farris and me a moment alone."

But David hesitated, and looked distressed.

"Sir, I would never do anything to hurt this party, or the American people," he said earnestly. "If you need me to, I'll gladly go if my presence here affects the party, or the candidates, negatively in any way."

McCoy opened his mouth to speak, but Mr. Farris quickly intervened.

"David, just hold on a second!" he exclaimed fearfully. "What makes you say that, man? Just wait awhile until we can discuss this and figure everything out, ok?"

Mr. Farris realized while he was speaking that Mr. McCoy was probably not going to be overly pleased with his sudden outburst, but the thought of losing David now was enough to give him a moment of panic. He tried to be assuring, but David still bore a strange sadness in his eyes as he nodded quietly to both of them, and closed the door behind himself.

Once again, it was just the two of them in the motor home. Mr. Farris gave Mr. McCoy a look just bordering on grumpy, and asked sarcastically, "Well, do you want me to keep him off the stage, sir?"

McCoy returned Mr. Farris' expression with a dangerous one as if to say, "Don't push it," and then retreated deep in thought, folding his arms and pacing back and forth. Mr. Farris twirled his hat in his hand uneasily.

McCoy shook his head. "No. I knew coming in that David would be a risk, and now that I've had the chance to meet with him and hear him speak, I believe he's a risk worth taking until we find out more. What he has to offer is more than we've ever seen as far as attracting audiences goes. We've been given national exposure by many big television companies, and they're going to turn David Connally into a celebrity." Mr. McCoy paused and sighed, but he didn't look upset. Mr. Farris restrained himself from another outburst, but this time one of joy.

"And as long as he doesn't mess up, the publicity he'll get us will be very good for the party and the candidates," McCoy went on. But then he pointed his finger at Mr. Farris.

"However, I'm making you personally responsible for him," he said firmly. "I'm going to have security down here soon, and it will be your job to make sure they keep everybody away from David, especially the reporters. We can't afford anyone to say something stupid. I don't want anyone here talking to reporters about anything that has to do with David, especially David himself."

Jack jumped nearly a foot when his phone started ringing boisterously on the bedside table in his hotel room. He had forgotten to put it on vibrate before going to sleep. With a yawn, he turned on the lamp and picked up his phone.

"Hello?" he mumbled groggily.

"Hey Jack! It's Aaron!"

"Aaron?" Jack sat up in bed, his surprise clearing the sleep from his head. He had to take a moment to comprehend the cheerful voice on the other end. "What, what's going on? Is everything ok? Is it your mom?"

"No, no, Mom's ok. Not great, but she was feeling fine enough for me to be able to get away, and she even suggested I come up and find you."

"Um, really?"

"Yeah! I saw on the website that y'all were setting up next in Bowling Green, so I got directions, filled up the tank, drove all day and night and day again, and guess what?"

"What?"

"I'm here!"

"Wait, you're here?" Jack's mind was whirling. "Where is here?"

"Kentucky, Jack! That's where you're at, right? I got a motel room."

Jack realized he was pressing his phone so tightly against his face that it was probably going to leave a mark on his skin, and eased up.

"Yeah, we just finished up tonight. But, Aaron…" Jack tried to collect his scattered thoughts that had been spinning around since Aaron had identified himself on the phone.

"Great! Well, I'm here to offer my services to you, Jack! You can still use me, right? With setting up and everything? That's why I'm here!"

"Aaron, are you sure you should be up here? I mean, I sure appreciate you coming all this way and yeah, I could use an extra pair of hands. But I'm concerned about you being so far away from your mother. Are you sure–"

"Aww, Jack, stop asking me that, of course I'm sure! I'm only a phone call away from her. And she's in a nursing home, for Pete's sake, it's not like there aren't a bunch of nurses there if she needs anything. I don't think I've been much help to her anyway," and Aaron's voice grew troubled. He paused, then added, "I feel like

I need to be doing something, making use of my time. And if you haven't replaced me, I'd like to come back, Jack. I would already be with you right now if the accident had never happened."

Jack rubbed his forehead. It wasn't that he didn't want Aaron. It was the idea of having to look after and worry about both David and Aaron together that bothered him.

"So, what do you say, Jack? Can you use me? Please?"

If anything, it was the guilt trip Jack felt himself beginning since Aaron had told him he had driven hundreds of miles that caused him to open his mouth with a 'yes' and told an exuberant Aaron that he would meet him tomorrow morning and bring him over to help clean up at the rally site before they got ready for their next trip.

"Awesome! Thanks, Jack! Oh, Jack?"

"Yes, Aaron," Jack sighed.

"It's kinda funny how David is such a big deal now, isn't it? I mean, the dude was just a hitchhiker when we found him, and look at him now! I've been seeing him on the internet and stuff."

"Definitely unusual, yep," was Jack's short reply, though in his mind he was thinking, *Is that really all he was when we found him?*

"Well, I'll see you tomorrow, Jack!"

"Yeah, ok Aaron. See you, kid."

Jack dropped his phone on the nightstand and rubbed his eyes so fiercely that he could see spots when he opened them. With his mind now going eighty miles an hour, all he wanted to do was crash and be dead to the world until six-thirty A.M. With a grunt, he picked up his phone again, wincing at the bright screen, and set it on silent before wearily turning off the lamp and rolling over into a sound sleep.

⸙ CHAPTER 6:

During the time when David Connally started working for The American Party and his popularity was exponentially growing, the Democratic Party was holding a meeting far away in Washington D.C. In the conference room of an extravagant hotel, the Democrats were discussing their party strategy regarding the upcoming primaries. With the Democratic National Convention being held at the end of May, they had four weeks to finish mapping out their goals and outline their priorities that would be stated at the convention.

The long, black, oval table in the room seated thirty, and every hard-backed wooden chair was occupied. The party members present sat with their leather binders on the table in front of them, opened to the meeting's agenda. Small, polished pen holders rested next to coasters at each place beneath fancy glasses of ice water, and a name tag propped up in front of every person. On larger wooden coasters along the center of the table were three or four heavy glass pitchers of iced water. The room was painted a dark coffee color, with a waxed wooden floor to match. One wall had a couple of small, narrow tables lined up against it, which held trays of catered food, plates, eating utensils, and a coffee maker. At the end of the room behind the head of the table a large flat-screen TV was attached to the wall. The ceiling had three large incandescent light fixtures hanging above the table, and on either side of the chandliers, oyster lights were fastened in rows all the way down to both ends of the room, combined to supply an ample amount of light.

The opposite wall from the food tables was an entire window, providing a fantastic view of the city of Washington. In the near distance, the single white spire of the Washington Monument rose proudly in the air, and beyond that, the Capitol dome was clearly visible in all its guilt-edged glory. But the people in the meeting were not interested in the window view. Heads were bent over their papers, some people trying to talk at the same time as others, and the scratching of many pens could be heard throughout the room.

One man who sat at the head of the table seemed to be in charge of the room more than anyone else. He also spoke the most, and everyone was silent when he had the floor. This man stood up several times while speaking, as if the importance of the points he was making warranted movement. He then would gaze pointedly around the table before resuming his seat. Each time he did this a few people shifted in their chairs and exchanged uneasy glances. No single person sitting at that table, even though they were all affiliates of the same cause, personally enjoyed it when Dominic York, chairman of the Democrat Party, chose to weld his eye-line to theirs.

With his heavy eyelids and apparent lack of blinking, York's eyes looked almost blank. There was something eerie about his gaze, not vacant, but perfectly devoid of emotion. Even when he was angry, or when he raised his eyebrows in questioning or surprise, those placid, penetrating eyes somehow remained unchanged. To make his appearance even more posthumous, the smooth, chalky skin of his face, drawn tightly over prominent cheekbones, also bore an unnerving resemblance to a cadaver. His tousled hair was an inky black, with short sideburns. If he stood very still, one might at first glance think him to be a colorless marble statue. But when he moved or looked about, there was something in his gait and demeanor that turned heads and stirred discomfort by the unsettling coldness in his face.

He stood and spoke like a man in control, one who knew all too well the power he wielded. He spoke quietly but in a very deliberate, determined manner, as if he was giving every sentence careful consideration before speaking it. When he wasn't talking, he sat at the head of the table, leaning on one arm of the chair and playing his fingers along the top of the table while listening to the discussion ensuing around him. Various prominent politicians were in attendance at the meeting, and every person had an opinion or idea they wanted to voice about the upcoming convention.

To the right of Dominic York sat an older woman. She sat very straight and rigid in her chair, with her hands resting one on top of the other in her lap. When York was speaking, she paid him very close attention, nodding frequently, and when he finished the two of them had their heads together soon afterward. When she wasn't speaking to anyone, or writing vigorously in her ledger, she was studying the other party members in the room. Her small blue eyes carried an expression of perpetual sharpness and intensity, set back in her stern, square face. The short, choppy cut of her gray-streaked blond hair, her stiff posture, and surly stern visage gave her a stark appearance that fell somewhat short of the usual feminine quality. Dressed in a stiff, scarlet pantsuit with pump heels and earrings to match, she looked tough and ready to take down anything or anyone unfortunate enough to stray onto her path. Everything about her persona gave off an austere air. She seemed untouchable, even just sitting quietly in the chair, as if in the harsh features of her face one could see this woman was a powerhouse of ferocity and fierceness just waiting to be unleashed in the political arena.

Occasionally she would smile at something that was said by one of her fellow Democrats, but even that human salute, meant to convey satisfaction or friendliness, seemed out of place, as if behind the smile there lurked something more calculating and cold.

This frosty iron-horse of a woman was none other than Senator Helen Kennedy, the leading candidate for the Democratic presidential nomination. At sixty-six years of age, Helen Kennedy was certainly one of the most energetic politicians in Washington. Her endorser, Dominic York, was the type to quietly but ruthlessly work his way up through political obstacles toward his ambitions by way of subtle yet lethal forces and means. He worked in the shadows. Not so with Helen Kennedy. For over a decade she had been the voice of liberalism in Washington, and stealth had never been a part of her campaign.

Beside her at the conference room table sat her campaign manager, Steven Sawyer. On the other side of Dominic York sat his personal assistant, Daniel White. Both Steven and Daniel were among those who spoke the least of all the people in the room, but they were no less busy, flipping feverishly through their ledgers, scribbling notes and checking dates, occasionally leaning over to speak in the ears of their superiors.

The business at hand was near to being concluded. Dominic York leaned back in his chair and rubbed his fingertips together, pleased and satisfied with the results of the meeting. Some of the other senators and congressmen in the room were standing up and mingling by the food table. Helen Kennedy looked up from her notes, and seemed surprised by the activity around her, as if she hadn't finished what she had wanted to accomplish on the agenda. She turned to Dominic York.

"Sir, I have one more item that I would like to present at this meeting," she requested. Her voice and expression were cold and imperious.

"Go ahead, Senator Kennedy."

His soft, husky voice fairly matched the expression in his eyes. Senator Kennedy pushed her chair back from the table and stood up. Smoothing down the front of her suit jacket, she cleared her throat to address the room.

"My fellow congressmen, congresswomen, and senators, there is a particular matter I should like to discuss with you before our meeting is concluded," she said loudly. The other people in the room stopped speaking to each other and all heads turned in her direction as the room fell silent.

"The subject I would like to discuss is The American Party. Have any of you been paying attention to this organization?"

There were a few nods, but most looked puzzled and shook their heads. Dominic York sat up and said, "That little grass-roots association down south. Please continue, Senator."

Senator Kennedy picked up her ledger and rifled through it until she came to the pages she was looking for. Pulling them forcefully out, she let her ledger smack back down on the tabletop, and held the papers up for all to see.

"For those of you who are unaware, The American Party is allegedly a non-profit political group started up by business owner

Rick McCoy from Montana." She looked down and began reading information off the papers in her hands, clearly paraphrasing. "The party's purpose is to reinstate ancient ideals as put forth by the Founding Fathers, and restore America to her former state of conservative honor of the past." Senator Kennedy read those words in a disparaging tone, jutting her chin out and shaking her head as if she couldn't believe anyone would dare to think such nonsense. "They endorse candidates running for political office, but only those candidates who meet the party's specific criteria. The candidates can be Republican, Independent, or even Democrat, as long as they are pro-life, hold conservative values (that includes traditional marriage, which obviously means they're against homosexuality), stand by the Constitution like it's their lifeline, and dedicated to putting their country before themselves. Oh, and they're all for putting firearms in the hands of the public, in spite of all the shootings that have occurred in this country over the years. That isn't a problem for The American Party. And with such specifics as these on their wish list," she added with a sneer, "it's astonishing they can even find one candidate to endorse. It seems they're on the lookout for what they consider to be the perfect patriot."

Senator Kennedy's voice was both irritated and mocking as she slapped the papers down and took off her reading glasses with an empathetic jerk.

"Normally, I would let them have their little game and they could go on thinking they're making a difference," she said quietly. "But unfortunately, that truly is the case! The party's routine is traveling around to different locations in the U.S. and holding rallies at which senators, congressmen, and other candidates they're endorsing or considering endorsing show up to speak. It's mainly Republicans who the party upholds, seeing as they're all closer in mindset than they would be with, say, a full-fledged Democrat."

Here, Senator Kennedy paused to allow a short murmur of laughter to pervade the room. But then her small, sharp blue eyes darkened and narrowed.

"Like I said before, I didn't have cause to think The American Party was of any concern at first. But after seeing the reports on the news, they seem to be gaining quite a bit of recognition and attention in the public eye. Not only that, more and more people are attending their rallies, and they're telling others. There are even some from our own party who have been to those rallies! Just one week ago I spoke at a fundraiser in the same town near where The American Party was holding a rally. The attendance number at the Democratic fundraiser was miserably pathetic in comparison to The American Party. Just sixty miles away, they were holding a rally with over three thousand people in the audience! Every news and television truck from every station you ever heard of was there to broadcast this party all over the media!"

Senator Kennedy again paused to catch her breath, her eyes flashing dangerously. Dominic York put his fingertips together and stared ahead, deep in thought.

"The American Party has already found some candidates they will surely try to get elected into the White House this year," Senator Kennedy went on, now calmer than before. "They're getting way more publicity than we can afford another party to have, and they're turning the people away from us. The Democrat party needs to take this seriously. Something has to be done."

Before she could sit down again, another senator toward the end of the table spoke up.

"Senator Kennedy is right," he said. "I've been following these people on the news as well, and they're drawing crowds like nothing I've ever seen in a grass-roots organization of this type. Every day more and more of our media time is taken up by what The American Party is doing. Usually, dealing with independent groups is like swatting a fly. But this is different."

A congressman on the other side of the table stood up.

"This guy that The American Party has seems to have a way of drawing the crowds from both official parties to hear their candidates. I mean, just who is this David Connally guy? Where'd he come from, and what is he doing? Is he even running for office?"

"From what I know, at first he was leading the audience in singing –I don't know why– and then they started letting him speak, like he was one of the candidates. I've heard some of the stuff he's said on TV, and he sounds dangerous," interposed another senator.

"Yeah, don't we have anybody who's checking this out?"

At this remark, several people began trying to talk over each other in voicing their concerns and demands. The noise was rising into a ruckus.

Dominic York stood up, and held up his hand without making a sound. He just waited until the room gradually fell silent once more.

"Thank you, Senator Kennedy, for bringing this item to everyone's attention so we are now all on the same page," he said quietly. Then in a louder voice, he said, "The Party has already been looking into this little matter of The American Party." He said "little" in a way intended to minimize the fears of those sitting around the table. "We are putting together a plan to deal with this issue. I'll be having a meeting with some people tomorrow to get the situation dealt with. Nobody needs to worry about The American Party or this Connally fellow. Everything will be taken care of."

Dominic's words, spoken with such unruffled confidence, were enough to reassure the Democrat party members present, and when Dominic adjourned the meeting, everyone closed their ledgers and stood up to get refreshments with an air of cheerfulness and satisfaction.

Everyone, that is, except Helen Kennedy. She remained sitting in her chair by Dominic, her arms crossed, and her face like stone. He too kept to his seat, as if he could guess she had more to say to him privately when the others left the table.

"Dominic, I don't like this at all," she said in a low voice. "This American Party is stealing our spotlight and if we aren't careful, they'll soon be stealing our votes. And I think most of that can be attributed to this David Connally guy. You've seen him, right?"

"He's a regular firebrand," replied Dominic, rubbing his upper lip thoughtfully. "I've seen the news reports, Senator. Don't think I'm trying to downplay the danger we're going to be facing if this problem isn't handled with care."

"But, it will be handled?" she persisted anxiously. "I'm warning you, Dominic, I'm not giving up the White House to some little ancient-principles, independent group just because some nobody has charisma and talks about America like she's the greatest thing ever."

She closed her ledger with a snap, and stood up. Dominic looked up at her.

"Frankly, I'm more concerned about Connally than The American Party itself, at the moment. He appears to be winning the hearts of the people with all that 'charisma' and 'ancient principles' talk," he said slowly. He stood up and straightened his suit jacket, brushing invisible flecks of dust from the front of it. Then he turned and looked Helen Kennedy in the eyes, and she looked back unflinchingly. "But don't worry, Senator," he said quietly, with a dark expression that suddenly overshadowed his face. His countenance changed from placid calm to a steely determination, made all the more frightening by his corpse-like eyes. "We'll take care of this Connally and his precious party long before the election. They'll never know what hit them. Now, would you like some coffee, Senator?"

It was early morning back in Bowling Green, Kentucky. Jack's crew gathered themselves in the service tent which Jack always provided for the candidates and his crew to protect them from the elements and also offer refreshments. This morning there was fresh coffee, doughnuts, muffins, bagels, fruit, and other various on-the-go breakfast foods. Also set up in the tent was a large television set that The American Party had given Jack for the express purpose of keeping everyone informed regarding the news.

This morning, as the rally was over and the candidates had gone home, Jack, Mr. Farris, and Jack's crew had the tent (and from Aaron's observation, all the food) to themselves. Jack had gone to collect Aaron and bring him to join the others. The rest of Jack's crew greeted their old buddy with cheers and slaps on the back, followed by demands to hear his account of the fiery truck accident that had knocked him out of work. Jack and Mr. Farris were standing near the entrance to the tent sipping coffee together. After they had talked for several minutes about the success of last night's rally, they began discussing travel plans for the next couple of weeks.

"So, we'll be in St. Louis tomorrow night," Jack said, cradling his coffee cup in his hands and releasing a huge yawn.

"Right. After that, I think we'll be in Tennessee, but I need to double-check with Mr. McCoy," Mr. Farris replied, taking a bite out of his perfectly toasted bagel. Then he eyed Jack and asked, "Hey, you sleep ok last night? You look exhausted."

"Ah, I guess because I am." Jack admitted with a sigh. He turned and nodded toward Aaron. Mr. Farris looked at the young man, then quizzically back at Jack. "Aaron Wright, one of my main guys who was hurt in the truck accident, called me when I was already in bed. He wanted to come up and join us here, but he's also worried about his mother. She's been real sick for some months now, and Aaron feels torn about leaving her, but he said he really wants to be with us."

Jack took a sip of coffee. Mr. Farris watched him thoughtfully.

"I told him he needed to do what he thought was best for his mother, which obviously would mean staying with her and making sure she gets the care she needs. But, he got up here without even telling me until he was already in town. I can't send him back now. He's a good kid, Aaron is. He's a case sometimes, but his heart's in the right place," said Jack.

"What about his father? Can't he take care of Aaron's mother, too? That would have made it easier for Aaron..."

Mr. Farris's words trailed off as Jack shook his head.

"His father is dead. I took Aaron on to work for me soon after that happened, and I've sort of looked after him."

Jack raised his coffee cup to his lips again, so he didn't see the little smile on Mr. Farris' face when he looked at Jack.

"You're a good man, Jack," he said simply, and finished off his bagel. Jack shrugged off the compliment and tried to hide his sudden uncomfortable feelings by asking if there were any more bagels.

"Yeah, I think so," Mr. Farris said, turning to peer back into the depths of the tent at the food tables.

"Good, because I think that's your third one, and I don't want you hogging them all," Jack teased, heading back into the tent.

"Hey, I haven't eaten a proper meal all week!" Mr. Farris

protested, following him. "You should be more worried about that old toaster you have in here. That piece of junk is going to catch fire one of these days and just explode."

"Watch yourself, this toaster and I go way back," Jack started to say, but his attention was suddenly arrested by the television screen. Across the bottom of the screen a scroll banner read in all capital letters, "THE AMERICAN PARTY BECOMING A PUBLIC PARTY."

"Mike!" Jack exclaimed, grabbing Mr. Farris's shoulder, his eyes glued to the flat screen. Mr. Farris followed his gaze, and quickly found a seat in one of the folding chairs scattered around the tent. Jack sat down beside him, both eagerly anticipating the report to come.

"That's Joann Walker," Mr. Farris commented as a young, attractive woman with long blond hair and a sweet face appeared onscreen in front of a long line of satellite trucks at the Bowling Green fairgrounds. When Jack turned a questioning face toward him, he added, "She's been assigned coverage of our party's activities and the candidates we endorse. I met her yesterday before McCoy got here. She seems like a pretty decent person–"

"We already have our own assigned reporter–?"

"Shh!"

"We have a special report in from Joann Walker today, who has been out observing the events of The American Party, a non-profit political organization which seems to be ever-growing in popularity," said one of the hosts in the recognizably exaggerated lilt of a broadcasting voice. "Joann, is it true that The American Party just held its largest rally yet, with all the leading candidates, there in Bowling Green last night?"

The camera cut back to Joann standing outside, holding her microphone and smiling confidently into the lenses. "Yes it is, Larry. As you can see behind me, these fairgrounds are where that rally was held, and I can tell you, it was packed solid. With the primaries only four weeks away, Senator Joseph Cane of Virginia told the audience here last night that he should get the nomination for president, and he was going to run on the Republican platform, and assured everyone he would stand strong against issues like abortion, gun control, and unsecured borders.

"However, many would say that the larger draw for the rally last night was not their official speakers, but actually the man who opened the night's events, David Connally. David entertained the audience last night for at least an hour before the rally began, leading the audience in one patriotic song after another. He really stirred up everyone's spirits. But then he actually began speaking to the audience, as if he were one of the candidates, though as far as we know, David isn't running for political office. He talked to the audience about how great America is, and how she could be even greater if the right people were elected."

The camera cut to show footage of David standing onstage, holding the microphone in one hand while passionately gesturing with the other as he spoke. Jack was impressed with how well he looked onscreen.

"That's a good shot," he murmured to Mr. Farris, who nodded in agreement, his hand covering the lower half of his face while he gazed at the screen.

"Nobody seems to know anything about this mysterious young man regarding his past, present, or future, but he certainly struck a chord with the audience," Joann Walker continued.

Jack stifled a moan. He wished she hadn't said that nobody knew anything about David. That was going to be bait for so many reporters and journalists to do their best in raking up his history, and being somewhat familiar with the world of media, Jack knew that whatever they could find (or not find) would doubtless have a discouraging spin that would only shed a negative light on David.

"Joann, what were some of the things David Connally spoke about last night that made him so popular with the audience?" the news host on TV asked.

"Well, Larry, he said that people should examine their candidates and vote for those who put America and her people above themselves and their agendas. He even said that America needs to go back to being a God-fearing nation, and take a stand in the world for what is right.

"The rally lasted almost four hours, and as people were leaving, I was able to talk to several present in the audience about what they thought of the candidates. For the most part, they seemed to think it was too early to tell who the right person for the president nomination was, but what was very interesting was that almost every person I talked to had something to say about how impressed they were by David Connally, and the message he was bringing them. It was like he had a way of communicating personally with them all that kept everybody spellbound."

"What did you think of what Connally said, Joann?"

"I think how he made the people feel makes perfect sense. It's like they finally found a voice for what has been engrained in the heart of Americans from the beginning, and many of them say they haven't heard truths like David spoke from politicians in a long time. What Connally said was refreshing and energizing, and I believe it's giving the people a resurgence of resolve to help America stand strong for what's right, and fight for the freedoms and rights that our enemies (even the ones in Washington, Connally said) would take away. And I have to say, Larry, everything he said made sense to me. Everyone present at last night's rally no doubt went home feeling that Connally gave them hope for a better America."

The camera cut to more scenes of David and the audience from the rally, followed by interviews between Joann Walker and some of the people who attended the rally when it was over. Jack and Mr. Farris both instinctively leaned forward to better hear what the general public thought of David.

Several thought he was great and that he was the best part of the whole evening, some were skeptical over what he said but still admired his passion, and a couple of teenagers Joann spoke to said David was really "cool" and looked like he really believed everything he was saying to them. But what Jack was quick to see was the pattern of how every person interviewed mentioned something about David's ability to motivate, inspire, or stir the spirit, and his passion for what he believed was evident in his every word and movement. Jack felt a surge of pride and fatherly affection for David that swept over him so suddenly, a wide smile split his face and he chuckled to himself.

Then Joann Walker appeared onscreen by herself again, saying, "The American Party really seems to be growing in popularity with the American people, and also seems like it's gaining more attention than the Republican and Democrat parties. When The American Party officially announces its candidate for the primaries this summer, it will definitely be an interesting race for the White House come November. Now, back to you in New York, Larry."

The camera cut away from Joann Walker to the studio headquarters and the hosts sitting around their wide, semi-circular couch together. They were speaking amongst themselves now, trying to guess who David Connally was, and where he came from. Jack suddenly felt a strong wish that David trusted him enough to tell him, so that at least he would have the satisfaction of knowing more than the news anchors did. But no, he was as mystified as they were.

He perked up when he heard Larry, the central news host in the studio, remark about David, "Well, whoever he is, he's sure helping those potential candidates backed by The American Party." Then he laughed jovially and added, "In fact, David Connally may be the greatest driving force of this party that they'll need to make any headway in the elections this fall."

Jack settled back in his chair as the news went to a commercial break. Beside him, Mr. Farris stretched his arms above his head, holding his elbows and grinning triumphantly as if they already carried the election in their favor.

"Did you hear that?" he exclaimed, nudging Jack. "Everyone loves him. David is our secret weapon we didn't know we needed. And every American is going to know who he is, every one!" He stood up and pulled out his cell. "I need to call McCoy. See you later. Oh..." He turned around again with the phone to his ear. "Did you need directions to the site in St. Louis, or are–"

"No, thanks, Mike. I got it."

"Boy, I tell you," Mr. Farris mused happily as he strolled out of the tent, "that Joann Walker certainly does her job right. She's going to make it big one day. Amazing."

His voice faded away. Jack was left still sitting in front of the TV. Around him, his crew members had returned to their conversation and breakfast. Commercials still propagated their products on the brightly flashing screen. Outside, a chilly wind was beginning to whip up the heavy edges of the tent flaps that weren't fastened, allowing the breeze to sail through and send paper plates and napkins dancing.

Every American will know his name. Jack couldn't restrain himself from rubbing a heavy hand over his eyes and down to his chin. Where would it end? With David gaining so much popularity and at such a rapid rate, what could stop him from running for office, if the praise and admiration of the people should, in the end, entice him with the idea of becoming a politician? He would certainly have the backing of the people to do so. True, he had no money for a campaign, and no background in politics, but then, George Washington had been a farmer and surveyor, and Abraham Lincoln a self-educated lawyer. Anything was possible.

Oh, David, how can I protect you when you insist on standing in the spotlight? The thought rose unbidden in Jack's mind, and before he could quell it, a host of raw emotions began flowing in faster than he could check them. Fear, confusion and even anger. And the more he dwelt on the anger, the more it encompassed his thoughts. He was angry that David wouldn't say "no" to going onstage in front of thousands. He was angry that the young man couldn't seem to simply and quietly stick with the job Jack had him here for. He was angry that David wouldn't trust him enough to confide in him. He was angry that he knew nothing of David or his past, and that he knew of no way to be able to reach out to him. He was angry that David's fame was on the rise, and he, Jack, was growing more and more powerless to stand between the young man and the harshness of a life of publicity. And he was angry that David reminded him so much of another young man, that every time David turned to look at Jack with that enthusiastic light aglow in his eyes, it was as if his own son were looking at him.

Jack sighed and wearily passed his hand across his face again. He knew deep down that his anger was superficial. Behind

118

the bitterness, fear and sorrow lurked as they had for many a month now.

The raucous laughter of the other men roused him from his painful reflections. Looking over at the cluster of men seated around a folding table, he saw most of them had their eyes fixed on young Aaron Wright, who was evidently in the middle of a lengthy joke, for a few seconds later, the laughter rang out again, and Aaron looked very pleased with himself. With his wild, gingery hair and friendly blue eyes, Aaron was the only redhead in the crew, and one of the most outgoing and easygoing persons Jack had ever met. When he and Aaron had first met several years ago, Jack almost didn't hire him, labeling the joking twenty-year-old as lackadaisical and unreliable. But when Aaron had begged for a second chance, Jack agreed, and soon discovered a very reliable hard worker in the skinny, fiery-topped youth. Breaking the ice was as easy for him as eating lunch, and when he had a mind to be he was a good worker. He caught Jack watching him, and turned red before smiling sheepishly and saluting him.

"Hey, boss, that was some news report, huh?"

"Yep. Sure was."

"Think it'll go to his head?"

Jack was startled. "What?"

"Well, I'm seeing more and more of David Connally on the news," said Aaron as he slowly stood up and made his way over to Jack with his drink in tow. "And everyone who talks about him can't say anything bad about him." Aaron sat down in Mr. Farris's vacated chair and drank a deep gulp of his soda. "Has he seen the reports?"

Jack studied him for a moment before carefully responding, "I don't know, Aaron. I guess David has seen some of them. After all," he added to himself in an almost disparaging tone, "how could he not?" Jack and Mr. Farris had privately agreed to try and keep David away from the news as much as possible for his own sake, but it wasn't as if Jack was going to be able to yank David away from every media outlet that talked about him.

"Well, I don't think it's going to make him any different," Aaron chattered on, cheerily oblivious, his gaze focused back on

119

the flat-screen. "David's not that kind of guy. All this attention he's getting, it doesn't seem like that's why he's doing what he's doing, you know?"

Jack twisted to look at him again, this time in surprise at the observation of his youngest crew member. He was slowly beginning to feel amusement steal over him, soothing the aching bitterness in his soul. Where before he had experienced minor irritation over Aaron's presence here, Jack now felt glad to have Aaron with him again. He had need of an optimistic diversion from his gloomy thoughts. "Well, why do you think he goes on that stage night after night, if not for attention? You heard some of the things he says out there. Why do you think he wants to get up and say them in front of thousands, and now even millions throughout America on TV?" he asked Aaron, half-playfully, but also genuinely curious as to what the young man's answer would be.

Aaron noisily finished his soda, looked at Jack, then back at the TV screen and said with a shrug, "I think he's up there because he can't not be up there. I guess...I guess you could say it's like he belongs where he is. It just seems right for him to be there."

Jack's amused grin vanished.

"Say..." Aaron suddenly tore his attention away from the TV, and twisting from side to side in his chair, scanned both sides of the tent. "Where is David, anyway? I haven't seen him since I got here."

For all the pondering he had given to David in the past fifteen minutes, Jack hadn't even considered where he was. In fact, Jack couldn't recall even seeing David in the tent at all that morning. Had he skipped breakfast? Jack stood up and dumped his crumb-covered paper plate and empty coffee cup in the trash can and parted the tent flaps with one hand as he called back to Aaron, "I'll find him."

The air was chillier outside the tent. Jack gripped the edges of his fleece-lined denim coat cuffs and balled his fists, crossing his arms to hold any degree of warmth against his chest. It shouldn't be hard to find David. He had no reason to leave the rally site, as they had already checked out of the hotel earlier that morning. But it still puzzled Jack that David wasn't socializing with the others. Where was he?

CHAPTER 6:

Jack's feet turned instinctively toward the area where the stage was setup. They would have to take it down shortly, he thought distractedly. He came up from behind the stage, near the motor home, and to his surprise saw Mr. Farris standing at the edge of the stage. He had his back toward Jack, and looked like he was observing something or somebody onstage, peeking around the corner while trying to stay out of sight. When Jack approached him, Mr. Farris looked over his shoulder and signaled him to be silent. Jack stopped beside his boss and craned his neck to see what he was looking at.

David was sitting cross-legged on the stage, his arms resting casually on his knees, reading to himself from the old black book Jack had come to recognize and associate him with. His head was bent over his reading, but what was visible of his face revealed sober contemplation. His lips moved noiselessly along with the words as he read them, but the only other motion he made was the occasional flick of his hand as he turned a page. He seemed so deeply intent on his study that Jack doubted if he knew he was being observed.

"He's been like this for a while now," Mr. Farris whispered. Jack looked at him.

"What are you doing here?" he asked.

"I called McCoy, like I said, and then I wanted to go find David and talk to him about the news report, since he wasn't there to see it," Mr. Farris said in an even lower whisper as David suddenly heaved a long sigh, startling the quiet. Both Jack and Mr. Farris waited for a few seconds, then seeing David simply rub his forehead with the side of his hand and turn the next page, stayed in their hiding place.

"I found him here about ten minutes ago, just like this," Mr. Farris's whisper continued. "I don't think I've ever seen a man read so hard. Not even in college."

"That's because nobody reads hard in college, Mike."

"I beg to differ–"

A soft slapping sound arrested their attention as David closed his Bible, followed by another quiet but heavy sigh. Jack couldn't understand the sad expression plainly written on the young man's face. Could this possibly be the same confident, happy, passionate orator from last night? What could he possibly have to be sorrowful about?

They both expected him to stand up and walk away now that he was finished reading, but he simply sat still for a few more seconds, his face concentrated as if gathering his thoughts. Then he rose up halfway and sank back on his knees. Folding his hands together, he bowed his head.

What followed shook Jack to his core. David, again, made no sound, but the pleading look on his face and his humble attitude were crying out a thousand words that Jack somehow felt would tear any soul apart to hear. In that moment, David looked like the loneliest, most heartbroken man living, evidently begging in tortured silence for something that he knew was too far beyond his grasp to obtain. It was a side of him that Jack had never imagined to see. He couldn't take his eyes off David.

Mr. Farris, however, turned away. "I'll watch a man read, but I won't watch him pray. That's between him and God," he murmured, and walked back toward the motor home. He paused to look back at Jack, who, after one long glance back at David, reluctantly followed him away from the stage.

Inside the motor home, the two men sat wordlessly at the small table, not bothering to turn on the light since the morning sunlight was streaming through the windows. Everything was very quiet.

"Jack," Mr. Farris said suddenly, with a very solemn expression on his face, "Should I be concerned?"

"What?" Jack sat up quickly and stared at him. "How do you mean?"

"David. Do you think he's ok?"

"Why wouldn't he be ok?"

"I know you saw him before we left," Mr. Farris pressed. "He looked like he was in pain. Do you think he needs help?"

"I..." Jack felt himself at a loss for words. The image of David on his knees flashed across his mind, and he suddenly wanted to overturn the table in his urge to get back to David.

"I don't know, Mike," he said finally, rubbing the back of his neck in frustration. "He always seemed fine to me before."

"Did anything happen between now and last night?" Mr. Farris asked.

Jack shook his head. "Not that I'm aware–"

Both of them were suddenly startled by a knock at the door. They looked at each other and stood up as the soft, quick knock sounded again. Mr. Farris walked past Jack to the door and opened it.

"David!" he exclaimed as the young man lowered his hand from preparing to knock a third time. "We were just..." But here he checked himself, glancing back at Jack.

"Mr. Farris, I was wondering if I might speak with you," David said politely. Then he noticed Jack standing in the trailer behind Mr. Farris and added, "Oh, good, you're here too, Jack. I was hoping I'd find you two together."

"How did you know we'd be here?" asked Mr. Farris, somewhat nervously, thinking perhaps David had seen them watching him after all.

"Well, I looked for you in the service tent just now and didn't see you, so the motor home was my next guess," David answered easily. Jack, peering over Mr. Farris' shoulder, studied the young man's face intently. His features were relaxed, and he seemed calm enough now. In looking at him now, Jack could almost forget the agonizing intensity that had so distorted David's face, if it were not for the faint shadow that left its trace in the young man's candid eyes.

Mr. Farris ushered David into the motor home, and gestured for him to have a seat, whereupon Jack and Mr. Farris followed suit.

"Is something the matter, David?" Mr. Farris asked.

David folded his hands on the tabletop and deliberated in silence for a few seconds, exhaling heavily as if a great burden was weighing on his mind. Then he said in a rush, "I don't know if I should speak at the rallies anymore."

Jack felt a surge of relief and joy, but then his initial reaction was overcome with sudden curiosity and concern. Mr. Farris closed his eyes for moment, and bowed his head.

"Why do you think that, David?" he asked quietly, looking back up.

123

↑THE SPEAKER

David kept his eyes on his hands. "I fear that in standing on that stage, I may be taking the focus off of the candidates, that I'm getting most of the attention they need from the people. I don't need to be the focal point. We're holding these rallies to raise awareness of how America should be."

Jack and Mr. Farris looked at each other.

"The American public doesn't have to listen to me to know how they should act to make this nation greater," David went on in a sort of feverish unburdening of his thoughts. "There are plenty of good men, better men, who can lead these people in their way of thinking. They don't need me. It's the men you're endorsing, that the party is endorsing, who need the attention of the public. I'm just, sort of," he paused and wrinkled his forehead. "The opening act."

He spoke those last words with a small, rueful smile. Finally looking up to meet Mr. Farris's gaze, who was sitting directly across from him, he unclasped his hands and spread them in a gesture of conclusion.

Mr. Farris sat back in his chair and drew in a long, deep breath.

"David," he began slowly, "before you think anything else, let me assure you that you are much, much more than just some 'opening act.'"

David nodded hesitantly. Jack reached over to squeeze his shoulder comfortingly.

"When I first asked you to go onstage a few months back, I did that because I was in a tight place, and you were the only one I could turn to, because I had seen once before what you could do with a crowd. I wondered how you could hold up with a bigger audience, and for a longer time. And you didn't disappoint."

David cocked his head with dull curiosity in his eyes.

"Now," Mr. Farris went on, "I admit that at the start I just needed somebody to fill in a time slot. But it very quickly became something much more important. You, David, showed us what the party has been missing. I felt it. Rick McCoy felt it. We needed something, somebody, to help us gain recognition and genuine connection with the American people. David, you have helped us do just that. And you're not doing this for yourself; you're doing it for them." Mr. Farris moved his arm in a sweeping gesture toward the door. "You're doing it for the people. You aren't stealing anybody's limelight. You aren't onstage to tell jokes and do politician impersonations. You aren't there as a sideshow." Mr. Farris stood up and braced his arms on the table for support, looking straight into David's eyes.

"We put you on that stage because you make a difference, David," he said firmly. "We have you talk to the people so they can see and imbibe your passion and enthusiasm for things that are true and have meaning. You are helping our potential candidates gain favor and interest in the public eye, not detracting from them, because you're talking about things that move people's hearts and get them thinking about both the past and future of our country. Then they're ready and willing to hear what our politicians have to say."

Jack was watching David's face closely during Mr. Farris's statement, and saw joy gradually stealing back over the young man's face. His eyes lit up, his color heightened beneath the party manager's words of praise, and his lips were curving slowly into the smile that Jack always associated with his cheerful disposition.

Mr. Farris came around the table and stood by David's chair. As David looked up at him, Mr. Farris reached down and placed a hand on his shoulder.

"David, what's important in all of this is that we're all part of something much bigger than ourselves. We're all cogs in a machine, working together towards a future that is hopefully much better than the present one we're in. It's not about me, or you, or Jack, or McCoy. It's about changing America, and helping get leaders elected into positions to turn her back from her downward spiral and onto the straight path again. Each of us have our own part. And you, David..." Mr. Farris patted the young man's shoulder. "You talk to the American people about things that matter. You remind them of truth and what it really means to be an American. You remind them of what was and what can be again...a country unsuppressed by greedy, tyrannical liberals and bureaucrats in Washington who want nothing more than in the name of progression to tear down what our ancestors worked so hard to build up, because they knew what was best for this nation. A country that is still the greatest in the world, with the greatest freedoms, but also that we must protect and can't take for granted. We have to fight for them, but it's worth the blood, the pain, and the heartache because our liberties, our rights, our Constitution, are worth it all. They're worth protecting from even our own leaders who would take them away from us and push their evil agendas on us that are ripping up our American values."

Mr. Farris' eyes shone bright with an oft-hidden fervor as he gazed unseeingly toward the window. David and Jack watched him in admiration.

"We need to give the people hope that there are still good men amongst us who recognize who the enemy is, and who will put themselves between that enemy and America and say, 'Do your worst, because we won't back down. Because I'm going to give my all for the good of this country.'" Mr. Farris said feelingly, shaking his fist at an invisible opponent. "That's why we do what we do." Mr. Farris looked steadily at David again. His voice was proud. "You give the people that hope, David," he said. "They need you. As do we. Please. Don't quit on us now."

David bowed his head. For a long span of seconds, the only sound inside the motor home was the soft ticking of the battery-powered clock fastened above the door.

"The people and the party need a patriot to stand up for us all," Jack said quietly.

"It's just..." David looked up suddenly. "Maybe I...maybe...I just don't know..."

He folded his arms across his chest, and then reached up with one hand to rub his forehead. He seemed to be struggling with his thoughts, warring internally against a desire to say exactly why he still appeared uncertain after Mr. Farris's reassurances.

Jack leaned forward. "What is it, David? Why are you saying all this? You can tell us, it's all right. You can trust us."

David's reluctance to indicate the cause of his preoccupation only served to further exacerbate both Jack and Mr. Farris. They exchanged glances, and Mr. Farris shook his head. Jack began wracking his brain back over the past few days to find some instance or occurrence that could have possibly altered David's mindset about his work. Had somebody spoken to him when Jack hadn't been around?

But that can't be, I'm always with him. Then it hit him. He had been near David the night before, when David was reaching the end of his hour onstage. Jack had been standing backstage when Mr. Farris had come to bring him to meet Rick McCoy. For several minutes he had been in the motor home with McCoy and Mr. Farris while David was finishing his speech, and he had no idea who David might have talked to when he first came offstage. Did a reporter speak to him? Jack was suddenly filled with alarm. Had one of the newscasters sneaked in under their noses? He turned to David.

"David, did somebody, anybody, talk to you after you came offstage last night?" he questioned anxiously. "Did..." he took a deep breath. "Did a reporter talk to you?"

David shook his head. "No, I didn't talk to anyone from the news," he said shortly.

"Well? Did anyone else talk to you?"

David's brow furrowed. His lips parted slightly, and Jack waited eagerly.

"I talked to...Senator Cane," said David finally, with a heavy sigh.

"Cane!"

Jack and Mr. Farris sat upright. "What did he say to you, David?" Mr. Farris demanded.

"Let's just say I got the impression that he wasn't overly pleased that I was there," said David with a wry smile.

"And you think Cane wanted you gone?"

"I think..." David said slowly, "that Senator Cane sees me as just trying to get attention from the crowd as an entertainer, like I'm a sideshow who's taking up his stage time."

The hurt in the young man's eyes when he confessed his feelings made Jack's blood run hot. His face reddened, and he half-rose from the table, muttering, "That stuck-up little–"

Mr. Farris quickly put a restraining hand firmly on Jack's arm and pulled him back down into his chair with a warning, "Jack!" But a tiny smile stole over his face, breaking his serious expression when he witnessed this fiery defense of David. With his hand still on Jack's arm, in case Jack suddenly took off like a rocket through the roof, Mr. Farris addressed David.

"Son, I don't want you to worry one more second about Senator Cane. Just put him out of your head. I know he's a vain man, and he sees the publicity he's worked for a long time as his due, but you can't let him take away what's yours. You have a right to speak, same as he does, and if he doesn't like that the party is employing you, he's just going to have to deal with that. I know sometimes he can be arrogant because he's so full of his own agendas, but he really is a very conservative fellow, and one of our best candidates for supporting. He wants to make a difference in the lives of the American people; he just needs a little more empathy sometimes."

David's face brightened up again as he listened to Mr. Farris's words, and as his old self shone through, both Jack and his boss felt surges of relief, though Jack was still angry at Senator Cane for belittling David. He moved his arm away from Mr. Farris's grasp and folded it atop his other arm. Mr. Farris gave him one more glance of caution before suddenly clapping a hand to his side, causing the others to jump slightly.

"Sorry, fellows," he exclaimed, pulling out his vibrating cell phone. "I need to take this, if you'll excuse me for a minute."

When he left the motor home, Jack scooted his chair over so he was sitting beside David.

"Look, David," he said urgently, "you heard what he said. What you're doing is invaluable to the party. It's gotta take more than some stuffed suits to shake your faith. You..." Jack inhaled deeply as he chose his words. "...you can't stop what you're doing, David. It's as simple as that. Mike is right. What you do is important. You really do give people hope because what you say, well, it means something to them that resonates in their hearts. "

As Jack said these words, he realized he was able to let go, just a little, of the oppressive weight he had been carrying around for the past several weeks. After listening to what Mr. Farris had said, and

David's own words and reaction, Jack felt that maybe he could finally accept David for what he was doing for the public while still caring about and protecting him. Perhaps he could back off a bit now. David was a grown man. He obviously knew what he was doing, and even more so, loved what he was doing. Who was Jack to deny him such opportunities as telling the American people things that were true and right and good about their country, instilling inspiration and reflection in the hearts of all who heard him speak?

Jack knew it would be a process in keeping such a perspective, but he also knew he needed to try. He couldn't be the over-protective nanny, much as he felt he needed to guard David. It was plain to see that David liked nothing better than to be where he was, doing what he was doing.

David looked up at Jack and his eyes brightened once more.

"Thank you, Jack," he said softly. "Thanks a lot."

Then Mr. Farris entered the motor home, cell phone in hand.

"Guys, I just got off the phone with McCoy," he announced impressively. David and Jack looked at him questioningly.

"He said the Blackheart Security detail is on their way, and should be down here within the hour. We better head back to the tent till they arrive. Jack," he added, "your crew should probably get started on disassembling the stage and everything. Remember, we're heading out to St. Louis in a few hours."

"We'll get on that right away, Mike."

"And one more thing," Mr. Farris added before they could stand up. "David, as of now, you work for The American Party instead of Jack," he said. His eyes flicked toward Jack, who was looking at David and failed to notice. Mr. Farris then held out his hand to David.

"Congratulations," he told him. "We're happy to have you working for us."

David shook his hand. "I'm happy to be of service to my country, sir."

Jack and David stood up, and along with Mr. Farris exited the motor home. The three of them made their way back toward the service tent, with Mr. Farris mentioning to David about the report

129

on the news that morning. Jack watched David carefully, but the young man received the news casually, as if he were being told a slightly interesting story that ceased to occupy his thoughts once it was told. If Jack had ever entertained the thought that David's ego might become inflated by his new-found popularity, that idea was now dispelled, and Jack felt foolish for even considering it.

Back at the service tent, Aaron welcomed David loudly into the group consisting of Jack's crew, and David joined them as easily as if they had been family. Jack and Mr. Farris got more coffee and resumed their seats by the TV, which had not been turned off in their absence, but muted for the sake of conversation.

As Jack sat down, he hollered toward his crew:

"Hey, y'all don't get too comfortable over there. You have fifteen minutes, then everyone goes back to work, hear me?"

There were a few quiet groans and good-natured grumbling ensued, to which Jack paid no attention. Mr. Farris checked his watch and settled back in his chair.

"Hey," he said suddenly, sitting up straighter as he gazed at the television screen. "Isn't that Helen Kennedy?"

Jack knit his brows as he studied the harsh profile of the unsmiling woman onscreen.

"She looks..." he tried to find the right description. "She looks kinda rough, doesn't she?"

"She looks like she's used to having everything her way, and she also looks like she'll be a tough opponent if she becomes the candidate for the Democrat party this fall," said Mr. Farris, shaking his head and taking a swallow of coffee. "From what I know about her, she's all about filling up Congress and the White House with socialist liberals and radical progressives. It might sound a little harsh, but she's a borderline communist herself."

Just then, their concentration on the television was broken as the sound of motor engines roared up close by. Jack and Mr. Farris both turned around to see two shimmering black SUVs pulling to a stop outside the tent. As they watched, eight armed security personnel began unloading from the vehicles. They were all heavily muscled men, dressed in dark clothing with combat boots, and each man carried either an AR15 rifle or other automatic weapon in his hands. That did not detract from the fact that every man also wore at least one or two handguns strapped to their hips. As they piled out of the vehicles and began striding toward the tent, their faces became clearer in focus, and every feature was stern, controlled, and icily professional.

As another man in a heavy black leather jacket stepped out of the passenger side of the SUV in front, the security detail stood at attention with their firearms. At a motion from him, the ranks of men advanced forward and surrounded the tent, their stance facing outward, while the man in the black jacket walked straight on in. He clearly appeared to be in charge of the unit, and looked neither to the right or to the left as he entered the tent with a brisk stride. Everyone automatically hushed their speaking when the newcomers arrived, and not a sound was heard except the tramping of the security personnel's heavy boots. Jack and Mr. Farris slowly stood up. From the corner where he sat, David observed the new arrivals with an expression of curious interest. Beside him, Aaron whispered hoarsely, "Whoa. You see those guns?"

The man in charge of the hired muscle held up his hand, and the men on either side of him stopped walking and stood in place while he continued forward a few more steps in front of them, and then stopped, too. Pushing back the lapels of his jacket and planting his hands on his waist, he surveyed the interior of the service tent in one sweeping glance before saying in a deep, rumbling voice,

"Is there a Michael Farris here?"

The sound of his thunderous voice startled everyone except his men standing behind him. Mr. Farris, who would not have admitted for the world the nervousness in the pit of his stomach, set down his coffee and approached the newcomer as though pushed forward by the force of his commanding voice.

"I'm Michael Farris," he said in a strong voice, as he eyed the newcomer up and down while trying to appear like he wasn't doing so. It was hard to do, for the man was truly a giant. His intimidating presence seemed to fill up the entire space inside the service tent. He stood well over six feet tall, a full head higher than Mr. Farris's hat. His skin was nearly as dark as the black vehicle in which he had arrived, and the muscles in his thick arms and chest bulged underneath his heavy clothing. The crown of his head was shaved completely bald, but he wore a small goatee. His dark brown eyes were without depth in their inscrutability. Every feature, every muscle, was completely under control of the constant gravity in this man's commanding demeanor. His military bearing inspired a feeling of awe and mild apprehension in everyone inside the tent, no less triggered by the numerous firearms he wore strapped to his muscular form.

When Mr. Farris spoke up, the big man moved toward the party manager and encased his hand in a grip of steel that he held for exactly two seconds with a strong jerk in greeting. His confidence seemed rooted enough to rival any politician.

"Mr. Farris, my name is Eli Farley." He pulled out his billfold and held up his identification. "I am Blackheart Security." He jerked his head back toward the ranks of men behind him. "This is my crew. We are here on behalf of Rick McCoy as this party's new head of security."

"Great," Mr. Farris smiled. "Let me just show you—"

But before he could go on, Eli Farley abruptly turned and walked toward Jack's crew, leaving Mr. Farris standing with his mouth open.

"Effective immediately, my team and I are in charge," Eli said loudly, looking around the tent. "We control any and all activities pertaining to security around this party. From this point on, no one goes in or out of this operation without our approval. From here on out, nothing happens without our knowledge. Is this clear?"

Jack's workers eyed each other in impressed silence and nodded hesitantly. Mr. Farris hurriedly composed himself for agreement, but Jack, his face contorted in confusion, stepped forward.

"Um, wait," he began, but Eli rounded on him with a glare.

"Do you have a problem with that?" he challenged.

Instantly cowed, Jack backed up, and Mr. Farris stepped forward quickly, placing a hand on Jack's shoulder as he stood slightly in front of him.

"No, there are no problems here, Agent Farley," he said, with a questioning look at Jack, who just shrugged and shook his head.

"Good," Eli grunted in approval. He then spoke up again for all present to hear:

"Now, is there a David Connally here, as well?"

Before David, over in the corner, could say anything, Jack now pushed past Mr. Farris and folding his arms, said gruffly, "David Connally works for me."

Eli studied Jack intently as if reading his mind.

"I was informed David Connally worked for The American Party," he said coolly. "I was also told about Michael Farris, but who are you?"

"Jack Webb. The party commissioned me to set up audio sound systems and staging for all their rallies." Jack responded shortly.

Eli took two steps toward Jack, towering over him. Jack stood his ground, but he could see the security agent was not intending to threaten him.

"Mr. Webb, as you can see, I am not the enemy. You need not treat me with suspicion. My team and I are here for the purpose of protection. We are highly trained security task force professionals, and elite gunmen, every last one of us. So," he added coldly as his eyes bored into Jack's, "in future I would ask that you show me more respect."

Jack fought hard to control the torrent of emotions he was sure could be seen in his face: abashed annoyance, defiance, and genuine respect for the giant in front of him. He couldn't explain why having a squad of heavily armed security personnel around gave him a nervousness that exhibited itself in frustration. Was it because he knew they were here to take over David's personal security, and up to this point he had looked upon that as his own special responsibility?

"David," he called out, without taking his eyes off Eli Farley. "Come over here, please."

David had risen from his chair when Eli had asked for him, and stood silently where he was until Jack called him over. As he slowly approached Jack, Mr. Farris, and Eli, open caution in his face marked his unsure feelings about what was going on since Eli's team had showed up. He walked over and stood between Mr. Farris and Jack, across from Eli.

Eli uncrossed his arms and held out his hand to David.

"David Connally? My name is Eli Farley." He waited for David's acknowledgment with a nod and a respectful, "Yes sir," before introducing himself.

"Mr. Connally, I would like to speak with you in private, if you would follow me."

David glanced instinctively in Jack's direction. Jack clapped him on the back and nodded briefly. Mr. Farris stepped closer to him and said quietly, "It's alright, David. These men are here to take care of us. Don't worry," he added when David turned to him in surprise. "Eli here will explain everything to you."

Eli gave a nod of assent, and held out his arm to indicate the way out of the tent, and for David to follow him. With one more look at Jack, David allowed Eli to lead him out into the windy morning. Outside the tent, four more armed men stood at attention with their weapons near the entrance. David's eyes widened when he saw them.

"Wow, looks like you have guys everywhere," he remarked carefully.

"There will be more stationed around the rally sites," Eli answered without breaking his stride or looking at David. "We need enough guards to hold the perimeter."

"Sounds like you're working a military mission."

"Ours is a mission of just as great importance."

When they were out of earshot of anyone else, Eli stopped walking and turned to David, who stood with his hands in the pockets of his jacket, expectancy written plainly on his face.

"Mr. Connally, I'm here to protect you," he said in a low voice, but less frigid and more kindly than he had used in the tent. However, he still spoke with clear authority.

"Do you know Rick McCoy?" he asked.

David nodded. Eli noted this with approval.

"Good. Then you are aware of what's happening. Mr. McCoy has enlisted me and my staff to give you the kind of personal security only the best money can buy. From this point on, I intend to do just that. From now on, no reporters will be granted access to you, so you won't be harassed in any way. I'm also informed to keep you from speaking to any reporters as well. Do you understand?"

David took his hands from his pockets and crossed his arms, a gesture Eli couldn't detect as fear or mere skepticism.

"I said, do you understand, Mr. Connally?"

"Yes sir, I do."

Eli put his hand on David's shoulder and turned him back to face the other armed security guards standing near the tent.

"From now on, one of my men will be with you twenty-four-seven. If there is the slightest problem, you see me. Understand?"

"Sir," said David, closing his eyes for a moment, "I understand everything you're saying, and I appreciate it, and Mr. McCoy's concern for me. But what I don't understand is why I need all this protection and hired guns in the first place. What's so special about me that I need a task force guarding me day and night? All I do is–"

"Mr. Connally, I don't know you, not yet, but I do know my mission. And that's you. I've crossed paths with McCoy before, and I know he only puts his time and emphasis into what really matters to him; what he thinks is truly worth investing in. If McCoy thinks you, Mr. Connally, are worth the protection of Blackheart Security, then he must feel you're pretty important to be guarding. And from the little he said to me about you personally when I spoke with him, he seemed pretty adamant about how important you are to his party, and he wants to make sure you have protection from television reporters and anyone else who might want access to you."

David slowly nodded his head.

Eli met his gaze.

"My team has never failed me," he said quietly. "If I can have your word that you will cooperate with us, everything will be fine."

"You won't have any problems from me," David answered, and the two men shook hands.

"Mr. Connally," said Eli with his first smile since he had arrived, "it's been a pleasure to meet you. And I give you my solemn word that I will do everything it takes to keep you safe from here on out."

"Thanks, Mr. Farley," said David with a returning smile.
"Call me Eli."
"Only if you call me David."

Sitting in the living room of his opulent D.C. residence, Joseph Cane watched the end of the Fox News report, then angrily grabbed the television remote and turned off the power. With the remote still dangling from his hand, he sank back in his covered chair and pinched the bridge of his nose, screwing up his eyes.

"What happened, Joseph?" His wife came into the room with a club sandwich on a plate and set it down on the small table beside him. "I thought you wanted to watch the news."

"I've seen enough for tonight," he answered wearily, rubbing his lower lip. He leaned forward and rested his elbows on his knees with his head down.

"Joseph? Are you OK?" Cassie Cane settled onto the arm of his chair and laid a gentle hand on his back. "What's wrong, honey?"

Senator Cane raised his head and stared vacantly at the blank TV screen in front of him.

"David Connally," he mumbled.

"David Connally? Why should he bother you, dear?"

"Because!" Senator Cane jumped to his feet and began pacing feverishly across the room. "He's out there when I should be! He's getting publicity that I both need and deserve! That should have been me featured in that news report. Did you see how often I was even mentioned? Connally was featured more than any actual politician! He's a nobody! Nobody even knows a thing about him!" He waved the remote at the TV in his state of agitation.

"Surely by now," said his wife in an attempt to calm him, "somebody must have–"

"No. If you try just Googling the guy, all you find is the recent articles, videos, so on. There's absolutely nothing about him or his background that dates before six months ago."

"Well, that's odd," his wife commented genially.

Senator Cane sat back down with a hard thud and rubbed his eyes so fiercely that his wife reached over and took his hand in hers, stroking it gently.

"I mean, what does he have that I don't?" he muttered, half to himself, half to his wife. "All he does is get up and sing a bunch of patriotic songs and say a few things about America. Anyone can do that. I have done that..."

"You used to praise America a lot more back when you were running for the Senate," said his wife, cutting into his scrutiny. He turned to look up at her. Her eyes had a far-off look.

"I remember when you were trying to raise the morale of the people by talking about our country and how great she is, and how blessed we are," she went on, still holding his hand in both of hers. "You had such a patriotic fire lit inside you, Joseph. I sometimes wondered how you didn't spontaneously combust in front of the audiences. I loved how excited you were to be helping this country, and how often you would arrange your speeches around the beauty and blessings of our nation, just because it was spilling out of you to tell. In a way, David Connally reminds me of you, a little bit, back when you were more in love with this country than...your work."

Her hesitancy over the last few words made him shift uncomfortably in his chair.

"You work so hard, Joseph, and I can do nothing but praise you for that. But it's almost as if you stopped caring—"

"I do care!" he exclaimed with more edge than he intended, and almost instantly regretted it.

"I didn't mean you don't care about the people, or this country," his wife said soothingly. "I meant that it seems you can only think now about satisfying Americans on the popular issues – and I know you have morals, dear, that you will never compromise – but it feels like you try so hard to stay popular with conservatives that you lost sight of the things David is talking about...and maybe that's why people love to listen to him—"

But the mention of David's name jarred the senator so that

he disengaged her hand, stood up again, and walked toward the television, standing with the remote in his hand behind his back.

"Well, I don't need an opening act," he said resentfully. "If it wasn't for David, I'd have carried the audience's attention at that last rally. That news slot would have been mine, and I'd be far more certain of getting the votes this fall!"

Behind him, his wife sat without saying a word, figuring it was best to let him have his tirade and get everything out of his system before interjecting with reason and sense to cool him down.

"I'm this close to becoming the official endorsed presidential candidate for The American Party," he said, turning around to show his finger and thumb a quarter of an inch apart. "I opted to join them because I expected this kind of grass-roots publicity would be good for my campaign. And now some nobody who's probably an illegal immigrant or something suddenly appears out of nowhere, and my public is suddenly his public. That should have been me. The American Party should have put their little entertainer at the end instead of the beginning when I could have spoken. Connally shouldn't be the center of attention when he isn't even running for office. If all he's doing is pre-rally entertaining, he shouldn't be getting my publicity!"

"So many 'shoulds,'" his wife said softly. "Joseph, your ego is as healthy as a horse and, unfortunately, nearly as big. It doesn't seem to me like David Connally is just out there to simply entertain the crowds. It's your own self-serving bias that put the idea in your head that he's trying to steal the people away from you. And since when have they been yours to lay claim to? The American public doesn't hate or despise you since they discovered David. I think you're jealous of the admiration and applause this young man is receiving because you think you're entitled to that instead of him."

"Cassie, I don't–"

"Yes you do, Joseph!" She walked over to where he stood with his arms now folded in front of him, turning him so that he was facing her. "Honey, I know you. You have never been able to stand it when someone in a similar field to yours wins the hearts and smiles of those you too are working to gain. When you work for something, you live in this dreaded fear that somebody else is going to come along and steal your hard-earned praise and attention."

She laid her hand against his cheek and smiled sadly at the chagrined frustration on his face.

"But I'll tell you this," she added in a sweeter voice, putting her arms around his neck. "You will always have the heart and smiles of one person that will always belong solely to you."

He sighed, and then raised his eyes to look at his wife, as if studying her for the first time in a long time.

"My perfect little wife," he said with his first real smile since the news report on television.

"Who is very proud of her husband," she returned, reaching up to give him a kiss. "Whether he's a senator or a lawyer..."

She paused before adding slyly, "...Or a college graduate who took an extra year because he failed his writing class..."

He gave her a warning look, but she smiled mischievously, undeterred.

"Twice," she finished.

"You know," he said, side-stepping her and grabbing the club sandwich and plate in either hand with a mock-injured air, "I was going to share this with you, but now I don't think I will."

"Oh, come on!" She burst out laughing.

He stalked across the room, then stopped in the doorway and turned around.

"May I remind you," he said, a broad grin growing on his face in spite of his earlier irritation, "that I only failed that class because there was a certain young lady who for some reason I felt compelled to spend most of my time in college with?"

"Oh, right, mm-hmm," she nodded, and her eyes sparkled playfully as she came around the chair and walked over to him.

"And when she wanted to go out on the weekends, it didn't leave me much time to do the assignments my professor gave me." Her husband took a bite of the sandwich as he spoke. "Wow, that's good."

"You bet it is!" She came up close to him and followed his example, taking a bite and leaving a drop of mustard at the corner of her mouth. Senator Cane set the sandwich on the plate and holding it with one hand, rummaged in his back pocket until he pulled out his handkerchief, which he used to gently wipe his wife's mouth. She smiled lovingly at him, and he put his arm around her with a sigh.

"What would I do without you, Cassie?"

"Make your own sandwich?"

"Hmm..." He knit his brows as if pretending to weigh options, then shook his head.

"Nope. You'll have to stick around. I can't do that by myself."

"Oh, all right, since I enjoy cooking and all," she teased him, and he laughed as if he had never been troubled by David Connally at all.

Rick McCoy sat in his office suite in Cincinnati, Ohio, with his coffee cup in hand while he surveyed some papers on the desk in front of him. He picked up one of the papers and held it up to the natural light coming from the windows for a closer look. As he did so, the intercom beside his desk phone lit up and a voice buzzed over the line.

"Mr. McCoy, Nathan Blaine is here to see you."

McCoy put down the paper immediately and pressed the answer button.

"Send him in."

The door opened a moment later, and a man entered the room. He was about thirty-five, and tall, with ears that stuck out slightly, and an oval-shaped face. His wavy brown hair was pushed back from his tall forehead, and his blue-gray eyes crinkled up endearingly when he smiled. And he did smile as he walked over to McCoy's desk. McCoy returned the smile as he walked around in front of his desk and reached out to shake the newcomer's hand.

"Nathan Blaine, it sure is good to see you again," he exclaimed heartily as their hands clasped in greeting.

"Rick McCoy, always a pleasure," Nathan returned. His voice was full of energy and good humor. McCoy gestured him to a chair in front of his desk, and resumed his own wing-back mahogany leather chair behind his desk again.

"Well now, it's been a few years, hasn't it, Nathan?"

Nathan chuckled as he crossed his legs and straightened up the lining of his gray sports jacket.

"Yes it has, Rick. Last time I saw you was about…oh…five years back, wasn't it? When one of your accountants had wandered off the reservation with a quarter-million dollars of your company's money?"

McCoy grimaced, then smiled to himself.

"Yes, those were…good times, Nathan," he replied, with a look that plainly said he felt the opposite way. "I do remember, though, that out of all the people we hired to find that scum bag, you–" he raised his eyebrows and flicked his hand at Nathan, "–were the only one who was able to track him down, and on the other side of the world at that!"

His remembrance ended on a note of admiration as he surveyed the private investigator sitting before him. Nathan made a modest gesture in acknowledgment of his field of expertise. Then he sat up straighter and asked, "So, what am I here for, Rick? Hopefully it isn't about another employee taking off with more funds? Because really, as much as I love my work, I'm not in the mood to chase some thief into the wilds of Australia again right now."

"Hey, isn't that what you do best?" McCoy questioned dryly, then grew serious. "No, I didn't call you in over theft or embezzlement, Nathan. In fact, what I brought you here for today has nothing to do with my company. Have you heard of a guy working for The American Party by the name of David Connally?"

Nathan knit his brows, nodding slowly. "Yes, I've heard of him. Seen him on the news once or twice, in fact. Has he gone missing on you?"

McCoy shook his head.

"So, what's the problem?"

McCoy drummed his fingers on his desk for a moment, then stood up and walked to the window. Nathan's gaze followed his movements until McCoy was standing with his back to the investigator. He took a deep breath.

"Here's my dilemma, Nathan. This young man is becoming extremely valuable to our party. I've heard him speak live, and talked with him myself. He seems like a pretty decent, stand-up fellow, a staunch patriot, and I've been told he's very dependable and a hard worker."

Nathan's eyes were bright and alert, fixed on McCoy like a hawk tracking movement. As McCoy paused, a little smile crept over the investigator's face.

"But?" he prompted knowingly.

McCoy sighed and turned to face Nathan as he leaned back against the window frame with his hands in his pockets.

"We don't know anything about him. His past, or even his present. No ID. No credit cards. No resident address. All we have is his name."

"Well, I suppose you haven't tried asking him." Nathan joked in an effort to lighten the atmosphere.

"As a matter of fact, I have," McCoy responded with a hint of frustration. He began pacing as he spoke. "And that's really where the problem lies. You see, this young man, whose popularity is daily growing by leaps and bounds, and who is becoming more and more important to The American Party because of it, is unwilling to discuss his past with anyone. At the present, every reporter who gets wind of him will be trying to find out who this David Connally is and where he came from."

McCoy finally sat back down behind his desk. Nathan rubbed his chin, looking puzzled.

"But how is it that they haven't found out everything about him already?" he asked.

McCoy smiled faintly.

"Because, Nathan, they're not you," he answered. He leaned forward across his desk. "I need you to find out everything you can about the last thirty years of David Connally's life, and I need you to do it fast before anyone else learns anything about him."

Nathan pursed his lips, deep in thought. He seemed hesitant to reply.

"Rick, you do realize that you're asking me to drop every case I'm working on and make this my first priority? That can be expensive, my friend."

"I understand, Nathan. We're going to make this worth your while, trust me." McCoy promised him. He again stood up and walked around his desk and leaned against the front of it with his arms folded. Nathan looked up at him expectantly.

"But Nathan, you have to get the scoop on this guy before anyone else," he added quietly. "The American Party has huge exposure with the public through Connally, and if there's any detrimental information in his past, he'll be a terrible liability that we really do not need. The damage control would be overwhelming."

Nathan nodded once more. "So you need me to..."

"I need you to do what you do best, Nathan Blaine," said McCoy, straightening up. "You find the trail before the blood hounds pick up the scent. I have every confidence that you'll find what you're looking for."

Nathan Blaine stood up and shook McCoy's hand with the air of a man on a mission.

"Understood. Where is Connally now?"

McCoy looked down at his phone, and slid his finger over the screen a couple of times.

"Here's the party rally schedule. They'll be in St. Louis tomorrow morning. And by 'they' I mean David as well," he answered.

Nathan smiled as if he had already found what he was assigned to search for.

"Well then," he said with a crafty expression in his gunmetal eyes, "if you will be so kind as to get me on the next flight out to St. Louis, then I guarantee I'll find out everything you want to know about David Connally."

"That's all I need to hear," McCoy said with a smile, following Nathan to the door. "Check in with my manager Michael Farris when you reach St. Louis. He'll introduce you to Jack Webb, and they will bring you up to speed on everything they know about David. And, Nathan," he added as Nathan opened the door. Nathan paused to look back at him.

THE SPEAKER

"I know you're already aware of this, but no one else is to know anything about what you find out except for me."

Nathan Blaine inclined his head. "But of course," he replied, almost theatrically. McCoy closed the door after him and returned to his desk with a smile.

CHAPTER 7:

David Connally's popularity with the American people continued to grow as time passed. The tranquility with which he met his rising fame contrasted starkly with the raging fever of the political parties and primaries running rampant in every possible media outlet.

Always on the road, The American Party was also gaining more and more news coverage, becoming a prime topic of discussion amongst many pundits and other party boards. Rick McCoy and Michael Farris were set up for several interviews, and though they were willing to comply, there was never a word mentioned about possibly interviewing David as well. The 'David Connally Phenomenon' as Mr. Farris liked to call it, was growing by leaps and bounds, more than anyone could understand or imagine. At every rally the crowds were larger and larger, more and more enthusiastic, and more and more vocal about their open approval and support of David. He was always welcomed by the audience with cheers and applause that warmed Mr. Farris's heart, and filled Jack with a cautious optimism. He felt better, even relieved, that Blackheart Security was now in charge of protecting David, for it took a great amount of stress off Jack's mind. Eli Farley, with his team of security personnel, certainly had their hands full keeping the media and enthusiastic people away from David. Plenty of news reporters were coming from D.C. alone, asking daily for interviews that were firmly declined.

It wasn't so much that they were afraid some random belligerent would try to hurt David, for it seemed there wasn't a single angry person in the audience at The American Party rallies. It was more the over-excitement and enthusiasm of the people that had Blackheart always within a few yards of David wherever he stood.

↑THE SPEAKER

"You never know what some crazy fool might do when they get too excited," said Eli darkly. "They lose their heads, and then somebody else does. It's like a domino effect."

"Or mob rule," added Jack.

But so far there didn't seem to be such a need for tighter security. At least not yet. It was plain to see the crowds loved David. They enjoyed and participated in his leading songs of patriotism. Somehow his way of drawing everyone in with his words of understanding about good people, good Americans who put God first, respected their government, and said no evil of their fellow man was winning their hearts. The loving way he spoke of why America is so special because she is the only nation where the government is the people, and talking about how the country is a beacon of light and hope to every other nation in the world because of her freedoms, promise of a better life, and daringly built on the power of entrepreneurship instead of mere conquest, filled every listener with a pride and joy that swept like a contagious fever across the country. He left more ardent patriots behind him in every city through which The American Party passed and held their rallies, not even counting the vast amount of television and radio coverage he was gaining.

"He isn't just giving us some boring history lesson," one starry-eyed observer said in answer to a question from Joann Walker one night after a rally. "He's speaking truths that we've been starving to hear from politicians but haven't been for so long. He doesn't stand only for America. He stands for what's right. America needs more people like Connally."

Those working for the media were astonished over how this man from nowhere, this fluke, was winning over so many people so quickly.

"We've never seen anything like this before," Joann Walker told the news headquarters with professionally controlled enthusiasm. "This is truly incredible."

Now that the 'fluke' was becoming something more than just a one-time coincidence, primary news stations were becoming very interested in this new phenomenon, and Joann Walker was working full time trying to get as much coverage as possible of the procedures and details of The American Party's events.

When the first week in June arrived, the Democratic Party held their national convention in Chicago to nominate their party's candidates for president and vice president. It had been determined a foregone decision that Helen Kennedy would easily carry the nomination, and she had chosen a fellow devoted Democrat by the name of Louis Wilson as her vice president; a man not nearly as liberal as she. In fact, he was one of the most hesitant, mealy-mouthed politicians to run for office. But her selection of Wilson for vice president seemed not to be all about dual strength, as Wilson had not done well in the primaries. It was thought by many that he was chosen because he wasn't one to present a challenge of domination to Helen as a female president. If this was the case or not, Senator Kennedy would not say, and if she cared what people thought of her running mate, or herself, she never said either. She had her eyes fixed on the White House, and she was determined to do whatever was 'necessary' in order to reach the prize.

During the DNC, there were many meetings about the Democrat Party's concern over the lack of interest in the voters over the Democratic platform and candidates this year. The American Party was often spoken of as a great threat to their party, and the Democrats could see that The American Party's star was drawing people from every other party like nothing seen before. It was really David Connally they were afraid of. He seemed to be posing the most serious threat to all of the Democratic candidates running for office.

When the DNC was concluded, a large meeting of the Democratic leadership was held in another Chicago hotel conference room to decide their next move. Present were the Democratic Party chairman Dominic York, Democratic presidential nominee Senator Helen Kennedy, her vice presidential running mate Louis Wilson, and many of the Democratic senators, representatives, and governors. As the meeting got underway, much of the strategy conversation was over how to take the house, the senate, and White House. But these conversations soon waned and the impending discussion, ever near the surface, emerged about what to do regarding The American Party and its enormous inroad into American politics. And, of course, David Connally, who had done so much to increase its popularity and value in the eyes of the people.

"The American Party has grown so exponentially that it could almost be considered a third party now!" Senator Kennedy complained. "They're trying the 'feel good' tactic, and it makes me sick. Sure, go ahead, promote conservative candidates with morally upright Christian values. That will take this nation to the top, oh yes. That's all we need, some do-good Bible-thumper leading America backwards instead of progressing into the future."

"Senator, I beg you to calm down," Dominic York said in his menacingly husky voice. "May I remind you that you have already won the Democratic nomination for presidency? We're halfway to controlling Washington, and you seem to forget that in your haste to worry over a minute issue that can and will be easily resolved."

His cold, mask-like eyes widened in emphasis as he spoke those last words. She stared at him for a few seconds in discomfited silence, then leaning toward him, muttered, "And how do you plan on fixing this problem, Chairman York?"

He smiled in an almost ghastly manner that gave his cadaverous appearance an even more blanched look, then turned to address the rest of the room.

"I realize you are all concerned about The American Party and this Connally fellow, but I'm here to alleviate your fears as of now. I will personally be setting in motion what needs to be done to show the people that The American Party is not in their best interests after all, and that this nation needs the Democratic Party to guide them and make their lives better. We'll see how the people react when they hear what our platform has to say about the rich supplying all of their needs, eh?"

Faint laughter broke out after this statement, and though a little skepticism remained, much of the worry was dispelled from the group. Dominic York, looking highly pleased with himself and certainly mysterious about something, stepped away and took Senator Kennedy by the elbow.

"Senator, you expressed a wish to know what I have in mind

for our little grass-roots rival," he said with an innocent lilt that made his voice even huskier. "How about you and I meet for dinner later, and I would be happy to discuss my plans with you."

She moved her gaze upwards, deliberating. "And Connally?" she asked pointedly.

"My dear senator…" York took her hand in both of his. "Did you really think I could leave him out?"

It would be only two more weeks until the Republican National Convention took place in San Antonio, Texas. Michael Farris and Rick McCoy were this time openly promoting Joseph Cane as a prime candidate for presidency, but so far had not put out an official announcement that he was their official candidate. Because The American Party had grown so huge in the media, and had gained so much popularity that their opinions and endorsements carried real weight with so many, the Republican party took their candidates, including Joseph Cane, into more serious consideration, and he was now a clear frontrunner for the nomination.

While the Republican Party was preparing for its convention in San Antonio, Rick McCoy was kept busy with phone calls and meetings. Whatever he disclosed to Mr. Farris, Mr. Farris asked permission to tell Jack, who in turn informed David what was going on.

David was so much an integral part of The American Party now that his name was practically synonymous with the organization. He was becoming so well known that he had a hard time escaping every Sunday morning, even with Eli's help. As promised, one of the security team members was always with David, whether he was off reading his Bible, eating lunch, or just helping set up for the rallies. Jack was at first a bit unsettled by Blackheart's presence all over the place, but after an awkward first couple of days, he slowly learned to accept they were there, and went about his usual business. He still felt a certain disquieting sense of watchfulness whenever he was working or standing near Eli's elite team, but then he reminded himself that this was for David's sake, and tried to shake off the feeling of discomfort.

A couple of weeks before the RNC, Rick McCoy got an important phone call and immediately informed Mr. Farris.

"Farris, I just got off the phone with Edward Martin," he told Mr. Farris over the phone. "You know who that is, don't you?"

Mr. Farris nearly choked on a mouthful of the sandwich he had just bitten into.

"Edward Martin? Not the Edward Martin who's chairman of the Republican Party?"

"The same. Mr. Farris, this is huge for our party. Martin wants to meet with me tomorrow to discuss some things of which he did not inform me fully, but if my hunch is correct, we could be looking at both support from and cohesion with the Republican Party."

"Wow. That's, that's incredible, sir!"

"Yeah, like I said, it's big. Imagine how much farther we could reach and expand with the official aid from the national Republican Party! But I'm being cautiously optimistic here, Farris. After all, I don't want us to get lost inside Team A or Team B. What makes us stand out and unique is in part because we're an independent party that's more concerned about people than politics, and aren't connected with other organizations."

"I thought what made us stand out was mainly due to David Connally, sir."

"Well, he's certainly helped us in that regard. Which reminds me, I now have an investigator on the case, and it's been given top priority. Don't go spreading the word, though. This is between us."

"Yes, sir."

"Alright then. I'll let you know how proceedings go tomorrow."

"Thank you, sir. I look forward to hearing about it."

The next morning Rick McCoy was in his Cincinnati office with his assistant, Jeff Dixon, going over details about the upcoming RNC. A sudden knock on the door caused them both to raise their heads, and McCoy called out, "Come in."

His secretary stuck her head in and said, "Mr. McCoy, Edward Martin is here to see you."

McCoy straightened up at once, and with a nod to Mr. Dixon, adjusted the lapels of his sports jacket and answered, "Thanks, Audrie. Show him in, please."

Audrie disappeared for a moment, and then reappeared followed by a man dressed in an immaculate navy suit with a fedora on his head. With all the finery he wore, all he needed was a little red flower in his buttonhole to look like a member of the mafia, thought McCoy. As the newcomer advanced into the office, both McCoy and his assistant took a good look at him.

Standing up, Edward Martin was just a few inches shy of six feet. He wore thick, black-rimmed glasses on his oblong face, which was partially obscured by his short, bushy goatee and mustache. His hair, already receding a fair distance back from his forehead, was light brown with flecks of gray here and there, including his beard. His small ears were flattened against his long head, and his dark blue eyes had a kind, knowing expression. He smiled without showing his teeth, making his cheekbones protrude out like wings and giving his head a contrast to his thick neck. He walked quietly, but the subtlety of his movements conveyed self-assurance and ease.

"Mr. Martin?" McCoy said, stepping forward with his hand out.

"That would be me, yes," returned the visitor, removing his hat with one hand while shaking McCoy's with the other. His voice was pleasantly pitched, soft, and bright.

"It's a privilege, sir. Allow me to also introduce my assistant, Jeff Dixon."

Mr. Dixon and Mr. Martin shook hands with equal enthusiasm. McCoy asked his visitor if he would like anything to drink before they got started.

"Coffee would be great, thank you," said the Republican Party chairman as he proceeded to follow the suggestion of his political counterpart by taking a seat. McCoy called his secretary back by pushing the buzzer on his desk.

"Audrie, would you bring us three cups of coffee, please?"

"Yes sir. Cream and sugar too?"

McCoy looked at Martin, who waved his hand and said he

would take his black.

"And I don't drink anything in mine, either," said McCoy, glancing at Mr. Dixon.

"It's the same for me," his assistant shrugged, his surprisingly deep voice resonating in the room.

"Just the coffee then, Audrie."

"Now, I have true respect for a man who drinks his coffee black," Martin exclaimed when the three men were left alone.

"I think it's one of those things that should be taken in its purest, original form," McCoy smiled.

"Like creating congressional legislation."

"Touché."

From the corner where he stood, Jeff Dixon smiled at their easy wordplay.

"But let's get down to business," said McCoy, parking himself behind his desk and folding his hands on top. Martin scooted his chair closer to the desk and placed his fedora on his knee.

"So, what are we here to talk about? Your phone call was, albeit a nice surprise, more ambiguous than what I'm used to."

Martin took his hat off his knee and set it in his lap so he could clasp his hands around his crossed leg. He leaned forward with his brows furrowed and his gaze intense, as if what he was about to say was very significant.

"Well, Mr. McCoy, it seems to me that we share a kinship in that many of those who adhere to the principles of The American Party are also members of the Republican Party. I've been following your media coverage for quite some time and frankly, I am perfectly astounded at the speed with which your party has grown and become such a favorite. Since what you're working for and what I'm working for gives us a mutual fighting cause, it seems to me that we should maybe..." He paused here, and motioned with his hand as if conveying the obvious meaning of his next words. McCoy put his head to one side, his eyebrows raised expectantly.

"It seems the Republican Party and The American Party should combine forces and work together to take back this country," Martin finished.

At that moment Audrie returned with a tray, and nothing more was said until the men had their coffee in hand and McCoy had sent his secretary away with his thanks.

"So, what do you think?" Martin demanded, smiling proudly.

McCoy blew on the dark liquid in his cup to cool it off, thinking long and hard about the offer.

"It's true that many of the men we support and recommend are also Republicans," he answered deliberately. "But for us, it's about what's good for the nation, and what's good for the people. Those are the things we're concerned about as a party, not the politics of the two-party system that have been fighting and squabbling to guide the country into the mess we're in today."

Martin set his coffee cup on a coaster on the desk, nodding rapidly and putting his hands up in a placating gesture as McCoy's words grew slightly more heated toward the end of his statement.

"Ok, ok, let me just ask you this. If Joseph Cane becomes the Republican nominee for president in two weeks, is The American Party going to support him?"

He felt Mr. Dixon move forward, and put out a quick hand to stop him before he spoke.

"We're not sure," he said in the same slow, careful manner. "Senator Cane is undoubtedly a great politician and he stands up for many things The American Party endorses. I like the guy–"

"So that's a yes, then?"

"We will reserve our decision until we hear what he has to say at the convention." McCoy's answer was firm. "If he is the best man, he will certainly have our support all the way. We will also be interested to see whom he selects for his vice presidential running mate. If he doesn't choose a suitable candidate whom we can get behind, we will simply have to work with those senators, representatives, and governors which fit the values of our party."

Martin sank back in his chair looking fairly satisfied.

"Fair enough. We will wait and see."

"Indeed we will," McCoy returned, raising his coffee to his lips again.

"But let me ask you another question," Martin added, and

McCoy inwardly cringed. He had been reluctantly anticipating the inevitable topic that was sure to come up in any political discussion these days.

"What exactly is going on regarding this fellow, this...David Connally?" Martin demanded. "You can't turn on the news without hearing about him. Do you intend to endorse him for some kind of office?"

"No." McCoy shook his head. It wasn't that talking about David made him uncomfortable; it was that eventually somebody was going to ask more about his past before he joined The American Party, and the ambiguity only served to exacerbate curiosity and disapproval. It also served as a constant reminder to those around the young man that even they didn't know anything about him, including McCoy. He hoped Nathan Blaine would have something for him soon.

"David Connally is not a candidate for any office," he said staunchly. "He is simply a good man who loves this country and her people. He only wants the best for this nation."

Martin twirled his fedora. He looked skeptical, as if he didn't believe McCoy's claim.

"But then, who is writing the speeches he's been giving at the rallies?"

"No one but him. But I assure you, Mr. Martin, that Mr. Connally is only saying what's on his heart. We don't direct him on anything he says–"

"Do you mean to tell me that you're letting that man just say whatever he wants out there without any approved script beforehand?!" Martin interrupted, sitting up with a jerk of surprise.

McCoy bit his lip, realizing how dangerous this sounded, but he knew enough about David and had seen him speak enough times that he was no longer worried about letting the young man continue unscripted before thousands of people and even live TV.

"That's right. And apparently he is saying exactly what the people need to hear, because neither of us have ever seen anyone like this – think about it, Mr. Martin!" McCoy stood up and paced restlessly beside his desk, keeping eye contact with Martin, who watched him in confusion.

"You have a man here who never speaks a bad word about anyone, talks about God as if he were his friend, and he teaches the people how to love their country, fellow man, and control their destiny instead of letting some power-hungry political machine slowly trample their civil rights in the name of 'progress', and moving into a 'new age', or whatever. Yes, I do pay attention to what he says, and no, I haven't found anything wrong with it."

Mr. Dixon raised his eyebrows at this sudden passionate outburst from his usually even-tempered boss. But even in his agitated state, McCoy kept his voice low, though it crackled with intensity. His bright blue eyes snapped like fire.

Martin rose to his feet, shaking his head regretfully.

"You're out in deep water, Mr. McCoy," he warned, setting his fedora carefully on top of his thinning hair. "And you, Connally, and your precious American Party may in all probability go down in a whirlpool."

"I believe that the people sincerely want to hear what David has to say," said McCoy, raising his head proudly. "He tells them the truth. He doesn't criticize any party or person for what they've done in the past, and that's certainly something, considering how often the most conservative individual usually has at least one or two negative things to say about some of our leaders in Washington. Rather, David encourages the people to look ahead, to make it better from here on, and to take control of their future and the future of this nation. At the present we are doing everything we can to find larger venues to hold rallies because of the massive crowds we have attending!"

McCoy slowly advanced toward Martin as he spoke, using his hands and raising his voice expressively in hopes of convincing the chairman of the Republican Party of David's value, but Martin just stood still with his arms crossed and a look of disagreeing indifference on his face. He looked exactly like he was waiting for McCoy to finish telling a story in which he had little interest.

McCoy could tell his visitor was not impressed, and sighed.

"Mr. Martin," he said, switching topics, "if Joseph Cane becomes your candidate, and we agree with his philosophy, ideas, and approaches to government, we will openly support and do all we can to help him. We seem to have a lot more pull with the media these days. But this party will remain dedicated to changing American politics to a party that puts the people first and the good of the nation second."

"The good of the nation second, eh?" said Martin coolly. "I should think that the good of the nation and putting the concerns of her people first would be one and the same."

"Mr. Martin, I'm sure I don't have to explain to you that government personnel do many things in the name of the people and claim their agendas are for the greater good of our country, when you and I both know that isn't true."

Martin acknowledged this with a reluctant, short bow of the head.

"Well, what about having Connally come and speak at our convention?" he asked, his face lighting up as if a light bulb had suddenly turned on inside his head. "We would, of course, have to work out what he's going to say to the people. I know you just let him say whatever comes to his mind, but, well..." and here Martin reached up to trace his upper lip, and let out a brief chuckle. "It would have to be a little different at the RNC–"

McCoy broke in with a shake of the head as he answered, "I don't really think David would want to do that, Mr. Martin, and I'm ninety-percent certain that if you came to him trying to put words in his mouth, he would be even less so inclined. That isn't his method, you see. He will only say what he thinks, not what you, me, or anybody else tells him."

"How can you be so sure?" Martin demanded, clearly nettled.

"Trust me," McCoy said. "I know how he works."

Martin uncrossed his arms, crossed them again, and rubbed his nose violently until it turned a bright red. He seemed out of ideas.

"Well then," he said gruffly, clearing his throat, "there's no deal. Isn't every news media reporter trying to figure out where this guy's from, and what he's been doing for the past thirty years? I heard you and your party don't even know anything about his past. Is that true? You just let some nobody you don't even know loose on the

American public with a warm, happy message about controlling their future–"

"That is true," McCoy cut in smoothly. "But we are getting that issue dealt with."

Martin stared at him, and McCoy could feel his incredulous, piercing gaze silently calling him a fool. He watched as Martin reached out his hand for one quick handshake out of courtesy before striding to the door, shaking his head as he went. At the door he stopped and turned back.

"Mr. McCoy, I hope for your sake that you're right, because when this all blows up, there might not be a single American out there who will want to be associated with or even care about The American Party anymore."

"You might be right, sir," McCoy answered lightly. "But right now, everyone wants to be a part of The American Party."

Dominic York sat at a small reserved table for two inside the spacious Mediterranean restaurant on 17th Street in Washington D.C., drumming his fingers lazily on the starched white tablecloth. He was surrounded by richly-dressed people focused on their meals and conversations, people who could afford to spend an evening at one of the most expensive restaurants in the nation's capital city. York also saw a few senators and representatives of his acquaintance scattered around at different tables. If one of them happened to look up from their seafood, ethanol-infused beverage, or dinner partner long enough to see York, they nodded and smiled, or raised their hand or glass to him. York gave a slight bow of the head from his seat in acknowledgment, and flexed his fingers in a return wave as he sat sideways with his legs crossed and one arm flung across the back of the chair while the other rested along the edge of the table. He wasn't here to be noticed by other politicians. He was here for an important meeting. An under-the-radar meeting.

The restaurant was longer than it was wide, with high ceilings, arched doorways, and polished wood floors. The air was rich with the smells of fresh pita bread, Italian meats and vegetables, and steaming pastas with their various sauces which permeated the heat in the room with their delicious scents.

Even though he was already aware of it before he came, York was glad to see there were no televisions set up inside the restaurant. He knew that if there were, there would surely be at least one tuned to a news station, and then he was bound to be shown something about that everlasting David Cornwell, or Connally; whatever his name was. York fudged the name more from vindictive spite than from actual absence of mind. He was only too well aware of Connally and his bothersome interference with York's cherished plans of taking Washington in the fall. York hardly dared admit to himself that this young nobody who sounded like he just walked off the set of Downton Abbey was causing more of a stir than was actually comfortable for York and his fellow Democrats. He had never witnessed such rapid growth in the popularity and influence of a grassroots organization, and he knew that was due mainly to this David Connally as their unofficial mascot, or whatever he was.

York checked his Michael Kors watch, which was turned on his right wrist so the face was looking out from the inside of his arm. He found it easier to read the time in this way, as it enabled him to use less energy in twisting his wrist around to see his watch. York never expended more energy than was necessary on the trivial, as it gave him time to fully exert himself in more important matters, like his work and planning for the upcoming presidential election which was mere months away.

"Forgive me for being late, Chairman."

York glanced up as Senator Helen Kennedy walked up to the table behind a waiter, who bowed and left the two of them together after he had seen the senator safely to her table.

"The traffic was terrible back on 9th," she said with a sigh, and York quickly stood up to shake her hand, smoothing down the front of his dark gray sports coat and vermillion necktie.

"You know, I'm rather surprised you chose this place," she commented, shrugging out of her violet coat and matching scarf, revealing a long, high collar black dress and a thick gold necklace that hung to her waist. "Don't you have to make a reservation a month in advance?"

"No worries, Senator," he said as he pulled her chair back from the table for her. "I'd already made the reservation in time for a meeting with a constituent from Illinois, but they had to pull out. I figured I may as well not let the reservation go to waste, and it timed perfectly with our meeting." He pushed her chair up to the table and sat down across from her with a smile.

Senator Kennedy took one glance round the busy room, playing with her gaudy finger rings. She then looked York straight in the eye.

"Alright, Dominic, please tell me you have something good, because Senator Cane just won the presidential nominee for the Republicans. That's mainly due to The American Party endorsing him, which means they've got way more clout than we gave them credit for, which means they will only have more and more influence in the future months. We can't underestimate them any longer, Dominic." She crossed her arms and pouted like a sulky child.

He nodded understandingly. "Senator, I know you're concerned and, seeing what The American Party is capable of, I can hardly blame you. None of us foresaw how Connally's popularity would skyrocket in the past couple of months, because none of us expected it. Because that kind of phenomenon just doesn't happen." York leaned back and relaxed his sitting position again. "Not without some kind of help from somewhere," he added thoughtfully.

Senator Kennedy stared at him through narrowed eyes. "What do you mean?"

"Well, I've been thinking." He sat up straight again and folded his hands. "Even with some kind of fluke like Connally, he has to have had some sort of behind-the-scenes aid to get him this far. Whether it's somebody intentionally writing all his speeches for him, or some kind of mind manipulation, something's going on with that American Party that I intend to find out about." He pointed down at the tablecloth for emphasis as he spoke.

A waiter brought them drinks and a pair of menus. Senator Kennedy refrained from speaking until he left, and then leaned closer to York.

"And just how do you intend on doing that?" she hissed. "Are you going to send some kind of spy into the midst of The American Party who's going to report back to you?"

York traced the edge of the filled glass in front of him with his middle finger and said nothing. He raised his head and gave the senator a hint of a smile.

Her eyes widened. "You are sending in a spy?"

He lifted his glass in the air, studied it a moment, then took a quick swallow. With a sigh of satisfaction, he licked his lips before answering.

"For now it's all very hush-hush, so I'd appreciate it, Senator, if you would keep this in confidence," he said quietly. She instinctively glanced around the restaurant again, as if afraid their conversation might be overhead by the other diners. "Though that is one of the subjects of discussion I had planned for this evening. I do have someone in mind for the delicate job you have just brought up, and I think he'll be just right for the task of learning everything that goes on inside The American Party."

"And you know for certain you can trust him?"

"Oh, his family has been devout Democrats for several decades at least. He's a young fellow, and from what I understand, very eager to serve his country. I have no doubt he will do whatever it takes to help make a difference in the days ahead."

York flipped his menu over and began perusing the dishes listed as if the conversation had dwindled to a smooth end. From his peripheral vision, he caught Senator Kennedy sitting very still. Seeing that she hadn't touched her menu, he looked up inquiringly. She was looking at him with a disappointed expression on her hard, heavily-powdered face.

"That's it?"

"I beg your pardon, Senator?"

"That's all you wanted to tell me? That you've enlisted the help of a spy to infiltrate The American Party? What about Connally? How is this going to send his ratings plummeting, Dominic? From what you said earlier, I expected much more from a mind like yours."

"My dear Senator, I told you I wouldn't leave Connally out."

"Then what–"

"Look."

York dropped his menu and for the first time all evening, his pale, sunken face seemed to darken, and his voice dropped into a ghostly whisper. Instead of pulling back, as most other people would have if they saw that expression on Dominic York's face, Senator Kennedy leaned in excitedly.

"What?" she demanded.

"I have...found...some people that are said to be extremely proficient at what they do-"

"Which is?"

York motioned for her to be quiet. "Please, Senator. Now, these people specialize in secret campaigns that...well...transform reputations, in so many words."

She knit her brows. "Smear tactics?"

"Do you think Connally would have half the popularity and goodwill of the masses that he does if they found out he was a racist, sexist bigot, and sleeps with female members of The American Party? Dear me..." York shook his head in mocking lamentation and heaved a sigh of pretend regret. "You just don't know what secrets people are hiding. Or could be hiding, if you have the right kind of power and money."

York took another sip of his drink, keeping his eyes fixed on Senator Kennedy to gauge her reaction to his ideas. She sat in silence for several seconds, as though turning the plan over in her mind.

"Do you know if hiring of these people can be traced?" she asked.

"I've spoken to others who have worked with them in the past. No complaints whatsoever, and I would take that to include confidentiality. These people are still in business, after all. What they do, it works."

She looked slightly skeptical, so York promised to have his assistant check the details, just to be safe. Then she seemed satisfied.

"I suppose I shouldn't ask how and where you found these people?"

He smiled in a way that looked more like he was just bearing his teeth. "I find that in some cases, ignorance is bliss, my dear

161

Senator."

"Well then," she said as she picked up her own glass for the first time and held it out to him. "Here's to the future of our government."

He clinked his glass against hers. "To the future of our country...with our beloved and fearless President Helen Kennedy at the helm."

A few weeks after the DNC concluded and Helen Kennedy had won the Democratic nomination for president, another secret meeting was taking place at the national office of the Democratic Party in Washington D.C.

It was late, past eleven o'clock in the evening. Dominic York and his personal assistant, Daniel White, were standing in York's luxurious office and speaking in low tones, even though they were the only ones still in the building.

Daniel rifled through his notes at a feverish pace. "Ok, here we are. Now, in about..." He paused to peer at the clock on the wall. "...fifteen minutes or so there should be a couple of people here to meet with us. I've been assured that they're the very best at what they do, so there should be no worries there."

"And nothing will be traced back to me."

"They leave no trails, and they get the job done quickly and efficiently," Daniel replied impressively. "You have nothing to worry about, sir."

York's mouth twisted open with an expression Daniel couldn't place.

"I'm not worried. But let me just enlighten you to the fact that the last time I hired an assistant to perform tasks such as this, I found him, well, incredibly deficient." York straightened up. Daniel scooted to the edge of his chair as though preparing to make a defense for himself, but his boss wasn't finished yet.

"My previous assistant broke promises. Couldn't deliver either on time or off. I've been failed enough times by the blunders and incompetence of others to show a little more caution whenever somebody tells me I have 'nothing to worry about.'" York held up his fingers in quotation marks. "I'm an extremely busy man, and I need someone I can rely on consistantly to help carry out my plans and never back down. What I'm asking is, are you that person, Daniel?"

"Um...yes...sir," Daniel mumbled, feeling like he was sitting in an interrogation room.

York had his blank, unblinking eyes fixed steadily on him as though trying to draw Daniel's thoughts out of his head by his gaze alone. Then he leaned against his desk and folded his arms. "Good. I'm glad we're still on the same page. I realize you've only been working here for...how long ago was it when you came to me?"

"About three months ago, sir."

"Of course." York smiled in a way that may have been meant as a sign of friendliness, but there are many different ways of parting one's lips and showing one's teeth. York seemed to have mastered the art of a fine sneer and grimace. And since he didn't often smile even when he was pleased, his face appeared even more hostile, which made his real smiles all the more hideous in his deathly features since the reason for his exuberance was often the misfortune of someone he considered an enemy.

"Still, three months isn't very long, and I know you've been working pretty faithfully to learn the ropes. I do acknowledge you've come a long way in a short time, Daniel."

York leaned down toward his assistant, and his empty eyes suddenly had a strange, sharply focused look. "But I've been around and done a lot before I hired you, and if you can't keep up, then you will be left behind. And then you can go back to that temp agency, or wherever it is you came from without any references from me. I need to know your loyalty to our party is unquestionable. Understand?"

Daniel suddenly felt heat flooding every inch of his face, neck, and hands while at the same time a shiver ran up his spine. York hadn't shouted. His voice hadn't risen above its usual pitch, nor had he made any violent movements. But his eerie calm and controlled level of menacing finality wrapped in open threat shook the assistant to his core, and for several seconds he could only sit in helpless confusion as he tried to find words to assure the chairman of the Democrat Party that his loyalty and time belonged solely to that organization.

"Mr. York, sir, I can promise you," he swallowed hard, and York watched him with raised eyebrows. "You just give me the instructions, and I will carry them out. I'll see them done."

York released another ominous smile that barely stretched the corners of his hard mouth. He reached over and grasped Daniel's shoulder, giving him a quick, hard shake. "Excellent!" he exclaimed, and Daniel felt his shoulders slump in relief. "Now, we have a few more minutes before our friends arrive." He squinted at the clock. "Have you met them?"

"No, and as far as I know, no one else has either."

York looked irritated. "What do you mean, no one's ever met them? How is that possible?"

Daniel bit his lip, looking foolish.

"Sir, I mean just that. I know it sounds crazy, but that's really all I can say."

York gave him an icy glare. "We don't do this kind of business with people we haven't met, Daniel. I was under the impression that you had already met with them."

"Sir," Daniel stood up, his hands outstretched pleadingly. "No one has ever met these people, but they do come highly recommended. They are just the right people for the job you want. Please, just give it a chance–"

"Dan, if I don't know who these people are, how can I expect them to fulfill my requests without talking? How do we know they aren't spies?"

The clock struck midnight.

"Sir, I–"

"Be quiet."

Daniel snapped his mouth shut. York was holding up a hand, his head cocked, listening to something.

Then they both heard it the second time. A soft, persistent rap at the door. York and his assistant looked at each other for the space for three seconds. Without moving any other muscle, York's eyes slid back to the door.

"Who's there?" he called out.

CHAPTER 7:

There was no reply save for a scratching sound. The next instant, a folded piece of paper was slipped under the door. York gave Daniel a shove with his eyes, and the assistant reluctantly approached the door, imagining all manner of strange beings on the other side of it, scooped up the paper, and retreated back toward York, reading it as he walked.

"Well? What does it say?" York demanded impatiently.

"Um, it says that only one person can be in here during the meeting, and that all the lights are to be turned off before the door is opened–"

"What!"

"–And if this does not happen in two minutes..." Daniel sneaked a hasty glance at the clock. "...there will be no one outside this door to talk to."

Daniel looked up from the paper at York, who for once looked visibly disconcerted. In another moment, however, all traces of bewilderment were gone, giving way to a reckless exasperation that Daniel wished he could share.

"Who are these people, the mafia? This is ridiculous."

"If, if you want to talk to them, let's just do what they say," Daniel suggested, devoid of any other ideas. He was seriously creeped out by this entire, weird situation, and the idea of letting in two strangers without the lights on who wouldn't even talk through the door but were lurking in silence on the other side made the hair on his arms stand up.

"Fine," York sighed as if the whole thing was a waste of his time. He waved his hand carelessly in Daniel's direction. "You go on. Turn out the light on your way out."

Daniel grabbed his coat and ledger, too happy to comply. There were two doors into York's office, the main entrance leading out into the hall (where Daniel knew the mysterious visitors were waiting) and the door beside York's desk that connected with his secretary's. Daniel nearly ran through this door, swiping at the light switch on his way out. As he closed the door behind him, he heard York muttering under his breath over the ridiculousness of the whole situation.

THE SPEAKER

Daniel scurried through the secretary's office, through the door connecting that office to a break room, and finally made his way out into a hall, trying to put as much distance between himself and York's office as possible. When he was sure the visitors had by now entered his boss's office, Daniel sagged against the wall of the hallway, clutching his ledger and coat to his chest. Leaning his head back, he let out a long exhale.

Maybe I should have stayed at the agency, he thought ruefully. He raked a shaky hand through his shiny brown hair, causing the short pieces in front to flop back on his perspiring forehead. Closing his hazel eyes, he took another deep breath. His square face was usually cheerful, with a tiny smile tugging on his lips as if he was always waiting to tell a funny story. Since he had started working for Dominic York, however, Daniel White, who had always considered himself a staunch Democrat, had lost some of his boyish and carefree attitude. Those had already been replaced by anxiety, uncertainty and now, fear. He didn't understand everything that went on behind York's closed doors, even when he was so often behind those doors himself. He felt that his boss wouldn't like him to pry into his business, although, as the assistant, Daniel was privy to much of York's political affairs. He thought he and York were on the same team, but then York had threatened him if he didn't do exactly as he was told, like a child threatened with punishment for disobedience. And Daniel hadn't even done anything. *Why does he have to be so...so ruthless with everyone?*

York sat behind his desk in total darkness. He waited until the sounds of his assistant died away, then he quickly stood up and faced his main office door. His time to answer was nearly gone. Clearing his throat, he called out, "Alright. You can come in. I'm alone, and the lights are out." A few seconds of silence passed. York stood with uncertainty in the dark, waiting for what, he didn't know. On instinct, he felt around the top of his desk and his fingers closed round a letter opener, the only potential weapon he could find to defend himself with, should the need arise. He also stayed behind his desk, near the door Daniel had left by.

CHAPTER 7:

Suddenly, there was a low, scraping sound that cut through the quiet like a razor blade, making York jump before silently chiding himself for being so foolish. In the faint moonlight spilling through the single window in the room, he watched, mesmerized, as the doorknob slowly turned from the outside. Clutching his letter opener by his side, he retreated one step, and waited.

The door opened two feet, and before he knew what was happening, York found himself face to face with two black-clad figures shining flashlights in his eyes. Blind from the brightness, all he could hear was the sound of his own breathing and the closing of the door.

☩ CHAPTER 8:

York put up one hand to shield his eyes from the flashlight beam, trying to size up his mysterious guests. He had expected secrecy, but not midnight meetings in the dark and being threatened with risk of optic nerve damage. He stayed behind his desk, trying to conceal the letter opener in his hand.

The two black-garbed figures stood side by side, motionless, with their flashlights in York's face, saying nothing. Then one of them, the taller one, took a few steps toward the desk.

"What is your name, and who are you?"

The figure spoke in a muffled, deep-throated way, as if disguising his voice. Neither of them lowered their lights from York's face.

York cleared his throat and said slowly, "I am Dominic York, chairman of the Democratic Party." The taller man lowered his light, and the other person standing a few feet behind him did the same. This provided just enough light to recognize that there were three persons in the room, but no faces could be distinguished. York felt the disadvantage of not being able to see the faces of the visitors while knowing they saw him. Without the lights and this covert interrogation, he was beginning to feel slightly ridiculous.

"Who are you?" he asked in a voice that would have made most people squirm.

But his visitors were not most people. "Who we are isn't important, Mr. York. You should know up front that you won't ever find out who we are, nor do you really want to. The important thing is that we're all on the same page here. Do you understand?"

York restrained himself from rolling his eyes. Even in the dark, he had an unpleasant feeling that these people would sense him doing it.

"I understand," he said.

"Now, we understand you're looking for some assistance with the competition."

"That is true, but–"

"Is there a problem, Mr. York?"

"Well, how do I know you are who you claim to be, and that you can do what you claim you can do?"

The tall figure stepped forward again, and York's hand tightened round the letter opener.

"You are one of the most skeptical clients we have done work for," said the tall figure with what sounded like an exasperated snicker. "We do not come with credentials or references, Mr. York. This is the way this is going to work: you have a job for us. We get it done. End of story."

"For the right price, of course," added the second figure, speaking for the first time. The voice was pitched higher than the tall person, making York wonder if maybe this was a woman.

"Of course," he repeated, turning over details in his mind. He fiddled with the letter opener in his hand, and without thinking about it, began standing it up end over end on his desktop, letting it slide through his fingers with soft clicks against the wood.

"But, how can I be sure that you'll do what you say, or more importantly, what I say?" he said.

The tall figure's unmistakable smirk shone through his deep voice.

"You'll just have to trust us, Mr. York. And after tonight, you will never hear from us again."

"Tell us what you want so we can get to work," the second figure added, displaying a seemingly restless attitude.

York decided that he may as well get down to business and hand out his instructions. If these neo-mafia people actually carried out his wishes and his plans worked, then good. But if they walked away with fatter bank accounts and did not deliver, York would find some way to make them pay.

He put down the letter opener, placed both hands flat on his desk, and leaned forward in his habitual pose when he was deep in thought or about to say something important.

"There is a man," he began, and the two figures slipped closer. "A man who can cause our party some real difficulties if he isn't stopped. I want him discredited beyond recognition."

"What's his name?"

"David Connally." York's mouth twisted bitterly around the name. "He works for The American Party, that pitiful little grassroots organization that has, unfortunately, gained much more popularity and influence in the political arena than my people and I thought possible."

"Do you have anything on this Connally now?"

York shifted his weight and suddenly wanted to cringe.

"Well, we don't really know anything about this person..." his words trailed off as a realization suddenly hit him. "And nobody seems to, as a matter of fact," he muttered to himself. "They won't let any reporters talk to him, and they won't talk about him to the reporters. I'm starting to wonder if they themselves actually have a clue about this guy, or if they're just letting him out there onstage because he makes everybody feel good..."

His musings were broken into by a forceful throat-clearing as the taller dark figure said, "What exactly do you want to happen to Connally?"

York's lips pulled back from his teeth in a smile that, in the bright flashlight beam mixed with black darkness, looked truly insidious.

"What do I want to happen to Connally?" he asked as if he were merely turning over the question in his mind. "I want him to crash and burn so hard that not even his own mother would stand to see his face, whether on TV or speaking at some pathetic conservative rally."

York spoke in such a matter-of-fact tone that it hardly seemed to match the ferocity of his intentions. The two figures in black shared a brief glance, and the tall one turned back to York.

"Twelve million."

"I beg your pardon?" York leaned forward.

"I said twelve million."

"Twelve million...what, dollars?"

"That's our price, Mr. York."

York's mouth fell open.

"Twelve million dollars?" he exclaimed, stunned. "Are you serious?" He let out a burst of disbelieving laughter. "I can't authorize that kind of money, guys."

The tall figure handed him a thick white card with a foreign bank account number on it. York stared at the card in his hand and then back at the people.

"Twelve million in this account by noon tomorrow, or we walk away."

York stood behind his desk, shaking his head as he tried to process what he had just heard while his brain worked overtime to figure out how to gather the necessary funds expected of him.

He looked up and saw both enigmas had turned and were on their way out. York quickly hurried out from behind the desk and called out for them to wait.

"Hey," he said.

They stopped in the doorway, but didn't turn around. York came within a yard of them and stopped.

"How will I know if you've earned my twelve million?"

He heard them chuckle as they continued on out the door. But the shorter figure turned slightly back over their shoulder before the door closed and said:

"Keep an eye on the news."

"This is Brad Kelso, bringing you today's stories on the morning news," came a lazy, self-assured voice from a man with a long face and half-hidden smile in the corner of his mouth. "We'll start with Janet Ellis in Chicago, reporting this morning from the Democratic Convention that's just wrapped up. Janet, tell us what's going on over there."

"Well, Brad, now that the convention is over and the nominees have been chosen, the candidates are heading back home to prepare for the fall election," said a woman with heavily shadowed eyes and thickly glossed lips. "I did catch up with some of them this morning as they were leaving and had a chance to speak with them, notably Senator Helen Kennedy, who took this party's nomination for president."

The camera cut to a shot of Janet speaking with Senator Kennedy, both of them standing with the large, empty auditorium behind them which had just recently been packed with enthusiastic Democrats ready to nominate their choice for President of the United States.

"Senator Kennedy, how does it feel to begin your first day as the presidential candidate for the Democratic Party?" Janet held her microphone closely under the senator's chin.

"Well, Janet, it truly is exciting to know that the party is looking to me to be the first female president of the United States. I believe that, come November, the people will speak, and will find their country's next leader by electing me."

Senator Kennedy appeared as calm and sure of her upcoming victory as if she had already moved into the White House. She was dressed in a bright green pantsuit that made her small, sharp eyes seem farther back in her wide face. Janet gave the camera lenses an impressed look before asking her next question.

"How does it feel to be a female candidate with a male vice president? Do you think that could potentially cause problems for you later on?"

The senator tossed her head. "I don't believe it to be an issue at all, nor should it be in the future. Louis Wilson and I work well together, and in that same spirit of a successful team, we will win this election."

"One last question, Senator: what about The American Party?"

Senator Kennedy's mouth tightened, and her back stiffened.

"They've had amazing growth and collected quite a following over the past few months, and most of the candidates who've been campaigning for the presidency have recently wanted a connection with The American Party, because so many people attend their rallies that it gives candidates a real publicity boost to be seen and associated with the organization," Janet pushed blithely on.

"What is your question, Janet?" asked Senator Kennedy in a strained, quiet voice. She was staring down at her hands as if she knew that if she let the camera see her face, viewers might run.

"Well, what are your thoughts on the seemingly overnight sensation The American Party has become, and all the attention it's drawing from both conservative and liberal sides?"

The senator finally raised her head, and seemed to be making a huge effort to keep her face looking professionally blank.

"It's just a fluke. Now that I'm the presidential candidate and the people understand that, we will begin to a see a shift in popularity and ratings from those of The American Party to those of the Democratic Party."

"But what about this David Connally, who seems to be the official spokesman of the organization and always gets people so excited at the rallies about The American Party, and makes more and more people, both Democrats and Republicans, want to be associated with them?"

Senator Kennedy viciously shook her head.

"You know, Janet," she said through her teeth, "it does seem like The American Party has chosen this guy to be their spokesperson or mascot, or whichever. And he's handing out a lot of religious ideas that he's feeding the people about doing what God wants them to do, and putting God first, even above government." The senator seemed to gain confidence in her words as she went on. "In fact, many of us are starting to wonder if The American Party is working with this Connally person to start a cult. The administration needs to get a senate investigation going regarding the activities of The American Party and David Connally. But, either way, Connally isn't a threat to my campaign, and certainly not to the Democrat Party."

With that, Senator Kennedy haughtily turned away from the camera, and Janet quickly shoved the microphone back up to her own lipsticked mouth again.

"Well, there you have it, straight from the Democratic presidential candidate herself. She's excited about the upcoming election and certainly not intimidated or worried in the least by

CHAPTER 8:

anything that might stand in her way. That's the news from Chicago. Now, back to you in New York, Brad."

"Thank you, Janet," said Brad Kelso, flashing a confident smile at the camera. "And, speaking of David Connally, while he has certainly had his fair share of the spotlight lately – why, you can hardly be involved in politics these days and not know his name – very little is known about his past. ABC News has been conducting an investigation into Connally's life and has turned up some interesting and quite possibly incriminating reports that Connally was in a Cuban prison for the past fifteen years. Why, we aren't yet certain. On a special report this evening we will have an eyewitness who claims to be Connally's former cellmate. Although there are conflicting reports on this story, it strongly appears as though The American Party is trying to keep David Connally away from any and all media reporters on this or any other issue concerning him. More for you on that topic tonight at six."

Nathan Blaine sat in a cozy hotel lobby, his gaze focused intently on the flat screen on the wall across from the small table where he sat alone with a Styrofoam cup of black coffee. As the news report concluded, Nathan looked down at his iPad on the table and took some quick notes.

"Cuban prison...huh..." he muttered, shaking his head. "Not likely, but also not impossible."

His cell phone vibrated against his side, and he plucked it out of the case attached to his belt.

"Hello?"

"Did you just see what I saw on TV?" Rick McCoy's voice was irate.

Nathan sighed. "Yes, I did."

"Well? Is it true!?"

McCoy sounded like he was about to burst a blood vessel. Nathan moved his coffee out of the way so he could rest his elbow on the tiny table.

"I don't know," he answered calmly. "But I'll be in Cuba before the day is out."

175

"You call me as soon as you know something."

"You know I will," said Nathan. He listened to the line go dead, then scooped up his iPad and coffee. "Time to fly," he murmured as he headed back to his room.

Senator Kennedy slammed the door of her limousine without waiting for the driver to close it for her. The moment she sat down, she dug through her purse and pulled out her cell phone.

"Good morning, Ms. President!"

"Oh, cut it out, Dominic," she hissed, rolling her eyes. If it hadn't been for the stressful interview she had just had to undergo, she would have probably reveled in the precipitate title.

"Did you just see what that little–"

"If you're referring to your sterling news interview, then yes, I did see that. Allow me to congratulate you, for you did very well."

"I did?" Senator Kennedy leaned back against the leather seat and rubbed her forehead as if nursing a headache. "Did I say everything right? I feel like I was losing my train of thought the moment she started asking about Connally..."

"You were perfect," York's voice purred through the phone. "You were subtle about the cult reference, and the senate investigation. If we hadn't already gone over it, I wouldn't have known you had rehearsed for that kind of statement."

"I just feel like I could have incorporated more in; something to really damage them."

"We plant one seed at a time, Senator. We can't take down The American Party and Connally in one full swing. This will take time, careful planning, and the right words and allegations dropped at the right moments. You're doing just fine."

"But...the fall elections..."

"I'm well aware of our time constraints, my dear Senator. But you have to trust me. I already have people working behind the scenes who, should they actually earn the ridiculous sum it cost me to hire them, will certainly make sure that our little mysterious patriotic friend is fully discredited, disgraced, and discharged long before November."

"Are you with somebody, Dominic?" He sounded like he was losing interest in the conversation.

"I'm actually about to have a singularly important meeting with somebody else who is going to get us special, exclusive insight to all the activities of The American Party...and David Connally."

"Well then," she said with a satisfied smile, "don't let me keep you."

"Good morning, future Ms. President."

She rolled her eyes again, but this time, she smirked.

"And to you...Mr. Chairman."

No sooner had he hung up with Nathan Blaine, Rick McCoy dialed Michael Farris. The party manager answered his phone from the site of the next rally, which was to occur that very evening. As he had done with Blaine, McCoy wasted no time on pleasantries when Mr. Farris answered.

"I assume you saw the report on this morning's newscast about David?"

"Yes, sir. I did."

"I want to speak with David. Now."

Mr. Farris sucked in his breath. He knew that if Rick McCoy ever demanded anything in that tone of voice, it was best not to argue. He hurried off to get David, and found him located him in the staging area, talking to Eli while he was setting up the audio system, which he still insisted on doing even though he was giving regular speeches now.

"David! You need to take this," Mr. Farris exclaimed, pushing his cell phone into David's hand. Eli folded his arms. "What's going on?"

David looked down at the phone. "Who would be calling me?"

"Uh, it's Rick McCoy." Mr. Farris said, staring at him as if he couldn't believe he didn't already have the phone slapped against his ear. "And you better talk to him. He sounds like he's about to go on the warpath."

David looked confused. "Why? What's happened?"

"Just..." Mr. Farris pulled off his hat and rubbed his temples. "Just take the call, David."

With a dubious expression, David held the phone to his ear. "Hello, Mr. McCoy. This is David."

"David, you're an upstanding guy, and I don't believe you have lied to me or anybody else. But there is a report out this morning that says you were in a Cuban prison for about half of your life. Is this true?"

David's mouth fell open. Mr. Farris and Eli, watching him closely, couldn't tell if it was fear of being found out or disbelief over such an allegation. But the next moment, they were assured.

"Mr. McCoy, that is not true."

"What about any other prison?"

"Sir, I've never been in any kind of jail or prison my entire life," said David firmly.

He could hear McCoy's inadvertent sigh of relief that echoed in Mr. Farris' mind as well.

"Thank you, David. I'm sorry I had to trouble you about this. It seems as though there are people who want to destroy your influence and reputation. You're doing such a good work, it isn't surprising somebody out there wants to tear you down."

"Yes sir," said David quietly. He shaded his eyes for a moment, and Mr. Farris and Eli both caught a passing look on his face that made them look at each other, puzzled.

"But don't let the wolves get to you, David, McCoy continued. "You're stronger than they are. Now you have a good rest of the day. I'll be there for the rally tonight, and we may be able to talk some more then."

David slid the phone down and handed it back to Mr. Farris without comment.

"Hey, David," said Eli, "you alright?"

David walked past him without a word. Mr. Farris and Eli shared one more glance of uncertainty as they parted ways, Eli to go after David and Mr. Farris to make some calls.

CHAPTER 8:

Back in his other office at the Democratic headquarters in Chicago, Dominic York ended his call with Senator Kennedy. As he did so, his assistant, Daniel, cracked the door and poked his head into the room.

"Mr. York, he's here," he announced.

York stood up. "Bring him in."

Daniel's head disappeared. York craned his neck as the door opened a bit wider, and a soft voice could be heard saying something to Daniel in the hallway. Daniel answered briefly, and then the door opened wide enough to let the visitor slip inside the office.

He walked slowly, as if hesitating over each step whether or not to keep moving forward. He was smartly dressed in a white polo shirt under a dark sports jacket with slacks and shiny brown Oxford shoes. He couldn't have been older than twenty-five, but his face was like that of a young boy. He was pale, with a strong, quarter-horse jawline flecked with last night's unshaven stubble. His full lips were pressed tightly together in a silent statement of declination to speak first, with dull blue eyes shrouded beneath sparse eyebrows. Overall, his appearance and demeanor seemed to say that he knew where he was and was aware of his surroundings, but he still wasn't quite sure why he was there. His eyes roved continually around the room as he slowly advanced toward York's desk at the far end of the office. If York hadn't already been assured of his political affiliations, he might have been suspicious of the young man's seemingly uncertain attitude.

"You must be James," York said, shaking the newcomer's hand with his twinge of a smile.

"Yes, sir. James Rivers."

The young man's voice was soft, rather bluff, and coupled with the low tone in which he spoke, he sounded like a child talking to his parent, unsure of whether he was in trouble or not. His handshake was gentle and brief.

"Please take a seat, Mr. Rivers." York gestured to one of the hard-backed wooden chairs by his desk.

"Oh, please," said his visitor with a quick wave as he settled into the chair, "call me James, sir."

"Alright then, James." York propped himself against the edge of his desk and crossed his arms while studying the young man intently. Now that James was sitting down he seemed more at ease.

"Dan!" York hollered suddenly, making James jump and then look around him in confusion.

Daniel stuck his head inside the office again. "Yes, sir?"

"Will you go get me and our young friend here some coffee?"

"Yes, sir. Any preference?"

"Bring us back two lattes." York stole a swift glance at James to make sure the choice of beverage suited him, and James shrugged with a noncombatant grin.

Daniel nodded, looked quickly at the newcomer, and left. York turned back to James.

"Good. Now, there are some things I would like to ask you, James. I understand that your family has been strong Democrats since Roosevelt."

"Oh, yes, sir," James sat up straighter and folded his hands across his lap. "My parents have been dedicated to the party since before I was born, and all of my family as far as I know has participated in Democratic administrations since the forties."

"And what about yourself?" York leaned forward, his colorless eyes penetrating. "Do you consider yourself attached to the party as well?"

"I do, sir."

"Excellent. I also understand that you've just graduated from Harvard, is that right?"

"This past spring, Mr. York. I'll be taking an internship with the Supreme Court this fall."

York nodded with approval.

"Now, a bright, obviously gifted young man such as yourself, fresh out of college with an interest and family history in politics, surely must be eager for the first opportunity to serve his country in any way he can, am I right?"

James nodded. He seemed to be growing more confident in where he was and what was going on with every affirmation.

"And surely you would be interested in helping the party, your party, in any way you can until the election."

"Mr. York, I'd be glad to serve our party in whatever ways I can be used."

York ran his tongue over his lips. His next words depended almost completely on James' character if he wanted them to strike a chord and enlist his aid. York knew he couldn't trust in family connections and history alone to get the response he wanted.

But at this point he felt nearly convinced that this James Rivers was perfect for the job he had in mind.

"Well," he said, moving away from his desk to stand by the window, putting James at his back. "It so happens that the party has a very special project that needs doing. It's extremely important, as well as very secretive..."

James twisted around in his chair to look at him. York turned his head slightly from the window so that James could see his profile as he added quietly, "I think only somebody like you could take care of this for me, James."

"Why?"

York turned around, his hands behind his back and his tall frame silhouetted by the sun shining through the window behind him into the dim room.

"Because you're young, untested but willing. You have a chance to make your country proud and you wouldn't turn down that chance, not if everything you've just told me is the truth. And because, well, you remind me of myself when I was entering politics for the first time."

"Really, sir?" James looked flattered.

"Absolutely. I was your age, or rather close to it, when I started working in Washington as an intern for one of my state senators. I fought hard to work my way up, and the rest, of course, is history." He smiled. James smiled back, then cleared his throat, stood up with his hands at his sides and said firmly, "I'm willing and ready to do anything the party needs me to do, sir."

York walked up to him and put his hands on James's shoulders, looking straight into his light blue eyes, which had hardened with resolve.

"That is exactly what I want to hear."

York released James with a clap on the back and returned to his desk. James remained standing, waiting for his instructions.

"There is a man who has the potential to harm the election of our presidential candidate, the ability to hurt the party, and the probability of changing America's Democratic two-party system."

James folded his arms and pursed his lips, nodding as he drank in the information. York pretended to be interested in some papers on his desk as he spoke. *Reel him in slowly.*

"He is a man who, ultimately, may prove extremely dangerous to this country, James. We need your help in dealing with him."

James walked up to the desk, put both hands on it, and leaned in.

"Just tell me what you need me to do," he said quietly.

York shifted in his chair, satisfied.

I've got him.

"Here's what I want you to do, James. I want you to go undercover and be an agent for the party. Infiltrate The American Party where the group using this man, David Connally, is operating. Convince them that, beyond a shadow of a doubt, you are a God-fearing, Bible-believing conservative who loves The American Party and everything that Connally and his friends say, and that you're willing to give of your time to help them and their candidates win the election. Convince them that you're even willing to pay your own way just to be a part of The American Party. They must be utterly trusting of you, James."

James's eyes flickered away from York's face for a moment. He bit his lip.

"Every day, I want you to call me at this number..." York scrawled some digits on a piece of paper and held it out to James with the numbers facing him. "And keep me informed of what's going on inside that organization. I want to know everything. Every little piece of news might have some bearing whether you think it's important or not."

James took the number and studied it wordlessly.

"I especially want you to keep an eye on Connally. If you find out one thing about him that could mar his character in any way, you let me know immediately. Understood?"

"Connally..." James spoke the name as though trying to engrave it on his memory. He tucked the slip of paper into his coat pocket, but his eyebrows were drawn closely together and he was still biting his lip. York pressed his fingertips together, waiting for his response.

"Um, I understand what you're telling me, Mr. York, but are you quite sure that's what you need me to do? I mean..." He trailed off doubtfully in his search for words. York's eyes narrowed.

"It's just, I've never done anything like this before, and—"

"Are you backing out on me, James?"

James wasn't looking at York's face, but at the desktop. All the same, he felt a shiver at the tone in York's voice. He shook his head.

"James, I'm sure you can do this. I have complete confidence in you. If I didn't think you were up to the task, I would have sent for someone else. The question is, will you do it?"

York held his breath. He really didn't want to have to start over with another candidate for this job, and he positively scoffed at the mere thought of sending Daniel White. James Rivers was his best choice, if only he could get the tug of doubt and moral consciousness out of his head.

"I want to help my party and do whatever is necessary for the good of America," the young man said slowly. York stood up, his fingertips just resting on his desk.

"I'll do it," James said at last.

"Good. Someone from my office will contact you with a bank account number and debit card to cover your expenses. But remember, James," and York ticked off on his fingers as he walked around his desk, "you've got to think, talk, and be one of them, every day, for us."

James nodded. His resolve had hardened once more, this time, York hoped, for good.

"When I came here, I didn't think I'd be helping the party this way," he remarked, with a short chuckle as he resumed his seat and York leaned against his desk again. York smiled leniently.

"But I won't let you down," James added. "And I won't let our party down."

"I know you won't, James. That's why you're sitting in my office today instead of somebody else."

There was a muffled thump at the door, as if something had bumped against it accidentally, followed by a more deliberate double-knock. York raised his voice, saying to come in, as the meeting was concluded and he had received the answer he was looking for. The door opened, and Daniel entered, looking huffy, hot, and out of temper. He didn't utter a word of complaint, however, as he marched in with a cardboard coffee tray with the two drinks from Starbucks nestled in it. He set them down on York's desk, and York picked up the one nearest him, taking a sip.

"Ah, thank you, Dan."

Daniel was not appeased by his boss's show of gratitude, but he just nodded as he handed the other latte to James and then slipped out of the office without a word.

⸙ CHAPTER 9:

Rick McCoy grabbed his phone almost before it started ringing. He had been walking around all day with one hand on it, edgily waiting for news down in Cuba from Nathan Blaine. Now, just as he was about to walk out the door to catch a flight, Blaine's name popped up on his caller ID. McCoy wasted no time and no words.

"What did you learn?"

"I visited at least six or seven different prisons down here, Rick. None of them have any records of a David Connally, and all the prison superintendents and personnel I spoke to had no memory of him being there. I even spoke with some of the inmates, and all but one of them, an older guy, denied knowing a man by the name of Connally."

McCoy grabbed onto the back of a chair to steady himself. "All but one? What did he say?"

"He said he'd known a fellow with the same last name years ago, back before he went to jail. He couldn't give me many details, and I traced the name down there as far back as I could, but hit a dead end. I think we can safely assume your David Connally hasn't been in prison, at least not in Cuba."

McCoy heard Nathan heave a long sigh on the other line. In his own mind, he was still uneasy, but more relieved than he had felt five minutes ago.

"I think this whole thing was a hoax, Rick. Somebody is out to get your man, or at least hurt his reputation. I hope you're keeping a good watch on him, because I have a feeling this isn't the last time they'll try something like this. I've worked jobs like this before where I chase rabbit trails leading to nowhere."

"I have twenty-four-hour security on him, and he isn't allowed to be near reporters or the media. Whatever is in his past, nobody is finding it out from him. He doesn't seem to have any friends outside of our organization, and he never mentions having any family. I don't know who would have any information on him."

"You leave that to me. If there's any history behind David Connally, I'll find it."

Sunday morning, Eli Farley drove to the hotel where David was staying off-site. He already knew David's room number, but all he had to do was look for the door with the armed, black-clothed, stone-faced guard standing in front of it. Eli tapped his man on the shoulder as an indication of relief from his position. The guard nodded and disappeared down the hall. Eli rapped two knuckles against the door.

"David? It's me, Eli."

"The door's unlocked!" came a cheerfully muffled voice on the other side of the door.

Eli's eyebrows rose. He reached down and turned the knob, gritting his teeth in frustration when it turned easily under his hand. Why did this hotel have to be the only obscure, out-of-the-way one in the area that didn't have automatic card key locks?

He slowly entered the small room. The bed was neatly made with David's Bible sitting on the end of it, and a white cotton, long-sleeve, button-down shirt was spread out on the bed so it wouldn't wrinkle. The curtains had been pushed back to let in the sunshine. Eli marched over and with one sweeping motion dragged the curtains back across the window. As he turned from doing this, David stepped out of the bathroom with a comb in his hand, wearing slacks and a white T-shirt with a towel draped around his neck. His hair was only partly combed, and he still had shaving cream on his face, which added to his rather comical, unfinished appearance.

"Morning, Eli," he said.

"David, you really shouldn't leave your door unlocked. It isn't safe."

David shrugged and tapped the comb against his hand.

CHAPTER 9:

"Well, with an armed guard at my door, I thought I'd probably be alright if I just left it unlocked for a short time while I got ready this morning." He glanced back at the mirror through the open bathroom door, then made a face when he saw his reflection.

Eli folded his arms. "I need you to cooperate with me, David. How am I supposed to guarantee your protection if you leave your door unlocked?"

David looked up in surprise. "What do you mean? I'm fine."

"Have you already forgotten what happened last night?"

Eli saw David pause in the act of wiping the last of the shaving cream off his neck and face. He slowly pulled the towel down from around his neck and disappeared back into the bathroom. Eli put his hands on his hips and shook his head.

Last night after the rally, David had been attacked backstage by what Eli, Mr. Farris, and Jack had at first thought to be a wildly enthusiastic fan from the audience. It took them but a few seconds to realize the "fan" actually turned out to be a seemingly intoxicated, belligerent man who yelled accusations about David being a mercenary liar who only cared about getting attention, and that he didn't care what happened to the country as long as he made himself famous, along with other, cruder accusations. He certainly appeared unhinged, and was advancing on David very quickly, pointing straight at him and presenting a grave threat. Mr. Farris had been standing near David, talking with Jack, when the man had come barreling toward them. Farris quickly thrust David back and moved to stand in front of him. But then he saw Jack moving forward to meet the shouter with one fist raised. He shoved past David as he ran past him to fend off the attacker, fury mounting in his eyes. Mr. Farris heard him cry, "No! Ryan!"

Mr. Farris knew Jack was going in for the punch, and in an instant, the loss of the reputation of The American Party flashed through his mind. He already knew what would happen if Jack got in a single hit on a member of the audience at one of his rallies.

"Jack!" he yelled, reaching out to grab Jack while still keeping David behind him. Jack's sleeve slipped through his fingers as Jack jerked his arm away. But before he reached the man, Eli got to him first, and tackled the assailant to the ground. Thankfully, he wasn't armed. Eli tore back his jacket to trap the intruder's arms behind him as he laid face-down on the ground. The man thrashed around under Eli's strong grip, but he was no match for the muscles of the head of Blackheart Security, however, and he soon realized it. He lay with his nose pressed against the cold dirt and muttered cruelly under his breath.

"How did this guy get back here?" Eli bellowed furiously as more of his security team raced up.

Jack stood still, his arm still raised, his chest heaving and his face red. Mr. Farris wanted to go to him, but he stayed in front of David with his hand pressed against his shoulder until Eli and three more of his men had raised the intruder to his feet and dragged him out, still hissing threats in David's direction, accompanied by disturbing inexplicable laughter. When Eli's men had taken the man away, Mr. Farris turned back to David. The young man looked visibly shaken.

"Are you alright, David?" he asked quietly.

David raised his eyes and stared after the direction Eli had gone. "I wish I could just give the speeches without the fame," was all he said. He reached up to smooth his hair back from his forehead. Mr. Farris noticed his hand shook.

"I'm afraid it doesn't work like that," said Mr. Farris gently, and he patted David's shoulder. "Or, at least, it isn't that way in your case. But this is the first time, out of all the thousands of people who have seen and heard you at all our rallies where something like this has happened. You remember what you told me Rick McCoy said to you on the phone. It's very possible somebody on the left is trying to work against us, and because you're at the forefront of our organization now, it looks like you're going to get some of that brunt as it comes. But don't you worry. Eli, Jack, and I are going to take care of you."

"How did he get in?" David repeated Eli's question.

"I honestly have no idea. But you can rest assured that Eli will find out and he'll take care of it."

David thanked Mr. Farris with a wordless nod and a quick

grip of the hand, still shaking. Then they both looked at Jack.

He hadn't moved from where he stood when Eli had tackled the intruder, but his arms now hung limply at his sides. His back was toward David and Mr. Farris. He stood so still that they couldn't even see his shoulders moving as he breathed. In fact, he looked as if he wasn't breathing.

Mr. Farris knew he needed to say something to Jack. He couldn't afford to let things come so close like that again. He walked over to Jack's side. Jack didn't look at him.

"Jack," he said quietly, "what were you thinking?"

Jack still said nothing. The side of his face that Mr. Farris could see was now deathly pale, and hard as stone. His mouth was pinched tighter than if his lips had been sewn together, and his nostrils flared fiercely.

"Jack," said Mr. Farris again, more urgently this time, "you were going to hit that man. I saw you. Do you understand what that would have done to this party's reputation? You should've known better. This is why we have Blackheart down here. If you had punched that guy – and you're working for The American Party–"

"He was going to hit Ryan."

Jack's voice was hushed. His eyes had a wild, glazed look.

Mr. Farris started.

"Wha...what? Jack, Ryan isn't here. That's David."

Jack kept staring straight ahead, shaking his head.

"I'm going to protect my son," he said feverishly.

"Jack!" Mr. Farris grabbed Jack's shoulder and twisted him around. "Jack, snap out of it. He's not your son. Are you listening to me?" He shook him just hard enough to jar his head a little. David stood rooted to the ground, his eyes wide as he watched them.

Jack looked at David for a long moment. He seemed not to be seeing David but rather seeing through him. Mr. Farris kept a grip on Jack's arm as he watched his face, his own eyes full of concern for his friend. But as he and David both continued to stare at Jack, they saw his eyes refocus, and his face visibly softened while he looked at David. He looked around him as if he had forgotten where he was. He reached up and covered his face.

189

"I...I'm sorry," he mumbled. He jerked his arm away from Mr. Farris, who reluctantly let him go. He and David both watched as Jack stumbled off toward The American Party's motor home, where they soon heard the door open and shut violently.

Mr. Farris heaved a long sigh, his hands on his belt while he stared up at the evening sky. He glanced over at David and saw the young man was still staring in the direction Jack had gone. A troubled confusion had settled over his fine features, causing a furrow between his eyes, which were filled with worry. *He has no idea*, Mr. Farris thought. He walked over to David and placed a hand on his shoulder.

"Come on, David. I'll drive you back to the hotel." he said kindly, though his voice was weary. David turned his head.

"Is Jack ok?" he asked.

"I'm guessing he never acted like this with you before."

"No. Did something happen? Why did he call me Ryan?"

Mr. Farris turned his face away. "Let's get you back to the hotel," was all he said.

It was this scene from last night that was still fresh in David's mind this morning. Eli could tell he was still dwelling on it by the look on his face when he mentioned it. But David didn't say anything. He simply went back into the bathroom, and a moment later Eli heard the sound of running water as David finished combing his hair.

"It could have been a lot worse," Eli remarked, walking over to lean against the bathroom doorway, his arms still folded. He tried to catch David's eye in the mirror, but David kept his gaze averted. "That guy could have been packing. Who knows what he might have done–"

"But, he didn't, Eli."

David laid down the comb and finally looked up to meet Eli's gaze in the mirror.

"Did you find out how he got in?"

Eli stiffened. "That's not something you need to concern yourself with."

CHAPTER 9:

David's eyes widened, but he let the subject drop. He walked out into the main room past Eli, where he picked up his shirt off the bed. As he slid his arms into the sleeves and straightened the collar, he cast a sideways glance at his guard. Eli stood in his usual pose: his muscular arms crossed across his broad chest with his military-booted feet planted exactly two feet apart. He wasn't really staring at David, but rather out the window.

"So, um..." David cleared his throat. Eli's gaze shifted back to him. "Have you protected many people in the past, since you became head of Blackheart Security? Or am I not supposed to ask?"

Eli's face wore a forbidding expression, but he slightly relaxed his stiffly arched eyebrows.

"You have permission to ask me whatever you like, David. However, I do not promise to satisfy your curiosity on every question, on account of client confidentiality."

"Of course," David said, buttoning up his shirt front. "I guess I was just trying to make a little conversation." He smiled. Eli offered no further comment, but inclined his head. David turned so his back was toward Eli. For several long seconds there was no sound in the room but the soft rustle of David's shirt as he finished buttoning his sleeve cuffs.

"I've guarded several people since I've worked with Blackheart." Eli's voice startled the silence in the room. David turned around. Eli unfolded his arms and leaned back against the wall. His eyes had a thoughtful look in them, and he seemed to be struggling between a reluctance to speak and a willingness to share his thoughts. David didn't say anything, but he quietly let his hands drop to his sides, waiting to see if Eli would continue.

"Most of them have been wealthy, famous people. People who put their faith and security completely in my hands, and the hands of my team. As long as they had their protection from the world, they didn't think twice about doing something that might put their lives in danger. No, because they had us, they thought they had free rein." Eli's voice was frustrated. "My job has been put in jeopardy countless times because my charges refuse to cooperate with the simple terms I give them to help me better protect them."

191

David walked over to him, pausing a few feet away. Eli met his gaze with unabashed resolution, and his eyes hardened.

"I take my job very seriously, David."

"I know you do."

"When I'm assigned to protect someone, I take full responsibility for their actions as well as my own. That is why I appreciate all the help you can give me in this, whether by not drawing unnecessary attention to yourself or simply keeping your hotel doors locked. Even with my men around you, something could happen unexpectedly. We're here for you, and I'll do everything in my power to keep you safe."

"I know." David nodded seriously. "You told me that when we first met. But if you're here to ward off danger, why are you worried something will happen?"

"We're here as a buffer, a shield. You don't pick up a shield if you don't think there's a possibility of danger. If something can go wrong, it usually does."

Eli let that ominous statement sink into the silence that followed.

David ran his tongue over his lips and threw his head back as if coming to a resolve. "I don't think most of the people who come to the rallies have the mindset that one man did," he said stoutly. He walked over and picked up his Bible, smoothing the shabby cover. Eli watched him. "The people who come, I'd rather imagine they care more about what I'm saying than they actually care about me," he went on. "I'm just a speaker. I'm no politician or a candidate to become one. If what I'm doing is a good thing, why should I be worried?"

Eli shook his head at such a naive statement. He straightened up and moved away from the wall. "The people don't come for the speeches, David," he said firmly. "They come for you."

David made a gesture of protest, but Eli held his gaze, hoping to convince him.

"You think I haven't seen what's going on? I may only be your protection, but I have ears, and I have eyes that see and hear more than just what's circulating in my team behind the scenes. You're an important man, David Connally. Why do you think Rick McCoy chose Blackheart? We're the best security that money can buy, and a man like McCoy wouldn't hire us on a whim. It's not possible to hire us on a whim. Everyone I've talked to, everything I've seen...people look up to you, David. They come to the rallies to support and listen to you."

David bit his lip. "I'm not doing this for the popularity, Eli. Isn't that what that man said last night? That I only want attention. It's not true."

"I know."

The two of them exchanged a brief glance of understanding, then David hefted his Bible in his hand, saying, "Well, I'm ready to go. You're coming with me?"

Eli looked at him as though he had asked the most trivial of questions. "Of course I am," he answered firmly, and headed for the door with David in tow.

They had to drive only a few miles to find the small church building, which was located in a less urban part of town. When David had asked Jack and Mr. Farris earlier about finding a congregation to worship with on Sunday mornings, Mr. Farris had made sure to look for an out-of-the-way establishment, a building that wasn't prominent in the area, to avoid extra attention for David. The one Eli and David were now parked in front of in Eli's black SUV looked like a school house from the 19th century. Small, with white paint curling back from the flat boards along the outer walls where it was peeling from exposure to the elements, and a tiny cupola on the pointed roof with a cross in place of a steeple, the whole building emitted an air of ancient quaintness. On the greenish-brown grass around the church building, a few cars were already parked.

David unbuckled his seat belt and slid out of the SUV. Eli followed suit, but hung back when David bounded up a few weathered steps to the door of the church building. On the third step, he paused suddenly, and turned around.

"Hey Eli, why don't you come in with me?"

But Eli shook his head.

"No. I can't. I'll be out here the whole time, though."

"Why can't you come in?"

Eli gave a short laugh that was almost self-deprecating.

"David, I'm your security detail. Praying and singing with a bunch of people isn't part of my job."

David smiled. "People with all kinds of jobs can worship God, Eli. You wouldn't be shirking your duty if you were still watching me inside. Why don't you just come in with me?"

Eli just shook his head again, looking up at the short iron cross atop the cupola. For the first time since they had met, David could see the uncertainty in the man's dark face. He started walking back down the steps toward him, his hand outstretched.

"Eli," he began, his voice gently pleading, but Eli cut him off.

"I'll be out here, and I'll come to the door in an hour for you," he said, and with a jerk, turned and walked swiftly back to the vehicle. David watched him go with a sigh. Then he looked down at the Bible in his hand, and back up at the building behind him. A smile came over his face, and he hurried up into the church building as if he couldn't wait to get inside.

A few days afterward, The American Party was setting up for a rally in Omaha, Nebraska. The crowds had grown to such a size that Rick McCoy had rented out the city's Convention Center, a modern behemoth of a building. Most of the entire front was glass windows, with metal columns between the panes. McCoy was very satisfied with the locale and, more importantly, the size of the convention center. He arrived there himself after the rally had already opened with David in the midst of his usual routine of leading the several thousand people present in songs that would be followed by one of his inspiring speeches.

But McCoy didn't stay to hear David. He met with Mr. Farris and Eli in the motor home office set up beside the convention center. McCoy started off by addressing Eli. He had heard, of course, about the security breach last week, and wanted to get to that first.

"I understand from Michael that you've been experiencing some security breaches, Agent Farley," he said quietly, his gaze piercing. Eli stood, as usual, with his arms crossed. "I also hear that

CHAPTER 9:

there have been some people trying to talk to David, and even some young women who were trying to reach him in his hotel room."

McCoy looked from Eli to Mr. Farris, as if both of them were seriously to blame.

"There are even some people who seem to be telling reporters that they saw somebody selling drugs to David. I thought we...I was paying for better security than this."

McCoy slammed his hand down on the table, startling an already-cringing Mr. Farris. Eli, however, did not move except for a flicker of his eyelid. But when he spoke, his voice was full of frustration.

"Several people have evidently been making false claims about getting to David and speaking with him," he said. "It's also true we have had a few cases of women trying to reach him, but I can personally assure you" he added with a burning look, "that no one has talked to David who doesn't have my authorization to do so. At our last rally we did have a man break through my security line, but my team dealt with it, and he never touched David."

"But the point remains, he got through," McCoy said angrily. "This is exactly what I've been afraid of. And I was certain that a security detail as prestigious and trained as Blackheart would have done a better job taking care of their charge."

Eli's arms unfolded of their own accord. He took a couple of steps toward McCoy, his face hard as a stone. A muscle jumped in his cheek. "Mr. McCoy, my team is the best you will find anywhere in this part of the country. But the fact is, in order to maintain the current level of security we have around him–"

"Which doesn't seem to be helping him much, does it?"

Eli's fists clenched at his sides. He gritted his teeth, then went on calmly, "In order to give David the protection he needs, I'm going to need your authorization to triple my security personnel from twenty to at least sixty officers for a twenty-four-seven guard."

McCoy grimaced when Eli said "sixty." His eyes narrowed.

"As David's popularity will only continue to grow, and more and more people flock to see him at the rallies or try to get to him in other ways, I won't be able to protect him unless I have more people."

THE SPEAKER

McCoy tilted his head. He studied Eli with his still-sharpened gaze.

"You said 'I,'" he said slowly. Eli stood motionless. McCoy moved to close the distance between them. "You alone take the full responsibility of protecting David."

"Indeed I do, Mr. McCoy." Eli's voice was both determined and solemn. "I have my men under my orders, of course, but I'm their leader. I give them orders, and I take the culpability for their actions, my own, and David's. Whatever happens to him, I'll bear all the blame."

Eli and McCoy now stood but a foot apart from each other. McCoy had to tilt his head back to meet Eli's gaze, but that didn't make him less imposing. The two men looked at each other in silence, each giving a promise to the other that didn't need words to seal them. McCoy inclined his head, and they stepped back from each other.

Mr. Farris spoke up.

"Sir, as you know, the audiences are doubling with every rally we hold. Tonight is the largest we've ever had, and we have every conservative candidate wanting to be on our platform to speak to the public. David, and David alone, mind you, has made this happen. We've had to use some of the Blackheart personnel just to keep people from getting up onto the stage. You wouldn't believe how unmanageable some of the people are at our rallies–"

"I think I can, Michael. But what stands out to me about what you just said is that you've been positioning the security around the stage area. If those men are out in front of the crowd, who's guarding the entry and exit points to keep people from getting to David?"

"But sir, that's why Eli's asking about more men! We need them all over the place."

McCoy rubbed the bridge of his nose and sighed. He turned to Eli. "You're talking about adding a lot of money to a lot of money we're already paying you. Could you do the job with forty people instead of sixty?"

Eli looked at Mr. Farris, who had folded his arms as he leaned back with one boot propped up against the wall behind him. He

196

nodded once.

"I'll tell you what I can do, Mr. McCoy," Eli proposed, "I can use forty Blackheart personnel for twenty-four hour surveillance and protection for David, as well as for the candidates while they're here. But at the rallies I'm going to need to hire at least ten local policemen who can be disguised in the crowd as ordinary attendees. They'll be our eyes in the audience who can tell us if any issues are going on that we can't see."

"The policemen will have to be off duty, of course," said McCoy.

"Yes. But if you want good security, that's the best I can do with what you're paying me."

McCoy wrapped his hands around his belt buckle and looked down at the floor, nodding his head in slow deliberation.

"Alright. Send me your cost estimates tomorrow and we'll figure it out from there," he answered briefly. Eli shook his hand, and said he would do so first thing tomorrow.

"And Mr. McCoy, if I may," Mr. Farris added as he pushed himself away from the wall with the toe of his boot, "we're going to need somebody to help me find larger venues for the rallies. I'm talking sports stadiums where we can have security at every gate, more room to accommodate the crowds, and better audio systems to communicate. Jack Webb has a good sound system, but it won't bear up enough as the crowds get bigger and bigger, and we have to look for a larger location every time. I mean, just tonight, the auditorium is standing room only! We estimate that there are at least ten thousand people present. Many were turned away simply because there wasn't any more space."

"I understand. When I get back I'll see about finding us some larger venues. Now, then..."

McCoy sat down at the motor home table and assumed his favored pose of settling slightly sideways in his chair, with one ankle resting on the knee of the opposite leg. Draping one arm along the back of the chair, he addressed both Eli and Mr. Farris.

"Next week is the RNC, and as soon as we know who their candidate for president is, I'll coordinate with Edward Martin, the chairman of the Republican Party, and any other conservative candidates as to the locations in the cities and states where we need to be. We'll do all we can to help get the best men elected."

"And David is certainly going to be of help there," Mr. Farris interjected with a chuckle.

McCoy let slip the smallest and briefest of smiles. A thoughtful expression crept into his eyes as he looked up at Eli.

"David is worth his weight in gold," he said quietly. "I know you'll make sure nothing happens to him."

"I will watch over him as if he were my own son."

Mr. Farris raised his eyebrows, but the sincerity that rang in the security guard's voice was impossible to mistake. McCoy stood up.

"I want to see David as soon as he's finished," he told Mr. Farris.

Mr. Farris promised to bring the young man in, and headed out to check his progress. At the door, he paused, and something caused him to turn and look at Eli. Eli stood silently in a corner, his arms folded and his head bowed. He presented a formidable aura, but Mr. Farris noticed the skin between his eyes was wrinkled and his mouth pursed in a tight frown that looked almost...sorrowful.

Jack stood off to the side of the stage where David was cheerfully but soberly giving one of his fiery speeches. Since David was spending so much time onstage during the rallies, Jack had had to get another member of his limited crew to help with the sound system. With such a large crowd he was fearful of not being able to reach the hearing of everyone in the audience. And because Aaron was the only person who was eager enough to volunteer to handle David's job of running the audio equipment for the rallies, Jack had to constantly supervise him. This was partly because he didn't trust anyone but David to work the system perfectly, and partly because Aaron was easily distracted. Jack didn't really fault him for this, having looked after him for so long and knowing he had many good intentions among his scatterbrained ways.

So while trying to keep one eye on Aaron, Jack managed to

pay careful attention to David and his words, as he did every time he was onstage. Jack also watched the people in the audience closest to David. Ever since the security breach last week, Jack had been on edge, and highly distrustful of the excited people at the rallies. It had been his idea to station more of Eli's men down in front as a buffer between the audience and David onstage. When he voiced the idea to Mr. Farris, Mr. Farris agreed and said he had been trying to think of different ways to protect David more when he was standing in front of everyone. The young man did present a vulnerable target without security down there with him.

"I'll have Eli station some of his men down there for tonight's rally," Mr. Farris had promised Jack a few hours before the rally in Omaha. Then he had given Jack a sidelong, penetrating look.

"Hey, are you ok? You had me kind of concerned the other night."

"I'm...I'll be fine, Mike." Jack didn't look at him.

"I heard you call him Ryan, Jack." Mr. Farris' voice was gentle.

"I'm going to go find Aaron. He's going to need some help with the sound system tonight," Jack said hurriedly, and walked away before Mr. Farris could say more.

Now David was halfway through his hour. Jack kept his gaze in rotation from David, to Eric, to the crowd, and back to David again. But the second time he swept the audience, Jack noticed something toward the back of the crowd that caught his attention more than usual.

It wasn't extraordinary for some of the people in attendance at the rallies to bring banners or signs with them, which they propped up or held high during the speeches. Several also brought American flags with them, and waved the bright Stars and Stripes with enthusiastic fervor. But the sign that captured Jack's attention tonight was different. It had only four words marked in capital letters on it, along with the flag colored in marker beneath. At first Jack thought it said JOSEPH CANE FOR PRESIDENT on it, but then realized he had mistaken the first two words. Squinting to see it from where he stood, Jack strained to make out the writing. He was going to need glasses soon. At last, the bearer of the sign shifted a little

199

to the side, holding the large piece of white cardboard so it faced more toward Jack, and ceased bouncing it up and down just long enough for Jack to catch the writing at last: DAVID CONNALLY FOR PRESIDENT.

Jack felt something squeezing up tight in his stomach, and it wasn't pride for David. As he continued staring out at that sign, out of his peripheral vision he noticed another one similar to it that also bore David's name. Then another, and another. This was no coincidence.

About a half-hour later, Mr. Farris collected David to have him escorted to Rick McCoy. Mr. Farris remained onstage to present the other speakers, as usual, while four of Blackheart's team led David away amidst thunderous cheers and applause that rose like a storm.

McCoy was standing when David entered the motor home office. David was rather winded after his passionate speech and singing, and carried a towel with which he sponged his damp forehead and neck.

"Good evening, David," McCoy greeted him cheerfully, and David quickly hung the towel around his neck and shook the other man's hand.

"Evening, sir. Is there something wrong?"

"Wrong? Why would you ask that?"

"Well sir, the last time we spoke, you wanted to know if I was a convict from Cuba," David answered bluntly, walking past McCoy to the mini-fridge. Opening the door, he stuck his head inside for a moment before pulling out a can of Dr. Pepper.

"Yes, that's true. But in my position, one can't be too careful." McCoy folded his arms and cocked his head. "How are you doing, David?"

"I'm doing just fine, sir," David replied, leaning back against the sink counter while pushing down the tab of his soda. The metal crackled and the soda released its carbonated pressure in a loud hiss.

"And how are Jack Webb and Michael Farris treating you?"

"Everyone treats me better than I deserve."

CHAPTER 9:

"Is it difficult for you with the constant security folks around?"

David took a swig of Dr. Pepper and swished it in his mouth for a few seconds before swallowing. "Honestly, Mr. McCoy, I wish all this security fuss wasn't necessary at all, but I do understand now why they're here," he said slowly. "Eli and his people are always looking out for me, and there have been instances where people had to be stopped or someone, including myself, could have been hurt."

At this last sentence, David met McCoy's eye line, and McCoy nodded soberly.

"Yes, I've been briefed on some of the incidents that have taken place, David, and I consider us very lucky to have Eli Farley and his team here with us." He approached David and his voice grew very earnest. "Neither the party nor I want anything to happen to you."

David bowed his head again. "That's very thoughtful of you, sir."

"Now tell me, are you enjoying the work?" McCoy stepped back and sat down at the table, pulling out another chair for David as he did so. David came over and sat down, putting his drink within close reach.

"Yes sir, there are a lot of wonderful people out there," he began, his face lighting up. "They're simply trying to live their lives in peace and comfort. I feel very privileged that The American Party gives me the opportunity to speak to and encourage those present at the rallies."

McCoy smiled at David's sudden animation when he spoke about the people.

"Most of the candidates treat me pretty well, too. They shake my hand and thank me for saying the things I do for the sake of the audience..."

David's voice trailed off for a moment. A tiny frown line appeared between his brows, but McCoy didn't notice.

"David, you're one of us now," he said. "We appreciate all you do. I want you to know that, and that we intend to do all we can to keep you safe while you go on doing your good work. Now, is there anything you need? Anything at all?"

David shook his head.

"No sir, thank you. Jack and Mr. Farris both take care of me like I'm their own family, and so does Eli. I want for nothing." He smiled radiantly.

McCoy looked past him and saw that on the small TV inside the motor home, the eight o'clock news had just come on. Seeing this reminded him of something else he had wanted to mention to David. He sat back in his chair and dropped his voice to a more serious level.

"David, let me ask you, don't you realize that in the recent news there are a lot of folks saying a lot of things about you? And they're not all nice things."

David cocked his head and raised his eyebrows. McCoy realized that Mr. Farris and Jack must have been keeping him away from the media so much so that he probably hadn't seen any news on TV for weeks now. With this thought, McCoy actually felt some relief. David didn't need to be worrying about what other people said about him, as long as none of the torrential accusations leveled against him in the media coverage were true.

"Some of those things are pretty obvious to all of us as lies told by some disgruntled Democrats or other ne'er-do-wells to merely stir up trouble or discredit you. But it seems like we have a larger danger lurking unseen behind even the most pitiful stories told about you." McCoy bit his lips and exhaled heavily. "It's my belief that some people are working very hard out there behind the scenes to destroy you, your reputation, and your influence. And it's only going to be worse from here on out until the fall election."

David took a long sip of Dr. Pepper and took his time swallowing it as he studied the tabletop. McCoy didn't push him for a response. Then another thought occurred to him.

"But David, this also shows us something good. It means that the enemy is getting scared. We're rattling them, and they don't like it. They know, whoever they are, that you are shifting the balance of things and influencing a whole lot of minds for the better all across the nation."

David rubbed his forehead, and ran a hand through his hair.

He quietly moved his soda can back and forth between his hands. McCoy waited, hoping he hadn't just planted a seed of discouragement in David's mind.

"Mr. McCoy," David said suddenly, raising his head as he spoke, "whatever they say about me in the news, the lies and the hatefulness...I can't change that. But as long as you, Mr. Farris, and Jack trust me, I intend to do all I can in turn to earn your faith and help the American people by carrying on with what I do here for the party. I'll speak to them and encourage them the best way I know how."

McCoy smiled broadly. "I think it's safe to say that you already have our trust, David."

"But more importantly than anything else, I care about what God thinks of me, what I say, and what I do."

At this, McCoy rose, and David, when he saw him stand up, quickly followed suit.

"You are a remarkable young man, David Connally," McCoy said, and David shrugged with a small smile. "We all care about this country, and we care about these people. Together, we want them to have a good government, the freedom guaranteed them, and a good life."

David nodded fervently, and McCoy reached out to shake his hand.

"You know that if you need to talk to me, all you have to do is ask Jack or Michael, and they'll get you in touch with me immediately. Or if necessary, I can come see you if it's possible for me to get away."

"Thank you, sir," said David, his eyes and voice full of the utmost gratitude and sincerity. McCoy smiled again, nodded, and then headed for the door. David watched him go.

"Oh, and David, if you wouldn't mind, could you just wait here until Michael comes back for you? There's a guard outside, but I just wanted to make sure you don't go wandering off alone."

McCoy tried to make his tone light, but there was a trace of authority hidden beneath his words of concern.

David nodded his consent. "Sure, I can stay put. The mini-fridge is full, so that should keep me busy for a while. I think I'll survive," he joked.

"Good man," McCoy said, though he hadn't really expected David to defy him. "I'll see you again soon. In the meantime, keep up the good work."

"Mr. McCoy!"

Jack broke into a trot to catch up with the man who was walking steadfastly away from him.

McCoy turned at the sound of his name. "Mr. Webb?"

"Mr. McCoy..." Jack paused to catch a moment's breath. "I thought you should know...about the signs."

"Signs? What signs?"

"The signs out in the audience, sir. They–"

"Well, what's so unusual about the people bringing signs with them? I don't see any problem with it, as long as none of them are inappropriate."

"No, sir, you don't understand." Jack waved his arms helplessly. "I saw at least five signs out there tonight that said 'David Connally For President.'"

McCoy's face changed instantly, and grew very still.

"Really," he said softly. He turned and looked back toward the motor home where he knew David was. A worried frown that nearly bordered on reluctance drew his brows together.

"Thank you for telling me, Jack," he said. "It's a strange set of circumstances we find ourselves in, eh?"

Jack crossed his arms. "What are we going to do?"

"Well, at present there's not much we can do. And right now I'm not sure we even need to do anything. So a few people are a little carried away by David's patriotism and their own. What's the harm in showing him their support?"

Well, you've changed your tune. "But sir, if this keeps up, other parties might think you're endorsing David as a candidate."

"I know. But let's just wait a little and see. There were only a few signs, right?"

"Five, at least," Jack muttered.

"Well, let's see what happens at the next rally. If there are fewer signs, then fine."

"And if there are more?"

McCoy rubbed his ear. He heaved a deep sigh, as if regretting what he was about to say.

"Then we may have to rein David in, just enough to show there's a line between David and the actual candidates themselves."

Jack's eyes widened as that bolt of surprise struck a nerve inside him. "You would do that to him? You can't do that, Mr. McCoy, you know what it means to him!"

"Look, Jack," said McCoy in a conciliatory tone, "I'm not talking about taking away his opportunity to speak or lead songs. We may just need to de-emphasize on David and emphasize more on the candidates themselves. David should start talking about them more, maybe. Maybe we're giving him a little too much time and not enough to the real speakers. Jack..." and McCoy put a hand on Jack's shoulder. "I like David. I care about him, and I want him to continue what he's doing."

"Then why would you –

"Because David is not an official candidate. He's just a man talking to Americans about America and singing a few songs. The focal point of the rallies shouldn't be just him. We're trying to support men who stand a chance for changing this nation by getting elected to office."

"And David isn't making a change where he stands now?"

"Jack, we both know he is. But remember, David is not a politician. We don't even know his history. What we do know is that he's a good person who genuinely seems to want to help people. But this is not about him. It's about the people and what's best for them and their interests. The American Party needs publicity to help those we support get noticed for their campaigns."

"So," Jack remarked with a bitter smile, "David is no more than a team mascot in your eyes. An entertainer who draws in the crowd so you can have the attention and publicity you want from the media and the people. Are you protecting the people's interest, or your own?"

McCoy's face darkened, and his eyes narrowed. He took a

forceful step toward Jack, who tilted his head back and stood his ground.

"You should be careful what you assume about people, especially when you don't know them," McCoy said, his voice a cold, quiet hiss. "David is worth more to me than most of the men we have sitting in government positions right now. He's gold to our organization, and I'll be the first to admit he has an uncanny gift for oratory. But our rallies are about more than just the 'opening act', as you might call it. You need to believe me when I say that."

Jack's face slowly depleted of its darkly sarcastic expression, and he swallowed hard to keep from speaking again, afraid of saying something he might regret.

McCoy sighed again, and with the exhale of air his anger seemed to evaporate.

"I have to go now, Mr. Webb." His formal use of Jack's surname again seemed to build a barrier between them that neither felt they had the energy or willingness to overcome. "But in parting, I ask you to please be more careful in the future. Farris told me about how you almost hit a man last week at one of the rallies–"

"He was a trespasser who broke through security! He was trying to attack David!"

"I understand, and Farris told me the details, but we can't have any court cases brought against us, which is undoubtedly what would have happened had you reached that man before Blackheart did."

Jack decided the best thing for him to do was simply nod in agreement and promise to behave better in the future. When he did this in a respectful tone, McCoy shook his hand and bade him goodnight.

Jack stood alone where McCoy had left him, shaking his head. If only it wasn't already too late to turn David back into just the sound man. Even with Blackheart around, Jack wished he could just take David away and hide him somewhere so he would be safe, and Jack would always know where he was and that he was in no public danger...

Jack shook his head and decided to go get a soda from the

motor home. But as he turned in that direction, he saw the Blackheart guard standing formidably before the door. That could only mean one thing. An image of a strong, smiling young man drifted to the front of his mind, followed by the harsh memory of an assailant shouting crude accusations. The dim echo of an explosion sounded in Jack's mind and gave him a jolt. Without one more glance at the motor home, he hurried back inside the convention center where some thousands of people still lingered, talking amongst themselves or to the irrevocable news reporters scattered throughout the crowd.

For once, Jack wanted to be as far away from David as possible.

The next morning, David was helping Aaron wind up the long, heavy wiring for the stage microphones.

"So, all I'm saying is that I think we could get even more people coming to these things if we had a snack bar. Am I right?" Aaron grunted as he shifted the thick roll of plastic-coated wire over his shoulder. David smiled.

"I don't know if there would be any food left for the people actually attending the rally, not if you were allowed anywhere near it." His eyes twinkled.

Aaron paused, pressing his lips together in deep thought. Then his face brightened.

"Maybe we should have two tables, one for the crew, and one for the rally attendees!" He grinned as if he had just solved a world problem. David laughed this time.

"You're a case, Aaron," he said. Aaron flicked his hair out of his eyes and shrugged cheerfully.

"Guess I should run my plan by Jack, eh?"

"It sounds like something Jack wouldn't have as much authority over as Mr. Farris would," David corrected him. But at the mention of Jack's name, he turned automatically and looked over to where the subject of their conversation stood, drinking his thermos of morning coffee and looking the very image of unapproachable loneliness. David had never seen him like this before. A wrinkle formed between his eyes.

↑THE SPEAKER

He was distracted by the ringing of Aaron's cell phone. The young man pulled it from his pocket, and a troubled expression swept over his face. He hesitated to answer it.

"What's wrong? Aren't you going to take that?"

"Um, nah, I'll call them back."

Aaron shoved the phone deep into the pocket of his jeans, and soon the ringing ceased. But the look on Aaron's face remained. David noticed, and asked if everything was alright. In response, Aaron sighed and rubbed the back of his neck, a nervous habit of his that David had often seen after Aaron had rejoined their team.

"It's my mom. She's been sick for a long time, and then it seemed like she started getting better. I thought it was safe to leave her where she is, in the nursing home, and come help Jack again. But I got a phone call last night after the rally that she took a bad turn, and I said I'd talk to them later today."

"Well, if that was the nursing home, don't you think you ought to talk to them now? They probably have an update on her health."

"I'm kinda scared to, actually," Aaron confessed, breathing out a short laugh to hide his nervousness.

David reached over and put his hand on Aaron's shoulder.

"Hey," he said kindly, "you don't need to be afraid. Maybe it's good news. Either way, wouldn't your mom want you to know?"

Aaron bit his lip, but he seemed slightly reassured by David's sympathy. "I guess so..."

He reached into his pocket, fishing for his phone. As he held it out and studied it for a moment, he clutched it tight and said, "I'll call them back real fast."

"Good choice." And David clapped him on the back before resuming his work, while Aaron scurried off to a corner with the phone already to his ear.

Once more, David glanced over at Jack. The older man's gaze was roaming over the room, but when his eyes met David's for just the briefest second, Jack's face went blank, and he looked away. David dropped the smile he had been fixing in place. He and Jack had barely spoken the past week. It wasn't because David hadn't tried to seek out Jack, but rather Jack seemed strangely reluctant to be near David. It more than puzzled Mr. Farris, who knew more than anyone there how protective Jack was.

The longer David stared at Jack, the longer Jack looked deliberately in another direction. A determined expression came over David's face. He put down the microphone wiring and walked over to where Aaron stood talking on the phone. When he saw David approaching, Aaron began nodding as if the person on the other end of the line could see him, and said quickly, "Ok, man, thanks a lot."

"Mom's doing a little bit better, but still getting over the last bad turn," he added when David reached him. David smiled in approval, and then as they both turned to walk back, he said softly, "Hey, Aaron?"

"You'll have to move to my left, dude. You're on my blind side," Aaron joked, pointing up at his milky right pupil with a grin. A surprised look came over David's face, but he hurriedly wiped it off with a nervous laugh as he moved to stand on Aaron's left.

"So, what's up?"

"Well..." David stole another look at Jack, who was now helping his men pick up signs and debris from off the convention center hall where the rally had been held. "It's about...has Jack ever been like this with you before?" he ended abruptly.

Aaron raised an eyebrow. "What do you mean?"

"Haven't you noticed? He's been pretty quiet and distant over the past few days. It's not like him. You had to have noticed. You know him better than I do."

Aaron turned and studied his old boss for several seconds, David watching him.

"I think you're right," he said slowly. "He's usually a lot louder. But he spends a lot more time with you than he does with me now."

David raised an eyebrow, but Aaron didn't sound bitter or resentful, merely stating a fact.

"It seems like ever since the night we had that security breach, he's tried to stay away from me. I don't know why. Did I do something wrong?"

"Pshaw. What could you possibly have done wrong? That

loser who got in, he's the one everybody was mad at. I have no clue how Jack could be upset with you over that. It wasn't your fault at all."

"Well, I can't explain why he doesn't want to talk to me." David sighed. "But I also can't connect a reason to anything before that night."

Aaron shrugged. "I don't know, man. Jack, well, he gets things in his head sometimes. Don't ask me to explain, because I can't. But it's like ever since..." Aaron suddenly stopped and made a quizzical face as if he had suddenly remembered something and needed to hide the fact. "Where'd I put that other microphone," he muttered as if to himself, searching around.

A meditative look pinched David's face. Then a light dawned in his eyes.

"I remember...he talked about his son."

Aaron looked up. "What? His son?"

"Yes. Do you know him?"

"Ryan Webb?"

"Yes," David repeated.

Aaron sucked a deep breath of air through his teeth and blew it out with a helpless gesture.

"Ryan died, David. About a year ago. He was shot down overseas."

David turned away. Aaron saw his hand shaking as he placed it quietly on the large speaker nearest him, as if for support. He said nothing, but his gaze shifted back to Jack with a heavy concentration that seemed to want to reach out and hold together the brokenhearted man on the other side of the room.

"Ryan was a hero," Aaron continued thoughtfully. He looked at David and added, "I'm actually surprised Jack's talked about him to you. He hadn't said a word about Ryan...well, for a long time."

"How," began David haltingly, then stopped. He bowed his head and shook it once, reaching up to scrub something from his eyes with the back of his fist. Aaron respectfully pretended to be interested in the overhead lights, while concealing his curiosity over David's reaction.

"How old, how old was Ryan? When did it happen?" he asked

finally, without looking at Aaron.

"Twenty-six. Just a few years older than me."

"Ah." David twisted his neck to the side with his eyes half shut, as if he had just been struck in the face. Aaron now looked at him curiously.

"But you didn't even know – did you know Ryan Webb?" he asked. Aaron regarded David as a charismatic figure swathed in mystery who seemed capable of doing anything he set his hand to. And even though he wouldn't tell a soul about himself and who knows what could have happened in his past, Aaron thought David was still one of the nicest guys he had ever met.

But David shook his head.

"I knew Ryan before Jack sort of took me under his wing, when my dad died about three years ago," Aaron went on in an unusually subdued voice, his eyes sober as he kept them focused on his work. "Jack was friends with my dad, and he gave me a job after Dad passed away, and always kept an eye on me and my mom. I got to know Ryan before he went into the military. I'd have joined too, except for this," and Aaron pointed unnecessarily at his blind eye, as David wasn't looking at him. "He was a really great guy, and always... always a good friend to me." Aaron's voice caught in his throat. He swallowed hard, directing his gaze to his hands. Then he looked up at David, who didn't say that Jack had called him by his son's name when he thought he was in danger.

"Ryan was a lot like you, actually. He even carried a Bible around with him everywhere."

Aaron was looking at him with renewed respect and curiosity. David leaned his head back and let out a sigh that seemed to drag itself from the deepest recess of his body. He closed his bright blue eyes and massaged his temple as though affected by a headache.

"Are you ok, man?" Aaron reached toward him, then paused, uncertain. He glanced around, then added in a lower tone, "Look, maybe I shouldn't have told you all that about Ryan Webb. Jack never talks about him, or at least he didn't talk about him before...I don't want him to get mad at me."

David lifted his eyelids and studied the imploring look at

Aaron's face. He seemed to be trying to get his eyes in focus. Blinking hard once or twice, he nodded slowly. "I won't tell him you told me. But Aaron," he hesitated, "thank you."

"What for?"

David quietly grasped the younger man's shoulder as he walked past him.

"Eric, I don't want to see that cell phone out one more time until lunch, you hear me?" Jack barked. From a few feet away, Eric Dodge made a face and quickly stashed the guilty phone in his pocket before turning to lift a heavy reel of speaker cable. As he carried it out the door past Jack, Jack cuffed him upside the head, but not hard. Eric turned his head barely in time to give a sheepish half-grin, and Jack pointed warningly at him. But a flicker of a smile crept over his face, too.

"Jack!"

The smile vanished.

Jack closed his eyes for the briefest of seconds, and steeling himself, turned slowly around.

David walked up to him, the usual smile on his handsome face. Jack bit the inside of his cheek. He felt like he had been turned inside out for everyone to see, and he hated the feeling of vulnerability. Seeing David about to try and engage him in conversation after what had happened served to only dance across Jack's already raw nerves.

"Hey, David," he muttered, hiding behind his phone screen as he searched desperately for any new messages that might make a legitimate excuse to pull him away. David stopped a few feet away, and as Jack chanced a glance up at him, he was surprised to see not only friendliness but warm sympathy and something else in David's candid eyes that Jack couldn't place.

"Jack, I was just wondering..." David licked his lips. "Would you let me get you some coffee?"

"What?"

"Or food? Or maybe a soda, or something?"

Jack eyed him sharply. "What for?"

David gave him a sad little smile.

"You've done more than enough for me over the past months," he said simply. "I'd like to return at least a little of the favor."

Jack bit his lip. Something felt off, but he could tell David was nothing but sincere. He also knew he couldn't put off talking to the young man forever. Maybe it was better if they went somewhere else to work out between them what had happened.

"I guess coffee'd be fine, but where are you getting the money to pay for it?" he asked pointedly as they fell into step beside each other.

David's smile widened. "Mr. McCoy has been paying me for working with the party for a few months now. And I think you knew that."

Jack felt his face flush. "Well, I have a lot to think about every day, so you'll have to forgive me if one or two things slip my mind once in a while."

The blatant bitterness in his voice seemed to startle David. Neither of them said a word until after Jack had left one of his men in charge of overseeing the clean-up process and the two of them had made their way out of the convention center building.

"Actually, I thought maybe we could walk," David said when Jack took out his truck keys. "There's a coffee shop just a couple blocks away. We can use the exercise, right?"

The forced joviality in his voice made Jack glare at him, but he slid the keys back into his pocket.

For the first block, not a word was spoken between the two men. An uncomfortable knowledge put distance between them, and secrets glued their tongues to the roofs of their mouths. Small talk felt inevitable as a weak avoidance of awkwardness, but so shallow that Jack nearly hated himself for speaking first.

"So our next rally is going to be in Missouri, four days from now," he heard himself saying, with an internal grimace. "And after that it's only a couple of weeks till the RNC in San Antonio, Texas."

"Ah, that's...good," David's voice faltered. Then he added, "Hopefully there won't be any more security problems."

"They're being pretty vigilant," Jack said, glancing back at the two Blackheart guards following a few yards behind them. Up ahead, a black SUV was slowly driving along parallel to the sidewalk. "That's the last thing we need right now. Everybody freaking out and saying things they don't mean just because–"

"Jack."

Jack stiffened, but his head turned unwillingly toward David. David had stopped walking and was looking at him with such an unfathomable expression that Jack felt that unwelcome vulnerability again.

"Jack, I need to ask you something."

Here it comes. Jack's hands balled into fists inside the pockets of his jacket.

"That night of the first security breach..."

"Yes."

"You called me Ryan."

"Yes." Jack couldn't think of anything else to say.

"Why?"

"It was just...just a slip of the tongue, David." Jack spread out his hands, still in his pockets, so that his jacket opened as if he were spreading wings. "It happens to people all the time. Is this why you wanted to get me coffee? To get me alone for interrogation?"

"I know you must miss him very much, don't you?"

Jack shot him a glare that was more of a disguise to conceal his horrified shock than anything else. He spluttered, "What...what do you–"

"To have a son in the military must be hard," David said without looking at him. He glanced over and saw an empty, weather-stained wooden bench sitting back from the sidewalk. "You probably think about him all the time."

Jack slowly let out his breath a little at a time. A dull pain, familiar and un-faded over the past year clamped around his heart. He stumbled over to the bench and sat down, burying his face in his hands like a man wearied of the world around him.

David sat down softly beside him.

"You must be so proud of him," he murmured.

Jack's shoulders were shaking. But when he raised his head his eyes were dry.

"Ryan has always given me reasons to be proud of him," he said hoarsely. He cleared his throat and blinked hard. "A more honorable man than I could ever hope to be, or find anywhere."

"It's really hard when somebody you love goes away from you," said David quietly. He was looking away with a very distant expression in his eyes, but Jack felt almost as if David had put his arm around his shoulders, his words were so gentle and warm.

"Harder than you know," he sighed.

David swiveled his gaze to meet Jack's eyes, and Jack was startled by the sudden, odd intensity burning in them. But then, just as instantly, the moment passed, and David's face was serene and calm, though lined with sadness as he now put one hand on Jack's shoulder. Jack shrugged.

"I'll be fine," he murmured, more to himself than to David. "Ryan made a hero out of himself. Kid really outdid my expectations of him. Although..." Jack's green eyes softened in spite of his fierce attempts to block every emotion boiling up inside. "I always knew he would do something great someday. Never had a doubt."

"It's really wonderful you had the privilege of raising him to be what sounds like such a fine young man. I would like to have met him."

"He was..." Jack stopped himself and took a measured breath, shooting a furtive look at David. Then his shoulders slumped, as though the weight hanging on them for so many months had finally grown too heavy for him to bear unhidden. "He was a good...a good kid. Then he was a good man."

David was silent.

"Then..." Jack took a shaky breath, steeling himself. He pressed both hands hard against the edge of the bench, wrapping his fingers around the faded wood until the tightness whitened his knuckles. "He was a good officer." Jack suddenly switched the direction of the conversation, as if he couldn't hold in what was clawing its way out of his insides. "I miss him so much, sometimes it hurts to breathe. Like I shouldn't be using up air that he could..."

He stopped again. A bitter hardness formed around his trembling mouth.

"I couldn't keep him safe. I couldn't protect him. If I had known, I never would have let him..." He floundered desperately for words as black grief encompassed his thoughts.

"Yes, you would have, Jack."

Jack turned to stare at him, eyes wide.

"You would have let him go because it was the way he wanted to use his passion for protecting others and serving his country. You told me so yourself it's why he joined up. He wanted to be where he was, Jack."

Jack's hard eyes bored into David's face. Something flickered in them that made him feel suddenly deeply frustrated which, when mingled with his sorrow, made him feel unprotected like cracked porcelain.

"How do you know what Ryan wanted?" he demanded bitterly. "You didn't know him."

David drew back, but then his expression softened. "But I do know you, Jack."

Jack choked back a scoff. "Well, my son and I were very different from each other. I wanted him to stay close, where I could protect him if he ever needed help. But Ryan...no, he had to get out there and 'save the world.'" Jack quirked his fingers in quotation marks. A warm moistness welled up in his eyes. He quickly dashed it away. Then, as if by the recall of a tender memory, the smallest of smiles pricked the corners of his mouth. "But I love him for his bravery. His noble courage. For wanting to help others. For..." Jack looked down at his hands as they twisted themselves together in his lap. He leaned forward, resting his elbows on his knees and steepling his fingers. "For helping me to realize that what he was doing was good. That it was right for him. He helped me let go just enough to let him slip out the door." Jack's face fell again. "And then he slipped right out of my life without warning," he whispered brokenly. He reached up one hand and rubbed it down the length of his face.

David clasped his shoulder again, giving him one quick, firm, steadying shake. For several seconds the two of them sat in silence, watching the occasional pedestrian trek by.

"I remember the last time we talked to each other," Jack said suddenly. He closed his eyes briefly, imagining the scenario playing out behind his eyelids. "It was just a few days before. He called me from where he was stationed. He could only talk for a few minutes, but he sounded so, so joyful. Even more than I had ever expected him to be in his position. But, that was kind of Ryan's default attitude. He told me he should be able to come home, hopefully, within the next four weeks, and that he couldn't wait to see me. The last words he said to me, right before he hung up, were, 'Bye, Dad. I'll see you soon. I love you.'" Jack's pauses between sentences were growing longer as he fought to steady himself. "So, the last memory I would have of him is being just excited. Happy..." Jack's face darkened. "I wish that was my last memory of him."

"You got a phone call," David breathed.

"Yes. It was a moment I'll never forget. I can't forget. My whole world just stopped. I don't remember anything that happened between that call and when I actually saw my son again...it was all such a blur. A horrible, sick, mess of a nightmare I didn't think I could ever wake up from."

Jack paused, his voice catching. "I'm still living in that nightmare."

David copied Jack's posture by leaning forward and clasping his hands, parking his elbows on his knees.

"It just..." Jack twisted his face and locked his jaw, blinking rapidly. "...It made me so angry. I was helpless to do anything. All I could do was stand on the other side of the glass and watch, saying his name over and over in my mind, willing him to just open his eyes. Waiting for him to look at me." He clenched and unclenched his fists, as if somehow by grasping and releasing the empty air he could find a balm for the self-imposed guilt and burning pain uncurling in his stomach as it had for so long.

"It's human to be angry. Anger gives us the idea of something to lift our heads above the water, to cling to so we don't have to face the depths of our grief. But you have to deal with the anger or else it'll consume you."

Jack shook his head. "When did you become so wise, David?"

David leaned back and shoved his hands in his jeans pockets.

↑ THE SPEAKER

"I guess the longer you live, the more you realize how valuable life is, but that there is something beyond that you have to be thinking about," he said slowly, a distant look in his eyes. "Eternity. Life on earth is about getting ready for life after earth. If there's anything about this life that God wants us to understand, it's that life is short. It's beautiful, unpredictable, and sometimes it gives out on us before we're ready to say goodbye. Eventually, we need to learn to let go, hard and impossible as that seems. But the thing is, you don't have to let go right away. And if you're a child of God, and the person you love was a child of God, the two of you will see each other again."

Jack laughed. It was short and harsh. "After that day, what little faith I had was totally depleted. My wife couldn't handle her own grief as well as my own, and she left me."

"I'm sorry."

"I didn't protect him like I should have," Jack groaned and pressed his palms against his eyes.

"No, don't go there. You can't blame yourself for what happened, Jack," said David firmly. "You've been through something which no father should have to endure, but grief, anger...it can spin your head until you paralyze yourself. It wasn't your fault. You've got to recognize that."

"But why was he taken from me? That's what I don't understand." Jack dropped his hands and rolled his head from side to side, casting his eyes around in desperate search of an answer he had never been able to find. David sat back and, clasping his hands together, he closed his eyes for a moment as if in the deepest concentration. Jack watched him pleadingly, as though David could tell him what he needed most to hear.

"When we lose someone we love, I don't think asking why helps us," he said, opening his eyes and heaving a sigh. "God isn't just going to speak to us and give us the answer we want. Sometimes things happen because of simple laws of nature, or an untimely accident, or a mistake made by another person that has resounding consequences." David massaged his brow. Jack's expectancy faded, leaking out of him like a deflating balloon. He didn't know what he had been waiting for David to say, but somehow he felt that only the man sitting beside him could have had the right words.

"But that isn't anything you don't already know," David added. "The truth is," he hesitated and looked away from Jack, seeing something in the distance that his companion could not. "The truth is...you can't try to find reasons for losing someone. No matter how hard you attempt to justify it, you just...can't. Because it isn't given for us to know why everything happens. What we do know, is that when we put our faith in God, trusting Him to take care of us while giving our tears and grief and broken hearts to Him, only there can we find true comfort. And peace."

Jack realized he had been holding his breath, and released it. He looked down at his empty hands dangling between his knees as he leaned his elbows against his thighs.

"Can you..." he fought the rough snag in his voice, "Can you do anything besides make sense and for once, not be so eloquent?"

David's face broke into a shivery smile before the corners of his mouth dropped faintly.

"I'm sorry," he said again. "I know I can't ease your pain or take away the burden you're carrying. But if I could, Jack...I would. I'd consider myself an ungrateful, selfish human being if I thought anything less."

Jack struggled fiercely against the tears swimming in his eyes, but now they overflowed, hot and unrestrained. David turned his head away, but his hand arm reached around Jack's shoulders in calm and silent sympathy. For several long moments, the two friends sat communicating without words. Two full hearts needed nothing to say. Jack wept quietly, his chest and shoulders heaving, but he felt David's friendly hand, and appreciated it more than he would ever say, though the knowledge of it made him weep even harder. He was aware of David's touch, but what he didn't see was the single tear that finally escaped David's long, dark lashes and landed unnoticed on his own hand.

When Jack finally raised his swollen, reddened eyes from behind his wet hands, David handed him a handkerchief from his pocket. The Blackheart guards stood at attention nearby. Their security SUV was parked across the street.

"I apologize, David." Jack finished mopping his face and then blew his nose. "I think that's the first time I've let myself..." he trailed off, crumpling the handkerchief into a ball.

"You don't have anything to be sorry about," David told him, patting his back gently before taking his hand away.

"And, you know..." Jack hesitated for one breath, then blurted out, "You remind me of Ryan, David. I guess that's why I...well, I'm just an over-protective old man–"

David snorted in disagreement.

Jack warmed with gratitude. "But I'm sorry. I've been obsessive and then, I guess, sort of blaming you for reminding me of my own son and my grief. That was wrong of me."

David sat very still. Then he slowly stood up and, shoving his hands deep in his jeans pockets, paced a few steps back and forth in front of the bench, across the short sidewalk to the curb and back. He finally paused, rubbing his chin thoughtfully, with his back toward Jack. Jack fidgeted uneasily, wishing he could unsay what he had just said. *Way to unnerve the man, Jack. It's like you just told him you're blaming him for your own foolishness.*

Suddenly David turned around and resumed his seat beside Jack, hands coming out of his pockets to cross his arms over his broad chest. He appeared to have decided something. But what came out of his mouth next was, again, not what Jack expected.

"Jack, from what I know about your son, I would take it as a very high compliment to be compared to him. I know that missing him must be at the back of your every thought."

"He's with me all the time," Jack murmured.

David's face worked like he was trying to recall a faded memory. "His absence is like the sky, spread over everything," he said, his voice distant. Jack recognized the words, and understanding dawned on his face.

"C.S. Lewis," he remarked, and David nodded. Jack shook his head and uttered a genuine chuckle.

"David Connally, you never cease to amaze."

David smiled faintly.

"He's my favorite author."

"Yeah, I think I've skimmed one or two of his works before, but then, I don't read much. Good literature is hard to find these days, anyway." Jack welcomed the subtle transition in topic after his emotional release. He felt...lighter, somehow. "You have to reach back decades to find the really good books."

"Kind of like a good man is hard to find," David laughed. He too, seemed relieved by the subject change. "You have to go seek him out."

Jack shot him a furtive look. "Yes," he said slowly. "And yet, occasionally, he'll come to you when you least expect it. For example, when your old truck breaks down on you in the middle of the night."

David's ears reddened, but he only gave a half-shrug and then looked down at his watch.

"Hey, we were supposed to get coffee," he said, as if he was shocked at how the time had flown by since they had left the convention center.

Jack gave him a knowing smile, still a little shaky from his tears, but he stood up.

"That's right, and you're buying." He pointed a finger at David.

David assumed a stiff posture with his hand to his forehead in a salute. "Yes, sir." His eyes twinkled. Jack gave him a teasing push as he walked past him, and David smiled to himself as he turned to fall into step beside Jack.

From across the street, a pale young man stood behind the glass of a convenience store window, his eyes trained on the pair until they disappeared from his sight.

⸏CHAPTER 10:

The following afternoon gave The American Party workers a respite from the usual flurried activity. The crew was gathered in the meal tent for lunch, talking and joking as usual. Only Mr. Farris wasn't present among them. Jack, shoveling steaming lasagna onto his paper plate, was quick to notice someone else who wasn't there.

"Hey, David," he called behind him. David, standing three people behind Jack in line for food, craned his neck to meet Jack's gaze. "What?"

"Have you seen Aaron?"

"No, actually..." David's eyes scanned the room. A puzzled expression crept over his face. "Come to think of it, I don't think I've seen him all morning."

"That's odd," Jack began, but was suddenly cut off by a yelp from his own mouth as a splotch of hot tomato sauce escaped the server and landed on his thumb. Sticking his finger in his mouth, Jack shook his head and walked away to sit down. David soon joined him.

"Aaron's usually at work on time, and you always know he's here. He makes sure of that."

David nodded thoughtfully as he balanced his plate on his knees. "You think maybe he's sick and still at the hotel?"

"He would have called and told me. What I really can't understand is how nobody noticed he was missing until lunchtime. Hey," Jack turned to David. "When did you see him last?"

"Last night at dinner. I remember because I distinctly heard him say he had to get back to the hotel from the restaurant as soon as possible because there was some show coming on he wanted to see. Some CSI show or something."

Jack chuckled, in spite of his uncertainty. "Yeah, that kid loves his crime shows. Beats me why you'd want to waste time filling up your mind with creepy scenarios that might actually stand a chance of happening because of all the freaks out there, but Aaron likes it." He shrugged and took a bite of lasagna, wincing against the heat.

It was then that Mr. Farris entered the food tent. He was closely followed by a young man in his early twenties, with wavy brown hair, cloudy blue eyes, and a wan complexion that gave him a very washed-out appearance. Most everyone in the tent looked up from mere habit when Mr. Farris came in, an automatic reflex when an entrance is taken up by a newcomer. But their eyes lingered curiously on the pale young man with the party manager.

Mr. Farris stood near the front of the tent and put his hand on the shoulder of the young stranger who stood beside him.

"Hey, everyone, could I have your attention, please?"

The chatter drained into silence. Mr. Farris took off his hat and wiped the back of his hand across his face. The days were growing steadily warmer, and nearly everyone in the tent was beginning to sweat around noon.

"I would like to introduce you all to James Rivers," Mr. Farris announced, patting the shoulder of the young man, who shoved his hands deep into his pockets and gave the room a tight-lipped smile. "He's just graduated from Harvard this past May, and has graciously volunteered to give the Party his time and help up until Election Day. He has a real passion for politics, and will even be working as an intern in the Supreme Court this coming January. I've had quite a discussion with him, and have determined that he has the Party's best interests in mind," Mr. Farris continued approvingly. "He will act as my personal assistant until November. I think he will make a good fit for our crew." Mr. Farris turned to James and gave him a friendly slap on the back. "What do you say, James?"

James passed an apprehensive smile around the room, bouncing on the balls of his feet. He took his hands out of his pockets, waving one aimlessly while rubbing the back of his neck with the other. He seemed at a loss for words as he tossed his gaze around the different faces staring back at him. Then he found David, sitting at the opposite end of the tent. His stare became instantly more fixed and intense.

"Well, I'm just, just real honored to be allowed to come work with you guys," he said, clearing his throat. "I watch, ah, I've seen your reports on the news and thought you guys were just doing an incredible job and...uh, I felt like I really needed to be a part of that and, uh, do what I can to help my country."

Mr. Farris beamed. Jack's eyes widened as he sucked in a quiet breath.

"As long as he doesn't say much, he'll be alright," he muttered. David nudged him with a small grin on his face, and Jack tilted his head in an apologetic manner.

Mr. Farris then took James around the tent, introducing him to everyone. When they reached Jack and David, David wiped his mouth and stood up. Jack followed suit, adjusting his belt.

"James Rivers, Jack Webb and David Connally."

"Pleasure," said Jack, adding a firm handshake to the greeting. James' hand felt cold and rather limp in Jack's strong grip. Jack glanced down at his own hand after their introduction and waited to make sure no one was looking when he shook his head.

"So this is the great David Connally," James remarked, as his and David's hands met. He seemed more animated and interested when talking to David.

David reddened, and waved the compliment away. "Ah, I wouldn't say that."

"Oh, I don't know, man. You seem to have a lot of people convinced," James said with a lopsided smirk.

"Well," David scratched the back of his neck. "I'm pretty sure not everybody." He folded his arms, sharing a look with Jack.

James wore a sphinxlike expression. "What? Anybody ever take a shot at you or something?"

Jack stiffened, but David chuckled. "Not yet," he said lightly. "I doubt I'm important enough for people to be that angry with me."

James' face broke into a smile.

"David's too modest for his own good," Mr. Farris said evenly. "He's one of our best assets. We have top security on him round the clock."

"That's right," boomed a deep voice behind them. James whirled around and saw Eli standing there, eying him penetratingly.

"Elijah Farley, Blackheart Security," he said, sticking out his hand. James looked noticeably awed, but he slid his hand nervously into Eli's, who wrung it firmly before letting go. James backed up a couple of steps, massaging his hand while letting out a weak laugh.

"Wow, you guys really go all out on security detail," he remarked, nodding toward Eli, who stood like a massive statue. "I didn't know you could afford Blackheart. Isn't that one of the top protection agencies in the country?"

"We have more sponsors now than we did at the start," Mr. Farris assured him. "I think we have David to thank for that. And Rick McCoy is a pretty successful businessman. He knows what he's doing, believe me. He wanted only the best for the best," he added, slapping David on the back.

David turned red again. James was watching him again, as if David was the most interesting object in the room.

"Hey!"

Startled, everyone turned toward Jack, who had let out a shout of surprise. His attention had wandered slightly from the conversation, and he was pointing toward the TV, a stupefied look on his face.

"That's, that's Aaron!" he cried, his eyes bugging.

David, Mr. Farris, Eli, and the others quickly followed Jack over to the TV. James ambled along behind them, mild curiosity in his eyes.

Sure enough, Aaron Wright appeared on the screen again, sitting in a plush white chair opposite a newsman in a gray suit and red necktie. Aaron wasn't looking at the camera. At the bottom of the screen a headline scrolled across reading: PATRIOTS OR PAGANS? CHARLIE WALTER'S EXCLUSIVE INTERVIEW WITH AN EX-AMERICAN PARTY EMPLOYEE REVEALS THE INSIDE STORY.

"What is this," Mr. Farris breathed, his eyes narrowed.

As if to answer his question, the man in the suit turned his face toward the camera, a well-rehearsed smile on his face.

226

CHAPTER 10:

"Good afternoon. This is the midday news special, and I'm Charlie Walters. Our top story today: Patriots or Pagans? will no doubt astonish and unnerve you, as we were approached by a former employee of the increasingly popular American Party who will give us the true story of what goes on behind the scenes in this supposedly righteous and conservative organization."

"Former employee? What is he talking about?!" Jack raged.

"Shhh!" Mr. Farris hissed, his wide eyes glued to the screen.

"Aaron Wright, who has traveled with the party from town to town as well as being close to David Connally, says he has the inside story of what really happens within the heavily guarded American Party camp," Charlie Walters continued relentlessly. "Today I'm sitting down with him for an exclusive interview."

He swiveled his gaze over to Aaron, who looked extremely uncomfortable. He kept rubbing his hands up and down his thighs, as if his hands were sweaty.

"Now Aaron," Charlie began, "you have been, or I guess I should say had been, an employee of The American Party for the past eight months or so, working and living with the group David Connally travels the country with?"

"Yes sir," Aaron mumbled, his voice a soft murmur. "That's true.

"And isn't it also true that you were fired just yesterday and thrown out of the camp because you simply objected to the activities that were going on there night after night?"

Aaron bit his lip. Even from where Jack stood he could see the sweat beading Aaron's temples. He still wouldn't look at the camera, and he barely raised his eyes to meet Charlie's.

"Yes...sir."

Jack clenched his fists against his sides. "That's a lie!" he seethed.

"And tell me, Aaron," said Charlie, leaning in to better catch Aaron's next response. "Is is really true that every night The American Party camp there is heavy drug and alcohol use which David Connally and even some of the security personnel are involved in?"

Mr. Farris gripped Jack's shoulder.

"That is true."

"That boy better not show his face around here again," Eli said hotly.

"And is it not the case that late in the night they allow prostitutes through security to entertain the crew, including David?" Charlie Walters went on. He looked almost as if he were enjoying himself, tearing down the reputation of The American Party. Jack closed his eyes briefly, imagining how many rapt viewers were watching this same interview on TV right now.

Aaron hesitated.

Jack held his breath.

"Isn't that what you told me went on there?" Charlie pressed.

Jack felt his last hope deflate. If Aaron denied the lie now, he would only cause more trouble and controversy that would only hurt the party more.

Aaron hung his head. "Yes, that's true."

Charlie Walters smiled smugly as he turned back to face the camera.

"Well folks, there you have it: the answer to the question we've all wondered for months now as to what really goes on behind the spotless facade and tight security surrounding the elusively enigmatic David Connally and The American Party's organization."

Eli slammed his hand against the power button and the screen cut to black. Stunned silence filled the tent. Jack pulled a hand down the side of his face, his mind racing. He felt himself silently screaming, *Why, Aaron?*

David voiced what they were all thinking. "For all the time Aaron and I worked together and how long I've known him, he was always an honest person, a good kid. Why would he say all these things about us?"

David looked hurt, making Jack feel even worse. Mr. Farris slowly released his hands from their iron grip on the back of the chair in front of him while letting out a long, slow exhale. He turned to Jack.

"That young man was under your watch," he said tersely. "I know you trusted him, and because of that I trusted you. But this is going to be dynamite in our faces, Jack."

"I know," Jack said numbly.

"Do you realize what he just did to us?" Mr. Farris' voice was rising. He jabbed a finger at the TV screen as if Aaron's image were still showing there. "This is the worst thing anyone could have possibly done to undo everything we've tried to build up! Do you know how many people would have seen that?"

"Look, I know Aaron!" Jack exclaimed, getting rough in his defense. "He would never do something like this! Something must have happened..."

"No, Jack. Nobody was holding a loaded gun on him. He wasn't forced to answer those questions the way he did." Mr. Farris turned away, disgust and anxiety showing in his eyes. "He was probably a spy the whole time," he muttered scathingly.

"Hey!" Jack protested angrily, going after him, but David grabbed his arm. Then the phone rang.

Everybody stopped talking. Mr. Farris' shoulders slumped. He reached down with a resigned look to his belt, but his phone was gone. He looked down and around himself, checking his pockets. The ringing grew louder, more insistent, as if matching the mood of the caller. Then James picked up the cell phone from where it lay on the table and pushed it toward Mr. Farris. Mr. Farris took it from him with a silent nod, then held it to his ear with both hands.

"Yes, Mr. McCoy," he answered in a falsely confident voice.

"Are you trying to be funny?"

"I'm sorry?"

"You sound like there's absolutely nothing wrong and that this is nothing more than a social call. Am I getting the wrong vibe from you here, Farris?"

Mr. Farris gulped. "No, sir."

"I assume you saw the report about one of your people."

"Just finished watching it. Sir, I swear I don't know what–"

"Michael..." McCoy's voice took a surprisingly weary turn. "What I'm about to tell you is just between you and me. We got a call from the local television station that a news reporter had asked for permission to do an interview in their studios late last night when no one else was around."

Mr. Farris marched out of the tent and didn't stop until he was several yards away. He leaned against one of the trucks and rubbed his eyes.

"I'm guessing that interview was–"

"The very one you just finished watching. As soon as I got this information, I sent Nathan Blaine down there to find out what was going on, because I knew it was going to be pretty ugly."

"Yes," and Mr. Farris winced as parts of the interview replayed in his mind. "Ugly is one way to describe it."

"I got off the phone with Nathan right before I called you," McCoy continued. "He informed me that Aaron Wright's mother had taken a sudden turn for the worse and was deathly ill. She had been refused treatment at the local hospital unless there was a ten-thousand dollar up-front co-pay. After pleading on his mother's behalf, Aaron was approached by this Charlie Walters, a real slime ball of a guy, who told him he could help get his mother's treatment taken care of if he would only agree to an exclusive interview with him. Apparently your man Aaron was so desperate for his mother's medical care that he was willing to agree to whatever they said. After the interview, which was around midnight this morning, Aaron and his mother arrived at the hospital in an ambulance. Aaron paid ten thousand dollars in cash for his mother's treatment."

Mr. Farris shook his head. "Poor kid. He must have been scared. He just wanted to help his mother."

"That's one way to look at it. But I don't think Walters just up and took the initiative on this one, Michael. I think he was hired to seek Aaron out, otherwise I doubt he would have even known about Aaron's mother. I think somebody is shadowing us."

"You think we have a spy in our midst?"

"Not necessarily, and for Pete's sake don't go spreading that around. But I think we've grown to the point that other people have taken an interest in us, for good or for bad, or both. Just keep your eyes open."

Mr. Farris could feel his already turbulent feelings swelling up again like ocean waves in a storm. "But Aaron didn't have to do this to us! Surely there was another way to take care of his mother without lying to the press! And tomorrow this is going to be in bold headlines all over!"

"You think I don't know that?" McCoy barked. Mr. Farris heard him sigh. "Michael, look. I've already submitted a report to one of the more reliable, unbiased networks. They'll carry the truth about this tonight on the evening news. I know this is asking a lot of you, but try not to worry about this. The truth will come out."

"Yes sir." Mr. Farris glanced back toward the tent. A torn expression passed over his face. "Sir."

"Yes?"

"Can I...can I at least tell Jack what you told me? About Aaron Wright? He's really fond of the kid, been taking care of him for years after his father passed...he was really upset."

He could almost hear McCoy nodding over the phone. "Sure, ok, fine. We're not trying to make Aaron out as a monster. But you keep an eye on David, too. We got a storm coming."

James Rivers stood awkwardly inside the meal tent, surrounded by jabbering people who were completely flabbergasted over the interview they had all just seen on the news. Theories and speculations about Aaron Wright's betrayal, who meant little to James, spread like wildfire. Everyone was guessing why he would do such a thing. James looked around. The man he had met named Jack Webb looked angrier than anybody else, and was fiddling with his phone as if debating whether or not to make a call. Eli Farley, the huge Blackheart Security agent who James couldn't compare to anyone more intimidating he had ever met, brooded with his arms folded. Every time his eye came to rest on James, the young man felt a shiver run up his spine. As if the security agent could see straight through him. As if he could see through the web of lies in James' head.

But when James looked at David Connally, he noticed that David seemed to be the only person not throwing out ideas as to how or why their fellow crew member had betrayed them. David had fallen back into his seat, his plate of food untouched before him. He had folded his hands and his head was bowed. James cocked his own head. So this was the man he was to keep his eye on. He seemed easy enough. Was David...praying? James scrunched his nose. Odd.

Then he realized he should probably report back to York. He had been here less than twenty minutes and already enough had happened to fill a phone call with worthy information. "I'm gonna have to up my minutes per month," he muttered to himself. Then he glanced around. Nobody was looking at him, so he made his way stealthily toward the front of the tent. He had just raised the flap with his hand when...

"Where are you going?"

James gulped. Eli loomed over him like a stronghold tower. James noted the knotted muscles in his arms.

"I, uh, I'm just going to, uh, use the facilities," he said as he jerked his thumb over his shoulder. He squinted up in pretend confusion. "Is that ok?"

Eli folded his arms. "What made you decide you wanted to work for The American Party?"

James' eyes widened. "Uh..." he scrambled for words, his mind racing. *Who does this guy think he is?* James felt almost angry, but his apprehension was stronger. He swallowed and licked his lips. "I, just, want to help," he said blandly. "Help my country. Do you have a problem with that?"

His voice grew more solid on the tail end of the question. Eli's face was as inscrutable as marble, but he slowly turned away. James felt that Eli's gaze was somehow still on him, however, as he scurried out and away from the tent. He headed around the corner and walked a couple of blocks toward one of the bridges spanning the Missouri River. As he marched out onto the bridge, hands pushed into the pockets of his jacket, James kept glancing behind him, turning his head from right to left. When he reached the center, he moved over to the railing and pulled out his cell phone. Scrolling through the contacts until he came to a nameless number, he pushed the call button, put the phone to his ear and waited.

Bikers passed him going in both directions, their helmets and reflectors blinking in the sun. Joggers hustled by in their neon

CHAPTER 10:

T-Shirts, plugged into their MP3 players. Regular pedestrians out for a stroll or intent on an errand moved to and fro at their various paces. The wind had picked up just enough to fan hair and clothing with a gentle lift, and the subtle scent of water and distant sounds of city traffic filled the air.

James shifted his weight and leaned one elbow on the bridge railing, tapping the toe of his shoe against the concrete. On the second ring, there was a click on the other end. "What do you have for me, James?" Dominic York's voice rasped through the speaker.

James twisted away from the passers-by and ducked his head, still leaning heavily against the rail. "I'm in. Michael Farris trusts me, and everybody seems glad to have me...except for one guy."

"We can't afford for anyone not to trust you, James. Why doesn't this guy?"

"Well, to make things worse," James gnawed his lip, "he's head of the security detail."

Silence on the other line. Then a long, slow exhale.

"So the head of security doesn't trust you. Well that's wonderful. The last thing we need is for some nosy guard to be snooping around. You better not give him a single reason to be suspicious."

"I haven't!"

York sounded like he was seething. Suddenly he said, "You said security detail."

James rubbed the back of his neck. "Uh, yeah. They actually have a pretty high maintenance deal secured...like I think David Connally gets twenty-four-hour protection."

"Really. I didn't think The American Party could afford... Wait, what's the name of the agency?"

"Ah..." James narrowed his eyes as if that would somehow help him think. The image on the side of a great, black SUV cut through his memory. He had walked past it with Mr. Farris on the way to meet the crew.

"Black...Blackheart! Blackheart Security." He grinned, proud of himself for remembering that small detail from his peripheral vision on such short notice.

"Blackheart? You're certain?"

"Yeah. Why?"

"As in, Elijah Farley, Blackheart?"

"That was the man's name, who I met and who said he was the head of security," James said, a little confused. To his surprise, York snickered.

"I can't believe Rick McCoy would get that kind of security for David Connally. Besides costing an inordinate amount of money, I guess McCoy doesn't know anything about Farley, or he probably wouldn't have hired him."

James frowned. "Why? What did he do? And how do you know about him?"

"Fifteen years ago, I was working under a senator. This was shortly before I became chairman of the Democrat Party. But this senator, who shall remain nameless, had a teenage daughter. He wanted extra protection for her, especially so because he was about to pass a bill in Congress that he knew was going to make a lot of people angry, and he wanted to make sure his daughter was safe. Just in case somebody tried to use her to get to the senator. So he hired a couple of agents from the CIA to take care of her. One of those agents was Elijah Farley."

"He was CIA?"

"Oh yes, one of their best, too, from what I know." York made a swallowing sound, and smacked his lips softly. James guessed he was probably drinking coffee or something.

"Anyway, Farley was devoted to that girl. He took care of her and looked out for her like she was his own daughter. But then one day there was an accident. The details were kept very hush-hush, but the public story went that the senator's daughter was found dead in a car wrapped around a tree by the side of the road. For some inexplicable reason, neither security agent had been with her at the time of the crash. You can imagine the chaos facing the CIA."

James whistled long and low. "I'll bet. But what happened to Farley?"

"He was disgracefully discharged for failing his duty so blatantly, and disappeared for a long time. Then one day he decides to come into the public spotlight again to head up a new security agency by himself."

"Blackheart," James said, comprehension dawning.

"Precisely. And frankly I'm shocked that anyone would go to work for him, let alone that anyone would hire him. But, surprisingly enough, he seemed so genuine and serious about his job that I guess somebody gave him a chance, and the rest is history. That agency is pretty large now, and Farley's got at least a hundred people in total under him. People forget as the water rolls under the bridge." York took another drink of coffee.

"So..." James scratched his ear. "Why do you think he started Blackheart?"

"Hmm? Well, to atone for his past, is my guess. He's trying to prove once again to the world that Elijah Farley is a force to be reckoned with, and that he's worth the investment. I'm fairly certain it wasn't because he felt such a keen sense of duty to go back into the security field."

James felt a new confidence blossoming in his chest as this piece of information sunk in. Eli Farley had messed up in his past, and was now trying to smooth it over by acting tough and over-protective. But knowing his secret gave James a sense of power. He wouldn't be so easily intimidated by the agent again.

"You still there, James?"

"Yeah."

"Well, do you have anything else for me?"

"Um..." James cast his eyes around, biting his lip as he tried to remember all the events of the past hour. "Everybody saw the report on the news with that kid who worked for The American Party. They were pretty keyed up about it. I guess he was originally a pretty decent guy; Aaron...ah, what's his—"

He stopped because he realized York was chuckling softly. "Those crazy people did a good job. Maybe my investment isn't blown after all." Then he spoke to James directly. "I saw that report myself. Rather tragic for The American Party, isn't it? Who knew they were hiding all that dirty linen. They'll surely suffer some repercussions from that."

⭡THE SPEAKER

"What I don't get is how that reporter found that guy." James paced back and forth. "How did he manage to get all that out of Aaron when everybody around me watching was calling them lies? There was nobody around. They didn't have a reason to hide anything."

"Of course, James," York said silkily. "Who knows what The American Party is up to afterhours though, right? No doubt that reporter was hired."

"Hired...yeah, guess that makes sense."

York let out another ripple of laughter that made the hair stand up on the back of James' neck in spite of being on the same side as the callous man he was speaking to.

"Now, in return for your informative report, I will tell you something as well. I'm hiring a private investigator to root out David Connally's history. If there's anything to be found behind that man, I want to know before anyone else does." York's voice turned hard. "He's obviously hiding something in his past, and I intend to find out exactly what it is."

The RNC got underway on the twenty-fifth of June in San Antonio, Texas. As the week grew long, it became fairly obvious to all that Senator Joseph Cane would be nominated for the Republican presidential candidate. There were even a number of people in the Republican Party who were asking Senator Cane if he would consider David Connally to run on his ticket as Cane's vice president. When he heard this question, the senator's ears turned scarlet, but he simply replied that there was still much to be decided and figured out, but with time he would reveal his choice for his vice president.

But even as he did his best to dismiss the questions about David Connally, Cane did think the idea over when he was alone. As much as it pained him to admit it, he knew somebody with David's popularity and influence would be a wise choice for the candidacy. But he was also all too aware of David's unique situation of having virtually no past history anyone could uncover, and how large a liability he posed regarding the fact that he would not only be a dark horse, but nobody knew anything about him.

Then the light bulb pinged. Cane realized this would be a

CHAPTER 10:

perfect opportunity to find something out about David Connally. While he did not consider David as a viable candidate for office, he knew that David could possibly be a great asset to the Republican Party, the conservative candidates and, more importantly, to himself. Cane thought maybe he could use David to build bridges between himself and The American Party in the upcoming election. It could only help Cane, after all.

With this thought in mind, he decided it might be worthwhile to at least visit with the heads of The American Party and try to get into conversation with David, learn his secrets about keeping the crowd's spellbound attention and how to win their love and adoration. The idea of choosing David as his potential vice president had crossed his mind, simply because he knew that if (and it was the biggest "if" Cane had ever considered in regards to his political actions) the public knew that he and David Connally were on the same ticket, Cane was sure to have more votes, not to mention admiration and respect for his choice of candidate. Cane wanted all the good influence he could muster at this crucial point in time.

"Well, Jeff, what do you have for me?" Rick McCoy murmured. His assistant, Jefferson Dixon, walked across the room and laid a single sheet of paper on the desk. He tapped two fingers on it, his eyes wide and serious. McCoy looked up from where he sat in his chair, eyebrows raised.

"Sir, this is the statistics chart we've been running on each rally The American Party has held this year. Look," Mr. Dixon ran his finger down the list to the bottom of the page. "This was our first. See how low the numbers are?"

"They aren't that low," McCoy bristled, but Mr. Dixon gave him a skeptical look. "Moving on, anyhow," he cleared his throat. "Now see here..." He moved his finger all the way to the last set of digits at the top of the page. "These are the numbers from our last rally before the RNC, in Omaha."

"Right before everything went sour on us, eh?"

"Well," Mr. Dixon scratched his forehead. "Just look at the numbers, though, sir! They've risen by at least sixty percent. That

Connally fellow sure knows what he's doing."

"Does he," McCoy muttered thoughtfully, studying the chart with a furrowed brow. He let out a sigh. Even with the report he had given to the news to combat the lies from Aaron Wright, McCoy still wasn't certain what all to expect in the backlash that was sure to come. Suddenly the office phone rang. Both men straightened up and looked at the little green light flashing on the handset. Then Audrie's voice crackled over the intercom.

"Mr. McCoy, I have Joseph Cane on the line for you."

"Senator Joseph Cane?" McCoy and Dixon exchanged startled glances.

"Yes, sir. He seems very adamant about speaking to you."

"Well, I don't have a special grudge against him, so go ahead and put him through."

McCoy lifted the desk receiver to his ear. "Rick McCoy."

"Mr. McCoy, this is Joseph Cane."

"Senator, thank you for calling. What can I do for you?" McCoy stood up and gestured aimlessly at his desk. Mr. Dixon quickly began clearing off the papers.

"So how is life treating you, Mr. McCoy? Your party must be busy gearing up for the RNC."

McCoy's eyes narrowed. Small talk. The surest sign and maneuver of a politician who wants something.

"We're currently getting ready for a rally in Oklahoma City. It will take place right after the RNC closes with its final decision for presidential nominee."

"Excellent, excellent," Cane's voice sounded grasping, like he was hedging around the edges of what he really wanted to say. McCoy's lips twisted.

"Look, Senator, you and I are both men with little time on our hands and valuable business to take care of. So how about you and I stop playing pretend and have a serious discussion, preferably concerning why you called me to begin with."

Mr. Dixon, his head carefully turned away while he shuffled papers, played a brief smile.

After a moment of silence, Cane laughed shortly. "Very well,

238

Mr. McCoy, I apologize. The reason I called is because I would like to schedule a meeting with David Connally. A private meeting."

McCoy raised his head. "With David? And why is that?"

"I would like to talk with him and ask him some questions. A man as successful as he is in the public eye doesn't simply go unnoticed by me. And as I am actually running for president," he added emphatically, "I think I might, ahem, do well to learn a thing or two." He cleared his throat. "This isn't like a media interview, Mr. McCoy. It will be just the two of us."

"Three of us."

"I beg your pardon?"

McCoy realized he couldn't pace around his office because of the phone cord, and sank back into his chair. "If you want to have a meeting with David Connally, I will allow it on the stipulation that I will be present as well. I mean no disrespect, Senator Cane, but we don't even let David near reporters. I'm sure you will understand the necessity?"

"Ah, if that's what it takes for your stamp of approval, Mr. McCoy."

"That's what it takes, Senator Cane. But we don't want to inconvenience you during the RNC with only two days to go..."

"Oh, there's no trouble there. I can fly up from San Antonio to Oklahoma City tomorrow and be back before the nomination is brought to the floor."

"Alright," McCoy said slowly. "I'll need to talk to David and make sure he's OK with all of this, and if he says yes, we're on go. It's not about politics. None of this is about politics. Not with David. He measures it all up against what he believes, and that always wins. I'm not going to force him to agree, Senator. This will be his decision."

"Of course," Cane chuckled, though it sounded rather forced. "This is his say. But I appreciate you setting this up for me, Mr. McCoy. And I appreciate all the support you've given me politically."

"The American Party, as well as me personally, will always endorse the men we find to hold the same values as the men who founded this country, Senator. I'll call you back after I talk to David. Is there a special number where I can reach you?"

Twenty-four hours later, three men were standing in a hotel suite in Oklahoma City. The suite was large and luxurious, with a couple of couches and several chairs to sit on. Joseph Cane was the last to arrive, as McCoy had driven to David's room first to make sure they were ready before the senator got there. McCoy noticed that David didn't look very enthusiastic about the meeting, but guessed maybe he was tired. Jack's crew had been working extra hard lately in preparation for the upcoming rally that would surely be their biggest one yet, and David had put his shoulder to the wheel more tirelessly than anyone else. And perhaps he was feeling down about his friend's interview on the news, McCoy thought. Whatever it was, he wasn't going to pry.

When Cane arrived and shook both McCoy and David's hands, his gaze lingered longest on David, and David looked back at him with a firm politeness that brought almost a sense of a guilt on the senator's head. After all, their first and only encounter so far to date had been less than friendly. But Cane tried to shake off the feeling. He had business to take care of.

After the men exchanged greetings, they all sat down, David and McCoy sitting across from Cane. The senator was unfazed by this interrogation-sort of arrangement, however. He smoothed his necktie, leaned his elbows on the arms of his chair and folded his hands.

"Now, gentlemen, I'm here with the understanding that this meeting is just between us three?"

"Senator, I can assure you that nobody except the Blackheart Security team outside the door is privy to the fact that this meeting is taking place," McCoy promised.

Cane smiled. "Great. Now, may I lead?"

McCoy raised an eyebrow. "You arranged this meeting, Senator. Lead on."

Cane wasted no words. "If I am selected as the Republican Party's presidential candidate, will The American Party support and back my campaign?"

McCoy pushed his tongue against his teeth. He thought Cane

had wanted to talk to David.

"A number of us in the party have met and discussed this matter over the recent weeks. Considering there are really only two possible candidates from both of the main parties, we would certainly back you over any other candidate today if you win the nomination."

Cane looked satisfied but as he opened his mouth, McCoy continued, leaning forward over his knees as he spoke. "We do not agree with every part of the Republican platform, and we do not agree with the Republican Party as a whole. But, based upon how you will run your primary, and the things I know you personally stand for, Senator Cane, I believe that you can count on our support. But I don't make the final decision. The American Party will meet in one week to prepare a list of all the candidates, from presidential to dogcatcher, who deserves our backing, and we will work with those candidates after announcing our endorsement for them."

Cane nodded seriously, hesitating to attempt speaking again until he was sure McCoy was finished.

"And please remember, The American Party's platform does not share the views of the two-party system, or the way the government has now been run for the past few decades."

McCoy did not hesitate here and make a quick apology to Cane, like the senator almost expected him to, and tell him it was no slight on him, or anything of the kind. His voice was firm, not unkind, but simply matter-of-fact and truthful. Cane folded his hands, pulling in his lips and shifting his gaze down toward his fingers.

"We believe in states' rights, and a very small national government that answers to the people instead of trying to control and monitor their every decision, whether it's healthcare or choice of firearms. We believe in freedom of religion, and by that we mean the religion of Christ. We do not support tolerance of extremists, foreign or domestic, who get a say to push their crazy agendas just because they're radicals and supposedly misunderstood and victimized by those on the right. The American Party believes in freedom for all, welfare for only those who truly need it, and we certainly believe in the entirety of the Constitution of these United States and all

241

her amendments. What I'm trying to say here, Senator, is that my colleagues and I expect the people we back to hold these same views."

Cane felt suddenly as though he were treading on sensitive soil. The wrong answer given or even a misplaced word might knock down his plans for support now. He sucked in his breath.

"Well, Mr. McCoy, personally I know I can adhere to your party's platform," he said carefully. "But you must understand that I will have to run as a Republican candidate because of the way the two-party system is structured." He spread his hands pacifically.

McCoy deliberated in silence while Cane held his breath, folding his hands over his stomach as he leaned back in his chair.

"I suppose you can't run as an independent."

Cane forced out a short laugh. "I'm afraid not. I'm already well known for my standing in the Republican Party."

"Well then." McCoy drummed his fingers on the coffee table beside him. "I will take what you have just told me to The American Party leadership meeting next week. You can be sure to hear from us soon after."

Cane nodded his thanks, and the conversation fell into a lull as he considered how to broach the subject that he had really come to discuss. He kept eying David furtively during his conversation with McCoy, and saw the young man, instead of being abashed or nervous, was staring back at him with an unreadable gaze. Cane felt like David was reading his thoughts. The hair on the back of his neck prickled. Eyes narrowing, he tilted his head and turned toward David, placing one hand on the table.

"And what are your plans in all of this, Mr. Connally?" he asked loftily.

David straightened up. He seemed surprised at even being spoken to, let alone asked a question.

"Well, Senator, I apologize, but I'm not exactly sure why I'm even here." He glanced at McCoy, laughing at his own ignorance. Cane pursed his lips, waiting the few seconds until David grew serious. Their eyes met again.

"I'm not sure what you're asking, but I've given my word to Jack Webb that I'll work for him and his crew until Election Day," said David. "I have further given my word to Mr. McCoy here that I would help out the party, being very careful not to embarrass it or bring any reproach upon it with my past or present behavior–"

"Well, it seems that promise has been a bit harder to keep, doesn't it?" Cane cut in. McCoy gave him a warning look. Cane raised his hand, then placed his fingertips down on the arm of his chair. "I'm just saying that with all the news reports and stories being spread around by the media–"

"Senator Cane, you're a politician." McCoy's voice was icy. "You ought to know better than most how the media distorts and stretches the facts, let alone tells the truth. And when they do tell the truth, they make sure it's the worst secret they can dredge up. But no one, and I repeat, no one, has found one fact about David here that would make me reconsider keeping him as a member of our party."

Cane watched McCoy put a hand on David's shoulder when he spoke, and the senator suddenly felt he had overstepped the mark.

"I'm sorry, to both of you. I didn't mean...that's not what I wanted to say to you, David," he stammered foolishly.

David lifted his shoulders passively. "Like I said, Senator, I've been fortunate in both my livelihood and opportunities to help others over the past several months. I intend to continue doing those things I've mentioned until Election Day, or until The American Party has no more use for me."

McCoy smiled at the assurance in David's statement. Cane hitched his chair forward, speaking directly to David.

"I have been paying very close attention to you for the last few months, how you work with the audiences you speak to, watching you grow in popularity and the way you're obviously able to influence people," he began earnestly. "The things you're saying to them are both religious and ring like the making of sound government and prosperity of the country overall. You talk to people about being good neighbors as well as good citizens. You've said nothing I would be opposed to upholding, and your unique ability to communicate with the people is, well..." Here Cane couldn't resist a chuckle for lack of knowing what else to do, "...nothing short of amazing."

David's face flushed as always when somebody praised him

so highly. Cane now put both hands out in front of him, holding them up as if he were holding an invisible box between them and bouncing them a couple of times for emphasis.

"Nowhere, in all my studies of this country's history, have I seen or heard of a man who had a connection and charisma with the people like you do. You don't try to guard your words so you don't offend anyone. You're not trying to win votes or raise approval ratings. So why are you out there behind that microphone night after night? What drives you so intently to speak to the people?" Cane pressed the pad of one finger against his temple, his thumb just under his jaw as he waited for David's response.

The young man blinked a few times, his arms still folded across his chest like they had been since the opening of the meeting. Suddenly he too pushed his chair forward and held out his hands, palms up. His soft blue eyes lit up with a passionate gleam impossible to ignore.

"Senator," he said, his voice tremulous, "I just want to remind people not only of the greatness of America and how much greater she could be, but of also the power and providence of God. Through His will and blessings this country stands, and only by His grace will she continue on. But America cannot thrive as she might if the people turn away from God. This nation's motto says, 'In God We Trust.' People say it, but do they believe it?"

Cane felt himself mesmerized by David's heartfelt words. At the same time, a voice inside him screamed, *how does he do it?*

"And Senator," David went on, emboldened, "I notice in your speeches you often say, 'Here is what I'm going to do for you.'"

Cane inclined his head. "That's right."

"But shouldn't it be more like, we need to tell the people how great they are, and move out of their way so they can prove the wonderful things they're capable of without the extra help from the government? Prosperity abounds and the economy thrives when people are allowed to work for themselves."

Cane drew back, his gaze sharpened. "Are you telling me how I should speak to my constituents and behave in office, Mr. Connally?"

CHAPTER 10:

"Not at all, sir. I just think it's something worth thinking about."

"Spoken like a true patriot." McCoy couldn't tell if Cane's words were sarcastic or sincere. "I'm certainly not the one calling the shots, but if the people had their way, you might just find your name being put forward for public office, perhaps even..." Cane pretended to study his nails. "...the presidency itself."

David's expression was oddly reminiscent of someone who had ice water dropped down their back. "Um, Senator," he stammered, lifting himself up by pressing his hand against the arm of the chair, and rubbing his hairline distractedly. "I can assure you that I'm not a candidate for the presidency, or any public office, for that matter. I'm only serving the people, in my own small way, and in the best way I know how."

Cane knew he meant it, and figured now was the time to tender the question he had been turning over in his mind for the past weeks. He gripped the chair arms as if he was about to rise from his seat.

"Mr. Connally, what if I were to ask you to serve this country and its people by taking your place at my right hand as my vice presidential candidate?"

McCoy half-rose from his chair, his previously contemplative smile frozen on his face. Cane folded his hands and leaned his elbows on the table, watching only David. David's blue eyes grew wider than before. His mouth half open, he started to lean forward, then fell back, his stare hopping between Cane and McCoy. Then slowly, a stunned smile spread over his face as if he were just comprehending a joke. Pulling one hand back through his hair and down the back of his neck, he flipped the other aimlessly in Cane's direction.

"I'm flattered you would consider me for such a role, Senator," he said with an amused glint. "But like I said before, I'm neither currently, nor do I have intentions of, running for any sort of government office. Surely," he added with a laugh, "you aren't serious."

"Oh, but I am. Very much so." Cane pushed his chair back and stood up, moving to stand behind it and holding the back of it for support with one hand, putting the other on his hip. "You have something special, Mr. Connally. I think you would make a wonderful asset to my team. I mean..." He laughed, and waved his arm in the direction of the window. "Look at what you can do already? But imagine what you could do with sponsors and an entire campaign team behind you. Think of the audiences that you'll reach, not just nationwide, but worldwide! If you want to make a difference and serve people like you say you do, Mr. Connally, I'm offering you an even bigger chance to continue doing just that, but on a global scale."

McCoy watched the mirth and shock fade off David's face as they were replaced with wonder and contemplation. He looked like he was actually seriously considering Cane's proposal. McCoy looked at the senator and saw his eyes glowing with expectation. McCoy was familiar enough with politicians and Joseph Cane himself to guess what was really going on. Cane wanted David not so much so that David could have an opportunity to continue inspiring and encouraging Americans, but to bring more attention and influence for himself. McCoy thought it a rather desperate ploy, seeing as Cane knew anything of David's past, or even if he was an American citizen.

McCoy felt like nudging David in the ribs to warn him, though he also knew David wouldn't rush into something like this. But he couldn't help speaking up.

"David's a good man. He's proven to all of us that he loves God and loves this country. I know he'll do everything he can to help change America and turn her back from going down the road of corrupt government and immorality, and make this nation what God and the Founding Fathers intended for us."

Clearly embarrassed, David raised his eyes to Cane's.

"I thank you again for your interest, senator." His resolve was firm. "But I'll have to say no to your proposition. I'm sorry."

Cane felt a stiffness crawl up his spine. Drawing up his mouth, he swallowed hard once, and then pushed a smile across his face that seemed more like a pained smirk.

"Well, now we know where we all stand," he said, his voice wooden. He cleared his throat and put on a softer expression as he bowed his head toward McCoy. "I appreciate your frankness on this issue. It is my hope that after the convention and The American Party's meeting that we will all be able to work together in harmony to bring America back to an ideal state."

McCoy nodded his head in respectful response, and David raised his eyes toward the senator's face once more before casting them down again. All three of them rose, the meeting concluded now that Cane had received his answer. He politely shook hands with both McCoy and David, then after lingering for a moment, released David's hand and scrutinized him again.

"I hope you men know that there are people in high places who have set in motion plans to ruin not only your reputation, Mr. Connally, but those of The American Party and its influence upon the election this fall."

"We are aware," McCoy answered calmly. "But that isn't anything new. Mud-slingers and evil-doers will always try to make themselves heard when truth and morality threaten them."

Cane was unconvinced, and shook his head. "They're afraid of what you mean to do: change the way things are now. There are some people who are willing to do whatever it takes to destroy you two and what you stand for. What I'm trying to say is just be careful. Especially you, Mr. Connally," he added with an emphatic nod toward the young man. "Every lie that can be told about you, they will tell. All of the money and power belonging to the corrupt holding office is at stake, and they will use it to your bitterest end and ultimately the end of The American Party and America as we know it. They'll manipulate this government they currently control in ways you haven't even seen."

McCoy and David stood in silence while Cane picked up his brown Fedora by the taper and settled it down over his eyebrows, pushing it back on his head.

"These next four months will be critical for all of us," he finished dourly.

"Come now, Senator Cane," McCoy smiled. "I know you have more self-confidence than that. We'll weather any storms that come, and by the grace of God, we'll turn some things around in government come this fall!"

Cane rubbed the bridge of his nose, smiled briefly, then nodded and wished them both a good day. As he walked out of the hotel suite, past the Blackheart guards at the door and out into the lobby where his own security team was waiting in civilian dress to escort him to his car, Cane replayed David's reactions and words from the meeting. His mind was in a snarl. Just who was this guy, that he, with all his sudden fame and impact, would turn down an offer of the vice presidency, when he so obviously could do so much more in that role? Who would do something like that? What was Connally thinking? What went on behind that calm face that nobody had yet found an image of in a single high school yearbook, online account or link, college, prison, bank, or employment record?

"He must have some kind of neural inhibition or something," he muttered as he slid into the plush leather seat of the car waiting to drive him back to the airport. He pressed his head back against the headrest and rolled his shoulders. "What makes a person of total obscurity pass up the chance of a lifetime?"

↑ CHAPTER 11:

The RNC closed out with a bang, Joseph Cane having taken the Republican nomination for president in a landslide. His acceptance speech was gracious and full of eager ambition to take over Washington, and his words were powerful enough that the applause didn't die down for several minutes after he left the platform. Cane was almost giddy with elation. Though he still felt the sting of David's rejection of the position as his running mate, he felt good about his chances. But the bitterness in his heart was still just dark enough for him to rear back his head with pride and arrogance in his eyes. So Connally thought himself above running for vice presidency under Cane? Well, thought Cane brusquely, if Connally wouldn't help him, he would pave his own way to the White House, and let that nobody in jeans and the strange accent go on trying to reach the masses on the small scale. It wouldn't matter after he, Cane, became President anyway. Once he began making the necessary changes in government that America so desperately needed, once he took care of what he felt needed to be done, David Connally would surely fade back into the obscurity whence he came. There would be no more need for him and his eloquent words about the greatness of America and her people, for Cane would be the one putting the words into action. The people wouldn't have to look to David Connally for hope any longer. Cane would realize that hope for them himself.

He had chosen a strongly conservative man by the name of William Stuart to be his running mate. Stuart's values were accepted by The American Party, which had their meeting in accordance with what McCoy had told Cane. The American Party leadership had been impressed enough with Cane's credentials and beliefs, as well as with his speeches and his choice of running mate, and had given Rick McCoy the go-ahead to inform the senator they would back him in his campaign for presidency. So in this way, Cane became not only the presidential candidate for the Republican Party, but also the official candidate for The American Party.

It wasn't two weeks before the Democratic presidential campaign began a full-scale attack on both Joseph Cane and David Connally. Half-truths and complete lies alike were spread around like wildfire on the news and the internet with the single intention of destroying the reputations of both men. It seemed some on the left blamed David personally for Cane's success thus far, and were intent on ripping him to shreds. The highest and lowest levels of degradation were reached. Women came forward declaring they had been assaulted by David in the past, or that he had treated them in a shameful way just because of their skin color. He was labeled a racist, and a religious bigot. Language experts gave interviews saying things like, "Connally doesn't even sound American. There's no evidence of any birth records to date, and he could be from Australia for all we know. And people are starting to root for this guy to run for some kind of public office. He's probably not even an American."

Cane was dragged through the mud by having his name thrown into similar situations, discounting the solid proof that he was born in America, however. Their enemies pulled out all the stops, doing their utmost to not only discredit the Republican nominees and David Connally, but The American Party's popularity among the people as well.

Rick McCoy was up to his ears handling the onslaught of the media and the press, which were of both public and private nature. He and Mr. Farris gave a handful of interviews to combat the lies being hurled and debated whether or not to let the media behind the scenes just to prove false the accusations about immorality going on after hours. McCoy even seriously considered letting David speak for himself and actually go on the air refuting the black lies told about him, but then he took pause. David's best defense now was to keep on speaking to the people; if he publicly tried to defend himself against the lies, he would only draw more attention to that negativity and perhaps even raise suspicions that he was trying to get out of something. McCoy decided to just do his best to protect David by keeping him away from the media and other news outlets, but let him continue to encourage and give heart to the crowds. Thousands of people still continued to show up at their rallies, the loyalty and enthusiasm of many patriots and those strong-minded enough to discard the lies were undimmed by the deceitful slander.

It was hard though, for their numbers did drop some, and McCoy had to grit his teeth more than once over an interview he watched with a person who claimed to have been very impressed with David Connally's speeches and had looked up to him until he heard about some scandal he had been involved in. He also had to endure reporters who blithely asked questions regarding complete lies told about David. Fortunately, that sort of occurrence was not very frequent. What was very encouraging was hearing the statements several people gave on TV who still believed in David and the good things he stood for, and that all the muckrakers needed to give up and stop deceiving everyone just to give corruption a more prominent seat in government.

Jack struggled more with all the smear campaigning than he let on. It hurt him to see David being dragged through such a mess just because he was trying to do and say what was right. Ever since their conversation about Ryan, Jack looked on David more and more as the son he had lost. A dig at David felt like a dig in Jack's heart.

When the Fourth of July rolled around, it was only four months from Election Day. Work was underway in St. Louis, Missouri, where McCoy had made arrangements for what The American Party anticipated to be their largest rally yet at the St. Louis Cardinals' Stadium. The American Party had taken on more staff over the past months, and as their organization grew, their fame continued to flourish with them. With the holiday coming up in July, McCoy figured it would only be fitting for their party to hold a rally on Independence day. People would be coming from all over the country to be a part of this national birthday celebration, to hear David Connally's words live, and join in what would virtually be the kick-off to the events in November.

↑THE SPEAKER

As The American Party took on more people and more followers, donations also began pouring in as well. Jack was able to get better trucks for carrying their equipment around, and they had obtained a motor home strictly for David's personal use so he could stay with the group instead of having to find a hotel off-site. This also made it easier for Eli and his Blackheart guards to keep an eye on him. At first David had protested for being given an entire motor home for only himself.

"It really isn't necessary," he told Mr. Farris when The American Party manager gave him the news. "I don't need all this space. At least let...I don't know...James can share it with me."

James Rivers and David had grown close during the weeks since James had come to work with them, or rather pretend to work with them. James tried by subtle conversation to draw something out of David regarding his past, and scrutinized him for character flaws as often as possible without seeming to pry, all the while disguising his info-mining as friendly conversations. But David stumped him. James even tried checking him online, but only found such news and data about him as was posted by others after he seemingly sprang into existence back in February. It was frustrating to have so little to report to Dominic York over their secret calls, but James still made every effort to be friendly and warm to David. David told him that, especially after Aaron left, it was nice to have another younger person around to talk with. So maybe it was no wonder David suggested the two of them share his new motor home since he didn't want it all to himself.

But Mr. Farris shook his head. "No, David, this is just for you. Believe me, we're all happy to have you staying in among us instead of having to be away in some hotel. It's covered in the budget, so please," and he put his hand on David's shoulder. "Just accept it and make yourself at home. Blackheart will be outside the door whenever you're inside, if you need anything."

David bowed his head as he took the key dangling from Mr. Farris' hand. "Thank you," he said quietly. But as he turned to look at what was to be his new home, a smile spread across his face.

Now, with everybody busy preparing for the special

Independence Day rally in the Cardinals' Stadium, James Rivers had barely a moment to spare for a phone call to York, Jack had barely a moment to spend in a quiet conversation with David, and Mr. Farris had barely a moment when his cell phone wasn't glued to his ear. Satellite trucks were parked as far as a mile away from the stadium, doing their best to cover the approaching events of the evening. Every parking lot within the radius of five blocks was near overflowing with the massive number of cars and people who had traveled from states far away to participate in this national holiday event. Senator Cane was scheduled to be present as the newly elected Republican presidential candidate, so between his own surveillance team and Blackheart, security was even tighter than usual, if that was possible.

But despite the whirlwind of activity and added security measures taken, David Connally remained at the center of it all with the calm tranquility of the eye of a storm. The Fourth fell on a Sunday this year, and Eli knew before David mentioned it to him that he would have to arrange for David to be privately escorted away from the rally site and delivered to church. This had been David's custom ever since Eli had arrived, to go to worship every Sunday morning, no matter where The American Party was currently stationed, even if the closest congregation was half an hour to an hour away. David and Eli had worked out a system where David would select the location for the church online beforehand and inform Eli. Eli loaded the map into the GPS of his unmarked SUV with tinted windows and had the vehicle ready for David in the morning to whisk him away with only Mr. Farris and Jack privy to the knowledge of his departure. Customarily, Eli dropped him off at the church building along with a few members of his security team in plain clothes to stand near every means of entrance to the building while remaining as inconspicuous as possible.

David spent every Sunday morning in this way. He also never stopped asking Eli to come worship with him, but each time Eli steadfastly declined. He always looked troubled when David extended the invitation to him, but continued to say no. David had begun asking Jack to come with him as well, but Jack, although wanting to spend time with David, hadn't set foot inside a church building since Ryan's death. He felt his faith was depleted, and somehow the idea of walking into the house of God was a rather daunting one to him. He wasn't sure yet if he was ready to try "making up" with God, as he put it. *Not that He'll probably be listening to me anyway. It's been a long time.*

In Philadelphia, the Democrat Party was hosting a Fourth of July rally as well, but to most it was evident that it was more of a counter to David and his rally startups than anything else. Many officials including the presidential candidate, Helen Kennedy, were scheduled to deliver speeches at the rally, which took place at Lincoln's Financial Field, stadium to the Philadelphia Eagles. A number of popular artists had been brought in to entertain the crowd by singing and rapping. The first song was a strange, pop version of The Star-Spangled Banner, but with every strain after it seemed like there was a contest among the performers to see who could come up with the most degrading rap about the Republicans, The American Party, Joseph Cane, or David Connally. All of them lacked good taste, and some were very vulgar.

At the Omni Majestic hotel several blocks away, a meeting was held earlier before the opening of the rally. Those in attendance included Dominic York, Helen Kennedy with both her husband and her campaign manager, John Locus, and a sum of other Democrat candidates for various offices. As usual, the focus of this kind of meeting was to see what could be done to undermine the reputations and efforts of their opponents.

Senator Kennedy stood up, facing the head of the table with a tight-lipped smile that held no trace of real humor. Her icy blue eyes arrowed straight at Dominic York.

"Well, Mr. Chairman, it seems that, in spite of your tireless efforts to put an end to the success of The American Party and David Connally, we are still facing major competition from them. Their numbers have scarcely changed at all! I had the impression you had this under control," she practically hissed at York. Her puffy, hard hands splayed out on the table top. "But evidently this is beyond what

– no, this is *beyond* beyond what we could never comprehend would happen. Why can we not put them under? What are we missing?"

York, ever serene, had begun to look ever so slightly more frazzled than usual these past few weeks. His eyes were more shadowed and his body seemed restless, as if trying to keep pace with the torrent of activity within his brain. Also, if anything, he was also far more irascible than normal.

"Senator, you're too hasty with your accusations." His words were terse and stern, with no flattery in them. Pinching the bridge of his nose, he squeezed his eyes closed for a moment, forcing back a rush of irritation. Hadn't he been doing everything he could think of to stop The American Party? Hadn't he forked over twelve million to those subpar mystery crooks for the sole purpose of ripping Connally and that infuriatingly confounding grassroots party to pieces? Hadn't he told every lie and supposedly dredged-up every secret that he could imagine to drag Connally's name through the mud? Hadn't he hired reporters, bribed officials, enlisted a spy, paid women to come forward making false claims against Connally? And wasn't he in the midst of bringing a private investigator into the mix as well? It was little wonder York felt Helen Kennedy's words were unjustified.

"I would like to assure everyone," he paused to look stridently in Kennedy's direction, "that everything possible is being done to ensure the downfall of Connally, Cane, and The American Party." He heaved out a heavy exhale, scratching the dark stubble just visible along his jawline.

Senator Kennedy folded her arms and leaned back in her chair, unimpressed, but quiet. A moody frown tugged at her lips, giving her a sinister appearance.

"I have spent tireless efforts and time on dealing with these problems," York defended himself, but also in a manner that suggested he wanted all to take notice of his indefatigable endeavors. "I can assure everyone here that I also have others working beside me in this course of action. So those who aren't doing much of anything to directly aid in putting the work of our enemies to a stop–" Here York again sent an arrowed glance toward where Senator Kennedy's seat was. "–I suggest you place your faith in me and trust me to do my best in this situation, with what I have."

As his gaze snaked down the table and around those seated there, several people shifted in their chairs, discomfort written plainly on their faces under that cold, lifeless stare that nevertheless carried a simmering menace beneath.

"I want to remind all the Democratic candidates and party members in general present that one of the things you can do to help in this case is to, as often and publicly as possible, point out to our electorate the shortcomings and flaws of The American Party and its members and candidates. Don't leave out the problems of their policies and standpoints, either."

"I'm sure I don't need to portend how crucial these times are for all of us," York went on, arching his hand, fingertips pressing into the tabletop. "We're living in a historic moment, and instead of getting to bask in it, we're fighting against the likes of some old-fashioned conservatives who think they can merge the old and new together and make ancient ideas flow with the changing times." York slowly stood up, his fingers now forming a fist that he raised up near his face. "But we're here to show the country that 'out with the old' is exactly what everyone needs. It's time to lay aside ideals formed by some men who lived hundreds of years ago who lived in a different world than we do now." His voice rose. "And we will prove people like David Connally wrong...this country doesn't need history lessons or religious romanticism thrown in her face. This country..." York's voice faltered, dropping his hand at his side as if suddenly weary. He bowed his head for a moment before raising his eyes to zone in down the length of the table. "This country needs a government that will take care of every need of its people, digitally monitor them closely so we can keep a tighter watch for any potential threats, and allow them to create their own definitions of ways of life as most satisfies them. It is absolutely essential," he went on, stabbing one finger into the air, "that we retain control in November. It is fundamental, in every speech or snippet of conversation, that the people understand when our party is re-elected, any and everything they want, we will give them. We want them to know that we, the party of the people, will be their own proverbial Robin Hood." York smirked, and a few people snickered appreciatively. "We are," and York paused again, knitting his brows, then smoothing out his forehead again, and lifted both hands as if explaining a simple statement, "the party of the people."

A murmur of concurrence rippled down the table. York slowly straightened up, dragging his hands back along the tabletop. Suddenly, Daniel White scurried into the room. He looked like he had run all the way from York's office in D.C., he was so winded. Heads turned toward him when he crossed the threshold, but he was looking only at Dominic York.

"Sir, I think you need to turn on the TV," he said breathlessly. He seemed both excited and scared, his eyes wide and restless. York raised an eyebrow, but reached for the compact remote and switched on the flat screen at the other end of the room. All those present craned their necks to see.

"Channel 8," Daniel muttered. York threw him a look before complying.

The channel belonged to the news station carrying almost exclusive live coverage of the rally in St. Louis, which was already gaining momentum as it got underway. The cameras were now focusing in on the stage, where David Connally was striding across it toward the microphone at the center, smiling broadly and waving to the thousands of cheering people like he couldn't find a better way to enjoy himself. As he took hold of the mic, grinning from ear to ear, he waved once more before calling out, "Are you all ready to sing 'God Bless America' with me today?" His reply was an eruption of applause and more jubilant ovation, and he grinned as he began singing the patriot song. Within seconds the entire crowd was singing along with him. The sound was deafening.

York rolled his eyes, his arms folded. "Why are we watching this?" he hissed at his assistant. Daniel bit his lips. "Just..." his eyes never left the screen, one arm outspread toward York in a plea to listen. "Just wait for it," he breathed. "Wait for the camera to change."

York groaned under his breath, but shifted his feet and waited. A few moments more, and another angle showed a view of the audience from behind David, looking out across the crowd over the young man's shoulder.

"There! See that?" Daniel exclaimed, pointing wildly at the audience.

York slowly moved around the table and edged toward the screen, widening his eyes as if to dispel the sudden scene before him. An unpleasant sensation roiled in his stomach as he realized what his assistant was talking about. Behind him, he heard Senator Kennedy's sharp intake of breath.

As the crowd sang, there were no fewer than two to three hundred signs being joyfully waved throughout the assembly that clearly said, "David For President!"

York knew he would be lying to himself if he tried now to dismiss this clarion harbinger as nothing more than a fluke. He could feel his hands clenching into fists, and realized his jaw was beginning to ache from how hard he was unconsciously grinding his teeth together. This was getting out of hand.

Helen Kennedy threw up her hands.

"Am I now running against two different candidates from two different parties?" she demanded furiously. "I want answers, York!"

"Yeah, is this going to be a three-party race?" John Locus asked, worry etching a scowl between his eyes.

York turned around and tossed the remote at, rather than to, his assistant. "Change the channel. Now." His voice was deadly. Daniel quickly switched to the news station covering the preparations for the Democrat rally in Philadelphia. Even with the buzz of uncertainty and anger flowing around him, York walked back to his chair in silence. When he came parallel with it, he stood still, placing one hand on its back. Drumming his fingers, he slowly turned around to face everyone. They looked back at him, waiting.

"Those signs didn't mean anything," he said curtly. "That's just the work of some infatuated, ignorant people who have been duped by the right wing into thinking they know what's best for themselves. Forget it." He waved his hand dismissively, as if brushing away a tiresome idea. "I told you already what we must do, which

258

is to remind people that we are the party who will stand by and uphold their freedom of choice, and defend their right to practice whatever lifestyle that suits them best. We will praise and encourage them for their courage to choose a life of homosexuality, and try to open doors for them so they don't have to be afraid of discrimination and prejudice. Everyone receives equal benefits under the law, and any alien in this country can have a right to vote, education, and citizenship." York put his hands behind his back and shrugged. "Could it be simpler? We appeal to the people with what they want, and provide the means of giving it to them by winning their votes. We accommodate the minorities. Have the government provide welfare for the needy. When you give people what they want, they will follow you anywhere," he finished triumphantly, a smile curling his thin lips.

"You leave the situation up to me. I'll sort everything out."

"Ed, are you seeing this?"

Edward Martin stood clenching his hat in his hands, his gaze fixed moodily on the spectacle before him. "I see it," he muttered, taking in the sight of the hundreds of signs waving that proudly read "David for President" on them. His brow furrowed, making him look like an angry mouse. Then he turned and strode past the man on his right.

"Get me Rick McCoy on the phone."

Joseph Cane had also not missed the unmistakable hopes for David to take political office. The very one Cane was after himself. The senator was in fumes. It was all his wife could do to calm him down.

"What did I do wrong?" he fretted feverishly. He paced back and forth in their backstage room. "I'm supposed to go on in thirty minutes, and somehow I get the distinct feeling that whatever I do or say isn't going to be half as much appreciated as Connally."

"Maybe you could sing a song for them?" Cassie Cane suggested with the slightest edge in her gentle voice. She had been through this kind of conversation with her husband so many times and was growing weary of it.

He frowned at her, then his eyes widened and he put a hand to his forehead, sinking into a chair.

"I won the Republican nomination for president, for crying out loud," he muttered, kneading his scalp. "But I've never gotten the same kind of ovation or popularity as that man. And how am I supposed to win the election without that?"

His wife came to him and put her hand on his shoulder.

"I think you need to focus more on the people themselves than on yourself, dear," she said gently. "This country has been suffering through some pretty sad leadership over the past several years, and she needs somebody who will stop putting the government first and put her people first instead." She stroked his hair. "If you are truly willing to do that, Joseph, the people will see that in you, and they will rally around you."

Joseph looked up at her, then shifted his gaze toward the door through which again seeped the sound of applause for David onstage. Cassie saw his forehead wrinkle again, and took his hand in both of hers.

"Will you do something for me? Don't think about David Connally at all when you go out there." She smiled. "And don't think about yourself either. You just think about this country. Make your words count so that everyone will see what a wonderful leader you will make as their president. Show them how much I know you care about this country, and don't allow yourself to be clouded by vanity. You won their vote for the presidential nominee. Now show them you deserve their respect."

Cane's eyes slowly softened. His fingers closed around his wife's hands.

"I love you, Cass," he said with a sigh. "But I can't imagine why you married me."

"Well, some girl had to make sure you kept your head and stayed the course," she said with a teasing grin. She kissed his cheek and then laid her hand there.

"Honey, even if you weren't to become president, I want you to know that I'll always be proud of you and always love you," she said seriously. "And doesn't that count for something?"

"Of course it does," he said, drawing her against him. As they embraced, he tried to shove the troublesome thoughts away from his mind, knowing his wife was right. But as they broke apart, he took hold of her shoulders and said firmly, "When I'm finished tonight, I need to meet with Rick McCoy as soon as possible. Will you get him on the phone for me the minute I come offstage?"

"Alright, Joseph. But remember," and she held up one finger, "no matter what you say, your true character will always shine through. Just be sure that what you want is what's truly best, not just to satisfy your personal pride."

The rally in St. Louis had come to a close, with wild success in The American Party's wake. Rick McCoy couldn't be more thrilled, but he had little time to enjoy the smell of the roses. Before the rally was three quarters of the way finished, he had had two separate phone calls from two very important men who both seemed very emphatic about speaking with him right away. Knowing what these men were like, and having an idea of what they had on their minds (McCoy had seen the "David" signs as well as anybody), the chairman of The American Party was not looking forward to the inevitable meeting.

Deciding it was best to just get it over with, McCoy summoned both men to his hotel room that evening. Upon arrival, Edward Martin wasted no time getting to the point.

"Mr. McCoy, I fail to see why people are allowed to bring those signs into the rally," he said, clearly irritated. His nostrils flared indignantly, and he didn't take the seat McCoy offered him. "Just what is The American Party trying to do, secretly push another candidate? I thought you were behind Senator Cane one hundred percent with full support!" He shook his finger in McCoy's face. "Are you now telling me that David Connally is also running for president? Is this your, your underhanded way of-" He couldn't seem to stop sputtering. The veins in his neck were standing out.

McCoy raised his hands, trying to placate and appease. "Look, Mr. Martin, let me first reassure you that this is one of maybe two times that signs like these have been spotted at one of our rallies.

We aren't trying to run David Connally for president or any kind of office. Think of him like...like a mascot of sorts, if you will."

Edward Martin tightened his mouth. A sheen of sweat glistened on his broad forehead. He searched McCoy's eyes for a long moment, as if trying to find a trace of untruth there. When McCoy didn't blink, Martin's shoulders drooped and he sat down beside Joseph Cane, who hadn't said a word since their greeting at the door. Martin seemed to be making his speech for him. The two of them exchanged looks.

"Well, I believe you then," Martin mumbled, pulling out a large handkerchief and dabbing his forehead wearily. "But you can't just allow this kind of thing to happen, Mr. McCoy. This kind of stuff pulls people in the opposite direction of where we're trying to lead them. If David Connally isn't any kind of candidate, he needs to maintain a lower profile. That means no signs. Is that clear?"

"David Connally has made it clear to you, I believe, Senator Cane," McCoy said, switching his focus to Cane, "that he isn't seeking any office."

Cane nodded.

"But we, The American Party, are certainly not going to restrict the people's freedom of speech," McCoy continued, giving Martin a hard look. "And that includes the use of these signs."

Martin turned red, and his small eyes narrowed. "Well then," he said stiffly, "you need to tell David to make it perfectly clear to the audience that he is not a candidate, nor will he be a candidate, and that Joseph Cane is the one everyone should be putting their support behind." Martin clapped his hand on Cane's shoulder, his eyes holding a warning as he waited for McCoy's response.

McCoy stood with his chin tucked and his arms crossed over his chest, deliberating.

"I both appreciate and understand your concern," he said quietly. Martin raised his eyebrows, holding out one hand toward McCoy, asking a silent question.

"I'll speak with David and request that he somehow communicates to the people that he isn't running for president," said McCoy.

"Good." Martin rose, and Cane followed suit. "But you won't mention what passed between us here?"

"Of course not. I'm on your side of the matter. Neither of us wants any emphasis to be taken away from our candidate," McCoy said, giving Cane a small smile.

"True, true!" Martin exclaimed, his good humor beginning to return now that the threat he feared promised to be dispelled. He shook hands with McCoy, as did Cane, and McCoy let them both out.

"Do we still have any idea who this guy even is?" Martin nudged Cane as they walked down the hotel hallway. The senator shook his head.

"They've got to have dozens of reporters and journalists out there searching for his history," he answered. "Somebody's bound to dredge up something before long. I just hope it doesn't have any bearing whatsoever on my campaign."

"It won't." Martin promised firmly. "It won't."

Dominic York sat alone in his office, fiddling with a small white card in his hand. Outside, the late afternoon sun warmed through the windowpanes, casting a glow over the room and causing dust particles to shimmer in the air. But York kept his eyes down, focused on the card. After a minute, he reached for the phone on his desk and dialed a number.

"Hello, yes, this is Dominic York. I sent you an email last week regarding...yes, that's correct. I was wondering how soon you might be able to...oh, well then, I'll be expecting you here?" York's eyebrows suddenly rose in confusion at the shortness of the reply. "Alright then. That may work much better, actually. The less you and I are seen together, the better." He chuckled dryly. "But I trust you to keep me updated with any and all information you find, is that understood?"

"That's what you're paying me for, isn't it?" replied the deliberately slow, cool voice.

York let out another short chuckle.

"I think you are just the man I need, Hicks," he said. "And I expect you'll get started right away? Excellent. We do sort of have a deadline."

When York hung up, he exhaled heavily, feeling more at ease now that he had another undercover agent working behind the scenes. On impulse he picked up the phone again and dialed a number from memory.

"Yes, it's me, and you can stop making that poisonous face when I tell you my news," he said in one breath, holding the phone to his ear with his shoulder while pouring himself some ice water from the decanter on the table beside the desk.

"What is it?" Helen Kennedy's voice was icy.

"I now officially have a private investigator on Connally's trail. And let me tell you, this guy's a bloodhound. He'll track down anything, and he's absolutely relentless. I know we're getting the best for what we're paying him."

"Oh, really? Kind of like those enigmas you hired to ruin Connally and The American Party? Because if you have the same kind of faith in this guy as you do in them, I may actually start worrying about your mental health, Dominic."

York gritted his teeth, sloshing some of the water out of his glass.

"Careful, Senator," he said heatedly. "Remember who you're talking to. I have more power than you currently do, and we're going to have to work together to take control in November, or neither of us wins. You need me. So let's be a little more civilized and respectful, shall we?"

Silence for several long seconds. If he wasn't sure that she was completely aware of the truth behind his every word, he would have assumed she had hung up.

"So this P.I...has he already started working?"

"As of a few minutes ago. If there's anything to find out about this unknowable David Connally, I am going to know it."

"Jeff, will you come in here, please?"

Jeff Dixon swiped closed the window on his iPad and strode into Rick McCoy's office with the tablet in his hand. "Yes, sir?"

CHAPTER 11:

McCoy looked up from his computer. "Do we have any new publicity updates from last Tuesday?"

Mr. Dixon's eyes narrowed in thought as he walked toward McCoy's desk. "The rally in St. Louis? We received quite a response, remember? Joseph Cane's rating went up by nine percent just after that one day." Mr. Dixon brought up another tab on his iPad and traced his finger down the screen. "Cane also took the URL domain for his campaign site. He's getting on up there, sir. He and Helen Kennedy are almost tied neck and neck now."

McCoy had folded his hands, leaning his elbows on the desk, his mouth pressing against his fingers as he nodded slowly in response to Mr. Dixon's report. "Good, but not good enough. Let's hope we can get enough publicity and support drummed up for him so he'll be above Kennedy in the approval ratings."

Mr. Dixon nodded seriously, his eyes flitting between McCoy and the screen in his hands. "Aren't they supposed to release that report this morning about the rally in Bristol last night?" he asked suddenly, as if only just remembering.

"I'm waiting for it now." McCoy pointed to the TV screen on the wall across the room behind his assistant. Mr. Dixon turned halfway around to look at the changing images onscreen. "It's supposed to air at ten."

"Well, that gives us a few minutes then," Mr. Dixon replied, glancing at his watch before taking a seat to the side of McCoy's desk. McCoy studied his relaxed posture for a few seconds, rubbing a hand over his chin.

"So, Jeff," he said. Mr. Dixon looked up expectantly. "What do you think of David?"

"Connally?" Mr. Dixon raised his eyebrows. He shifted in his chair, crossing one ankle over the opposite knee and pulling his shoulders back. "Well, I'd say he certainly has a talent for winning audiences. He claims to not be much of an orator, but his vocabulary and speaking skills, though maybe leaving a little to be desired, seem to imply the opposite. He's one of the most patriotic men I've ever heard publicly, but we still don't know his nationality, and that accent especially." Mr. Dixon shook his head. "No, it's not a bad thing, but he sounds more House of Parliament than House of Congress, if you know what I mean."

McCoy drummed his fingers on the desktop. "Well, it doesn't seem to matter much to the people. You heard about the signs."

"Yes. Have you spoken to him yet?"

"No." McCoy massaged his forehead, letting his eyes slide shut. "I don't even know how you go about telling somebody what Edward Martin wants me to tell David." He opened his eyes, waving his hand flippantly. "Hey, David, I think you need to tone down all the nationalistic passion so you don't draw too much attention to yourself. And oh, while you're up there before thousands of people, I need you to somehow work into your songs and patriotic speeches that you are definitely not running for president so we don't scare our candidates and the Republicans."

Mr. Dixon bowed his head, sighing as McCoy finished his frustrated ranting.

"Well, there are also all those stories and accusations against Connally as well. It's hard to wave those away when we don't know much about him. Have you heard anything more from Nathan Blaine lately?"

"He's supposed to report back when he finds anything," McCoy answered tiredly. "But I haven't heard from him for a few days. I hope that just means he's still digging. If I know Nathan, he won't give up." He looked down at his hand resting on the desk and slowly raised it at the wrist before thumping it back down. "It just irks me that Martin would actually ask me to have David 'tone it down', or something, and convey he isn't running for...I mean, it's not like he's even said anything in his speeches about wanting any kind of political support for himself."

Mr. Dixon leaned forward, balancing his iPad on his knee.

"Sir, I know it seems like an odd request for Martin to make, but you can surely understand where he's coming from. He's doing everything to back and build up his presidential nominee. Cane is a safe candidate, and he's well established. Connally is an unknown, a dark horse, if you will, though I know he isn't running. And yet the people love him. In Martin's mind, Connally represents a very potential threat."

"Well, he shouldn't at all, because we're supposed to be on the same side," McCoy returned hotly. He pulled a hand down his face and looked at Mr. Dixon. "Sad, isn't it, that we're the United States of America, and yet we're divided into all these political factions."

"Political correctness will be the death of us, eventually," Mr. Dixon answered soberly.

"You got that right. When man starts caring more about not offending other men than what God thinks about his decisions, you know we're in trouble."

"Breaking News this morning: David Connally continues to bring record numbers to rallies of The American Party," a clear, professional voice carried into the momentary lull in the room, and McCoy quickly turned up the TV volume. He and Mr. Dixon stood up and moved closer to the screen.

"We're going to Joann Walker at the Bristol Motor Speedway in Bristol, Tennessee, where the latest American Party rally was held last night," the announcer went on airily. The camera cut to a shot of the now familiar woman with the sweet, angular face and rolls of long blond hair. She stood at the starting line on the track of the speedway when she began her report.

"Good morning to all of you in New York!" Her voice was as light and breezy as the weather itself. "It's pretty early here at the Speedway, but there are already rumors swirling and accusations surrounding David Connally, who spoke here for the rally last night, as per usual..."

"Here it comes," McCoy muttered, sharply drawing a breath.

"It was reported that there is now proof that David had been in prison for the last twelve years. However, there appears to be no hard evidence that anyone has come forward with to substantiate that claim to back the accusation."

McCoy stopped holding his breath and widened his eyes as if he had been squeezing them shut.

"Also, a newspaper in Canada has reported that a children's home in Ontario had fired David on allegations of child abuse, and perhaps even child molesting."

"What," McCoy actually yelled, and felt Mr. Dixon's hand on his arm for a brief moment. The office door opened, and Audrie stuck her head in.

"Is everything ok, Mr. McCoy?" she asked hesitantly. "I heard–"

"Shush-shh!" McCoy waved wildly at her, still staring at the screen. Eyes wide, she slowly backed out of the room.

"However, the news affiliate in that area reported today on their morning broadcast that the local police gave information that they had never received such a report, but that they would look into it."

"It's...it's relentless," McCoy said numbly. Mr. Dixon watched him sympathetically. He glanced back at the news, then quickly tugged McCoy's arm. "Look, sir, it's Michael Farris!"

"Ah, something hopeful," McCoy exclaimed thankfully as his colleague appeared onscreen beside Joann Walker in his conventional Stetson and boots.

"The Democrat candidate for president, Senator Helen Kennedy, is stating that The American Party knew about these allegations all along, but that they have purposely kept them hidden from the public. Here now is Mr. Michael Farris with The American Party to give us some information concerning those accusations," Joann said, turning the microphone under her chin toward Mr. Farris, who smiled politely.

"Hello, Joann, it's good to be here with you this morning."

"Thank you, we're glad to have you on the show," she returned brightly. "What do you make of all these charges and hearsay coming from basically all over the county against David Connally, The American Party's leading man?"

Mr. Farris expanded his chest and wet his lips, then turned his gaze directly to meet that of the eager reporter.

"You know, Joann, to anyone really paying attention to these rumors, it's fairly obvious they're part of a smear campaign. For instance, David has been accused of being a child molester in Canada, an inmate in a foreign prison, involved in drug dealing in Seattle as well as in a prostitution ring in Las Vegas, and among many other things, he has been allegedly doing all these things at the same time! And you know something, Joann? Each of these stories began to surface just a few days after the conclusion of the DNC. And although none of these really bear answering, I will say that they are, each and every one of them, lies. Not one bit of evidence that could hold up in court has been submitted that could prove even one of these stories true."

"Atta boy, Michael," McCoy said under his breath, impressed at the easy manner his manager carried and his smooth handling of the situation.

"But, Mr. Farris, why won't The American Party let us or anyone else speak to David about these charges?" Joann pressed.

Mr. Farris lifted his chin.

"Well, Joann," he began, crossing his arms, "it's like this. David is simply an employee of The American Party, trying to be of help to the American people, and he doesn't need to defend himself against a bunch of lies that have no factual basis whatsoever. It's obvious that the American people see this for what it is, and that those who care to seek the truth will not believe these false reports. Joann, you were here last night, and in the stands of this race track there were about sixteen thousand people who came to hear and see David." Mr. Farris turned to wave his hand out toward the now empty space around them. "Those people also came to hear Joseph Cane, and all those in this area who followed him from the state governor and senate races to the point where he is now. Both Senator Cane and David Connally received standing ovations at the end of their presentations," he added proudly.

Joann waited a few seconds before asking another question, studying Mr. Farris critically, as if she couldn't quite make him out.

"Well, Mr. Farris," she said finally, "many are saying that The American Party keeps David behind more security than even the president, and that you're hiding something by not letting anyone see or interview him after his time onstage."

"Joann, it's as simple as this: David is not a candidate for any political office. He knows that. We know that. And now you know it. He is an employee of ours who has found himself in a very unique situation none of us could have foreseen." A small smile crept over Mr. Farris' face. "He simply entertains and encourages the audiences with patriotic songs and words of wisdom to help build up their enthusiasm and joy. Because of this, we see no need or reason for him to have to talk to the media."

Joann dipped her head in silent acknowledgment before turning back to face the camera.

"Well, there you have it from the horse's mouth, as they say," she smiled, and Mr. Farris nodded. "The American Party has revealed their take on this development on David Connally. Now, back to you in New York."

McCoy reached for the power button without thinking about it, and silence filled the room. He walked back to his desk, tapping the remote against his palm. Mr. Dixon followed him a few steps before stopping. "Sir?"

McCoy sank into his chair.

"I don't think he could have done better with what he had to work with," he said slowly. "I'm glad at least that he didn't have to give an interview to a left-biased network."

"I agree with you there." Mr. Dixon stood in front of the desk, fingers already flying across his iPad screen. "Is there anything you need, before I send these emails?"

"You're always one step ahead of the game, Jeff," McCoy smiled broadly. Then he shook his head. "No, you go on. I have some calls to make."

When he was alone again, McCoy let his smile fade. He got up and walked to the window, leaning his shoulder against the glass.

"Nathan, please have something for me soon," he pleaded silently. "And please let it be good."

CHAPTER 12:

The American Party was once again packed up and hitting the road to Indianapolis, where their next rally was scheduled to be held on the coming Saturday. In the second truck behind a Blackheart Security SUV, Jack glanced behind him at the long line of vehicles beginning to leave the staging area and chuckled.

"What?" David asked him from the passenger seat.

"All this reminds me of my time working for the Barnum & Bailey Circus," Jack answered thoughtfully, shifting gears. David craned his neck to see the group behind them. The group had swollen to quite a caravan of equipment trucks, security vehicles, and communication vans. The American Party could now boast about twenty vehicles altogether, which were presently in a convoy heading northeast to US-70.

"Except the circus had even more trucks than we do, obviously," Jack went on, checking his rearview mirror. "And most of them smelled like animals."

"Well, at least we don't have that problem," David laughed.

Jack chuckled too, but then his smile faded as a thought resurfaced in his mind. He had been thinking about it for a long time now, and finally felt he needed to say something.

"Uh, listen, David..." he began reluctantly, staring straight ahead at the road but clearly conscious of the young man's curious eyes on his face. "I think there's something you should know."

"Ok." David's voice was composed and mellow.

Still without looking at him, Jack swiped his hand down on the blinker and pulled up the ramp onto the interstate. "Well, do you remember, back in Kentucky, when we had our rally there?"

"Of course," David replied.

"It was the next day, when Blackheart arrived, and I'd picked up Aaron."

"Yes, and speaking of which, how are you doing, Jack?"

Jack tried to shrug off the pressure from the concern he heard in David's voice. His hands tightened around the steering wheel.

"I know Aaron's almost like a son to you, Jack."

"And I know the kid was worried sick about his mother and, unfortunately, would do anything to keep her from death's door," Jack returned shortly, trying to curb the sudden flare of bitterness in his chest. "I just wish he had come to us. We could have taken up a collection or something. I know Mike would have backed that idea a hundred percent." He sighed and rubbed his forehead. "I can't believe Aaron would betray us like that."

David stared out the windshield and for a few seconds, they rode in silence. Then David turned his head. "You were going to tell me something?"

Jack drew in his lips and took a deep breath. "Yeah...I just... well, you remember what day I'm talking about. The rest of us were in the food tent and you weren't."

"Yes..."

Jack rolled his shoulders, feeling himself shrinking away from David. "Well, Mike and I came looking for you."

For the first time, he felt David tense beside him. When Jack didn't look at him, he let out a long, slow exhale. "You found me," he guessed quietly.

Jack nodded, still keeping his eyes averted. "You didn't see us...but we saw you."

"When I was...?"

"Yes."

David stayed quiet for so long that Jack was afraid he was very upset. Yet, at the same time, he didn't quite understand just what would make the young man so angry about being seen in prayer. But then, Jack couldn't forget that expression of...it couldn't aptly be called anything other than agony, etched across David's face all those weeks ago. He had a burning desire to know exactly what it was that caused such turmoil in David's thoughts, but he almost dared not ask.

"I'm sorry," he said, breaking the heavy silence at last. "We should have said something, or I should have told you sooner. I didn't want you to feel like we interrupted your privacy or anything..." he trailed off feebly. "It's just, you looked so...distressed. I was worried something was bothering you."

David sighed, a sound so surprisingly mournful that Jack took his eyes off the road to look at him in alarm.

"I appreciate you telling me, Jack," he said simply. Then he looked out the window, clearly finished with the subject. Jack felt like a marionette whose strings had suddenly been cut.

"But...David, would you mind telling me what it was that troubled you so much? You looked like you were in serious pain, and that really concerns me."

When David said nothing, Jack felt frustration growing inside him. "I thought by now you trusted me at least a little. Maybe I was mistaken," he muttered, turning his head away.

"I do trust you."

Jack tilted his head but said nothing.

David sighed again, looking down at his hands. "There are some things that every man wants to leave behind him along the way, and just because I don't wish to speak of my past, it doesn't mean I don't because of a lack of trust in you, Jack. You've shown me nothing but kindness, and given me so much. I couldn't ask for a better friend. But I...I made a promise that I can't forsake. I guess all that I can ask in return is that you trust me with my own silence."

His final words held a question in them. Jack looked over at him, and his face softened. He took one hand off the wheel and took hold of David's shoulder.

"I trust you more than any other man I know," he said simply. "I won't deny that I wish I knew more about you, but that's your business, not mine. But you have to realize this, David..." He paused, searching for words. "You have to understand that the more you don't disclose about yourself, the harder people will try to uncover the truth, whatever that may be. You've already gotten a taste of the ugly side of that with all the media spreading lies."

David leaned his head back against the headrest and let his eyes slide halfway shut. "They can say whatever they like, but that's not going to affect my soul. God knows my heart, and that's enough for me."

Jack put both hands back on the steering wheel, trying hard not to stare at David. *Where does this guy get all that confidence and peace in himself?* David didn't seem to care one bit about being publicly slandered. Jack felt his incredulity and admiration for the young man grow.

In the back seat, James, who was pretending to be asleep, cracked one eye open, tilted his head ever so slightly to the side, and began typing a message on his phone.

It was several hours later, well into the afternoon, when Eli, who was leading the caravan in his black SUV, signaled for the rest of the convoy to take the next exit off the highway. They all followed him down the off-ramp and drove a few miles down the frontage road, which led them to a small country town not far from the freeway. Eli pulled up at the nearest gas station parking lot with its display of old, dusty pumps that matched the old, dusty buildings and streets.

"What's going on, Eli?" Jack called out, rolling down his window. Eli jumped out of the SUV and casually slammed the door. The pattern on the soles of his combat boots made tread marks in the fine layer of dust coating the pavement. The others started opening their doors or rolling down their windows to hear.

"I just received a report over my police scanner," Eli told Jack, draping his arms over the edge of Jack's truck window. "About twenty miles up the highway there's been a serious accident involving at least two semis and several other cars. It caused that part of the road to be completely shut down, and there wasn't any sense in getting caught up in traffic waiting for the road to be cleared."

"Ok," Jack nodded. "Good thing you pulled us off the interstate in time before we hit all the traffic. But what are we supposed to do until the wreckage is all cleaned up?"

Eli straightened up and looked around.

"I recommend that everyone just relax for a while," he answered. "There's a convenience store right over there." He gestured toward the small shop connected with the gas station. "I'll keep an ear open for the police scanner and will let you know when the accident is cleared up and it's safe to get back on the interstate again."

"How far do you estimate this will set us back?" James piped up from the back.

"Hopefully, no more than a few hours."

"Do you know if anyone was badly hurt?" David asked, leaning forward to look past Jack at Eli.

"I think so, David. The report mentioned at least one fatality." David pulled back, his eyes somber.

Jack pulled himself out of the car and raised both fists up toward the sky, stretching and then twisting his torso at the waist from side to side a couple of times. As the other drivers and passengers began getting out of their vehicles as well, he walked around a few yards, taking in the scenery.

There wasn't a soul in sight, not even visible inside the gas station store. The wide main street stretched down the entire length of houses and small shops, disappearing over a small rise. Vintage lamp posts marched every hundred feet along the cracked sidewalks, and wooden park benches, withered by sun and rain, were scattered about. The store fronts looked as if they had seen better days, with peeling paint, streaked windows, and faded advertisements. And the perpetual dust infiltrated everywhere. A hot wind was blowing, making Jack feel like he was in the Oklahoma Dust Bowl.

As he shielded his eyes from the glaring sunlight, he noticed a sign across the road. Made of rusted metal and riddled with several bullet holes, it leaned warily to one side, lazily guarding a gravel road that branched off the main street through town. Jack squinted and read the words: "SHOOTING RANGE AHEAD." The sign sparked an idea in his mind like fire on flint.

"Hey, Eli," he called, walking back over to where Eli, David, and James stood in a little knot of conversation. They all looked up when he came over. "Do you think we could go do some shooting?"

Eli raised his eyebrows. "Where?"

Jack jerked his thumb back toward the sign. "There's a range down there. It'll be fun. A good way to unwind, but responsibly," he added.

Eli's lips twitched. "And what better way for a man to relax then firing off a few rounds?"

"But you don't even have any guns," James said to Jack, a sardonic smile on his face, as if he couldn't quite believe they were serious.

Jack just smiled.

"Oh, we've got guns."

He jerked his head toward his truck, and as the others watched, he walked over and opened the side door behind the driver's seat. James' eyes widened when Jack folded the back seat forward and revealed a stash of three rifles, two shotguns, and four handguns, neatly imbedded up behind the seat, along with a small stockpile of ammunition.

Eli smirked. James was aghast.

"I've been sitting on that this whole time!?" he exclaimed, his eyes popping.

"Yep." Jack lifted out one of the shotguns and checked the chamber. He grinned at James, who turned pale. "Driving all over the country, you never know what you're gonna run into. But I think a man should always be prepared for anything. Also, who says you can have too many guns?" He winked at David.

"Now, I know you're a responsible man, Jack," said Eli, unfolding his arms to pick up one of the rifles. He raised it to his cheek, barrel pointed toward the ground as he looked down the scope. "But as a professional security guard, I have to ask if you have permits for this arsenal of yours."

"Absolutely I do," Jack responded airily. He patted one of the handguns and smiled. "It's called the Second Amendment."

The others chuckled at his answer, and Eli shook his head, but he was grinning. "Is that a .357 magnum revolver?"

"Smith & Wesson," Jack told him. Then he added confidentially, "And don't worry, Eli. I've got licenses for every one of these."

James still looked unsettled.

"What's the matter, boy, never seen a gun before?" Jack asked him. James tried to smile, and shrugged, scraping the toe of his boot across the pavement. "I don't think I've really shot a gun before," he mumbled, rubbing the back of his neck.

Jack and Eli both stared at him. "Well, let's do something about that!" Jack said, slapping him on the shoulder. James stumbled half a step forward, pressing his lips together in a tight smile that looked more like a grimace.

Jack shoved two of the handguns into his belt and grabbed a .50 caliber military ammo tin filled with magazines, along with a couple of ammo boxes. Eli handed one of the rifles to James, who looked at it curiously.

"Don't point that thing at anybody, including you!" Eli warned him, shoving the end of the barrel away from James' own face. "Keep the barrel aimed at the ground or straight up at the sky at all times."

"But it's not even loaded..."

"Doesn't matter. You never know if a bullet might be in the chamber, even if you checked it. It's a good rule of thumb to never point a gun at people, loaded or not."

Jack grinned at David, expecting him to share the mood as he offered him the other rifle. To his surprise, David shrank back from the weapon, a strange reluctance in his candid blue eyes.

"Something wrong, David?"

David seemed to hold his breath for a moment, then his hands closed around the stock and barrel of the rifle. "Thanks," he said carefully.

"Yeah...sure," Jack said cautiously. He couldn't say why they were speaking almost in a mysterious code he didn't even understand. From the corner of his eye he watched David examine the gun in his hands with a care that seemed to be torn between interest and unwillingness. What kind of a man doesn't like handling guns, Jack thought.

He pushed the thought away as he turned to face the others. "Come on boys, let's do some target practice!"

They loaded the guns back into the truck and drove across the street, pulling off onto the bumpy gravel that spat up even more swirling dust when the tires hit it. Several crew members followed Eli and Jack down to the shooting range while the others stayed behind to relax or explore the promises of the convenience store.

When Jack had driven about a quarter mile down the gravel road, he saw a shack up ahead with another sign reading: "No Operator Today. Shoot At Own Risk. $5 per Gun. Please Shoot Responsibly." Jack followed the arrow on the sign pointing to a metal box for the money deposits.

"Let me tally these up here," he muttered, reaching back to pull out his wallet. Thumbing through it, he silently counted out a small pile of dollar bills and handed them to David.

"Here, you're closer. Will you shove those in there?" He pointed to the metal box.

David nodded once, and getting down from the truck, thrust the money into the deposit box.

"Alright, we've paid our dues. Now let's have some fun!" Jack said with a broad smile, putting the truck back in gear.

David climbed quietly back into his seat and buckled his seat belt without a word. Between them, the rifle Jack had handed him rested with its barrel pointed at the roof, closer to Jack's side than David's.

When they had driven past the operator's box and gone a few more yards, the gravel road spread out and ended in a disorganized parking area. A beaten path led away from the gravel toward a line of trees, through which could dimly be seen the cleared space for the range. They all got out of the vehicles, and Jack handed out firearms and ammo with gusto.

"They should already have some old targets set up, but I think I have some Coke cans or something in the back we can shoot at, too," he said as they began trudging along the worn path with the grass stomped down underfoot.

"Doesn't look like people have been out here in a while," Eli remarked, looking around as they emerged at the clearing. Old wooden rails had been set up in a wide U-shaped perimeter, open

278

where the faded, well-used targets stood at the opposite end from the crew. Behind the targets, a tall mound of pale earth rose well over ten feet, grass and weeds sprouting out of it here and there. Rusty tin cans, mildewed cardboard boxes, shiny bits of glass bottles, and even large plastic laundry detergent containers littered the shooting area. Bullet casings and shotgun shells peeked out of every inch of ground.

"Doesn't look like anyone has been here in a while," Jack said, setting down his tin of military ammo on the railing. "It's a regular ghost town. I didn't even see anyone in the convenience store."

"Oh, I'm sure they had somebody in there," Eli laughed. "They wouldn't leave a place like that unattended. A shooting range, maybe. But not a convenience store."

Jack smiled. He and Eli had warmed to each other considerably since Blackheart had first arrived, and now Jack felt almost as comfortable around Eli as he did with Mr. Farris or David.

"Let's move those targets around," he instructed some of his crewmen. "We'll place a few up closer for the handguns, one about halfway down range for rifles, and then see if you can get one or two set up at two-hundred yards at the end of the range."

"Ambitious, aren't you."

Jack grinned at Eli. "That'll be for the more experienced people."

He turned to James, who stood awkwardly holding the shotgun Jack had given him, attempting to keep the barrel pointed straight at the dirt.

"So, you've never shot a gun, son?"

"No," he mumbled, turning a little pink.

"Well, there's no better time to start learning than now!" Jack told him buoyantly. "And this way I'll be able to teach you how to do it the right way from the start, too. Come on," he added as James walked reluctantly over to him. "I'll make a marksman out of you yet."

For the next several minutes, Jack worked with James, explaining what each firearm he had brought was called, the ammunition capacity, and how to load, aim, and fire all of them. James learned quickly, and the more he shot, the more he seemed to enjoy it. Jack watched in approval as James smoothly lifted one of the revolvers, loaded it, spun the chamber and snapped it shut, then took careful aim at the target, his arms stretched taut, hands cupped carefully around the stock. His finger just resting against the trigger guard, he cocked the hammer and drew a deep breath before firing.

Jack squinted at the target, hand shading his eyes from the sun.

"Wow! Great job, James!" he exclaimed, and James grinned proudly. "You nearly hit the center."

"I think I like this one the best," James said, turning the small gun on its side on his palm, weighing it expertly. Jack smiled at the professional sound in his voice.

"Yeah, that little snub-nose .38 has been good to me for as long as I've had her," he answered, as if the gun were a pet he was very fond of. James looked at him, then back at the gun in his hand, studying it. Jack clapped him on the shoulder.

"I told you," he said, beaming. "Anyone can learn to shoot. And as long as you're always responsible and safe about handling firearms, there's no reason not to own one. Or ten. Well done. You are now officially a member of our crew, James."

James turned a little red, but stammered out a babble of thanks.

"Can we try some quick-draw shooting?" he then asked eagerly.

"Not while I'm around," Eli told him firmly, stepping forward. "I'm not going to take you to the hospital when you shoot yourself through the foot."

James seemed cowed for a moment, then he lifted his chin and studied Eli. A sliver of a smile, barely visible, played on his face. "You don't think I'm careful enough, that I'll let some sort of accident happen because I'm not responsible?" he asked.

Eli stood very still. Then his bright eyes narrowed. He walked up to James, and James couldn't resist taking one step back. The expression in Eli's face was frightening.

"Playing with guns is a dangerous past time. Especially when you get others involved," he said in a low voice, danger barely disguised beneath.

"Yes, well, even careful people can make mistakes, can't they?" James said, matching Eli's tone, even though he was aware of his fingers tightening nervously around the small gun in his hand.

Eli's eyebrows were drawn together so closely that he looked absolutely fierce.

"Of course they can," he answered stiffly.

"Hey guys," Jack called to them, "come over here and let's see who shoots straightest, alright?"

"Fine." Eli didn't break eye contact with James. "I've always considered myself a straight shooter."

They rejoined the others, and some of the other crew members who had come down to the range with them were given the opportunity to shoot some of the handguns at the closer targets. A few even ventured a shot at the target halfway down the field with Jack's AR-15, but none were able to hit the two-hundred yard mark.

During all this time, David stood a little apart from the rest. He had placed his rifle against the railing, resting the butt of the stock against the ground. He then stood back with his hands in his pockets, calmly surveying the scene before him. Eli stood next to him, cradling a heavy semi-automatic rifle in his arms. As ever, his eyes were watchful, alert.

Jack lowered the shotgun from his shoulder after firing off six shots in quick succession at the halfway mark. He nodded at James, who hurried down the range to check the target.

"You hit the bulls-eye every time!" he hollered back at Jack.

Jack pumped the force-end, and the last shell flew out of the ejection port.

"I was a pretty fair marksman in my day," he said proudly. "And I always had an affinity for guns. I guess I still got it!"

He turned around and saw David and Eli silently observing the proceedings.

"Eli, why don't you bring that MP5 over here and show these boys how it's really done?" he suggested teasingly.

Eli chuckled, and shifted the gun in his arms.

"This gun isn't for target practice, Jack. Defense and

protection only."

Jack dismissed this with a wave of the hand, then turned to David.

"Hey David!" he exclaimed, "You haven't shot once."

David just smiled a little, but said nothing.

"You done any shooting before?"

David pulled his hands out of his pockets to cross his arms, hunching his shoulders.

"I'm ok," he said simply. "I don't need to shoot."

Jack's eyes widened. "You're worse than Roy Rogers was. Here," he gestured toward James, who started goading David on as if he himself had never been afraid of handling the guns earlier.

"Yeah, C'mon, David! Are you afraid of holding a gun? Don't hand in your man card, man!"

Some of the other crew members also started chiding and razzing David about his refusal to shoot, good-naturedly, but rather relentlessly. David took the teasing with a mild grin on his face, but still made no move toward the firearms.

Jack folded his arms.

"We're not going back to the car till everybody shoots. Come on, David." Jack tilted his head, widening his eyes teasingly. "I'll help you," he offered, sending everyone else except Eli into fits of laughter. With how strongly built and muscular David was, it seemed strange to everyone that he would be reluctant to shoot a gun. He looked made to model weapons, Jack thought.

David continued to shake his head, and Eli, watching him, thought he looked a little more distressed with every goad from the others. He leaned toward David.

"If you don't want to shoot, we can go back to the car," he said, low. David turned his head toward Eli's voice, but didn't look at him. Tiny, fine lines were etched above his nose. But he smiled and even chuckled a little at the jokes being tossed at him about his not wanting to shoot.

James, with a sense of arrogance in his new ability to shoot, stepped toward David, confidence exuding with every move.

"Come on, David," he repeated, as if to a kid. "Jack said we're not leaving till you shoot, so what's the problem? Go on, it's fun! Are you afraid I'll just show you up?" he added, smirking.

"David," Eli said quietly, but with urgency.

David seemed lost in thought. He responded to neither James nor Eli, but kept his eyes down, chewing on his lower lip. Jack stopped smiling, wondering if he had gone too far with the teasing. But David wouldn't say anything, so how was he to know?

Suddenly, without a word to anyone, David uncrossed his arms and walked straight up to the small wooden table where most of the guns were laid out. He didn't hesitate a second, but reached directly for Jack's M14 rifle and magazine sitting beside it. Jack hurried over.

"Wait, hold on a sec, why don't we start you out with something smaller. You don't want to shoot the .22 first?"

But while Jack was still speaking and walking toward him, David picked up the rifle, deftly loaded the magazine into the magazine well, pulled back and released the bolt, all in one fluid motion. He barely looked to see what his hands were doing. Jack paused mid-step as David quickly raised the rifle to his shoulder, switching off the safety, and without delay fired three shots that echoed like cannon fire throughout the quiet woods around them. After the third shot, he pointed the barrel toward the sky, leaning the gun back against his arm as he looked at the target. Then abruptly he turned around, walked past a stunned Jack, laid the rifle down in its previous position, and walked back to Eli without a glance at anyone else.

The others stared at him in complete silence, awe and amazement on their faces. Eli looked at David, then pulled out his binoculars to check the targets downrange.

"What was that? He didn't even hit anything!" James said smugly.

Eli, still peering through his binoculars, realized what he was truly seeing, and a big smile spread over his face.

"My man didn't miss," he said loudly. They all turned to see what he was talking about.

"What, yeah he did!" James pressed, irritated. "Look, no new bullet holes!" He pointed at the halfway mark.

Eli lowered his binoculars. "Three in the center. Two hundred yards."

James' mouth fell open.

David reached Eli and kept walking past him, saying quietly, "I'm ready to go back now."

Ignoring the gawking stares of everyone else, Eli nodded, shoving his binoculars against James' chest. "Don't drop those, or I will shoot you in the foot myself."

As he and David walked away, James raised the glasses to his eyes. Sure enough, the target furthest away, the one no one had been able to hit, was punctured in the middle by three neat bullet holes from Jack's M14.

"So where'd you learn to shoot like that?" Eli asked David as they walked back up the path to the trucks. David shrugged.

"Must have been my lucky day," he replied.

Back at the range, Jack leaned against the table of guns, shaking his head. "Now why would he refuse to shoot when he can shoot like that?" he mused aloud. The others around him were still at target practice except for James, who looked completely crushed.

"I guess Connally has me beaten here all square," he muttered, trying to laugh it off but scowling heavily at the same time.

Jack looked at him. "Now, you're only learning this stuff today. I guess David has more experience with guns than anyone knew about."

"Ain't that the truth," James said, coming over to lean against the table beside Jack. He twisted to look back at the guns behind him, and picked up the .38 again.

"The thing is, I can't seem to keep my hand steady," he complained. "I'm alright until just before I pull the trigger, in that split second I feel my hand start to shake a little. What's with that?"

"It's probably just nerves."

"Nerves nothing! I–"

"James, it's ok to be a little nervous when you're around guns for the first time. They are weapons, after all, and it's important to have a healthy respect for them. Just remember, there's no need to be afraid of the gun if it's in responsible hands. They don't fire on their own."

James watched Jack while he spoke, nodding slowly as he listened. "But what about my hand?" he asked again.

"Well, if it keeps happening, take a deep breath. Allow yourself time to really take aim and be comfortable holding the gun. Remember you are the one with the control."

Jack straightened up and reached down to pick up the rifle David had used. His eyes traveled along the length of the barrel.

"And also," he added distantly, "remember that you're only aiming for an inanimate target, an object of plastic, metal, or wood. You're not aiming at a living being."

James looked down at the small gun in his hands. "Yeah..." he said slowly. Then he snickered. "I can only imagine how shaky I'd be in that case, right?"

But Jack wasn't listening. He looked up from the rifle to the bend in the path where Eli and David had disappeared from view. Dimly he recollected the sharp sound of David's shots, the smooth, professional motions of preparing to fire, the quiet calm of his expression and lack of wanting to draw attention to himself. The way he handled the rifle, it was as if he went out shooting every day of his life. Jack took Eli's binoculars and scanned the two-hundred-yard target again.

"I've never seen anyone shoot like that," he said with a low whistle. Then he and James caught each other's gazes. "Except a military sniper," Jack added quietly.

↑CHAPTER 13:

Throughout the summer months of July and August, the country saw a rising sweep of wonder resembling what few in American politics had seen before. With each subsequent rally of The American Party there was an ever-growing number of signs saying, "David for President!" being waved eagerly by enthusiastic members in the audience. It seemed like at least a quarter of the people were caught up in a fervent desire to see this man as their national leader, regardless of party affiliation. And it didn't stop with the rally crowds. The media took to the arena in full swing, as it always did with politics. Nearly every news broadcast regarding the upcoming election contained some vein about David, The American Party, and the unofficial push for this zealous but mysterious young patriot to take the helm in the White House. Such reports were met with skepticism, excitement, outrage, disbelief, and ridicule, but every word spoken about him online, onscreen, or by word-of-mouth only served to raise David Connally's fame across the nation.

Almost every week there seemed to be some new tale about David having been allegedly involved in immoral or criminal activity in his past. Those behind the fabrications were working overtime to discredit and humiliate him, but the more lies they told, the more unbelievable the accusations sounded. As the false stories piled up, those who had begun to doubt the young man's character and motives seemed to finally realize what was really going on. The lies carried less and less of an effect, for few now actually believed them, even some who claimed affiliation with the Democrat Party. As usual, neither The American Party nor David commented on any of the stories told.

More and more people were sitting up and taking notice. The left wing was growing even more increasingly aggressive against the right while stepping up their campaigns of changing America's future by stepping away from the traditions of old. The American Party continued with their promises to restore America to her original founding system of smaller government with special emphasis on stricter adherence to the Constitution, quality education for all, elimination of the IRS, and government officials being accountable to the people. Everyone paying attention could already tell this would be an election to change the course America was taking. A year of change, for either the best or the worst.

When Jeff Dixon brought Rick McCoy a letter someone had written to ask the chairman's assistance on changing the election laws so David Connally's name could be put on the ballot, even this late in the race, concern coursed through his mind.

"What do they think I want to do, sneak David to the front lines and bring him out as a dark horse to the surprise of all?" he said, crumpling the letter in his fist. "These people don't know what they're asking. The idea of asking me to help change laws." He grimaced. "We still don't know a thing about this guy, and here they are, wanting his name on the ballot anyway."

"Maybe David is getting too much time and attention onstage?" Mr. Dixon suggested mildly. He gave his boss a knowing look. "Perhaps you'd better talk to him about backing out of the spotlight after all."

McCoy let the wadded piece of paper fall to the desktop and brushed it off into the trash can. "That will be all, Jeff."

On the first of September The American Party and Republican Party were set to hold the largest rally yet, more of a convention in itself. It was to take place at the Los Angeles Rose Bowl. On the day of the rally, McCoy was up to his neck in details and organization when he got a call from Edward Martin.

"Do you have time for a quick meeting before the rally?"

"Uh..." McCoy looked up and saw Mr. Dixon holding a pile of papers for him to go over, then swatted at the air for him to leave them. "I'm really busy right now, Edward. Can we do this later?"

"Certainly. How about one thirty?"

McCoy straightened up in surprise. Martin didn't take the hint.

"Alright, I might have a very small window of time then, if I'm able to get everything else taken care of that I need to this morning," he said, trying to keep the irritation out of his voice.

"Excellent. I'm sorry to give you such short notice, but I think this is very necessary."

"Mm-hmm." McCoy's eyes strayed to the unfinished work left on his desk clamoring silently for his attention. "Alright, one thirty. I'll see you then."

He hung up almost before the other man had time to say goodbye. As he put down the phone, he scrunched up his eyes. "Jeff!"

Mr. Dixon strode back into the room as though he knew exactly when he would be called for. "Mr. McCoy?"

"Jeff, I have a feeling that our friend, Edward Martin, may have just roped us into a meeting I would very much care to avoid at this time."

"So you know what he's going to say?"

"Well, I think we can safely bet that he'll undoubtedly have at least a few things to say about David."

In the suite of an L.A. hotel room, Rick McCoy, Jeff Dixon, Joseph Cane, and Edward Martin met together several hours before the rally started. For this occasion, Martin had called the meeting, and he appeared anything but settled over the circumstances they were in.

"Gentlemen, I thank you for meeting with me today," he began, somewhat cordially. But McCoy could tell just by looking at him that Martin was not in a tranquil frame of mind. He seemed to have developed a twitch since their last encounter, and his smile didn't reach his eyes. McCoy knew that whatever came up in this meeting, Martin would probably find a way to connect their discussions back to David. If Martin had been watching the news lately, and of course he must have been, there was no possible way he couldn't know about people wanting David to be president.

"I first wanted to lay some concerns of mine out on the table," Martin said diplomatically. "Mr. McCoy. I seem to recall you saying you would handle this, but apparently The American Party is not well equipped to stop the people from displaying their signs and banners supporting David Connally for president." Martin spoke in clipped words, his voice tight as he emphasized his words with jerks of the head. McCoy didn't break eye contact with him, but steadily looked back into Martin's irritated eyes, offering no comment. He knew Martin wasn't finished.

"This is getting out of hand, and the opposite of what I meant about us working together," Martin went on feverishly. Sweat was already beginning to pop out on his forehead. "The TV cameras broadcast it all over the country, all this publicity cooked up over David's alleged secret campaign run for president. And it's not getting any better. It's getting worse." Martin pressed his hands against the table top. His eyes bored directly into McCoy's. "Reports have come to me that in almost every state in the union people are working to get laws changed and David's name on the ballot." Martin leaned over the table, undisguised anger in his voice. "Rick, if you and I are going to continue working together, you will put a stop to this."

McCoy looked around the table. Jeff Dixon was watching him steadily, a question in his eyes. Joseph Cane sat with his arms folded, his face both sullen and worried. McCoy shook his head. *Men with power, or a taste of it, always worry about any imagined competition to their plans.*

"First of all, Edward, it's nice to finally be on a first-name basis with you," he said. Mr. Dixon smiled as he quickly lowered his head to look at the ledger on the table before him.

"Secondly, as I have already told you, we cannot restrict the First Amendment of the people who come to these rallies. Do you really think my team and I are secretly egging them on and supporting their ideas about David being president?"

Martin swallowed at the look on McCoy's face. But he pressed his lips together tightly, still angry. Still unconvinced. But McCoy could tell that he was listening.

"Because that isn't what we're doing at all. I gave you my word that The American Party would give full support to your man, Cane, here. But I can't stop the people from putting David's name on the ballot. We are and have been doing all we can to make it perfectly clear to everyone in our party that David Connally is not our candidate. We don't endorse him in any way as a candidate, we don't think it's helpful for the signs to appear as they do, but as long as this is a free country there's nothing we can do about that." McCoy studied Martin, who was now openly glaring at him. "Maybe the Republican Party should spend a little more money on signs for the true candidate," he suggested quietly.

Cane looked up and turned a shade of red, his eyebrows drawing together. Martin pulled back as if he had been insulted.

"There is no need for you to tell us what to do with our budget, Rick," he said with a glare.

"I apologize. I don't mean to offend you," McCoy replied honestly. "We are partners in this same endeavor after all, aren't we? But, Edward," he added slowly, "I think that you're getting a little too uptight about David. You seem to be seriously worried that he presents real competition for your candidate, yet he's not even running for office. I shouldn't think, if you had the right man for the office, that you had any need to be concerned about a patriotic guy who happens to be very popular with the American people right now."

Martin raised his chin. "Are you implying that Senator Cane is wrong for the office of president?"

"I never said that, nor do I think it," McCoy said. "But I do wonder why you're so insecure about David, and why you find him so threatening to your plans this fall."

Martin bristled, his long, oval-shaped face scrunching up.

"Connally has no campaign, no plans, and no preparation to lead this country. Yet he seems to act like that's exactly what he does have and what he is doing. For all we know, he really could be plotting to take the White House by gaining the support of the people."

McCoy let out a snort of laughter. "Do you actually believe

David is – I can't believe you actually used this word – plotting to win the election?" He shook his head again. "Wow, Edward. Maybe I was wrong. You aren't worried. You're paranoid."

"I'm concerned about the welfare of my party, and I intend to see that Joseph Cane becomes the next president of the United States, not some nobody we know nothing about!"

McCoy stood up. "And haven't I been telling you that we're on your side about this? Haven't I been–"

"Well, you're not doing enough!" Martin interrupted, waspish. "Somehow, The American Party needs to take control of this situation and stop your people from drafting David Connally for president! I asked you to speak to David about this, Rick," he added. "Did you?"

McCoy shifted his feet, glancing down at his boots.

"I have not spoken to David," he said at last, looking straight at Martin. "I thought it best, after careful deliberation, that he doesn't have anything more to be self-conscious about. David is not trying to undermine anybody, least of all, you," he said quickly as Martin began to splutter indignantly. "He doesn't need anyone telling him to back off the patriotism, and I'm not going to be the one to do it, either. I don't know how I can convince you to believe me when I say that David," and McCoy leaned over the table, pointing downward to emphasize his point, "is not trying to do anything except bring people hope, encouragement, and wisdom about the future by reminding them of the past."

"Mr. Martin," Jeff Dixon said in a conciliatory tone, "these aren't 'our' people, as you said. Most of our audiences are made of up both Republicans and Democrats now who are calling for David to be president. Perhaps you should voice your concerns to them."

Before Martin could respond, McCoy cut in.

"And Edward, I was under the impression that we were here to discuss how we're going to be working together in the next couple of months, not how to stifle one of our own from speaking, and not about pulling against each other."

Martin fixed him with a stony stare. For a few awkward seconds, the chairman of the Republican Party and the chairman of

CHAPTER 13:

The American Party stared each other down, one gaze baleful, the other mild but unmoving.

Joseph Cane broke the silence. "Gentlemen, this really is a serious issue, and especially sensitive to me. It's nothing short of embarrassing for me to be up on one of your stages, speaking to an audience waving a sea of signs endorsing David Connally for president, when I'm there for the purpose of running my own campaign." He rolled his shoulders. "That is the campaign that actually exists and the one the Republican Party is graciously backing with their full support."

McCoy responded, "What, you think David doesn't find all this unwanted attention embarrassing too? He's rallying up the people to give you their vote, and here they continue to insist he become their candidate! He doesn't want that any more than you do. But I'll remind you, Senator Cane, this is a free country. That's something The American Party is neither able nor willing to forcibly put a stop to, though we are making it very clear that, as a party, we are not endorsing David for president. You guys get yourselves some more signs of your own."

Martin took a deep breath, drawing up his mouth while his eyes narrowed to slits. "Rick, I find it really hard to believe that you are actually taking any of these very real concerns seriously."

"Edward." McCoy pinched the bridge of his nose, squeezing his eyes shut in frustration. "I wouldn't be having this discussion with you if I didn't care about what you're saying. I'm being perfectly sincere when I tell you that I want us to work together, which means I wouldn't let David try to sneak around you like you so adamantly accuse him of doing, even if he wanted to, which he doesn't."

Martin scoffed. "I want your word that you and The American Party will do everything in your power to put our candidate, Joseph Cane, first. And that you will do all that you can to squelch this unauthorized (not to mention ridiculous) effort to draft David Connally for president. We have two months until the election, so I need your word. Here and now."

"Alright." McCoy uncrossed his arms and strode right up to Martin, standing almost nose to nose with him. Martin, confused and a little startled by McCoy's sudden terse movement and the fierceness in his eyes, fell back a step.

"You want my word? Well let me tell you something, for the here and now." McCoy's voice was low, yet every word was enunciated with an unmistakable meaning. "We don't know anything more about this guy than the rest of the country. To our current knowledge, David Connally is unable to even meet the qualifications for becoming a presidential candidate. He doesn't have a birth certificate. We have no records of his past. We don't even know if he's an American citizen. And if he isn't, by law he can't be president anyway."

Martin pushed his glasses up and sniffed, simply because he seemed so rattled by McCoy's stern and uncomfortable attitude that he didn't know what else to do. Cane and Mr. Dixon watched their interaction with both anticipation and apprehension.

"Now," McCoy continued, stepping away from him and moving around the corner of the table toward his chair. "As to giving our word to back Senator Cane, I can assure you personally that at this point The American Party has full intentions of continuing complete support for your candidate." He turned around, one hand resting on the table. "My party will never back somebody who isn't qualified." He dipped his chin, his gaze perfectly steady and sincere. "You can depend on that."

Martin licked his lips. He turned to Cane, then looked back at McCoy. Something in the other man's eyes finally seemed to hit home, and Martin's shoulders slumped in compromise.

"Alright," he said with a heavy sigh, shaking his head. "I guess that'll have to be good enough for us. For now."

"Well, I'm glad to know we'll still be able to work together to make this country great," McCoy told him, relief evident on his face. Martin merely nodded and mumbled something unintelligible as he quickly shook McCoy's offered hand, disapproval still written in his eyes as he picked up his hat. Cane stood up, his own feelings anything but satisfied. But at least now everything was out on the table, and everyone knew where they stood.

McCoy left the room first, but as he turned the knob, he thought of something. A smile spread across his face and he faced the other men, resting his other hand on the doorjamb.

"On the other hand," he said innocently, as if stating an obvious but overlooked truth, "If there weren't any problems, with the qualifications, I mean with David, I think he'd make quite a candidate, you know?"

Martin and Cane stared at him, their eyes wide.

"Just a thought." McCoy shrugged. "See you fellas tonight at the Rose Bowl!"

While The American Party was gearing up for their rally in California, the left wing was preparing a news release for one of their own. Helen Kennedy was vamping up her campaign even more with only a couple more months until November. As The American Party focused on David Connally and Joseph Cane, the Democrat senator was sitting down to an exclusive TV interview in Richmond, Virginia. As Helen's profile appeared on camera, the headline scrolling across the bottom of the television screen read: "On the Campaign Trail with Senator Helen Kennedy"

"Good afternoon! I'm Lindsey Caldwell, here with Senator Helen Kennedy, who as we all know, took the Democratic nomination for president earlier in the year, and has been unfaltering and steadfast in her campaign. Thank you for being with us today, Senator."

Senator Kennedy graciously tilted her head. "Of course, Linda."

"Well," said Linda, straightening her notes and flicking her hair back as she made herself more comfortable in her chair, "I'm so glad I'm finally able to sit down with you and ask you some questions about your campaign. First of all, I think our viewers would like to know, is it harder for a woman to run against a male candidate for the presidency?"

Senator Kennedy didn't even blink.

"With my experience working in Congress, particularly the Senate, and also my work with the present administration, I believe I have all the credentials necessary to be the greatest president this great nation has ever had. So no, I don't find it difficult to run against a man, and I'm certainly not intimidated by the opposition.

I've won elections against men before, and I see no problem with doing it again. It doesn't matter the gender of the candidates. What matters is, can they lead the country? And see, Linda," she added, leaning forward with a newly passionate edge in her voice, "this isn't really about me. This is about our country. Why, if I knew that my opponent would make America stronger and do a better job than I could, I would fold right now." She waved her hand and chuckled, Linda joining her, an incredulous smile on her face.

"Oh, you wouldn't do that!" she exclaimed, an almost fawning note in her voice.

Helen Kennedy smiled and demurely smoothed her hands over her lap.

"Well, I have no cause to!" she returned. "I did say 'if', remember?"

Linda cleared her throat. "Well, how does it feel to have your husband with you on the campaign trail?"

Helen brought her chin up, every inch the diplomat. "He understands what is expected of me and what I must do as a presidential candidate. He supports me and stands beside me every step of the way. We are a team, and we want people to know that."

"Of course, and I'm sure that's inspiring to many. But Senator, do you believe that your candidacy and the Democrat Party will prevail in the upcoming election?"

"Linda, I think there's little doubt that I will be the next and first female president of this country. I know this because we are the party of the people." Senator Kennedy's voice was dauntless. "We will serve the people and, as a government, supply their every need."

"Is it true that you intend to unveil a new strategy for helping the people of this country who are so much in need?"

"Yes, and I'm grateful for this interview because it gives me an opportunity to really explain what my administration plans to do within the first hundred days of my tenure as president. With full control of the House and Senate, we will work together to implement the greatest national treasure for the people."

"Oh, that sounds promising!"

"Yes, it's called the Basic American Rights Act," said Senator

Kennedy proudly. "This new law will guarantee to every person living in this great nation, well, the basic rights of life." She laughed brightly. "This law will provide everyone the simple needs of free housing, food, and healthcare. It will be known as the BARA. It will ensure that the government guarantees each person who can't afford those three basic rights, they will be provided for them. If they can't afford decent housing, the government will subsidize and, or, make this housing possible for them. If they can't afford the necessary food essentials for life, this government will provide it for them."

"How so? Food stamps?"

"Oh, something a bit more sophisticated than food stamps," the senator said smugly. "It will take the form of a pre-loaded ATM debit card from my administration to cover the monthly food expenses. And last but not least, all the medicals needs that are out of reach for them will be met through the healthcare provision in the BARA."

"Well, Senator, that sounds like a wonderful thing for the needy in this country. I commend you, but I would also ask how will your administration pay for this type of unprecedented care?"

"Trust me, Linda. We have studied this new plan and it's not going to cost the American people one extra tax dollar. When the BARA is passed it will require every wealthy company and corporation, and individual millionaire and billionaire in this country to simply pay their proper tax. This tax will be imposed upon the rich so their fellow countrymen will be able to have their basic needs met by aid of BARA. And to make this as fair as possible, the government will help each corporation and wealthy individual determine what we know to be the fair and proper tax. When this is determined, the IRS will be mandated to make certain of closing all loopholes. They'll also make sure that tax can be easily met from the surpluses of these excessive profits designed to line the pockets of the rich. In addition, we'll be able to lower the national debt by trillions in lieu of the surplus from this tax."

"How will all of this be implemented so that everyone receives their fair share?" Linda asked.

Senator Kennedy turned to look directly at the camera.

"The plan is simple," she said confidently. "We, the government, will determine the fair tax, and the people will determine who is qualified and eligible to be a receiver of BARA. In every town and city we will establish community organizers, much like the ACORN organization. They will determine among themselves who is qualified to receive the benefits of BARA. With this group working under the federal government there will be no need for the state governments to be involved in the rights of the people. Because, frankly, Linda," she added in a conspiratorial manner as she turned back to the interviewer, "I think we all know Washington will always be able to manage what's good for the people better than the states."

Linda nodded thoughtfully. "Well, let's shift gears a little. With all your confidence and obvious preparations for entering the White House this fall, what are your thoughts regarding The American Party and their spokesman, David Connally? He's been telling the people things like..." She consulted her notes. "...Benevolence and welfare should be left up to churches, businesses, and other charity groups who are better qualified to administer benevolence than the federal government. Now, you just told us that you think the federal government would actually be better qualified to serve the needs of the people?"

The senator gave a tight-lipped smile and waved her hand flippantly.

"Well, everyone knows that's ridiculous, Linda. No one in their right mind would trust businesses and churches to administer help to the helpless. Everyone knows that the government is best suited to supervise these types of aid programs. The people can't take care of themselves without the federal government to help them. They need us to rely on."

"Well, David Connally has also made statements to the effect that God expects a person to work if they want to eat," Linda pressed on, watching Senator Kennedy for her reaction. "He said that each state should provide a job for everyone who is able, and if they won't work when they're capable of doing so, that they shouldn't receive governmental aid. Except, he said, for the sick, disabled, and mentally ill."

The senator straightened up in her seat, raising her chin and clenching her jaw while trying to maintain the smile on her face. "Linda, let me assure you that what David Connally claims God says and what the federal government should actually do are two very different things."

"But what about when he said that God expects people to love their neighbors like they love themselves, and to do good and be of help to others as they themselves would wish to be treated? And to pray for your enemy as well as your neighbor?"

Senator Kennedy scoffed, but her eyes were narrowed, and her face was steadily turning red.

"You see," she began, then paused with a forced chuckle as if she couldn't believe she was even speaking about such a topic. "That kind of talk only goes to prove that these people in The American Party are simply not in touch with the needs of the people. This David and his party friends need to learn about the necessary separation of church and state, and to look to their government, not to a God, for their fundamental needs and rights. And as soon as I'm elected, Linda, you can be sure that I'll be having Congress, the FBI, and the CIA formally investigate this American Party, and bring to justice all these radical elements who are trying to destroy America's future and proper way of life."

"Well, what do you make of the ever-growing crowds and popularity that follow The American Party and David Connally? It's pretty evident that many love David and want him to succeed in some kind of political office, perhaps even the presidency itself."

"It should be quite obvious to every single informed American that this Connally guy has been involved in some of the worst perpetration of both national and moral law. We still don't even know the full truth yet regarding any reports of his history before he joined The American Party. Some call him a diehard bigot, prejudiced toward African-Americans and Hispanics, and that he's against gay marriage and abortion for any reason. Personally, I have reason to believe he's only in this for the millions of dollars he must receive from The American Party, and therefore has no qualms about deceiving the American public. All these charges against him have been proven true, and therefore the idea of him ever taking office is nothing short of laughable." The senator laughed here, as if to better illustrate her point before going on. "Soon enough the American people will wake up and vote for the party that truly has their best interests at heart."

"So you don't think that Joseph Cane, who is backed by both The American Party and the Republican Party, has a chance in November even though David seems to be the spokesman for them all and has drawn in quite a following?"

Senator Kennedy ran her tongue along her lower lip, taking in a deep breath and closing her eyes for a moment. When she opened them, her gaze was very sharp indeed.

"Frankly, Linda, I don't want to hear any more about this man, this David Connally. He is not a candidate, and he isn't even an American. Why should anyone listen to him? Has he given one good, sound piece of political wisdom since he started speaking for The American Party? No. Has he laid out any actual, working, reasonable plan for helping this country? No. So tell me why the people should pay attention to the words of some low-living, uninformed, Bible-thumping fundamentalist? What difference can it make? There isn't any room in the government for anyone with such views, and the government has never lied to the people like The American Party is now doing. It's just how it is, Linda."

Linda, her head tilted to one side, nodded slowly, then turned to face the camera.

"Well, that concludes our interview with Helen Kennedy, a strong, confident prospect for our next president."

Jack turned off the TV and turned to Eli, who stood beside him in the refreshment tent, arms folded and eyes slit as they watched the end of Helen Kennedy's interview.

"Well," Jack said after an awkward pause, "talk about a frightening prospect for our next president!"

"She certainly intends to change the country," Eli said in his deep voice.

Jack added, "And you heard her talking about how sure she is that David isn't even American, even though we don't know that for sure, and how all those awful rumors about him are true."

"Yes, she's a vindictive woman. I fully believe she will do whatever it takes to get into the White House this year," Eli said.

"I wonder..." Jack paused in the act of pouring himself a cup of coffee. "I wonder what happens in a person's life to make them that way. You aren't born with that kind of cynical outlook."

"Good and bad things happen to both good and bad people," said Eli slowly. "You either let the bad things twist you into somebody else, somebody you were never intended to be, or you make sure the good eclipses the bad, and allow yourself to grow, to become a better person for the trials."

"You sound like a preacher," Jack mumbled around the rim of his coffee cup.

"I only speak from what I've found to be true in my own life."

Jack lowered his coffee and gazed intently at Eli. "And I suppose something drastic happened to you at one point in the past that could have sent you in either direction, like you say?"

Eli's face was sober as he ran the edge of his thumb up and down his opposite wrist. "I made a mistake. Once. It could have crippled me forever, but I decided to fight back. To take back what I considered my due. If I had stayed where I was when I was down, I wouldn't be where I am today."

Jack's eyes shifted to the side.

"Guess we both have something in common there," he said quietly.

Eli looked down at him, being almost a head taller, and a slow smile spread across his dark face.

"You protect David. You look out for him." He spoke it as a fact, not a question. "A person with that much care in their heart, it usually comes from a broken piece of their past."

"Well, I think I can say the same for you," Jack returned. "I know you're getting paid for this, and it's your job, but surely by now you truly care about protecting David as more than just a client?"

"He is a good, worthy man," Eli said in a matter-of-fact voice.

"He is the kind of man I would give my life for without hesitation. He has taught me some things I didn't expect when I first took this job. I think I've learned more from listening to his speeches and watching him than I have anywhere else."

"You ever go to church?"

Eli raised his eyebrows, cocking his head. "A funny question coming from a man I've never seen leave his work on a Sunday morning."

Jack gave a wry smile and shrugged one shoulder. "I guess I had a better chance at religion several years ago than I do now. I'm not so sure that I'm ready to follow a God who could have prevented a tragedy from happening that took away basically everything that gave me reason to live."

"You know, David invites me to go to church with him. Every Sunday. Has he ever asked you?"

"He used to ask me more, but I kept telling him no." Jack's brow wrinkled. "Like I said, I don't think I'm ready for that kind of thing. But what about you? How come you never take him up on the offer?"

Eli chuckled shortly, but his eyes were grave. "I guess I could say the same thing as you, but with a twist. I suppose I do believe in God. I think He's capable of using both good and bad people to carry out His will. But..." he hesitated, hooking his thumbs into his pockets. "I guess I have a hard time putting my trust in flawed human beings. I go near a church building, and I feel like I'll only be judged if I step inside. You have people who have this unshakable faith in a Somebody they can't even see, but it's been my experience that even people who call themselves good and caring will look down on you for the mistakes in your past that they can only pretend to really understand. Because you just can't know exactly what another person has gone through, or is going through.

"Well, I guess everybody really is fighting a battle of their own. And you can't make assumptions about anybody."

Eli dipped his head and took out the walkie on his belt. "I better check in with Branson and see how David's doing."

"I think he's rehearsing for tonight, isn't he?"

"Yes, and I think it's about time for a guard change." Eli held the walkie up to his mouth, stopped, and looked at Jack.

"David thinks a lot of you," he said quietly. "If he were your own son, I don't think he could admire you more. He talks about you often, and your kindness to him in being the means to an opportunity he couldn't have dreamed of."

Jack turned his head to the side, feeling foolish for the sudden warm moistness in his eyes. Eli nodded to him in silent understanding as he walked away.

↑CHAPTER 14:

In the final week of September, autumn was beginning early in the south. Though the weather remained warm, there was an underlying crispness in the air, and the leaves were tinged with dull brown streaked with red. The light itself looked different with the autumn equinox slowly changing. The atmosphere seemed charged with the promise of summer on its way out.

"So, Jack, where are we headed today?" David said at breakfast one morning. Jack looked up from the map he was studying, then turned it around and slid it across the cafe table.

"Memphis," he said around a mouthful of scrambled eggs. "Our next rally is late tomorrow afternoon, so we gotta hit the road soon as we're done here. You nearly finished?"

"You're asking me, and that's your second plate?" David joked, his eyes roving over the map. He usually studied their routes before their next trip. Jack suspected it was to check and see if there were any places worth sightseeing around the areas where they set up. Although he usually stayed close to the site wherever they went and didn't go anywhere much besides to church, David had in fact a few times wanted to go out and see a few sights around the area. This only happened when Eli or other Blackheart personnel accompanied him, of course.

"Hey, I've been working all night getting us packed up and ready to go," Jack protested. "I think I deserve a little extra for everything I burned working, don't you think?"

David didn't answer, his brows were drawn tightly as he gazed intensely at the map. His finger traced a line along the road through the boldly printed "Memphis".

"Would it be possible for me to take out one of the cars tomorrow, after we set up in the morning?" he asked without looking up.

"Ah..." Jack tilted his head. "Why and wherefore are we going?"

David lifted one shoulder. "I just wanted to go see some places around the Tennessee area where we'll be staying."

"You talking about going down to Graceland? See Elvis' place? Oh, you'll probably want to get yourself some Memphis barbeque, too. It's pretty amazing."

David gave his little half-smile. "Well, I was actually thinking about heading in another direction, although the barbeque does sound good. There's someplace else I need to go."

"Someplace else?" Jack repeated curiously. For all he knew, David had never spent time in Tennessee. How would he know of anywhere else to go?

"Um, well, you do need to check with Eli so he can clear you for taking off. And of course, there's no question about taking a guard along with you."

"Actually..." David looked down at the map again. "This is a place I need to go alone, Jack."

Jack put down his fork.

"You can't be serious."

"I need to do this without any security people tailing me," David said firmly.

Jack leaned back in his chair, hooking his thumbs into his pockets. This was the first time David had made a request to go someplace without security, and obviously for personal reasons that Jack felt he wasn't about to divulge.

"Well, David," he scratched the back of his neck, turning his head to the side as he tried to decide on the wisest answer. "You can go where you like, certainly. Nobody is going to stop you. But I really feel like you should take at least one of the security people with you. If it was just Eli I would be fine. I mean, if you're out and about and somebody recognizes you..."

But David was shaking his head, polite but adamant.

306

CHAPTER 14:

"No, Jack. I need to do this alone."

"David..."

"Trust me, please. I'll be fine. You can give me your cell phone if you're really that worried. I'll just be a few digits away."

"You're not the only one who could get in serious trouble here if I let you do this."

"I shouldn't need more than a few hours. I'll be back in plenty of time before the rally."

Jack knew he wasn't going to budge. David's sky-colored eyes were hard with resolve.

"Oh...ok," he said reluctantly, mentally face-palming at the same time. "Just be careful. And, David?"

"Yes?"

Jack drew his shoulders up to his ears. "Ah, don't let Eli know I let you go, or we're both in big trouble. Understand?"

He expected a good-natured grin, but David's face was quiet and serene.

"I won't," he promised.

"Alright, guys! Microphones sound good, and the stage looks good," Jack hollered as he and his crew completed their setup at the Liberty Bowl Stadium. "Y'all go get yourselves some lunch and take a break, but be sure you're back here in a couple hours, ok?"

James walked up to Jack, who was leaning on the podium with a toothpick between his teeth.

"Well, James," he said thickly, shifting the slender piece of wood to the other side of his mouth, "What d'you think? Could you stand for some lunch about now?

"Yeah, definitely," James smiled thinly. "Are we going out to eat, or should I bring something in?"

Jack stretched, clasping his hands together behind his head. "You know, I could really go for a barbeque sandwich right now," he remarked, his stomach rumbling in agreement. "And since everybody else is going to lunch, how about you go grab us some? It'll just be the two of us."

James cocked his head. "What about David?"

307

Jack slowly took his hands away from his head.

"Well, he's not going to be eating with us," he said slowly. "Ah..." he glanced around, then gestured for James to come closer so he could speak more quietly. "He's going out for a bit. Security doesn't know he's leaving (which I'll probably pay for in a pound of flesh later). So don't tell anybody, is that clear?"

James nodded vigorously. "Um, so, where's he going, anyway?"

Jack shrugged. "He wouldn't say. I guess that's just as well. If Eli asks where he is before he gets back, I'll need all the ignorance I can get, am I right?"

James mustered a laugh.

"At any rate, that leaves more barbeque for us!" Jack added jovially, trying to distract James' mind from the fact that David was sneaking out. James played along, giving Jack the idea he wasn't thinking about it anymore, but as he hurried off to get lunch all he could think about was his next phone call to Dominic York.

"Mr. York, it's me."

"I know, James. I have your caller ID. I trust you have something new to report."

James pressed himself back against the seat of his car, one arm draped over the steering wheel while the other elbow rested against the window frame as he held the phone to his ear. "Yeah. Well, we're in Memphis. And Connally's beat it."

"What?"

"David's gone off somewhere on his own, and apparently nobody knows where or why. Not even Jack."

"Who is Jack?"

"He's like David's handler."

"I thought that's what they had Blackheart for."

"Well then, I don't know. I just know he and David are close."

"Ok, fine. That's not important here anyway. So nobody knows where Connally went?"

"Nobody. Jack said not even security knows."

"Hmm..." York deliberated on the other end. "Interesting. He usually has a guard round the clock, doesn't he? So why give them the slip now?"

"I...I don't know," James mumbled, wishing he had some impressive ideas to share.

"Well, this could give us some of the answers everybody's been looking for, James. Good work. I'll call up my P.I. and have him do some digging. He's already in the area, and if he's any kind of detective he'll already be tailing Connally."

"Ok." James hesitated. "Is there anything else?"

"I have nothing more to say to you, unless you have more to report?"

"No, that's all."

"Well then, James, you have a nice day with your new friends."

As David pulled out of the parking lot in one of the cars leased by The American Party, he didn't see the car parked across the street that stealthily turned around and began following him as he drove away. Nathan Blaine stayed a good fifty yards or so behind David as he followed along behind him. Then as they both passed an alley a few hundred feet down, a smaller black vehicle pulled out of it and began trailing along after Blaine. Thirty seconds later, a large SUV containing two Blackheart agents drove out of the parking lot after David and began following everybody else.

Jack watched them leave.

"I'm sorry, David," he said softly. "You should've known I wouldn't let you go anywhere alone. I can't lose my job, and I can't lose you."

The small convoy of cars and their drivers, unaware of being followed, headed east out of Memphis, traveling for close to two hours. Nathan Blaine, gripping his steering wheel in excitement over a possible lead, grew even more thrilled when they entered the small Tennessee town of Henderson. Surely that could mean only one thing to David, and Nathan's hunch was correct. A few minutes later, David turned into the parking lot of Freed-Hardeman University.

Within minutes, he stepped out of his car, and stood gazing

up at the old brick buildings and the sign curving inward with the letters FREED-HARDEMAN UNIVERSITY across it. Nathan parked several spaces away, sitting in his car as he watched David. Several spaces down from him, the small black car from the alley slid into a spot, the driver settling back in his seat as he too kept his gaze on the young man.

In his early fifties, Wayne Hicks continued to hold the constitution of an ox, the stealth of a fox, and the eyes of a hawk. When trained on a target, Hicks was as relentless as they come, honing in but holding back until the moment of perfect opportunity before swooping in like a falcon in the dive to seize its prey. There seemed to be some sort of charge running through his veins not unlike a perfect machine that, when filled with oil and kept in good condition and connected with electricity, performed its job faultlessly. Hicks never let himself slow down or fall behind. His job was his entire life, and he had dedicated himself to scouring for the truth and stripping away the facades people were always attempting to keep up. Hicks often grumbled to himself that the world would be better off if nobody wore a mask but just showed themselves as they truly were, no matter what it was, so long as they were being honest. It would make jobs like this far easier.

Now, Hicks' eyebrows drew closely together in his habitual thoughtful expression as he watched David. In his mind, he was only thinking, but to most his thinking face looked much more like a sour scowl. Frown lines were permanently etched into his forehead and between his nose. His eyebrows were almost constantly drawn down together, giving him a morosely forbidding expression. His tall forehead appeared even taller by his receding hairline, though he still retained a patch of reddish-brown hair that dropped down over his forehead when it wasn't combed back like it usually was. He had crows-feet around and under the intense, dark blue eyes that were so fierce in their focus, and narrow sideburns that reached halfway down to his firm jawline. His mouth seemed fashioned for strictness, making his profile a brooding, meditative one, as if he were always calculating his next move or the move of his target.

It was this iron-willed man who Dominic York had hired to

follow David Connally. And Wayne Hicks was doing just that – by also following Nathan Blaine. When Blaine made a move, so did Hicks.

As David walked onto the Freed-Hardeman campus, Nathan Blaine slid out of his car, glancing around nonchalantly as he raised a pair of sunglasses to his face and slowly began strolling along after him. Unnoticed by Nathan, Wayne meandered casually behind, looking up at the buildings around them as if he was interested in the architecture. And neither investigator, both assuming they had no reason to be followed themselves, saw the Blackheart men park and start to walk after them at a safe distance as inconspicuously as possible, wearing civilian clothes.

For the next forty-five minutes or so, David traversed the campus. He strolled along with his hands in his pockets or swinging freely by his sides as he visited different parts of the school, oblivious to the men tailing him. He went out onto the Commons and walked the perimeter of the Quad. He spent some time at the Walk of Fame and then headed down to the Loyd Auditorium. He then switched sides and walked over to look at the Heritage Towers. It was a fine day, sunny and crisp outside, with gold and red leaves floating down from the trees and blowing gently across the pavement. David whistled softly as he walked, often pausing his tune each time he stopped to look more closely at a particular spot on the campus. Blaine, closer to him than the others, saw him smiling faintly to himself more than once as if recollecting some memory connected with the area.

He then headed back up the north side of the campus, stopping to go into the Loden-Daniel Library, where he stayed for several minutes before continuing on up in the direction of the Henderson church of Christ building. David stopped a few times to sit on one of the benches spread around the campus, leaning his elbows on his knees and clasping his hands together, just looking around as though he was reliving old memories of time spent in this place. Watching him, Blaine's brain was having a field day.

They followed him all the way up the church building and then saw him cross White Avenue to the Alumni House, which he simply stood in front of for several long seconds without going in.

Blaine and Hicks, from their respective locations, both were thinking along the same lines. Why wasn't he going inside? He just stood there, looking at the building as if trying to decide if he wanted to go in or not. Finally, he took one step toward the door, then stopped, backing up as he shook his head. A smile that was almost sad stole over his cheerful face. He turned and began walking quietly back the way he had come. Blaine, Hicks, and the security guards followed him all the way back to the parking lot where he got in his car and drove away. Blaine hurried back to his car, almost bumping into Hicks who was rushing past him to get to his own vehicle. Neither of them saw the guards go back to their SUV as well. They all followed each other following David back to the rally area, the investigators disappointed that he didn't make any other stops. He simply took the same route back to Memphis.

But disappointment wasn't the only thing Blaine felt. He finally had a clue to the mystery surrounding David Connally, and he was now more determined than ever to pursue this trail wherever it led.

Unbeknownst to Nathan, Wayne Hicks was having some very similar thoughts.

Later that evening with the rally underway, David was operating the audio system while the candidates were onstage speaking. Jack and Mr. Farris stood off by themselves, talking together backstage. Mr. Farris glanced over at David.

"It's hard to believe, isn't it," he murmured.

Jack followed his gaze. "What, David? You're not just now figuring that out."

Mr. Farris tipped his Stetson back and crossed his arms. "No, I mean, this guy's really something else. Not just in the way he can control a crowd, but that he would want to come back here when he's done and return to this kind of job, content to just stay behind the scenes."

"Well, there's no way he can stay behind the scenes anymore. He's way too popular for that now."

"I know, Jack, but that's not the point. See, a man with power usually wants to go on wielding that to his advantage. And I've never seen such chemistry between a man and a mob as I have with David and the American public. Now, what do you think an ordinary man would do with that kind of influence?"

Jack shrugged. "Peddle it for himself. Go on gaining fame and notoriety until he has all the power he wants."

"But David isn't like that at all. He loves the people and he loves talking to them, but when he's done, he's done. He walks away completely detached from all his popularity like it's a coat he can just take off when he's done in the spotlight. And then he comes back to work like a regular member of your crew." Mr. Farris shook his head, a smile of incredulity on his face. "Now you tell me, how does a man gain that kind of mindset, eh?"

They both looked at David again. The young man had both hands on either side of the headphones he wore, then he brought them down to rest on his knees while he sat looking from the equipment he operated out toward the stage. From where he was stationed, he could see part of the audience and the current speaker. When the candidate's words earned a burst of applause, David smiled as proudly as if the crowd's approval had been for himself.

"You know," Jack said, low, "the other day when we were out at breakfast, some guy came up to our table and started telling David how much he admired and respected him for standing up for truths and reminding people what it means to live in a great nation, and so on. But the kicker is, this guy tells us he's been a die-hard Democrat practically his whole life. But he was so moved by what David's been saying that he had true respect for him."

"Well, people with open and honest hearts can only agree with truth once they find it," Mr. Farris nodded. "I think we've become so biased in our thinking that because there are two major factions in American politics we're forced to side with one or the other. The truth is that there are good people and bad people on both sides. Just like in war. No single party is wholly pure and has the best interests of the nation at heart while the other is totally evil. That's why people like David, who doesn't belong to either the Republicans or Democrats, simply stand for what is true, good, and best. People have a thirst for that. They don't get enough of it. And it's people like David who will make America stronger as a nation under God. Party affiliations don't always label what's in a person's heart."

"No, but they often give a pretty good idea."

"Yes. But as your little story just proved, truth may be often ridiculed, but ultimately it will stand when everything else falls."

Mr. Farris' cell phone rang.

"Oh, hold on, Jack. This is..." he checked the caller ID, then frowned. "This is nobody I know, apparently. Give me a minute, would you?"

Jack waved him away, and Mr. Farris walked off toward the hotel lobby that was connected to the stadium, holding the phone to his ear.

"Hello? Who is this?"

"Are you Michael Farris?"

"Yes, but may I ask who's calling?"

"Mr. Farris, my name is Nathan Blaine, and I was hired by Rick McCoy as a private investigator to look into some things regarding David Connally. You can check back with him to confirm my story."

"There's a lot of big names in there. Go on."

"Well, this is unorthodox, and I would ordinarily report straight back to Mr. McCoy, but I can't seem to reach him right now, so I'm coming to his number two man. I know you run everything by him, so I thought maybe you could give him some information for me."

Mr. Farris waited warily before saying, "What is it?"

"Today I believe I found the most credible clues to date to tell us where our mysterious friend came from. Tomorrow morning while you guys are breaking everything down, I'm going to investigate some more, look into that information and hopefully find out more than what I've been coming up with for the past few months."

"Alright, well, what do you want us to do in the meantime?"

"Just keep an eye on David while I'm checking this out."

"What do you think we've been doing all this time?"

Nathan laughed.

"Hey, Mr. McCoy doesn't keep me informed of everything you guys do; it usually works the opposite way. No offense to anyone."

"Ok," Mr. Farris smiled. "Say, where are you headed, anyway? Or are you not allowed to say where you found this profound clue?"

"Freed-Hardeman University."

"Freed-Hardeman?"

"I can't say more right now. I need to be sure of some things first. Check records and such."

Mr. Farris tried to adjust his speeding thoughts. "Well, if you still can't reach McCoy, let me know as soon as you know something, and I'll get the info straight back to headquarters."

"Yes sir. If I can't get hold of McCoy, you'll hear from me."

Mr. Farris clipped his phone back onto his belt with a frown. As he walked slowly back toward the stage area, a young man in a hooded sweater and a baseball cap pulled over his eyes brushed against him as he passed through the door, hurrying to get by him. Mr. Farris barely gave him a passing glance, his mind was so preoccupied. A clue. They had a clue.

James Rivers was afraid he had been recognized by Mr. Farris when he rushed by him, but the man didn't stop him or call his name, so hopefully he hadn't seen his face. James whipped out his cell phone, eager to relate what he had just overheard before the information evaporated from his mind.

The next morning, Nathan Blaine returned to the university, eager to find more clues connected with David's past. He was too preoccupied to notice Wayne Hicks following him back to Freed-Hardeman. After James called Dominic York concerning Mr. Farris and Blaine's conversation on which he had eavesdropped, York contacted Hicks with the information, and so both investigators were headed back to the same place.

Nathan revisited the same locations David had the day before, keeping his eyes peeled for anything that might reveal a link to the young man. But as he tried to see what David had seen, he was forced to come to the disappointing conclusion that no names on the buildings or any of the little local spots David had walked were of help to him in his search. All the while, Hicks tailed him like a silent shadow.

Nathan finally sat down on the Commons. As he tilted his head back to look into the blue sky, a wrinkle creased his forehead.

"What am I missing?" he muttered to himself, tapping his fingers against his arm. He had the strongest feeling David must have attended this college. His behavior the day before had provided ample evidence that he was very familiar with the campus. And he had just seemed so at home there. Besides, Nathan thought to himself as he trudged up toward the administration building, why would David take off without security just to visit some random university? No, Nathan decided as he opened the door of the administration building. Something else was going on here.

The building was fairly deserted when he entered. The only other person he could see was a middle-aged woman sitting behind the registrar's desk. Nathan walked up to her.

"Hi," he said lightly in response to her friendly smile. "I'm wondering if you can help me."

"I can certainly try."

"You see, I'm looking for the records of a former student here."

"Yes sir, what year was the student here?"

"Eh..." Nathan's mind raced for a moment. "I don't know the exact year, but it would be in the records for the past ten years."

"And the student's name?"

"Connally."

The registrar pulled her wireless keyboard and mouse closer. "Is that with two Ls?"

Nathan nodded.

The woman turned to her computer and began a database search while Nathan lounged against the high desk, wetting his lips in anticipation.

After looking intently at the screen for a few minutes, clicking, scrolling, and typing her way through several pages, the registrar looked up at Nathan.

"There have been four students with the name Connally here

in the last ten years," she said. He immediately straightened and tried to peer over the desk to see her screen. "But let me see..." She clicked the mouse again, adjusting her glasses with the other hand. "Three of them were women."

"This would be a male," said Nathan eagerly.

"I see, and there is the one male. Was his first name Rudolph, and was he from Germany?"

Nathan's shoulders slumped.

"No," he said bitterly. "Is that all you have for Connally?"

"Everything for the past ten years," she said, her voice sympathetic to the disappointment on his face. "I'm sorry you didn't find what you're looking for."

Nathan nodded, crestfallen.

She tilted her head, her face brightening. "Wait a moment," she exclaimed as he turned to leave. Nathan turned. "Maybe you should go over to the Loden-Daniel library," she suggested. "Ask for Marian Carter. She's been here longer than I have, and knows most of the students, past and present. She also has some records over there that I don't have here."

Nathan hurried back, hope once again filling his eyes. "What records would she have that aren't here with you?"

"Well, I know I don't have the Mission's Training School files, and Marian does."

Nathan raised an eyebrow, but he thanked her sincerely before hurrying back toward the library.

The door had barely closed behind him when it opened again, and Wayne Hicks approached the registrar.

"Good morning," he said evenly. She looked up at him.

"I'm looking for a friend of mine. He was supposed to meet me here with information for some research we're working on together, but I don't see him." Hicks looked around innocently.

"Oh," the woman said slowly, realization dawning on her face. "There was a man in here just a moment ago – you just missed him! He was looking for records of somebody named Connally?"

"That's him!" Hicks exclaimed, sounding relieved. "I hope he's not trying to avoid me!"

The registrar laughed, then added, "He just went down to the Loden-Daniel library to do some more digging. I'm sure you can find him down there."

"Thank you very much," Hicks said with a syrupy smile.

Nathan entered the Loden-Daniel library and quietly made his way past the small groups of students huddled around tables while they studied. He approached the librarian's desk and found an impeccably dressed elderly lady with soft white hair rolled up in a bun at the nape of her neck. Her glasses were attached to a thin silvery chain draped around her neck. Her smile was pleasant and her voice sweet when she asked, "Can I help you, young man?"

"Are you Marian Carter?"

"I am."

"Then, hopefully, yes you can. I'm looking for a male student by the last name of Connally. I believe he's been here in the past ten years, though which year exactly I'm not certain."

She nodded thoughtfully. "Did you have Sarah check the records in the administration building?"

"I did, but, eh, Sarah there couldn't help me. She sent me to you, thinking you might be able to."

"Oh, well that's sweet of her," the little woman beamed. "It's true I probably do have some files over here that she doesn't..." Nathan gave her an impatient smile. She put a wrinkled finger to her chin. "Well, let's see now. I've known several Connallys here down through the years..." She suddenly turned to her computer. "Please, have a seat while I check my files."

Nathan looked around and pulled out the nearest chair by the nearest table. His knees bounced up and down as he tried to wait patiently, hoping his luck was about to change.

"Alright," Marian announced, and Nathan jumped up. "I have records for a total of six Connally's: four men and two women. Now to narrow it down for the year span you requested...What is the student's first name?"

"Ah..." Nathan hesitated. With David's fame, he was unwilling to give more than David's surname. "What names do you have listed?"

"Well, for the men I have a Rudolph and a Byrom...but the latter passed away in an accident near the campus about eight years ago."

"And the other two?" Nathan demanded as politely as possible. "What about the students in the Mission School?" he added, remembering what the registrar had told him.

"I know almost all of them, but I don't remember a Connally being in that school any time during the past ten years..." she trailed off as she pulled out a record book and looked through it. Nathan waited on pins and needles.

"I'm so sorry, but I can't find a record of any Connally for that time period."

Nathan clenched his fist against the side of his head as he leaned his elbow on the desk, slumping against the hard wood. "Perfect," he muttered.

She watched his demeanor as she slid the record book back in its place.

"Are you quite sure the man you're looking for went to school here?" she asked.

"You know," Nathan said with a heavy sigh, "I truly believed he did, but now..." He shook his head, gazing in another direction. He suddenly felt as worn out as if he had run all over campus instead of walking. This was proving to be one of his most challenging, not to mention discouraging, cases yet. "What a day."

He decided to leave, but when he looked back to thank the little librarian, she had disappeared. He looked around curiously and saw her coming back through a door to a room behind her desk. Her arms were piled with wide, thick volumes in leathery shades of black, brown, and maroon. Nathan's eyes widened.

"These may not be of much help," she said, panting slightly as she walked around the desk. Nathan hurried to take the books from her arms. "But we do have all the yearbooks from the school stored here. These are only some of the collection; the rest are back there. But feel free to look through them and see if you can find who you're looking for. Maybe he changed his name or something."

THE SPEAKER

Nathan looked down at the stack of yearbooks in his arms, then back at Marian, who was smiling as if she had found the answer to all his problems.

"Thank you," he said sincerely, and she bobbed her head cheerfully.

"Just let me know when you're done with those and we can get you some more!" she called over her shoulder as she walked back to her computer.

With this new prospect before him, Nathan carried the yearbooks over to the table and sat down once more, opening the top book on the stack. These all appeared to be from within the last ten years. Nathan resigned himself and began thumbing through the pages. "Ok, David, where are you..."

Wayne Hicks quietly walked into the library and looked around as he moseyed along the shelves, pretending to be searching for a book while keeping an eye out for Blaine. Coming around a corner of a reading section, he quickly backed up when he saw Blaine sitting at a table with his back facing him. Hicks slid out of sight and peered at him through the slim space between the tops of the books and the bottom of the next shelf. Blaine appeared to be going through yearbooks. Hicks caught a glimpse of a page with rows of similar-looking photos. Hicks suddenly felt an urge to chuckle. At this rate he wouldn't have to do hardly any sleuthing on his own. If he just kept following this guy around, Blaine would find his clues for him, and Hicks could do the rest.

Marian kept an eye on Nathan while he hunted though the pages, evidently growing increasingly frustrated with his lack of information. With the end of each book, he let out a heavy sigh and let the back cover fall with a thump. Rubbing his forehead, he started on with the next one. She watched his unsuccessful search for about fifteen minutes between pauses in her own work, when she suddenly brightened up and hurried into the back room behind her desk again. Nathan didn't see her, he was still so engrossed in his search. She walked back out a minute later holding a much older yearbook.

CHAPTER 14:

"You know, I do recall another Connally from the Mission School, but that must have been almost thirty years ago," she said, as if talking to herself. Nathan rubbed his neck and looked up, only mildly interested, as it gave him an excuse to momentarily break from the seemingly endless poring over yearbook pictures. Marian brought the book over to his table and spread it out beside him, flipping gingerly through the pages.

"I appreciate this, but that can't be Dav– the man I'm looking for," he tried to tell her wearily. "It's too far back."

"Connally! There it is!" she exclaimed brightly, smoothing her hand across the page and pointing at a small picture. Nathan sighed and slowly dragged his eyes up to the smiling face at the end of her finger.

And for a moment, he couldn't have been more certain that he was looking at a picture of David Connally himself.

Nathan's initial reaction was a start of amazement, half-rising from his chair as he bent over the picture. "That can't be!" he muttered excitedly. "There's no way..."

Then as he looked closer, he could see that it wasn't David at all. The resemblance was eerily striking, but this was a different man. He had the same sandy hair, same strong jawline, the same charming laugh lines around his blue eyes, and the same smile so warm and inviting that Nathan had to blink several times and look hard to make sure it wasn't David. But no, this was somebody else. Nathan's gaze traveled over to the name beside the photo, and his finger stopped underneath the black printed letters.

"Robert Connally."

Very much interested now, Nathan pushed the other yearbooks aside and sat down, pulling the old one towards himself. "Can you tell me anything about this man?"

"Let me see now..." she cocked her head. "If I remember correctly, he came to Freed from Oklahoma, studying to go into mission work."

Nathan watched her intently, silently begging her not to pause.

"I believe his family was in the oil business. He lost his mother

321

to cancer, and his father died in a freak plane crash in Canada. Poor boy. But he still wanted to come to school and learn how to take the Gospel to foreign soil."

"Yes, yes," Nathan tried not to sound too demanding or impatient, but he felt he was hot on the trail now. He could feel his right knee start to bounce again.

"Anyway, he enrolled in the Mission School after he finished his degree. Oh, and his wife was a real sweetheart of a lady." Marian smiled reminiscently. "I remember her very well, now that I think about it...gracious, how long ago it's been!"

Nathan looked up quickly at the word 'wife.'

"He had a wife? Is there a picture in here of her, too?" He flipped feverishly through the pages.

"There should be. She was in the Mission School too. Here..." Marian turned over a few pages and showed him a picture of a lovely young woman with bronze-colored skin and big, dark eyes that matched the color of her long, flowing hair. "This is her."

Nathan stared at the picture. Her smile was similar to the young man's on the other page. Nathan flipped back to Robert's picture and compared the two. Both of them looked to be in their mid-to-late twenties. And when Nathan looked closely at the woman's picture again, he saw one side of her smile was tilted up more than the other...an expression he remembered seeing David Connally give time and again on TV. The name beside the young lady's picture was Nalda Caballero.

Nathan sank back in his chair, his mind in a whirl. Could it be that David hadn't attended Freed-Hardeman after all? Had he come here only because...and Nathan hardly dared to hope...maybe he was paying a tribute visit to honor his relatives who went to school here? Maybe even...his parents?

Nathan flipped through the book again, coming to rest on a page showing a photo of Robert Connally and Nalda Caballero together. Only this must have been after they had gotten married, for beneath the picture somebody had scribbled, "Congratulations and good luck to the Connallys and their mission work in Tanzania!"

Marian looked fondly down at the picture.

CHAPTER 14:

"Yes, it's coming back to me now. Such a sweet couple. If you just give me a moment, I'll draw up their personal files. Mission students provide the schools with their family history. I'll just check the archives..."

Delighted that he had found some kind of true lead at last, Nathan waited while she pulled up the files and printed them behind her desk. She brought them over and sat down next to him.

"This library wasn't here then, it was just a chapel," she informed him. He crossed his arms on the table and leaned forward, intrigued. "Many of the student couples at the time would meet here and then get married at the chapel. And that's exactly what these two did." She tapped her finger on the picture of the Connallys.

"The young woman, Nalda, I do remember her well." Marian rummaged through the papers she had printed out. "She and all her family came over from Cuba."

"Cuba!"

"Yes. Is something wrong?"

Nathan shook his head, but all he could think of now was his recent trip to Cuba and how at the time he had no idea how close he had been to cracking the political mystery of the decade. "Nothing. Please continue."

"Well, the boat Nalda's family used to cross over to the states was caught in a terrible storm. Everybody on board was lost except for two: Nalda and one of the crew members. They were stranded on an oil rig in the Gulf of Mexico, where they were fortunately rescued. The oil workers took her to Galveston, Texas after they found out the poor girl had lost all of her family. You see," Marian said, leaning conspiratorially toward Nathan, "there were some Cuban families living down there."

He nodded. "But what happened next?"

"Well, some members of the church tried to help Nalda," Marian said, clearly enjoying telling the story. "I believe she was nineteen years old at the time. Anyway, she had some nurse training in Cuba, so the church down in Galveston helped send her to nursing school down there.

"When she completed nursing school, she came here,

interested in doing mission work. That's when she and Robert met, both of them realizing they shared a love for the mission field that eventually turned into love for each other. After a year they graduated and got married here in the chapel – when it was still a chapel, that is. Ah, I remember that day...though I guess I haven't thought of it in years. They made such a lovely couple!"

Nathan digested this information in silence as he took out a notepad and pen and began to furiously write.

"I did feel sorry for them, though," Marian said regretfully.

Nathan's pen slowed. "What do you mean?"

"Well, neither of them had any living family. They were all the family each other had. But I suppose that did make it easier for them to go out on the mission field – no ties here or anywhere else."

Nathan stood up. He felt he suddenly needed to be on his way as quickly as possible.

"Thank you, ma'am," he said as he hurriedly gathered his things together and pushed his chair back under the table.

"I hope this was of help to you," she ventured.

"Oh, believe me," he grinned jubilantly. "It was."

Hicks ducked back around the corner of the bookshelf behind him as Nathan rushed past him. The excitement in his voice before he left was enough to assure Hicks that Nathan was on a lead, and Hicks casually followed him out of the building. With any luck, Nathan would lead him right to the source of the secrecy surrounding David Connally.

"Hello, this is Farris."

"It's Nathan Blaine again. I found something about David today, but I'd rather meet you in person to talk about it instead of speaking over the phone. Could I meet you somewhere?"

Mr. Farris automatically looked around and said, "What if you just swing by the stage area here? We're getting ready to move out to Dallas, but I have time to meet with you if you want to come by."

"That's what I'll do. See you in a couple of hours."

Mr. Farris was talking with James when he got a text from Nathan saying he had arrived.

"Listen, James, I need to go, but just tell Jack that for me and I'll meet up with you guys later." He slapped James on the shoulder as he walked past him. James started down the hall, but stopped and looked after Mr. Farris. He hesitated a moment, then hurried quietly after him.

Mr. Farris went into the lobby of the hotel where the crew, Jack, David, and everyone else connected with The American Party were staying. Nathan Blaine rose from the decorative sofa in front of the large stone fireplace in the middle of the room as he approached.

"Michael Farris?" he asked, extending his hand.

"That's me, and you must be Nathan Blaine."

"I'm the only one here," Nathan smiled. Mr. Farris looked around, and it was true that the lobby was deserted except for the two of them. "It's nice to meet you. I'm actually on my way out but I'm glad I was able to talk to you in person first."

"Oh, well, I'm glad too. Now what did you want to tell me?"

"Well, again, I can't say too much about it, but I think I found the answer to where David may have come from."

"Well, what about him?" Mr. Farris demanded. "Is he a jailbird? Drug smuggler? Is he even an American?"

Nathan worked his jaw. "I do not know that he is an American citizen."

Mr. Farris put his hands on his hips, shifting his feet and shaking his head as he looked down at the polished tile floor. Why his disappointment at this news was so sourly choking he wouldn't admit even to himself; that he had actually thought David might possibly have been a presidential candidate, and now the last chance for that hope seemed wrecked.

"Are you absolutely sure?" he asked without looking up.

"I'm...ninety percent sure he's not," said Nathan slowly. Mr. Farris raised his head. "Only ninety? Well that's ten percent of hope left for us."

"Well, to prove it one way or another, I would have to go to

Africa."

"Africa? Why Africa? He's clearly not African."

"I'm not ruling out anything at this point, Mr. Farris. And that's where I'm on my way to as soon as we're done here. If McCoy has no problems with it, I'll take the earliest flight to Tanzania."

"Is David from Tanzania?"

"Like I said, Mr. Farris, there's still much I don't know. But I should be back in a week or so, and then I think we'll have our answer for sure. I have a hot trail under me right now, and it's the best I've found yet that's worth following."

"Then I guess you better get going," Mr. Farris agreed. "I'll tell the office what's going on and what you've just told me. Jack and I will, of course, keep an eye on David till you get back."

"Good." Nathan nodded solemnly. "I hope you'll continue keeping him away from the media, too. I don't think he should be talking to any reporters."

"Oh, we're already on top of that."

"Alright then." Nathan checked his watch, then slapped his pockets, smoothing down the front of his jacket. "I guess I'm off, then. I haven't been to Africa in a long time. I hope the shot I had to get last time still carries over."

Mr. Farris smiled in return, his eyes earnest.

"Be careful out there, Mr. Blaine. And please let us know as soon as you find out anything. The earlier, the better."

"Oh, definitely. I will," Nathan replied. He and Mr. Farris shook hands, and Nathan exited the lobby into the late afternoon.

Mr. Farris stood by himself for a moment, deep in thought, then turned around and walked back through the lobby to the elevators.

CHAPTER 15:

James waited until he heard the elevator doors slide shut behind Mr. Farris before edging out from behind the big stone fireplace in the lobby. He looked outside at Nathan's retreating figure.

"Wow, this is big," he murmured, twisting his hand around in his pocket to find his phone. "I better tell York."

York was in the middle of dinner when James called.

"What?" he asked tersely, still chewing.

"Nathan Blaine is leaving the country tomorrow."

York stopped chewing. "He found a new lead?"

"I just heard a whole conversation between him and Michael Farris. He's pretty sure that David is somehow connected with Africa."

"Africa," York echoed Mr. Farris' skeptical response. "Where in Africa?"

"He said he's taking the first flight out of Memphis to Tanzania."

York swallowed his food and took a sip of coffee. "I'll let my investigator know immediately. Good work, James."

As Jack was getting ready for bed that night, he turned on the television for background noise. He wasn't surprised to see a news report with David's name in the title. It was a regular occurrence by now.

"This is Shaun Hanson, your national conservative news host, with a special interview tonight with the acclaimed and nationally recognized blogger Todd Morris, senior writer for Web America.

↑THE SPEAKER

Todd, thanks for being with us tonight."

Todd Morris, a man in his mid-thirties with a pleasant smile and lively eyes, nodded enthusiastically in response. He folded his hands and propped up his elbows on both arms of his pastel chair. "Thanks for having me! I always appreciate the opportunity, Shaun."

"Let me begin by saying that, to the best of my knowledge, you have written more than anybody else concerning the political rise of David Connally. What got you started blogging about David?"

Todd smiled as if he had received a great compliment.

"Well, it really began, if you want technicalities, back in April when I was visiting my sister in Nashville. She begged me to go with her to hear this guy who was singing for The American Party. I wasn't really interested, and frankly, thought it sounded a little weird." He laughed. "But you know sisters, eventually she convinced me. That was my first time to see David Connally live. And I can tell you, it was certainly an amazing experience being a part of that crowd while he led us in singing some of America's most patriotic songs, and then got everyone all riled up for the political speakers. And just before he left the stage, I remember, he made a few comments to the audience. You or I might call those comments political, but I don't believe he meant them to sound that way at all, actually. I believe he was simply speaking from the heart about his love for God and for America."

"And what was it exactly that he said which made you write about him consistently for six months?"

"Well, he said several things we already know: that America is made of the American people, and that we have been provided the God-given right to select our leaders, and that we as the people truly hold in our hands the power to make this nation great again. It was kind of like reminding us that we really are in charge, not just those up in D.C. Whether we succeed or fail, we the people will be responsible for what happens."

Shaun leaned forward. "So if you were to summarize for the sake of our audience tonight, what would you say is the message that David Connally is trying to get across to the American people?"

"I think David has a lot of messages to get across!" Todd

laughed again, rubbing his forehead with the back of his knuckles. "But in all seriousness, some of the things he's said are very straightforward and simple, while others are unique and complex. He has said things like, America needs reminding of who the government really is, and that all politicians - the president, senators, governors, congressmen, you name it - should not be allowed to be influenced by lobbyists. Or that men and women should be elected to office based upon what they intend to do for the country. I think he expects every politician to put their country first, which is, you know, fairly obvious. Ha, some people are saying he's like the next James Madison because of his belief in a smaller federal government with much more power granted to the state governments."

Jack sat down on the end of his bed, his toothbrush sticking out of his mouth while he watched the TV screen.

"David also seems to believe that the people should hold their elected officials accountable for their moral and ethical values, and that those who fail to uphold these principles should be immediately discharged from office," Todd went on. "I recently heard him say that benevolence and welfare should be administered by churches and private organizations rather than the government itself. And he has said the people have a right to jobs, and that instead of seeking to make it easier for those who don't have jobs, the government should do its best to provide jobs and make it possible for people to work. The people thrive in a system where the government gives them the opportunity to achieve the American dream. Then you get out of their way and let them work for themselves. The American people need an environment where they can create, enterprise, and work. I mean, can you think of a way to better the economy? Any man or woman who is mentally and physically capable of working in the private sector should have priority in getting jobs, with the focus on government jobs being second priority."

"So he's basically saying if you don't work, you don't eat."

"Exactly. And that's not David being mean, it's him saying that any able-bodied man or woman should be able to have a job that brings them steady income. The government needs to take more responsibility in creating those jobs, not taking them away or trying to worsen the jobless situation by making the unemployed more comfortable in their jobless state. The government needs to make sure there is work available. But you see, David also says that those who can work should help support those who cannot. I think he believes that even those who are truly needy should receive aid from their fellow man, not the government.

Jack got up to rinse his mouth and hurried back to finish watching the interview.

"And speaking of help, he has told the people that government shouldn't give away welfare to other governments in pecuniary form. But for any place in the world where there's a disaster, the American people can certainly send other forms of aid. It would just be better if it wasn't in the form of money."

"But if some country needs a dam built or something, shouldn't we give them money for that?"

"Well, I think David would say in that type of circumstance that private American corporations should oversee the work being done and can provide help for that country," Todd answered.

"You've spent so much time listening to him and writing about him that you're already able to predict his mind!" Shaun laughed, and Todd joined in.

"If I may change the subject, though," Shaun said. "I have heard that he has said that America shouldn't be involved in the U.N. Is that true?"

"Yes, you heard right, it's absolutely true. David said that while America should be friendly and peaceable with all nations, we shouldn't allow a body of foreign officials to oversee this country, nor should America be in the business of overseeing other countries. Our primary focus should be governing ourselves in a good and proper manner."

"Is he telling the people anything about election reform?"

"I'm glad you mentioned that," Todd grinned. "He's basically said that we shouldn't elect people who speak evil of others, or who criticize past and present officials to make themselves look better. His view is that we can't change the past, so we shouldn't elect people who spend their time complaining about it instead of moving forward to make things better. He advises that we elect people who spend less time talking and more time doing what they can to improve the future of this great nation, yet the best way they can do that is by looking back to the beginning when it all started with the dream the Founding Fathers had."

Shaun glanced down at his notes. "Well, is there anything else David has said that's particularly stood out to you, Todd?"

"I think one of his more powerful points is that the government is mainly here to protect our civil rights and liberties," Todd replied. "And that government is to ensure our domestic well-being without encroaching on our lives and creating laws that pretend to work for our benefit but in reality only serve to push the agenda of those in power."

Jack felt himself grinning without realizing he had started to. "Atta boy, David," he said softly.

"Well, those are some good thoughts, Todd," Shaun Hanson said to his interview guest. "I wish we could visit some more, but we're almost out of time. If any of you viewers would like to read more of Todd Morris' work following David Connally, check out his blog on Web America. You can also follow Todd on Twitter or Facebook. That's our exclusive for this evening. You all have a good night!"

CHAPTER 16:

The flight that Nathan Blaine found himself on that night was bound for Amsterdam. After he boarded the plane and slowly made his way up the aisle, his carry-on knocked against the knee of a passenger already seated. Nathan hurriedly pulled his luggage closer to himself.

"My apologies, sir."

"Don't worry about it."

The man's reply was as cool and polite as the smile he sent in Nathan's direction. Nathan nodded in return, and continued up the aisle. After a few steps he turned his head just enough to look back at the other man, who was now opening a newspaper on his lap. Nathan's brow furrowed, but he wasn't sure what it was about the stranger that suddenly seemed vaguely familiar to him. With a shrug, he turned around and made his way to his assigned seat, several rows behind the other man. As he leaned his head back and stared out the tiny airplane window, he tried to shake off the uneasiness tugging at the back of his mind.

When his flight reached Amsterdam, Nathan headed straight for his next gate of departure. He had a layover of a couple hours, so he decided that instead of just sitting at the gate for the whole time he would go grab a bite to eat. When he returned, he noticed with another sudden twinge of disquiet that the same man he had bumped into on the flight from Memphis was now sitting in the same gate area Nathan was to fly out of. When Nathan walked past him to a seat, the man barely raised his eyes, but Nathan caught a flicker of movement, and an inexplicable sense of annoyance flared up in his chest. He sat down several seats away from the stranger and didn't look at him for the rest of his wait till the plane arrived. It wasn't until he was on the plane for Tanzania, looking at his notes on what he had discovered at Freed-Hardeman University, that he realized the other man had sat down across the aisle, three rows up.

"What's wrong with you, Nathan?" he muttered to himself, rustling his papers in an effort to refocus. It was just a man who happened to be on the same flights to Tanzania that he was. And there were others on the plane besides the two of them. So why that troublesome nagging sensation he was feeling? It must be the jet-lag; it always messed up his system, no matter how often he flew overseas for his work. Nathan finally put his notes away and leaned back, shutting his eyes and letting the soft roaring of the turbine engines lull him into a restful sleep.

The circling of the British Airways jet woke him, and he looked out the window to see they were beginning their descent into the Mount Kilimanjaro Airport in Arusha. The view of the famous mountain from the sky was magnificent. Beautiful, huge, and imposing, the flat-topped peak was dusted with snow like powdered sugar. Wisps of cloud hazed around it, shrouding the mountain in obscurity near the top. Nathan studied it with admiration as he set foot on African soil.

He wasted no time in securing passage on a small plane that would fly out of Arusha in a few hours to Dar es Salaam, the capitol city of Tanzania. No sooner had he walked away from purchasing his ticket when Nathan saw, out of the corner of his eye, the same man who had traveled with him from Memphis approaching the same counter he had just left. Nathan's eyes narrowed. Could somebody really be following him? But how could they know to do so, and that he had been going to Africa? The only person he had told besides Rick McCoy had been Michael Farris, and the two of them had been alone during that conversation.

Nathan stood waiting for his luggage by the baggage carousel; he kept one eye discreetly on the man as he spoke with the person behind the ticket counter. He booked passage and turned around, and Nathan quickly looked in another direction. He looked down at the carousel, watching the various pieces of luggage drift around until their owners dragged them off and toted them away. Nathan finally saw his plain brown suitcase moving toward him, and involuntarily stepped forward to take it. He hadn't taken three steps with it when a polished voice suddenly arrested his motion.

"Excuse me, I believe that's mine."

Nathan looked over his shoulder in surprise, and was even more so when he saw it was that same man. The man who might or might not be following him, dogging his steps for some unknown reason. Nathan blinked.

"Ah, I think this is my suitcase," he said, the courteousness in his voice just tinged with coolness.

The stranger took a step closer, the same civil smile of decorum frozen on his face. He pointed to the name tag attached to the handle of the suitcase. Nathan glanced down and read it silently.

"Not to seem rude, but if you and I do share the same name that would be a remarkable coincidence," the man said with a casual shrug.

Coincidence indeed, Nathan thought. There were far too many coincidences happening today. He read the name tag once more to commit it to memory before shaking his head as he handed over the luggage.

"My apologies...again, Mr, ah, Hicks" he said awkwardly, though still trying to maintain his smile so as not to show hostility. He looked over at the luggage carousel and saw his own suitcase about to disappear round the bend again.

"I'm sure it's not the first time this has ever happened," the other man returned, hefting his luggage. "Enjoy your stay in Africa."

Nathan couldn't see his eyes. They were hidden behind a pair of especially dark sunglasses. But he didn't like how the man's smile widened knowingly as he turned away, or the tune he started whistling before he was out of earshot.

"Wayne Hicks," he said quietly as he retrieved his suitcase. "First thing I'm going to do when I get to Dar es Salaam is find a Wi-Fi connection. This guy needs looking into."

Nathan did his best not to give his suspected rival more than a furtive glance every now and then during their flight to Dar es

Salaam. He didn't know whether Hicks was doing the same thing with him whenever his eyes were turned away, but he didn't want the other man to suspect him of anything in return. Let Hicks think he was getting away with whatever he wanted to get away with. Nathan was sure he would find out plenty about him when he had access to research.

In the meantime, it felt like the plane would never arrive at its destination.

Once they reached Julius Nyerere International Airport in Dar es Salaam, Nathan immediately gathered his gear and set off through the terminal, being careful to keep Hicks in his peripheral vision. He had the hunch that if he really was being tailed, Hicks would keep him in sight at all times. He tested this by lingering near one of the restaurants and ducking into a gift shop under pretext of browsing. Whenever he stopped, his dogged shadow would, too, and always be apparently devoting himself to another past-time close by. Nathan was growing not only increasingly irritated, but also worried. Not for his own safety so much as that of David Connally's. If this Wayne Hicks had been able to successfully tail him in secrecy like this without Nathan having discovered him until now, who knows how long ago he had started? And what was he, anyway? Nathan's mind raced to find an explanation. A reporter? Possibly. Another investigator? That was more likely, but Nathan knew McCoy hadn't hired him. The best probability right now was that he was hired by somebody on the opposite side.

Which would only mean that Nathan couldn't be too careful about whatever he discovered about David Connally on this continent.

There's nothing you can do about it right now, he told himself, unwillingly enough. Do what you came here to do, and remember that McCoy hired you because you're the best. This guy isn't going to find out anything you don't let him.

Feeling somewhat foolish for standing in the middle of the walking area having this private pep talk with himself, Nathan got moving and entered customs, keeping an eye on Hicks as he, too, passed through the process. His passport stamped, Nathan left the terminal, walking jauntily along as though he had no idea he was being followed. When he reached the airport entrance, he stopped and called for a taxi. Without looking around before he got in, he said simply, "The U.S. Embassy, please."

He didn't have to check who got in the taxi behind him to know that Hicks was still on his trail.

Weary from travel and jet-lag, Nathan stumbled out of the taxi and gazed up at the clean, simple architecture of Dar es Salaam's United States Embassy building. Tilting his head from side to side, he popped his neck and drew his shoulders back before marching into the embassy.

He inquired at the front where he might find information about Americans who lived in Tanzania, and was directed to the desk of a government official. Nathan questioned the venerable older man in his uniform with respectful inquisitiveness. But his curiosity was only met with negative answers as the official assured him there was no record of any American currently in the country with the last name of Connally.

"But if he had lived here at one time and then left, would there be a record of that?"

"No sir, those records would have been transferred back to Washington D.C."

Nathan massaged his forehead.

"I'm looking for a David Connally," he said, finally resorting to using David's full name in his desperate search for answers. "He would have been here in the last ten years."

The old man checked for him, but shook his head. "I can find no record, sir."

"Ok then...do you have a Robert Connally listed? He may have been a missionary or something."

The old man peered over his glasses, his mouth puckered in annoyance at the frustration in Nathan's voice.

"There are many missionaries who come and go. We do not keep track of them all. They are here on their own and usually do not become permanent residents."

Nathan rubbed a finger up and down the bridge of his nose, squeezing his eyes shut. Weariness was clouding his thoughts. He couldn't believe he had come all this way for a dead end.

"You might make your inquiries at the Missionary Society offices," the old man told him after a pause. "They're located on Queens Boulevard."

Nathan nodded mutely and thanked the official for his help before leaving the embassy. He noted the taxi that continued to follow him, but tried to ignore it. If he hadn't found out anything, Hicks hadn't either. He directed his driver to the Missionary Society on Queens Boulevard and forced his eyes to stay open during the ride there.

It was an old building his taxi pulled up in front of. Nathan didn't spend any time looking at it. He shut the car door and headed straight for the entrance, stifling yawns while he walked.

Inside it was quiet, the atmosphere tranquil. Nathan noticed a receptionist behind a desk, and through a door to his right a couple of men were reading in a small library. How many people behind desks had he spent time talking to this week? He suddenly felt an urge to turn around and leave. But the receptionist was smiling at him in a friendly way, and he had nowhere else to go for information. Nathan approached the desk.

"How can I help you?" she asked kindly. There were laugh lines around her eyes and mouth, and her blond hair was pulled up in a curly ponytail. She had a youthful, eager-to-please look about her.

"I'm looking for a missionary by the name of Robert Connally," Nathan answered, trying to keep the disgruntled sound out of his voice.

"Alright...let me see..."

She began the familiar task of searching through record books on the shelves behind her. Nathan stood with his arms hanging uselessly by his sides, waiting for the inevitable news that would bring him more disappointment.

"Robert Connally...hmm...when was he here, and what part

of the country was he working in?"

"I think he may have been here in the past thirty years. As to where he's been working, I honestly don't know."

"Ok...do you know what denomination he was affiliated with?" she asked, still intently searching through records.

"Well, I don't know that...either."

"Hmm. Well, let's see what we can find..."

Nathan was relieved enough the receptionist seemed so friendly and eager to help that he didn't feel so foolish for coming up with unknowns to her questions. She continued combing her files anyway.

"Is there any other place that would have a record of missionaries coming to Tanzania?" he ventured. She put her finger on the page to mark her place and looked up, biting her lip in thought.

"Some of the independent or non-denominational missionaries wouldn't have checked in here with us at the Missionary Society. They would be pretty hard to find," she added, not without sympathy. Nathan nodded, and she returned to her search. After a few more seconds she closed her ledger and turned back to Nathan. He read her answer before she spoke.

"I'm sorry, but I don't have any records here of a Robert Connally registered with the Missionary Society," she said.

Nathan felt as though he had hit an all-time low. He couldn't remember being stuck at a dead end like this before in any of his previous cases. The discouragement was almost overwhelming, and he was so tired.

"Well, thank you for your help," he said simply, his voice dull. "Could you recommend a hotel for me?"

The receptionist listed her head, studying him directly, but not intrusively. Nathan thought he could detect more sympathy in her expressive eyes. He glanced away.

"You know, you might check with the newspaper office tomorrow," she suggested. "Perhaps they can tell you something we can't here. And as far as hotels go, the Royal Palace is very nice."

Weary and dispirited, Nathan nodded his thanks and returned to his waiting taxi. He was almost too exhausted to care that Hicks was still following him.

The Royal Palace was a very nice hotel indeed, but Nathan was too intent on finding any room with a bed in it to take much note of all the opulent furnishings he passed by in the lobby.

"I don't want to talk to another person for the next twelve hours at least," he mumbled under his breath when he shut the door behind himself and leaned back against it. He felt sapped of energy. He took a shower before his nap, and after curling up in bed soon fell into a dreamless sleep.

He awoke all of a sudden, his eyes flying open as if he had been shocked.

"What..." He rolled over and looked at the small clock on the nightstand. Through the heavy window curtains a strip of city lights peeked through. The clock read seven thirty P.M. Nathan groaned. So much for sleeping straight through till morning.

But however viciously jetlag had thrown off his sleep cycle, or how much he still wanted to be passed out in bed, his stomach did feel uncomfortably empty. Before, he had been too exhausted to notice. Now he suddenly felt weak from lack of food. He hadn't eaten since arriving in Dar es Salaam.

He went downstairs to the dining area, and as he sat down at a table for one, he noticed there were several other people sitting there as well, enjoying their dinners and talking amongst themselves. Then his eye caught the long profile of a figure at a table across the room, several yards away, but still distinct in his vision. The man was sitting with an empty plate in front of him, evidently long finished eating by the looks of his utensils and napkin disarrayed on the table and his near-empty drinking glass. He had a notebook open on the table, and was making tiny marks with a pencil that been sharpened so many times it was shortened to be almost invisible in his fist. When Nathan entered the room, he saw this man look up and watch him discreetly until he had seated himself.

This Hicks guy is pretty persistent, whoever he is.

He ordered his meal, and his thoughts began turning again to the reason of his journey here. He had no idea how or when to make his next move. He highly doubted the newspaper office could help him. Now he didn't know what to do next or who to turn to. He had no leads, no ideas. In fact, he was running out of hope at this point.

Suddenly a female voice said from his right, "May I join you?"

Nathan looked up. The friendly receptionist from the Missionary Society stood beside him, smiling hesitantly.

"Oh...certainly." He stood up while her smile widened, and she sat down opposite him.

"I felt badly for you today because I couldn't seem to help you," she told him as he resumed his seat, folding his arms on the table. "So, this evening I went to the home of one of our retired missionaries who has lived and worked all over Africa for the past fifty years."

Nathan played with the salt shaker, waiting.

"When I asked him if he'd ever heard of a missionary by the name of Robert Connally, he told me he had."

The salt shaker slipped from Nathan's hand and fell over with a thump.

Excited at the impression her news had made, the young woman hurried on with her information.

"Evidently, your Mr. Connally worked with a group that claimed to be non-denominational. The missionary I spoke to thought your man's group went by the name, 'the church of Christ,' and had done a lot of work throughout the country."

"Church of Christ," Nathan repeated softly.

"The missionary thinks he's probably not in the country anymore, but he said that Mr. Connally worked with a native by the name of Charles...ah...Charles Darweshi. He also told me that if you were looking for him, the best place to go would be the Robert Connally Hospital. It was founded by the man himself, and it's located in Mbala. I'm sure you'll find what you're looking for there!"

"Where is Mbala in relation to Dar es Salaam?"

"It's southeast, in Zambia. Is everything alright, sir? Was this information helpful to you?"

Nathan realized he was clutching his fork with such intensity that his knuckles were turning white. He quickly opened his hand, stretching the taut tendons. Excitement bubbled through his brain, now wide awake. So there was a ray of light through the murky fog at last.

"Yes, yes, everything is alright," he said with his first smile of the day. "And you have certainly been of much help. May I buy you dinner?"

She smiled in return.

"Thank you, but I must decline your kind offer. I was just worried about you being unable to continue your search – you seemed so downhearted earlier – so I wanted to see what I could do to help. I can tell this is important to you. But I must get home now. My husband is ill and he will be needing me." She stood up. Nathan did as well.

"Again, thank you so much for everything," he told her fervently, shaking her hand with as much gratitude as he could put through the gesture. "Oh, one more thing. Do you know how I might reach Mbala?"

"There is one flight every day from the airport here in Dar es Salaam. I'm unsure of the time it leaves, though."

He thanked her profusely once more before she left. It wasn't until after he watched her disappear when he remembered he hadn't even asked her name. She had just provided him with his most crucial piece of the puzzle yet, and he didn't know who she was.

He finished his dinner and paid the tab, keeping aware of Hicks across the room. Since he knew Hicks couldn't possibly know anything about the woman or what she had said to Nathan, he knew this was his opportunity to get Hicks off his tail once and for all.

He walked up to the main desk of the hotel, turning his head ever so slightly as if he were examining a picture on the wall when he was really checking to see if Hicks was watching him.

He was.

Nathan spread his hands along the edge of the counter.

"What time does the next train for Mombasa leave?" he asked loudly.

"There is an early train departing at six A.M., sir."

"Great. Could you check the price on a private compartment

CHAPTER 16:

on that train? I'll also pay extra for somebody to pick up my ticket and bring it to my room."

The clerk studied him with a puzzled expression. Nathan was still speaking louder than necessary.

"Yes, sir, we can do that for you."

Nathan nodded vigorously and provided the money and tip.

No cost too large, he assured himself as he handed over the currency he had exchanged at the airport. He then went back to his room for the night. As soon as he locked himself in, Nathan unpacked his laptop and plugged it in, waiting impatiently for it to boot up.

"Alright, Mr. Mysterious Wayne Hicks," he said roughly. "Let's see what you're up to."

Twenty minutes later, he leaned back in the hard hotel chair and rubbed his chin. Case-within-a-case jobs were not fun, and he was growing tired again, his short high from the new information the receptionist gave him at dinner finally starting to wear off. Nevertheless, he had found sufficient details on Hicks to know he wasn't in Africa at the same time as Nathan, let alone the same hotel, by coincidence.

"Sneaky little P.I., aren't you," he said, adjusting the angle of his laptop screen. "Well, you can do your best to keep up with me, Hicks, but I think I have the lead now. And I'm not giving it up to anyone."

Wayne Hicks waited until Nathan had entered the hotel elevator before approaching the front desk himself.

"Excuse me, but I'm supposed to be meeting my friend here," he told the clerk smoothly. "He and I are going on a business trip but he forgot to tell me what time we set out, and I think I just missed him. Would you mind giving me the time you gave him so we're both on the same page?"

The clerk promptly disclosed Nathan's asking about train times for Mombasa, including his request that a bellhop go and retrieve his ticket and bring it back to his hotel room.

Hicks rubbed his tongue across his upper gum, his sharp expression ever calculating.

"Look here, I'll double the amount of money he gave you if you get me a ticket for the same train and have it brought to my room," he told the clerk.

"Yes sir," the clerk agreed readily. "We are happy to oblige our customers in whatever way we can."

↑ CHAPTER 17:

After arriving at the train station the next morning, Nathan deliberately hung around on the platform area for a while to make sure Hicks was there. He soon saw his rival standing in line at the ticket counter, and waited to make sure Hicks had seen him before slowly meandering over to the train and boarding. He went straight to his compartment and sat down to wait. Soon he saw Hicks pass by the small window in the door, and hurried to look after him. Hicks went down a few more yards and entered another private compartment. Nathan checked his watch. Five minutes to departure. He needed to move quickly.

But not too quickly. He couldn't risk Hicks seeing him before the train was moving at full speed toward Kenya. With luck, the other man wouldn't even know Nathan wasn't on the train before it pulled into Mombasa.

Nathan got his luggage and slipped quietly out of his compartment, making his way back up the car in the opposite direction from where Hicks sat smugly in his own private quarters. No doubt he thought himself very clever to have tailed Nathan this far without being detected, Nathan thought with a grim smile. He could hear the conductor calling out a last warning to any passengers still loitering on the boarding platform, and picked up his speed. By way of the dining car toward the end of the train, he waited for a few final people to get on before ducking out the door. He hurried off the platform just as the train began to move along the tracks, steadily picking up speed as it moved toward Mombasa...in the opposite direction from Mbala.

Nathan took off his hat and waved it regally after the train. If he had cared, he would have liked to have seen Hicks' face when he arrived in Mombasa and realized Nathan had planted a false trail.

"Enjoy your stay in Kenya, Mr. Hicks."

Without returning to the hotel, Nathan learned the daily flight to Mbala out of Dar es Salaam was at one o'clock and sped to the airport, urgency gnawing at him. He boarded the plane and reached Mbala in the early afternoon.

Mbala was an old colonial town, sitting on the edge of the plateau that made up much of Zambia's land area. Far from urban markets and threaded with poor roads which made transport difficult, Mbala presented a very different picture than the shiny, bustling city of Dar es Salaam. The air was hot and dry, and the land was mainly flat, but small hills broke the surface here and there. Open grassland stretched for miles in every direction from the town.

Nathan didn't see any hospital, and it was a small village. He turned to the flight attendant handing him his bags.

"Which way to the Robert Connally Hospital?" he asked.

He soon found himself headed on foot down a dirt road off the main street running through the town. The brush and vegetation grew in sparse clumps alongside the road, the wide plains visible between them that stretched far away to the distant hills. Nathan gazed up into the sky, feeling his skin absorb the sun's heat. Coming to a bend in the road, he rounded it and stopped short.

The size and appearance of the hospital complex seemed oddly inappropriate for the wildlands surrounding it. The cluster of white, squared buildings looked out of place out here in their sterile city display. Like they just took a hospital from Dallas and dropped it here, Nathan thought, impressed. He walked up to the front entrance and walked through the revolving door, feeling a rush of cool air wash over him.

The lobby was large and furnished like any modern-day clinic. Nathan made his way to the information and visitor center. A young man with dark skin sat there reading a book, and a young woman in a nurse's uniform was visible through a glass pane in the office behind him, typing on a computer.

CHAPTER 17:

Nathan walked up to the window but as he did, the office phone rang and the nurse began talking. Nathan stood still, drumming his fingers against his thigh while he waited. The young African looked up from his book and watched him for a few seconds before suddenly speaking up.

"Is there something I can help you with?"

His accent sounded like David's, British but with a more exotic lilt.

Nathan glanced over at him, not expecting the sudden offer. "Ah, I'm looking for a Charles Darweshi. I understood he would be somewhere around here."

At the mention of this name, a strange expression passed over the young man's face. "He was here, but he passed away about a month ago."

Nathan stared at him, blinking rapidly. "Of course...just another rabbit trail leading to nowhere," he mumbled. He turned around, pressing his back against the counter and gazing blankly out the hospital front doors. The young man seemed to sense his distress, and got to his feet.

"One minute, please," he requested, holding up his hand. Then he closed his book and walked quickly down one of the several halls branching off the main lobby.

With nothing to lose and nowhere to go, Nathan sat down next to the chair the young man had just vacated, settling in for another wait to see what the helpful stranger would do.

He wasn't absent for long. When he returned, he brought another African man with him. He looked to be in his mid-thirties, dressed in the outfit of a safari hunter. He walked with the stride of a man who knew how to hold his own. He didn't waste any time on pleasantries, either. "I understand that you are seeking Charles Darweshi," he said in a deep voice.

Nathan had stood up as they approached, and paused in the act of holding out his hand in greeting.

"Yes, I am," he said uncertainly. "My name is Nathan Blaine." Who was this guy? The local game warden?

"Well, it is my misfortune to tell you that he has recently

347

died."

"Yes," Nathan repeated, trying to gauge the flat expression in the man's eyes. "This young man already told me as much."

"Why were you looking for him?"

"I was told that he worked with a man named Robert Connally."

The man suddenly leaned forward and reached his hand forward. Nathan automatically shook it. The man had an intense brightness in his eyes now. He seemed to have decided something. "My name is Jonothan Darweshi. Charles was my father. Perhaps I can be of some help to you."

Nathan felt his own countenance brighten. Maybe this wasn't a dead end after all. "Did you know the Connallys?" he asked eagerly, questions bubbling up on his tongue. "Robert and Nalda Connally?"

Jonothan nodded briefly. "Come." He gestured to something behind Nathan. "Look."

Nathan turned around again and followed Jonothan's pointing finger. Hanging above the main entrance to the hospital was a large portrait of the same couple Nathan had seen in the yearbook at Freed-Hardeman University. And right below the portrait, incased in glass, was a long hunting rifle. He didn't understand how he had missed it.

"They are the Connallys you speak of. This is the hospital they founded, and which was named after them."

Nathan could hardly stand still. He had found them! All the way out here in a tiny African town, he had found the Connallys at last.

"Is there any chance that I could meet them? I have some questions..."

He stopped when Jonothan shook his head.

"Robert and Nalda are no longer with us in this life."

His voice was even lower, now soft and sad. Nathan felt the familiar dejection sinking like a stone in his stomach. Could he have somehow been mistaken? Gotten lost in a false lead along the way? Followed the wrong trail? Forcing himself to speak clearly, he asked, "Did you know the Connallys, then?"

CHAPTER 17:

"I knew them very well." Jonothan's eyes were distant.

"Well then," Nathan sighed, feeling like he was grasping at a wild chance, but knowing he needed to take it anyway, "maybe you knew if they had a son. A son named David?"

Jonothan's face split suddenly into a wide smile, showing strong, white teeth.

"Ah, yes. David is my brother," he said serenely.

Nathan didn't know whether he was more taken aback over the fact that he had found someone who actually knew David and his family personally, or that that person had just claimed to be related to David, who certainly wasn't an African like this man.

He pointed up at the Connallys' picture.

"Is David the son of the people in that picture?"

"Yes."

"Are you their son as well?"

"No, but David is my brother all the same."

Nathan scratched his head, but decided not to pursue the subject any further for the moment.

"Is David Connally around here?" he asked carefully.

Jonothan's smile faded.

"No. I have not seen him in a year's time. When we last spoke, he told me of his intentions to leave Africa." He squinted at Nathan. "Why are you so interested in David?"

"Because the David whom I believe you and I are both talking about has come to America, placed himself in a position of extreme popularity, and people want to know who he is and where he came from. That's why I need you to tell me more about him."

Jonothan looked at him very seriously.

"Is it your intention to harm David in any way?" he asked gravely.

Nathan drew back. "Of course not. I only want to know the truth about a remarkable young man who seems to have an entire country calling for him to lead them."

Jonothan turned away. "Come with me," he said over his shoulder. Nathan hastened to follow.

His guide led both him and the other young man with them

349

out onto the deck that wrapped around a large part of the hospital. There were few patients out there now. Jonothan gestured to a couple of chairs near the railing, with a view looking off toward the main land area of Mbala.

"Please, sit," he said. He asked the other young man to bring them tea, then sat down opposite Nathan.

"I can tell you about David Connally," he said. "But it is a long story, and not all of it a bright one."

"You know, I could go for a long story about David Connally right about now," Nathan told him.

Jonothan didn't smile, but he bowed his head in assent. Then he began the story.

"My parents met the Connallys a little over thirty years ago when they flew over from America. I was only two years old at the time, with two older sisters. You see, Robert and Nalda had previously contacted my parents by mail to ask for their help translating, and to be their guides while the Connallys served as missionaries here. My family and the Connallys would travel from village to village around East Africa. Everywhere we stopped, Robert Connally would preach and spiritually minister to the villagers. Nalda and my own mother provided medical care to the locals and any others who had need of it."

At this point in Jonothan's story, the young hospital attendant returned with a tray bearing two cups of hot tea. Jonothan thanked him and had him place the tea on a table between their chairs, handing one of the cups to Nathan as the young man left them alone once more. Nathan balanced his cup and saucer on his knee, his eyes fixed expectantly on Jonothan's face.

"Our work was slow in the beginning, but as the years passed the Connallys became more and more accepted by the people, and villagers began to look forward to their visits. Our little missions group became known because we traveled as far as the border of South Africa, all the way to Ethiopia, and on occasion even to the Congo..." Jonothan's eyes had that distant look again. "Sometimes we would go east into Zaire, Uganda...but the home base was actually here in Mbala. The southern compound where they lived was where this hospital is now."

"But David?"

"As far as David and I were concerned, he and I lived day to day around the work our parents were doing. David and I were like any boys. We grew up learning from our parents as well as from the customs of those we were around. But mostly we would torment my older sisters every chance we had," he added, breaking suddenly into a hearty laugh at the memory. Nathan's eyes widened. He tried to picture David Connally as a small boy purposely trying to irritate girls. It was tough attempting to conjure that image.

"We became each other's closest friends, David and I. Our friendship was strong, thicker than blood, as you might say."

"Brothers," said Nathan with a little smile.

"Yes, brothers." Jonothan said softly.

"Well, as we grew older, our parents would hold us accountable to complete the tasks they gave us, expecting us to help out every way we could. Life is hard in the African bush. By the time David and I were teenagers we were working full time alongside the adults with whatever task happened to be at hand that we could help with. I remember the Connallys had two trucks and two Land Cruisers. One truck carried all the medical supplies that David's mother and my mother used in their medical work. The other truck carried a portable platform, audio system, and our personal belongings like food and clothing. We were often on the road for sometimes months at a time."

Nathan took a sip of his tea, almost missing his mouth because he was so engaged in Jonothan's tale.

"Robert Connally was a hunter as well as a preacher. Many times he would be called upon by desperate villagers to kill a rogue lion, elephant, or some other animal that was terrorizing a nearby settlement. On occasion he would go out and shoot a game animal for a village on the brink of starvation. And of course, it was always fun for us boys to go along whenever we were allowed to."

"I bet you begged to go along every time," Nathan guessed, amused.

"What boy wouldn't?" Jonothan agreed with a smile.

"We traveled as one family together. I can remember many times when I was sitting around a campfire with all of them. We told stories and sang songs. Sometimes the village leaders accompanied us for our evening fellowship."

"That sounds nice."

"It was a blessed time. But it went by far too quickly. My father had been in charge of keeping all our vehicles running, so even as a teenager I had taken an interest in vehicle maintenance and repairing equipment. However, David wouldn't let me touch the audio system. He wasn't being spiteful. He just wanted to be the one to operate it while his father was preaching in the villages. If memory serves me correctly, he got quite good at handling all those wires and dials. Not that it was overly complicated, but you understand my meaning."

Nathan nodded. "Did the two of you have hobbies when you weren't working?"

"Yes. Whenever we had time to spare, David and I hunted. Our fathers taught us everything they knew about firearms and stalking game. We both became very skilled with firearms."

"And just how skilled was that, Mr. Darweshi?"

"Oh, please call me Jonothan. My father was Mr. Darweshi," Jonothan told him. "And I can tell you from my own experience that I have never seen David's equal in handling a firearm. He could hit any target you put in front of him, and at the longest range. I never saw him miss. His father taught him well."

Nathan clinked his cup against the saucer. "Could you tell me a little more about what his father taught him?"

"Robert Connally actually instructed us both from an early age about the importance of helping others. To be kind and share the love of God with everyone we came in contact with. And David had a unique ability to communicate well with just about everyone. We all noticed this about him when he was still a boy. He had a way of making those he spoke to feel like they were the most valued individuals in the world. He was personable. He liked people, because he cared about their souls. He worked with the villagers, trying to help them apply God's teaching from the Bible to their everyday lives. It made no difference to him whether it was the village chiefs or the outcasts. David wanted to help them all understand God's principles so they could be better people for each other and for themselves. He did his job well, and everyone appreciated his help and guidance, even though he was only a young man."

"He put others before himself."

Jonothan nodded firmly. "Always. Because he understood that his God had put *him* first. And I'll tell you something else about the Connallys, they were constantly helping others. Whenever tragedy struck or a need arose, somehow and some way it was always taken care of to some extent. Sometimes it was my father helping a villager in need of new oxen because theirs were killed by wild animals, or maybe one year the gardens didn't grow because of a famine in the area, but food would show up. Maybe it was a village needing building materials because their homes had burned. The materials would turn up, but they were always anonymous. From talking with my father, I know the Connallys performed countless acts of Christian benevolence and then some. They gave willingly of themselves, their money, their time, and they gave God's Word to every soul they encountered."

"I do have a question for you," Nathan said slowly, swirling the contents of his cup. "Did David like to sing?"

Jonothan broke into a broad smile again. "He loved to sing. He sang all the time. Sometimes it was even annoying because he never seemed to stop. You could hear him humming or whistling all over the place. He would sing with others or by himself. He really liked getting groups of people together, just to sing for a while. Before every gospel meeting, he would lead the villagers in songs, and then the nearby settlements would hear the singing and knew that worship had begun, or that a special singing session was going on. And even though all the Connallys learned to master Swahili, everyone, native and white man alike, loved to hear David singing in English." Jonothan's voice grew very affectionate as he spoke.

"Well I have to say, in all my years, I think I would have to agree that I've never seen a normal person enjoy singing as much as

David does," Nathan said.

"Nor have I," Jonothan agreed, swallowing more of his tea.

"Well, where was I...about five or six years ago, when we were in our mid-twenties, my sisters had gotten married and I was seeing the young lady who is now my wife. David was the only one of the young people in our family who was unattached. I think his parents were worried he might not find a girl. But David wasn't worried. I remember he told me he was praying about it, and that God's will and plan would be worked out for good in time. Then a year later, a beautiful young native woman from Kenya by the name of Elizabeth Tumelo came out to the mission to work as a nurse with David's mother, Nalda. It was as if our prayers and hopes for David were answered, for the two of them hit it off from the moment they met. Within a few months they were so deeply in love that David told me often that he was seriously thinking about marriage. I warned him to be cautious and not rush headlong into this kind of commitment, but he had a pretty good head on his shoulders, and I trusted him more than anyone else I knew. By the end of that year, David and Elizabeth were married. And you couldn't have found a couple more in love, or more dedicated to God and each other. And I never saw David happier in his entire life than he was after he married Elizabeth."

Jonothan stopped here, folding his fingers together as if he were finished. Nathan was hard at work putting the details together in his mind. David was married, and to an African woman. Nathan thought of the cruel accusations hurled at David over the past year and remembered him being labeled, among other things, a racist. Well, this would certainly put that lie to rest forever. But where then was his wife?

Nathan then realized Jonothan wasn't speaking any more. When he studied the African's face, he saw a deep melancholy in his eyes that he didn't understand. Jonothan laced and unlaced his fingers, his lips pinched together. He bowed his head and shook it slightly in mute answer to Nathan's hesitated question.

"Mr. Blaine," he said at last, raising his head, "I have told you much about David Connally, including the best parts of his life. You no doubt have found many answers already in my story this far. I only ask that you consider if you really want me to continue. You must ask yourself if you truly want to hear the rest."

Nathan sat back, confused.

"What? Of course I want to hear it! If there's anything left to tell about David Connally, I need to know. It's part of my job, Jonothan."

Still, Jonothan hesitated. Reluctant.

"Do you mean..." Nathan stared. "...that something happened? To Elizabeth?"

"Do you want to hear the rest of the story?"

The African looked at Nathan with such intensity that he immediately nodded.

"Yes. I do. Please," he said firmly.

"Very well," Jonothan sighed.

"Three years ago, we were all encamped for the night about six hours south of Arusha. We had had a wonderful Gospel meeting, and were preparing to pull out of camp and head back home to the compound. But one of the trucks had an engine problem, and we couldn't get it started. I tinkered with it, as engines were my specialty, but to no avail. We decided that we were going to have to go for parts, so my parents and I headed off to a nearby town to see if we could find the truck pieces needed. We also agreed with the Connallys beforehand that my family would go on to the next town to visit one of my sisters there, so we took the Land Cruisers.

"David decided to stay with the broken truck until I returned with the parts. Robert, Nalda, and Elizabeth, who was now six months pregnant, wanted to stay together with him for the night. But Elizabeth wasn't feeling well, and David insisted the three of them take the working truck and go on ahead without him. When I returned the next day with the parts, David and I would fix the truck and follow behind the others. That way his wife and parents would be able to make it home that night and rest. They didn't want to leave him behind, but David wouldn't let them stay. He kissed his wife, and sent her away with his parents."

Jonothan took a deep breath, drawing his shoulders back and slowly rubbing his dark hands down over his knees.

"The road they took in the truck would take them through the great animal reserve between us and home. When they were within two miles from the northern edge of the park, the truck broke down. All of us knew what was to be done under such conditions: stay in the vehicle until daylight or one of the patrolling rangers finds you. But for some reason..." and Jonothan raised a fist and pressed it against his temple, shutting his eyes briefly. "For some reason I will never know, all three of them – or I guess I should say all four – Robert, Nalda, and Elizabeth carrying her and David's unborn child, decided to get out and walk the last couple of miles to the reserve ranger's station. I supposed they wanted to get a lift home from there."

Nathan found himself gripping his teaspoon very tightly.

"I don't know why they didn't wait," Jonothan said, low. He wasn't looking at Nathan. "But they didn't. And it was dark, so they... they didn't see the pride of lions intending to cross the road at the same time the Connallys were passing by. I don't think Robert even had a chance to get his gun off his shoulder before the lions attacked."

Jonothan covered his eyes, leaning his elbow heavily on the arm of the wooden deck chair. He sat like that for almost a minute. Nathan sat frozen in his seat, trying not to let the shock show through on his face. Part of him wanted to dismiss this part of the story. To forget what he had just heard.

Jonothan's voice startled him. He was still covering his eyes with his hand, but he was speaking nonetheless. He sounded as though every word was torturous, pain being drawn from his memories which he hadn't spoken of for a long time.

"The next day when David and I reached the reserve, the ranger's station reported that one of our trucks had been abandoned near the northern end of the park. We went straight there, and finding no one, we began to search for David's family."

Jonothan pulled his hand down the front of his face, dropping his hands into his lap.

"About a mile past the truck we...discovered what appeared to blood on the edge of the road, and it looked like something had been dragged off into the bush. That's when we started thinking the worst. We only had to...to travel a short distance down. Following the trail of blood and broken brush, we came upon their remains." Jonothan swallowed hard. "The vultures had already come. All that was left of that lion-feeding frenzy was more blood, broken bones, human hair, and Robert's gun."

Nathan felt a chill of horror writhing in his stomach. He didn't know where to look. Suddenly, he felt unspeakably rude that he had so callously made this personal friend of the Connallys relive such an awful, tragic past that connected him with David.

Jonothan had tears in his eyes and his hands shook. He seemed not to see Nathan.

"You know, I remember exactly what David looked like on that morning," he said, tilting his head almost as if he were recounting an everyday occurrence. "I remember his face. I never...never saw a grief so, so untouchable. I stood there looking at him looking at the scene of the death of his father, mother, wife, and unborn child, and I felt that even if I laid my hand on his shoulder, he would not come back to me. Sorrow was too inappropriate a word for the storm that I knew was inside him. I saw it in his eyes. The life was gone.

"He would not talk to me. He didn't respond to anything I said. He wouldn't say a word. He just stood there. After a while he sat down on the ground, but he never made a sound. He kept his head bowed and his eyes closed. We stayed there for hours.

"And then suddenly, he stood up. He picked up Robert's gun and walked away in the direction of the lions, still without a word to me. And even though we had been close for thirty years, I sensed he did not want me to follow him. I watched him walk away with his father's gun in his hand. And that's when I realized..."

"What," Nathan asked, his voice barely above a whisper.

Jonothan rolled his head against the back of his chair. "I realized that when the lions killed his family that they had killed David, too."

"A few days later, I had managed to get our trucks back to the compound. The local villagers and I had gathered all the remains of David's family and buried them as a memorial. Right up there."

↑THE SPEAKER

Nathan turned his head as Jonothan pointed past him. About a quarter kilometer beyond the hospital a small hill rose into the sky. Nathan looked at it, then back at Jonothan.

"They're buried there?"

"Yes. And after it was done, David returned. He visited the grave, then went back home, collecting supplies and all the guns and ammo he could find in the house. I was not here at the time, and he didn't contact me or my family for a long time. The most I heard about him was news from the cities that he had begun hiring himself out to anyone who wanted any lions killed.

"For the next two years, I believe that is all he did. It was as if he blamed the lions for the death of his wife, child, and parents, and that he sought revenge. But I knew him too well to believe that."

"He didn't blame the lions?"

"No." Jonothan shook his head. "He blamed God. And I knew that was something he would have to work through on his own. I couldn't help him, not that he would have let me."

"Meanwhile, all those who knew David and knew what happened were praying for him every day. I prayed every day, and so did my family. We were amazed by the number of people who contacted us asking about David and telling us they were keeping him in their prayers. People he had helped in the past, people he had taught, people he had gotten to know and who loved him.

"Then, a year ago, David just showed up at the hospital. By that time the building was completed and we were taking in patients daily. I happened to look out the window and I saw him pass by. I thought he was going to come in, but he just went up that hill to the stone marker for his family. I followed him for a distance, but I didn't speak to him, or let him know I was there. I remember. First he stood at the grave. Then he knelt down. Then he lay face down on the ground, and just curled up like he was trying to hold all the broken pieces of himself together. I couldn't make myself go up there. I kept others from going. He was up there for two days and two nights. I watched over him. But what I didn't expect was what happened on the second night.

"Dusk had fallen, and I could still see my brother up there

at the grave, hurting. But then villagers started coming out from the surrounding area. They were all holding candles that lit up the darkness like a thousand stars. And they just kept coming and coming. Somehow, they knew David was there. They all walked up to the hill and circled around the base, some standing higher up on it than others, but none too close to David or the stone marker. There were so many people who knew David and his family, and had come out to support him in his hour of darkness. That silent candlelight vigil showed such honor and respect for this family that had done so much to help change lives in Africa...and there David just sat, lifeless, in front of his family."

Jonothan's voice cracked. Nathan's respect and admiration for this man had grown so quickly during his story, and he saw no unmanly weakness in the tears falling from his eyes. "I will never forget it as long as I live. It was the most beautiful, heartrending sight I will ever behold, all those lights in the darkness, as if they were all trying to dispel the shadows overcoming David's life. Oh yes," Jonothan sighed. "I do believe a part of my dear friend died along with his family. His heart was still beating, his lungs breathing, his blood still warm. But the David I had known my whole life was gone forever. And I remember, when that thought was going through my mind, far away in the distant stillness of the night, a lion roared."

"David came down to the hospital on the third day, and I met him at the front door. He was so changed, altered. I almost didn't recognize him from the man he once was. It was as if those two years had not only been hard on him physically, but mentally too. But something else about him was changed. Something was different. The vengeful fire burning in his heart seemed to have died at last. In those two days and nights spent at the grave of his family, something had happened that caused him to finally make peace with God, and the blame was gone." Jonothan set his eyes on the distant hill. "When he came down from that hill, we knew he could move forward at last."

"What did he say to you?"

"Nothing. He handed me his father's rifle and walked past

me down to his house. He just put it in my hands and walked away without saying a word to me. But the next day he came back up to the hospital, where he knew I'd be waiting for him. He came in carrying a duffel bag with everything he owned inside. Then out of the blue he just hugged me, our first real contact in three years."

"Take care, my brother," he said to me, and I could see the heartbreak in his eyes.

"Where will you go?" I asked him.

He told me, "I'm going home, Jonothan. To start a new life."

Then he gave me a letter stating that all of the property and assets belonging to the Connally family now belonged to the church and the hospital. He then put his hand on my shoulder, and he smiled at the tears in my eyes.

"I will never forget you, brother," he said to me.

"And then he walked away, leaving his past behind him in the wilds of Africa. I knew he would never dwell there again. And that was the last time I saw David Connally. The last I heard of him was from a mutual friend who told me one day that David had passed through South Africa and was taking a ship out of Cape Town across to the United States." Jonothan smiled suddenly. "He would love going back there. His father taught us both so much about American history, and taught David especially to love the country his parents came from. Just listening to Robert Connally talk about America made me see how much he and Nalda loved their homeland. I know he had filled David's mind with very fond thoughts of the 'Land of the Free', and kept him up to date with publications and current events happening over there. I'm sure if that's where David is, then he is happy."

Nathan sat very still. Then he set his tea cup carefully on the tray.

"The gun," he said. "The rifle in the lobby of the hospital–"

Jonothan nodded.

Nathan looked off toward the hill. If he squinted, he thought he could almost make out a white marker, tiny in the distance.

"Thank you, Jonothan," he said. "Thank you for telling me David's story."

Jonothan bowed his head. "He is a good man."

"Yes," Nathan heard himself say. "Yes, he is."

The sun was beginning to set, filling the sky with scarlet, orange, and dark purple. Flames seemed to devour the western half of the horizon.

"It's late. You are welcome to stay the night here at the compound."

But Nathan shook his head as he stood up. "No, I need to get back as quickly as I can."

"But there are no more flights out of Mbala today."

Nathan paused. He had forgotten about that.

"Please, feel free to spend the night," Jonothan offered again, and this time Nathan agreed. Jonothan led him back through the hospital. As they passed underneath the picture of the Connallys, Nathan looked up at their gently smiling faces, and then over at Robert's gun. They all held such a deeper significance to him now.

"The domestic quarters are just down there. I shall have a car take you back to the airfield tomorrow," Jonothan told him when they were standing outside. Nathan turned to face him.

"Jonothan, I'm very grateful to you. You gave me answers I didn't even realize I needed to know. And you helped me understand the heart of a man that much of the world doesn't seem to know, yet they love him because he loves them."

"That is the way David has always been," Jonothan replied. "Loving and well-loved in return."

He turned to walk back into the hospital. Nathan stood there, smiling to himself as he walked in the opposite direction. Suddenly he stopped and hurried back.

"Jonothan!"

The other man looked over his shoulder, his hand on the door. "Yes?"

"Was David born in Africa?"

The corners of Jonothan's mouth turned up.

"When my parents met the Connallys thirty years ago, his mother stepped off the plane carrying a baby in her arms. He had been born but a few days before they left America."

↑THE SPEAKER

Long after Jonothan had re-entered the hospital, Nathan stood there under the beam from one of the outdoor lights, deep in thought.

And far off in the distant stillness of the night, a lion roared.

CHAPTER 18:

"Good afternoon! I'm Lisa Lyons, and we are here today in the home of Bruce Baxter, the author of the best-selling new book, *Prophet or President: The David Connally Phenomenon.* Bruce is a Pulitzer Prize-winner, and with ten books already on shelves written in the investigative journalist field as well, he has turned his attention toward a book on what he calls the 'phenomenon' of David Connally. His book hit shelves just a week ago and is already number three on the New York Times Bestseller List. Bruce," the news reporter added, turning away from the camera to face the author, "I want to congratulate you on the success of your new book."

"Thank you."

"Did you have any idea it would become so popular? I heard the printers are having trouble keeping up with the demand!"

Bruce chuckled, turning his head to rub his hand under the wavy, dark brown hair at the nape of his neck. His small blue eyes, which looked green when he looked toward the light, twinkled merrily.

"Well Lisa, I'm very honored and humbled by the overwhelming response to my newest book. In some ways I am very surprised my book is so popular...but then in some ways I'm also not surprised at all."

"What do you mean?"

"Well, I'm surprised by how many people bought the book, but not surprised by their desire to learn more about David, his story, and what he's really been saying to the American people."

"Tell me, Bruce, is it true that you are one of the extreme few outside of The American Party organization who had the chance to

363

personally meet David Connally?"

Bruce nodded, his lips pursed and eyes unfocused as if drawing back on a memory.

"That is true. I do have some contacts within The American Party, and although they wouldn't let me actually interview David, I was allowed to just visit with him for about, oh, ten minutes in the presence of a guard and others. And I gotta tell you, Lisa, this young man who has the country in an uproar..." Bruce spread his hands, searching for the right words. "Let's just say it was a very eye-opening and thought-provoking conversation. And from that time forward I began investigating and chronicling everything he was saying to the people."

"I think our audience would like to know, from all your experience and research, what you personally think of David?" Lisa asked.

Bruce covered one fist with the other hand, resting his chin on them for a moment. Then he straightened up, bringing his hands apart and back together with a smart clap.

"Well, what can I say? My impression was that he is a very kind, very humble young man. He cares about people. And from what I heard The American Party say, he never speaks poorly of anyone. He seems to have a very positive outlook on life in general, Lisa."

"But then, do you have any ideas why The American Party still refuses to let anyone interview him?"

"I believe it's as simple as this: David isn't their candidate. He's a great singer and superior speaker, but he really isn't out there trying to campaign. He works for The American Party. The election is coming up here soon, and they want to make sure the candidates they support are getting all the publicity possible. David could be viewed, in the roughest use of the word, as an entertainer, a sideshow, though we all know he's much more than that. He also loves God, and he loves America and wants what's best for her."

Lisa adjusted her skirt. "Tell me more about the title of your book, *Prophet or President*. What made you choose that title?"

Bruce settled back in his armchair, rubbing his chin. He

folded his arms.

"I think that's pretty self-evident. Many of David's loyal followers tend to revere him sort of like a prophet trying to lead them back to the truth, away from evil. I know there are others who believe he should, in fact, be the next president. However, it was clear to me early on that he wasn't going to voice himself as a political candidate, so I decided to focus the better part of my book on the 'prophet' angle. His messages, his religious teachings, leanings, if you will. His political message does factor in, but that's only a fraction of what he's really saying."

"I was able to read your book recently, and I was fascinated to the last page," Lisa exclaimed in a professional gush. "What I really liked is how you summarized everything David's been saying over the last, what, half-year, in a way that you couldn't really get from just watching news coverage."

"Well, you see, it's only when you put everything that he's been saying together that you can truly see the depth of the message he's been trying to present to the American people," Bruce explained. "Even while I was preparing this book, the message stood out so clearly in my mind that this is a godly man who was telling the nation what God would have them know. It's not like some type of new revelation, no, far from it. What David is doing here, is simply taking the teachings of the Bible and presenting them in such a way that if God were here in human form among us, that is probably very close to what He would say to us. There's a common theme in all of David's speeches."

"And that is?"

"Repent," said Bruce simply. "David has, in essence, told the people that their destiny, their welfare, and the welfare of generations to come hang in the balance. The nation has reached a point in time where, if she does not repent of her ways that lead her away from the God we have put our trust in for years, we may have no chance of turning back later."

"And what is he saying that we, the people, need to repent of, Bruce?"

"To my understanding, this is what he's saying: as the

American people, we have been blessed by God as the greatest nation on earth. Now, that's indisputable, of course." He smiled. "But he's reminding us that we are also a nation built not only on the foundations of sacrifice and freedom from oppression, but godly principles as well. Principles the Founding Fathers believed in with all their hearts. But now, years down the road, we have turned our backs on many of those principles and have headed down a road to destruction. It is we, the people, who must turn this country around both religiously and morally if we are to continue to truly be one nation under God. We are in sore need of repentance of this moral decay that has so rampantly engulfed our society."

"Well, if that's what David is saying, did he also have an application to make? How is he expecting the people to do that?"

"I'm glad you asked," Bruce smiled again. "I actually wrote about this in chapter seven of my book. See, in our unique, God-given government where the people elect their governors, the people are responsible for setting up the kind of leaders who will uncompromisingly stand for the truth, both religiously and morally. And throughout that process we must rid ourselves of any and all government leaders who are unwilling to extract corruption, or those who try to oppose the cleansing of moral decay. David has said that those with power who have been acting immorally, or are unethically involved in corruption of any kind, should be punished and removed from office. David is also very strong on the points of abortion and homosexual marriage. We must do away with the slaughter of innocent children, and rid the land of the other perversion that people call 'gay' marriage. And I have also heard him talk about the country's need to repent of how we've been sanctioning religions such as Islam over the one true religion of God and His Son, Jesus Christ."

Lisa furrowed her brow. "And do you believe that if we as a nation do not change and become the godly nation God created us to be, that we could be in real trouble down the road?"

"From my own readings and my investigations into world history, I believe everything David has said. I don't think we're heading toward trouble. I think we're already there. Regimes and

366

empires have fallen time and again throughout history because they didn't place their faith in God, and who knows how long God will put up with us in our present state. If we don't change, I think we can only be promised inevitable ruin. If God so chose, He could have this land turned into a third-world country ruled by some fascist dictator in a matter of days. It isn't entirely impossible. I believe that as a nation of people under God, we need to repent before it's too late."

THE SPEAKER

↑CHAPTER 19:

It was early on Saturday morning. The Cowboys Stadium in Dallas, Texas, was bustling with hundreds of people getting ready for The American Party's rally there that evening. Jack gathered his crew together and they all stood around holding their coffee, awaiting his instructions, David among them.

"Guys," Jack said slowly, his hands on his waist as he turned from side to side to see them all. "This is going to be the biggest rally the party has ever had anywhere, and that goes double because not only are all of The American Party bigwigs going to be here, but a big group of the Republican leaders as well. The Republican presidential candidate and his people will be here, and the chairman of the Republican party will be flying in with all his people too. It's going to be standing room only."

Jack paused, suddenly aware of how big this all really was. He looked around at his men, his eyes coming to rest on David.

"We've never dealt with anything like this before," he said, clearing his throat. "This will probably be the biggest political rally of its kind that this nation has ever seen. And I don't think that's bragging."

Some of the crew laughed. Jack smiled and addressed David. "Are you ready for this, David?"

The young man looked around. Every pair of eyes was now on him. He gave a half-shrug, smiling rather sheepishly.

"They're just people. Just people who need to know what God has in mind for this country."

Jack's smile turned down just a little. He walked up to David and looked straight into his eyes.

"But David, are you ready for tonight?"

David blinked. "Yes, sir."

From the doorway, Eli eased his shoulder around the doorjamb, his gaze focused on David, too.

Jack patted his shoulder. "Ok then, everyone, let's get to work," he said, raising his voice. "We all know what we have to do."

Mr. Farris stood outside the coffee vendor talking on his cell phone when Jack walked up to him later. From where he sat across the way, James saw them greet each other, and quickly dropped his work to sidle over, wanting to see if maybe he could find out anything more to tell York before tonight.

"Hey Jack," Mr. Farris said after he ended his call. "How's it going back there?"

"Everything's under control and running like clockwork," Jack said exuberantly.

"Fantastic. I love it when everyone's prepared. Can I buy you a coffee?"

"Hey, I'm always good for coffee," Jack joked. He couldn't help it. He had such a good feeling about tonight. About David. Jack knew the reason they had come this far was because of David, and when once he had been afraid, all he could feel now was pride and admiration for David.

James bounded up to them as if he had just noticed them while passing by.

"Hey, Jack, Mr. Farris," he nodded to them both. "What's going on? Anything new happening?"

"Nope, everything's great," Jack said. He raised an eyebrow. "Aren't you supposed to be helping with the signs and banners?"

"Uh, I'm on a break."

Jack smirked. "You have fifteen minutes, kid."

Mr. Farris looked down at his phone. "Excuse me."

He turned away, already talking.

"Yes, Mr. McCoy. Yes, we're all doing fine down here. Preparations are coming along..." He looked at Jack over his shoulder, who quickly made a motion of reassurance. "...fine. We'll be ready before tonight...Wait, he did what?!"

Jack and James watched him curiously.

"He'll be here tonight?" Mr. Farris exclaimed in an infuriatingly vague manner. Jack tried to get his attention, spreading his hands in a question.

"Wow, that, that makes all the difference in the world! Yes, sir, we'll be ready for you this evening. Yes, Joseph Cane and his wife are here, and almost all the other Republican candidates have arrived who are scheduled to speak tonight. Edward Martin will be coming down with you, right? Ok. We will make all the arrangements for you this morning. This is incredible news. Will we be able to settle this matter tonight? Ok. Yes sir, see you tonight!"

Mr. Farris lowered his phone and slowly turned around. "Nathan Blaine."

"Who? What's wrong?" Jack couldn't tell from Mr. Farris' expression if he looked like he had either seen a ghost or won a million dollars.

"The investigator Rick McCoy hired to check up on David! He found the answers to all of our questions."

Jack's breath caught. "He found out where he came from? His past? All of it?"

"All of it," Mr. Farris told him. "And at this point I'm both nervous and excited at the same time. Blaine will be landing in New York and flying out to Dallas in a few hours. He should be here before the rally starts. We'll be meeting with him later on this evening."

Mr. Farris was starting to get that look when he had a hundred things to think about all at once. "We need to bring The American Party motor home around and get it all cleaned out, park it inside near the door. We'll meet in there tonight."

"I'll get some guys on it right away," Jack promised, and sped off with one last slap on Mr. Farris' shoulder. Mr. Farris whipped his phone back out to make another call, walking in the opposite direction.

Both of them had forgotten about James standing there, even though Mr. Farris had distractedly handed him his coffee cup when striding past him, already intent on another phone conversation. James looked back at Jack hurrying away, then at Mr. Farris walking away, then walked over to the nearest trash can. Turning Mr. Farris' coffee on end, he watched the brown liquid stream out of the paper cup before dropping it in.

"Sorry, Jack," he said. "Looks like my break's gonna be a little longer than fifteen minutes."

He moved off in a different direction from the other men and called York, telling him what he had just heard. Unfortunately for him, York was in a bad mood, which did not improve over the course of the conversation.

"You have to be in that meeting tonight, James. I need to know exactly what's going on in there!"

"But, but I can't do that!" James cried. He tried to placate the angry Democratic chairman. "But look, I'll find a way to know what's going on in there."

"Frankly James, I don't care what you do, or how you do it. But you just make sure that I know everything said in that meeting, got it?"

"Yes, sir."

"Now listen, I'm flying out to Dallas tonight. I'll let you know when I'm on the ground. Stand by for further instructions. And James?"

"Yeah?"

"Do not mess this up."

"I won't, Mr. Yor–"

But York had already hung up.

The giant Cowboys Stadium was lit up at its finest, the seats packed to maximum capacity. Vehicles were still lined up in the parking lot as a tidal wave of people poured into the stadium. The noise was deafening. Television anchors, news reporters, pundits, cameramen and news channel vehicles squeezed in everywhere they could find a spot. Security had been stretched to the highest and tightest level.

Later that evening, the taxi that Nathan Blaine had hired

CHAPTER 19:

pulled up at the VIP gate and was stopped by the security guards. After showing his identification and the guard confirmed he was registered as a VIP, Nathan was allowed to enter the premises. Twice more he was stopped by Secret Service personnel while making his way back to the American Party motor home.

When he opened the door, Nathan found Rick McCoy, Jeff Dixon, Joseph Cane, and Edward Martin waiting for him. When he saw Nathan, McCoy's face broke into a big smile. He stood up and shook Nathan's hand with fervor.

"Well done, Mr. Blaine!" he said, beaming. "I understand from your email that you have found all the answers to the questions everyone's been asking about David Connally."

"I have, Mr. McCoy."

"Well, I only have one at this point. Is he an American?"

Nathan looked into McCoy's eyes, then took a second to look at each individual in the room. He could almost feel the intake of breath as they waited to hear his response.

He turned back to McCoy, as if they were alone in the room.

"Our friend David Connally is without a doubt...an American citizen."

McCoy nodded briefly, but his eyes betrayed the joy he was feeling. Nathan nodded back as if to say everything was alright now.

"Wait."

They looked at Joseph Cane, who was now on his feet. His face was pinched with surprise and even a little fear.

"He doesn't have any problems in his past? Where's he been for the last thirty years, then?"

Nathan looked to McCoy for permission, and with that he sat down, causing Cane to slowly do the same.

"David has lived almost his entire life in Africa. But he was born in America. His parents were missionaries overseas."

"So," Edward Martin spoke up, his voice dull. "What does this mean for The American Party now?"

McCoy folded his hands.

"I think it's very clear to all of us here that the American people want David for their president."

Martin shifted, a warning in his eyes.

"And now that we all understand that he is qualified–"

"No!"

"I think The American Party may have to come together and consider if he will be our candidate," McCoy finished, his eyes on Martin.

The Republican Party chairman was furious.

"This is unacceptable! You gave us your word back in June that Joseph Cane was to be your candidate! And now, weeks away from the election, you just change your mind on us? What kind of deal is this? Where's your loyalty?"

"In June we didn't know what we know today," McCoy said quietly. Martin stood staring at him, his hands clenched and shaking at his sides. "It was our belief that David wasn't qualified to be a candidate for the United States president. In June we didn't realize that most of the electorate would change their minds and want him for president no matter what. And as far as The American Party is concerned, we still only want what is best for America."

"And you think Connally is what's best," Martin sneered.

"You know something, Mr. Martin? I do. And based upon Nathan's report, as well as the desire of the people, I believe The American Party will do everything possible to see David Connally elected as our next president."

Martin's face turned an alarming shade of pink. He opened and closed his mouth, but no words came. Joseph Cane was very quiet and still, standing with his arms folded. He appeared to be studying the warp and woof of the motor home's carpet.

"But you gave us your word that Joseph would be your candidate!" Martin repeated, finding his voice at last.

McCoy bowed his head.

"Mr. Martin," he said respectfully, "The American Party made a decision in June to back Joseph Cane because he was the best qualified candidate to our knowledge at the time. Now things have changed. And may I remind you that at no point did my party enter into contract with either the Republican Party or Senator Cane that our backing would always be guaranteed. The decisions that The

American Party makes must simply have to do with what's best for the nation."

Cane raised his head. He studied McCoy.

"And with all that in mind, combined with the knowledge about David we now possess, it's obvious that The American Party needs to give him our full support now."

"So you intend to stop sponsoring me so that you can turn your efforts toward David. Try and make him president," said Cane suddenly. "Is that correct?"

But Martin interrupted McCoy's reply.

"If it is your intention to put David Connally forward as a candidate, I don't believe the Republican Party has anything more to do with this organization." He tilted his chin, looking down his nose at McCoy, though standing up McCoy was the taller of the two. "We're leaving."

He stalked to the door, then turned around when he realized Cane wasn't behind him.

"Joseph, what are you doing? Let's go."

Cane stood in the same position, rubbing his hands back and forth over each other. He looked deep in thought.

"You go on ahead, I'll be right out," he told Martin.

"Jeff, will you take Nathan back to his hotel?" McCoy added. His assistant nodded. Nathan walked to McCoy and shook his hand again.

"I'll work on a formal investigation report tonight that will be made public tomorrow morning," he said. "Soon the world will know the truth about David Connally."

"Truth only the best private eye could have dug up," McCoy grinned.

When the door closed behind the others, only McCoy and Cane remained in the motor home.

McCoy was the first to speak. "Senator, I want to apologize to you. The party and I have supported you from the beginning, and I like to think of you as a friend. But we never expected a David Connally to come along and just, well, sweep the people off their feet, so to speak."

↑THE SPEAKER

Cane continued to stand silently as before, rocking back and forth on his heels with his arms crossed.

"But we have a man here who has put God first, and has made this nation understand what she's been forgetting for years: what God would have the American people to be. And I won't bore you by quoting statistics or approval ratings. I know you know all that. I also hope you know that this isn't about anything personal whatsoever. But The American Party will support the candidate most needed by the country, and we actually have the people's full consent."

Cane walked slowly over to the table and stood behind one of the chairs, trailing his hand over the back of it. He chewed his lip, his eyebrows so low that he seemed almost like he was glowering. McCoy waited in silence while the senator mulled over his words.

"I cannot go against the Republican Party," he said slowly, his eyes meeting McCoy's. He cleared his throat. "But I am all too well aware that David Connally is the man that the people want for their next president." He shook his head, his smile resigned and defeated. McCoy lowered his head in respect.

"I would like to ask one favor, though," Cane added.

"Of course."

"I wish to speak with David privately before any announcement is made."

McCoy studied Cane, trying to figure out the motivation behind such a request. Cane didn't break eye contact.

"Alright, then, senator. If you will wait here, I'll send him over as soon as he comes off the stage."

Cane sat down again, and McCoy reached for the doorknob.

"You know," Cane suddenly said from behind him. McCoy turned around. "I can't believe I'm actually saying this..." Cane bent his elbow and rested his arm on the table. "But if I had to vote today...I'd vote for David Connally."

McCoy cocked his head. A little smile crept over his face. How much had it cost Cane to admit that? McCoy turned the handle and opened the door.

"You know," he said over his shoulder, "I believe so would the rest of America."

James pulled his black sweater hood farther down over his forehead and cheeks as he walked quickly along the sidewalk. A few blocks from the Cowboys Stadium, a glistening black limousine with tinted windows was parked by the curb. Four security personnel surrounded the vehicle, and when he approached, they searched James for weapons. When he had been cleared, one of the guards opened the back door, and James slid into the limousine.

"What did you find out?" Dominic York asked him.

He sat opposite of James' seat, wearing his usual three-piece suit and eerily blank but intense gaze in his cadaverous face. But he wasn't the only other body in the limo. Helen Kennedy sat across from him wearing her usual brightly-colored pantsuit, her puffy blond hair pulled back from her stony face in an unflattering style. Both she and York seemed clearly irritated to have found themselves in such a desperate situation.

"From what I could gather from the bug, they found evidence that proves David Connally is an American citizen," James said bluntly.

Helen Kennedy shook her head in disbelief similar to Edward Martin.

"That can't be..." she moaned.

York sat in silence, which to James was almost more disconcerting than an outburst of rage.

He stumbled on.

"Um, Rick McCoy told everybody in the meeting that he plans to have The American Party nominate David as their candidate, officially, and do everything he can to make David president."

"They can't do that!" Senator Kennedy raged. "The election is less than six weeks away!"

"Unfortunately," York spoke up gravely, "they can."

"What!"

"Don't you see?" York rubbed his eyes, scowling. "They've obviously been working toward this for months, maybe longer. I don't know how Connally could win in a landslide, but there's really little doubt that he would take the election away from us."

THE SPEAKER

York leaned his head back against the headrest. "The presidency would go either to Connally...or to Cane."

He and Kennedy looked at each other, each trying to devise a way out.

James looked from one to the other, frowning.

"I don't understand," he piped up. They both looked at him in frustration. "The American people aren't going to elect somebody who's lived his whole life in another country, will they?"

"The entire Democrat Party has been working on this man for months," York told him slowly. "We've tried to take the spotlight away from him, and when that didn't work, we tried using his publicity against him. Nothing has worked. Every tactic taken has backfired on us. James, it doesn't matter who he is, where he's from, or what he's done in the past. He's changed the people. They hang on his every word. If he gets the candidacy, they will elect him."

Kennedy was nodding, her face grim.

"If that happens, and an independent third-party candidate becomes president, our party's influence could be lost for many generations to come."

"She's right. If Connally is elected, this nation will never be the same again. If we're not in power, the people will be deprived of what our government can do for them," York said distantly, tilting his head as if he was turning something over in his mind.

James sat with his hands between his knees, unsure of what to do with himself. The mounting pressure from their stares was causing a burning redness to creep up the back of his neck.

"We can't allow this to happen," Kennedy said to York. He didn't answer her. He turned to James, and for once, the corpse-like expression in his eyes was no longer dormant, but hard as granite, and burning like fire.

"James," he said, his voice very cold, "if nothing is done about this, America will be lost. This cannot happen. *You* cannot let this happen."

James stared at York, squinting in confusion as he tried to read the unspoken message in the other man's eyes. James straightened his back.

CHAPTER 19:

"What are you suggesting I do?" he asked.

David waved jubilantly to the adoring audience as he finished his time on stage with his customary final words, "God bless America!" Sixty thousand people continued to shout the phrase back to him, along with his name in a joyous chant as he exited the platform. Everyone could hear the unanimous cry, "David Connally for President!" that the audience carried on in an unending shout.

David didn't acknowledge this, but simply toweled off and drank the water handed to him as Mr. Farris gave him a passing pat on the back on his way up on stage to introduce the candidates speaking that night.

Jack was waiting for David, and grinned at him over his folded arms when he sat down with his water. David peered up at him.

"What?" he demanded. "I have something in my teeth?"

"Like that would make any difference to the people," Jack scoffed. Then he sobered, his smile growing softer. "You did good out there, kid. You told them what they needed to hear, not just what they wanted to hear."

"But I guess those two coincided tonight," David chuckled. Jack gripped his shoulder and shook it a little. "I'm proud of you."

"That means a lot, Jack. Thanks."

When Mr. Farris clicked off the stage again in his cowboy boots, he drew David aside.

"You're needed over at The American Party HQ right away."

Jack drifted over. "Mind if I tag along?"

"I don't, but David needs to get going. McCoy just called me and said Joseph Cane wants to meet with David in the motor home."

"Joseph Cane!" Jack stood closer to David. "I'm definitely coming now."

"Hurry!" Mr. Farris urged them. "Oh, and David, great job out there. They all love you."

He dashed off on another mission, leaving Jack and David to head over to the American Party motor home, two Blackheart agents tailing them.

Outside the door, David stopped.

"What do you think he wants to talk to me about?"

"I don't know, but I trust Rick McCoy, and if he thinks it's ok to leave you relatively alone with Cane, there must be a good reason."

David nodded, and opened the door. He and Jack entered, leaving the two guards posted outside.

Cane stood up when they walked in, and shook both their hands.

"David, if it were up to those people out there, you would be the next president," he said with a little smile.

David turned red.

"I am not, and never will be a candidate for the presidency, sir. I'm simply a man who wants to tell my fellow Americans what God would have them know so that we can again be a righteous nation in His sight. That's all."

"I know," Cane answered. "But is it, really? I've listened to everything you've said, and David, I believe in you."

Jack realized his mouth was hanging open, and quickly closed it.

Cane's sincerity was nothing but genuine.

"I believe in you," he pointed at David. "But, I've come to also believe in something more important. I have believed in God, but I also know that in my pursuit of a rising political career, I have placed Him on the back-burner for a long time. Listening to you..." Cane's hands dropped to his sides as he looked at David. "You reminded me of what matters most, and that isn't a seat in the White House."

David lowered his head.

"I love America, like you, and I want what's best for her," Cane said passionately. "I am willing to give up my candidacy if you would consider becoming president. I'll gladly help you in every way I can. I would even serve as your vice president. What do you say? Will you lead us?"

David lifted his chin and wet his lips. Jack smiled and put a hand on his shoulder, nodding at him in a reassuring way as he took his hand away again.

"Senator, I love God and my country more than anything,"

David's voice trembled. "But as much as I love her, I know better than anyone that I am not the one to lead this beautiful nation. If you believe in everything I have said, then there is no one else more qualified to be the president of this city on a hill than you."

Cane swallowed hard. His eyes grew wide and he blinked rapidly.

"I'll tell you what I'll do," David promised, looking from one man to the other. "I'll leave, right here, right now. I'll sneak away and go into hiding until I can leave the country. That way, when I'm out of sight of the people, you can go out there and tell them what you believe. They will see you and what you stand for. They will make you the president of this great nation."

Cane spread his hands.

"David," he shook his head. "Are you sure this is how you want it?"

David cocked his head and gave his little half-grin.

"Both of us need to do what's right and best for America. And now we both know what that is."

Cane strode up to David, taking his hand firmly in both of his.

"I will go back to the people tonight. And I give you my word, with God as my witness, that if I become president, I will govern this land based off the principles you have laid down from God's Word," he said, his voice almost fierce.

David gripped his hand in return, too overcome with emotion to speak.

Cane nodded respectfully to Jack as he passed him on the way out.

David stood where Cane had left him. Incredulous, Jack watched Cane leave.

"Who'd have thought."

He then walked over and stood in front of David.

"David, do you really mean what you said? You're really gonna just give all of this up? Slip away like you did something wrong? Throw away everything you've built up?"

David looked steadily at him. "This isn't what I'm here for, Jack."

Jack sat down, rubbing his face. "You...you are the most remarkable person, David Connally."

"Jack."

Jack looked up and saw to his astonishment, there were tears in David's eyes.

"I can't...begin to put into words how thankful I am that you decided to take me with you on that truck ride back in February," the young man said, his voice breaking. A tear escaped his eyelashes, and the sight of it broke Jack's heart.

"I never dreamed I would see America like this. Or that I would find so good a friend." He brushed the tears away and tried to smile. Jack slowly stood up, put his hands on David's shoulders and looked him in the eye.

"David," he said tremulously, "I'm glad our truck broke down in Florida, because that's how you found us. And I could never have imagined..." He fought to keep his emotions in check. "I never could have imagined what a fine friend you would be to me."

David bit his lips, his eyes red-rimmed. His face twisted in an effort to hold back more tears.

"David, you brought Ryan back to me. By having his same joyful, patriotic, compassionate spirit, and the motivation to change things and make them better than they are. Having the hope to see the world not as it is, but as it should be. For that, I thank you. Thank you for bringing me back my son."

A tear slid down David's cheek. Jack pulled him into a firm embrace, wiping the mist from his own eyes.

"You can take the world, kid," Jack whispered. They drew apart, and David lifted his chin. Never had Jack seen such faith and strength in a single person. It gave him courage. Hope.

"I will never forget you," David told him.

"Where will you go?"

David looked at Jack, but Jack knew he didn't see him. He was seeing beyond. Into another future.

"I'm going home. To start a new life."

Jack closed his eyes. "Then this is goodbye for good."

But David was shaking his head. "Not forever, Jack."

Jack clasped his hand in a silent farewell. He then turned to leave.

"Oh, Jack?"

David stood alone by the table. He was smiling.

"Take care of her," he said.

"Who?"

"America. Take care of her."

Jack smiled, nodding his head as he shut the door behind himself.

James wiped the sweat from his upper lip, then dragged the back of his hand across his damp forehead. Ducking to avoid another security patrol, he hurried between the parked vehicles, making his way to those belonging to The American Party.

"C'mon, Jack, where'd you park your stupid – oh there it is."

James scurried over and picked the lock on the driver's side door, his attempt successful on the third try. By now he was drenched in sweat, his heart pounding a crater in his chest. Any minute he would be spotted. He wrenched the door open and fumbled around, searching...

"Ah, there you are."

The area around the motor home was quiet, almost deserted except for the security personnel. James passed by Joseph Cane, who had been met by several secret service men on his way back from speaking to David. James smoothly glided out of the way and stood with his back toward the motor home as Jack exited the trailer and walked away.

Seizing his chance, James rushed up to the motor home, calling the attention of the guards.

"You guys, there's some protestors trying to break through the front entrance. Eli needs all of the security people on level one down there to help right away!"

They eyed him suspiciously. "Can you confirm that?" one of

them asked.

James danced from side to side, his face flaming red, his brain in a flurry. If he couldn't convince them to go...

"Look," he snapped, hoping his fear was disguised well enough as irritation, if you get on your walkie right now and talk to Eli, I'm sure he'll confirm me. Go ahead."

The guards looked at each other, now unsure. The one who had spoken took out his walkie in an undecided way. James tasted blood in his mouth and realized he had bitten so hard on the inside of his mouth that he had cut his cheek.

"Alright. But we're sending reinforcements back here. Somebody's gotta keep an eye on Connally at all times."

"How long before they get here?" James asked.

"Maybe five minutes. Hey, you listen to me."

James found himself fixed eye to eye with the burly guard.

"Nobody goes in this motor home and nobody goes out. Not until the guards arrive. Got it?"

"Oh, I got it!" James nodded, relieved they had not called his bluff. "But hurry, before Eli comes looking for you himself."

The guards stalked away. James was alone.

David was leaning up against the table with his back to the door, his arms folded and his head bowed. When the door clattered open, he looked up.

"James? What are you doing here?"

James didn't answer. His face was so despondent that David crinkled his nose.

"Hey, is something wrong?"

James was looking everywhere but at the man standing across from him.

"David," he said soberly, "you've been saying all along that each of us must do what's best for his country."

David tilted his head, seemingly a little confused by James' strange demeanor.

"Yes, yes I have said that. I have only said what God would want us to do so we can be a better nation."

CHAPTER 19:

"If the country does what you say, America will change forever. It won't be the same again," said James, even more quietly than before.

"You're right. This nation would be a far better place if we would just do what God expects of us."

David turned away from James as he said this. He didn't see James close his eyes and grip something behind his back.

"David."

"Yes?"

David was opening the mini-fridge, reaching for a bottle of water.

"You have to do what's best for this nation. But so do I."

He pulled out the snub-nosed revolver stuffed in his waistband, raising it slowly in front of him, aiming at David's back.

"I can't allow you to be the next president."

He pulled back the hammer.

Eli was overseeing security procedures at the front gate, but turned around when the two guards from the trailer came hurrying up to him.

"What are you two doing here?" he demanded. "Who's watching David?"

"What?" they looked at each other, stunned. "James Rivers just came to us saying you had called a security breach and need everybody on level one at the front!"

Eli froze. "James told you that? Is there anybody watching the trailer?"

"We left him there with guards on the way–"

Eli didn't wait to hear the rest. He took off running in the direction of the motor home, the guards close behind him. They had just exited the stadium area and could see the trailer ahead of them.

A single gunshot split the air.

"NO!" Eli roared, sprinting even harder. He saw a figure running out of the motor home toward the parking lot.

"Stop! Stop, you coward!" Eli screamed, but the man only ran faster. Eli took out his own gun, firing off almost his entire clip, but

385

THE SPEAKER

it was dark and the fleeing man was darting between cars. Unable to get a clean shot, Eli dropped his gun arm to his side, leaning over his knees to drag snatches of air into his burning lungs. The other guards raced ahead of him to the motor home, one stopping short on the steps, his eyes wide. The other guard looked inside and slowly walked in.

Eli looked up, regaining his oxygen, and hurried over. He saw the faces of his guards and pushed roughly past them into the motor home, unwilling to let himself believe anything until he saw...

The light was still on inside the motor home. A bottle of water had rolled under the table, the cap partly twisted off. Tiny red flecks speckled the front of the mini-fridge and the surrounding area. A pool of blood was seeping toward Eli's shoes. Nearby lay a small revolver, carelessly tossed aside.

"I heard shots! What happened! Where's David? Let me through!"

Eli dropped numbly to his knees as Jack fought off the guards' half-hearted attempts to keep him out of the motor home. Jack came to the door and stood stock-still.

"David..."

"The coward," Eli hissed, his voice wracked with pain and fury. "The coward. He shot him in the back. Wasn't man enough to face him even as his murderer."

Jack couldn't feel his legs. He didn't know how he moved them, but he suddenly found himself stumbling to his knees beside the body. He looked down and saw the blood on his own hands from bracing himself against the floor.

Eli reached out a shaking hand to feel for a pulse, but they both knew there was none.

"I have failed," said Eli calmly. His dark eyes were brimming with agony. He raised a bloody hand to his forehead, turning his wrist so the liquid wouldn't touch his face. "I couldn't keep him safe. This is my fault."

Jack looked down at the corpse. The hot tears welled up in his eyes. He stroked the soft, sand-colored hair.

"Please," he whispered brokenly, his vision a blur. "Please

CHAPTER 19:

don't. I can't lose both of you. Just open your eyes, David. Open your eyes, please."

He reached down and clutched one of the lifeless hands, still warm, expecting the fingers to twitch at any moment. The helplessness was overwhelming.

"Why?" he whispered. This couldn't be real. He was in a nightmare. A horrible, sick, twisted mess of a nightmare. All over again.

Eli knelt down on the other side of the body. He looked at Jack, then down at the blood.

"David," he said, his voice low and shaking, "I promised to take care of you, and I have failed."

Jack looked up at him, still holding the lifeless hand in his own.

"But I swear this to you, on my life," Eli vowed, "that justice will ensure your death will not be in vain. Whoever did this will never escape me. This I swear."

With that, he abruptly rose and walked out of the motor home.

Jack stroked the hand he held one last time before gently setting it down. Then he sat back on the floor, pressed the back of his now-crimson palm against his eyes, and began to weep.

"Are you certain?" Nathan Blaine stood by the hotel phone in his bathrobe. Behind him on the lamp-lit desk, the draft of his formal investigation report lay spread out in sheets.

Nathan's eyes closed briefly and he looked up at the ceiling, holding the receiver against his chest for a few seconds before resuming the conversation.

"I appreciate you telling me. I'll be in touch."

He walked slowly across the room, passing the desk and the abandoned report. Sitting down on the end of the bed, he stared at the wall.

"I guess we all knew you were too good for us, David," he said softly. He let his thoughts drift back over Jonothan's story, remembering David's life through the eyes of his best friend. He

387

closed his eyes and pictured David walking down a bare dirt road in the grasslands of Africa, a cheerful whistle on his lips and a smile on his face. He pictured a beautiful African woman holding a baby in her arms, standing at a bend in the road. Waiting for David. She saw him, and smiled, raising one hand in greeting. Then another couple was standing there beside the African woman, an older man and woman who bore such strong resemblance to David. David smiled even wider when he saw them, and broke into an excited run. He joined his family, embracing all of them with joy and tears of happiness. Then they all walked around the bend in the road together, reunited, this time, for good.

It was the second Tuesday of November. Election Day.

Joseph Cane stood in a fancy room by himself, gathering his thoughts together. He paced back and forth, his face sober. He stopped alongside a mirror, taking time to gaze at his reflection for a minute. But he wasn't looking to see if his tie was straight or his cuffs jacket wrinkled. There was something else in the face in the glass he sought, and he was afraid of not finding it.

The door opened, and Cassie Cane slipped into the room. Beaming, she walked up to him and as he faced her, began adjusting his tie.

"Well, Mr. President," she said, smoothing down the front of his jacket one last time. "Are you ready for your victory speech?"

"I think I am, Madam First Lady," he said gently. She kissed his cheek.

"Well dear, they're all out there waiting for you."

Cane looked toward the large door.

"Yes. And I want this one to be for David."

She took his arm, and they walked out of the room together, passing the a TV on the wall displaying the footage and turnout of the election.

"Well folks, this election has been called for Joseph Cane within an hour of the California polls closing," a senior reporter said. "In all my years covering elections, I've never seen such a landslide. We had a record percent of voter turnout this year. In fact, almost eighty-percent of the electorate voted today. This is the first time in half a century that a presidential candidate won nearly every state in the union the way Cane did today. Not only that, but it was a vast majority win for the Republicans in both the house and the senate. That's quite remarkable when we remember how just a few months ago, Joseph Cane and Helen Kennedy were neck-and-neck. This is certainly not something the Democrats will be able to recover from for a long time. The people have spoken, and America will not be the same as she was before.

"Just a moment, we just received a breaking news bulletin from one of our news affiliates in Chicago," the reporter exclaimed. His face was eclipsed by a different reporter standing in the windy street of downtown Chicago, who wasted no time in launching into his story. "It has been confirmed that James Rivers, wanted by police since the death of David Connally for his suspected involvement in Connally's murder, was this very evening gunned down as he was leaving his hotel in what appeared to witnesses to be a drive-by shooting. Authorities haven't yet commented on any suspects for James Rivers' death, but hopefully we'll find out something soon."

"A great man once said, that a country is only as great as its people," Cane spoke into the microphone during his speech. "Personal responsibility make a nation what it is. The peace and security of America depend on the responsibility of we who call it home. And it is our dear, blessed home. The home of the free, the home established by the providence of God. And that's why it doesn't matter what my agenda is, so long as we are all working together to build America up to be as great a nation as she once was. A nation founded on the principles of God."

Jack muted the volume on the TV in his living room back home. While Cane's victory speech continued soundlessly on, Jack looked down at the small book in his hands, smoothing his hands over the faded cover. It had been worn to softness by much use. There was a small bloodstain on the corner of the leather and the pages. Jack held it in his lap as he had done every day for the past few weeks, never opening it, only letting his hands drift over the cover. But today, he thought he was ready. He closed his eyes for a moment, taking a deep breath as he braced himself for...what? He didn't know. Then he slowly opened the book.

Whatever he had expected, it certainly wasn't this. Every page was underlined – doubly underlined – with tiny notes crowding each other out of the margins. Here and there was a splash of color from use of a highlighting pen. Jack thumbed through the pages, his emotions growing stronger with every turn of the leaves.

He stopped on a page where one of the passages was circled, an arrow drawn from it down to a little knot of words written off to the side below it. Jack held the book close to his face to read the encircled words:

"And I will ask the Father, and he will give you another Helper, to be with you forever, even the Spirit of truth, whom the world cannot receive, because it neither sees him nor knows him. You know him, for he dwells with you and will be in you. I will not leave you as orphans; I will come to you. Yet a little while and the world will see me no more, but you will see me. Because I live, you also will live."

Jack followed the arrow down to the bottom of the page and read David's thoughts he had written about the verse:

My life is in You, Lord, as is my strength. You will not leave me alone in my grief forever.

Tucked between that page and the previous one was an old photograph, folded in half. Jack drew it out and carefully unfolded it, holding it up to the light.

The first face he saw was David's, smiling brightly in the way he always had. Jack felt a lump in his throat. He looked at the other people in the picture: a lovely, dark-skinned woman standing beside David whose waist his arm was around, and her arm was around him. Another couple stood on either side of the two young people in the middle. The gray-haired man had his hand on David's shoulder, and the woman with honey-colored skin and a gentle smile had her arm around the shoulders of the woman standing with David. The background scenery featured a grass and mud hut raised above the cracked earth, along with a landscape revealing miles of grassland beyond. Far off in the distance, a spindly tree leaned toward the camera, and the faint outline of a hilly ridge peeked from between the low clouds.

"So there you are," Jack murmured. He saw some writing on the back showing faintly through the front of the picture by the light from the window, and turned it over. There, scribbled in David's handwriting, was a simple message.

I love you and I will see you again.

Jack looked up and saw the victory speech was over, and the news was showing a clip from one of David's older speeches. He quickly turned the volume back up, leaning forward to see David alive again.

David was smiling and waving to the audience, the familiar joy in his face unmistakable. They played scenes from him leading the rally crowds in song, then cut to a clip from the last time he had spoken on camera, at the Cowboys Stadium in Dallas.

"America is the only nation with the motto 'In God We Trust'," he said. "Because that's the only way to live, and in regard to America, only when the people of a nation bring themselves under God can the country as a whole be truly great and blessed. We have a duty not only toward our country, but to our Creator. To be a good citizen, one must first be a good person. But being a good person is not enough. We must give God our all. He wants the best from us, and we owe Him no less than that. America is a Christian nation. That's the base she was founded upon, and the only way she can remain the greatest country in the world. Freedom of speech and democracy are important, but serving God should be our highest priority. And obedience to God isn't for America alone, but the greatness, prosperity, and abundance of freedom and blessings can abound for any nation that trusts in the Lord! The Constitution isn't something merely handed down throughout generations because of tradition. It came as a result of blood, toil, tears, and sacrifice from the hearts of men who only wanted what was best for their beloved country: to escape tyranny and oppression, and forge a government of the people, by the people, for the people, that would be the blueprint for centuries to come. And the Founders knew it would be successful because the only truly successful political system in the world is the one standing behind God.

"God's blessings have been on America from the beginning," David said as the camera slowly zoomed in on his face. His voice rang with hope. "His hand can clearly be seen in our past. So take courage, because we have the richest history behind us, and the brightest future ahead of us. But only if we stand for what is right and for what is true. If we are brave, and place our faith where it belongs. Not in the government. Not in things of this world. But in God."

THE END

"Of all the dispositions and habits which lead to political prosperity, religion and morality are indispensable supports. In vain would that man claim the tribute of Patriotism, who should labor to subvert these great pillars of human happiness, these firmest props of the duties of Man and citizens. The mere Politician, equally with the pious man, ought to respect and to cherish them. A volume could not trace all their connections with private and public felicity..."
(George Washington, 1796)

Other Books from this Author

Reader's Favorite gives *The House* a five-star review.

The House by Lacey Deaver is a good Christian story from beginning to end. Cheri is a troubled young woman running for her life. She hides in a truck in Seattle and, after three days without food and water, she escapes from the truck in a small Texas town. Cheri has no money and no place to go, so as she wanders the town she is picked up by the local Sheriff who brings her to the "house" of Margret and Carl Hanna. Daniel is a long time friend of the Hannas and often stays in the guesthouse. Cheri is mean and angry at the recent development in her life. Margret and Daniel befriend her over time and slowly she changes. The strength of growing friendships and belief in God is the crux of this heartwarming story.

The House will make you smile and make you cry, but mostly it will keep you glued to the book until you reach the end. It is a very fast paced story and only took a few hours of reading to finish, but I was really sorry to come to the final page and leave my new friends behind. Lacey Deaver is a marvelous storyteller. She has spiced the book with just enough suspense, drama, romance and uncertainty to keep me reading with great anticipation of the ending. I absolutely adored each of the characters and the plot is flawless. This book is perfect.

-Reader's Favorite review   **www.ReadersFavorite.com**

Also available in E-book form

Reader's Favorite gives *Good & Evil* a five-star review.

Good & Evil by Lacey Deaver is an excellent book. Jack Krantz is the 'disbelieving in God,' mean man. Tyler Emerson strongly believes in God and always does the right thing. Jack is a very rich man and wants to become richer, even if it means destroying other people. Tyler is wheelchair bound and without means of income and believes God will provide for all of his needs. Jack has taken Tyler's wife, destroyed their business partnership and is now trying to evict him and his sister Elizabeth from their home. When Jack has an accident that comes very close to killing him, it is Tyler who visits him every day in the hospital, trying to convince him to accept Jesus or risk going to Hell. Though no one can see or hear the two spirits following Jack on his path of recovery, the reader hears the debate of who shall claim him upon his death. Each argument is backed with a biblical truth and each paragraph ends in a passage from a book in the bible. The ending was one I did not at all see coming, but was a perfect finish.

Good & Evil was very different in a very good way. I was totally caught up by both sides – liking one and being disappointed for the other. The story could have been a standalone but the bible quotes made it so much more realistic. I found myself wanting to help Tyler and witness to Jack because Lacey Deaver made it seem so real. Whether or not you believe in God, this is a great book, pitting good against evil in man and how it can play out. Do not pass up Good & Evil; it is an inspiration.

-Reader's Favorite review   **www.ReadersFavorite.com**

Also available in E-book form

Books from WVBS

–Searching for Truth Study Guides–

These study guides, written by **John Moore**, area great resource as a companion to the *Searching for Truth* DVD, or used on their own as a workbook. The material is suitable for individual study or used in any Bible class setting. The text follows the same chapter structure and is nearly a word-for-word transcript of the DVD.

The study guides include extended question sections, including a "Section Review" after each section and a "Chapter Review" at the end of each chapter. To close-out the chapter there is a "Digging Deeper" section, which includes additional verses on the subject matter that are not used in the text. The answer to every question can be found in the Answer Key section at the end of the book. Additionally, six teaching charts are included in the book. These 8.5 x 11 inch, full-color charts cover popular issues such as, "The Book of Daniel & God's Kingdom," "Where do we go when we die?," "Modern Churches Timeline," "The Ten Commandments?," Baptism's significance, and the Church as God's spiritual house.

English Study Guide   Spanish Study Guide

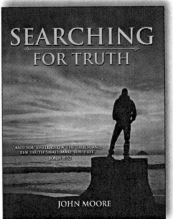

Over 120,000 printed!

Russian   Korean   Swahili

Also available in E-book form

Reader's Favorite gives *Transformed: A Spiritual Journey* a four-star review.

Transformed: A Spiritual Journey by Lance Mosher is a profound and inspirational book that documents the important events of the author's life. This spiritual autobiography is peppered with events in life, topics of conversation, and dialogues that speak about the author's emotional and intellectual struggles. The book shows the providence of God and will help readers with open minds to wrestle with themselves and the Lord. The book has spiritual answers to many questions that are already in the minds of readers, and will convince readers about the truths that exist in their beliefs. The book teaches readers to love and respect God, pray regularly, and lead a clean and good life.

The book is uplifting and helpful to all those who want to contemplate the teachings in their lives and the entire essence of their existence. The author's simple and succinct style makes it easy for readers to connect with what he is trying to convey. The author pulls readers into his world and many of his experiences are relatable. The book helps transform many readers, where the truth will set them free instead of debates, opinions or speculations.

God's presence is again reiterated through the author's words and he does an excellent job by helping readers understand Jesus Christ. This thought provoking book is definitely a good guide for all those readers who are trying to understand the Bible and the Lord in a better way.

-Readers' Favorite review   **www.ReadersFavorite.com**

Also available in E-book form

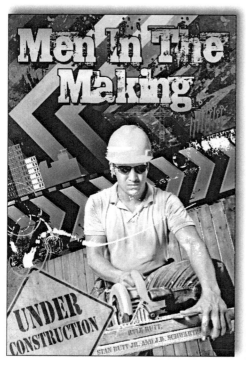

Reader's Favorite gives *Men in the Making* a **four-star review.**

In Men in the Making, authors Kyle Butt, Stan Butt Jr., and JD Schwartz talk to young teenage boys about what it means to grow from adolescence into manhood based on God's biblical standards. They candidly and creatively address such topics as how to choose proper role models, why a godly man should defend the weak, ways to show honor to elders and other adults, how to get along with your parents, winning the battle against sexual temptation and, most importantly, how to choose the right woman to marry and spend the rest of your life with - all this from a Christian perspective. The added bonus to the book was that the authors listed links at the end of each chapter that take you to other sites where you can receive instruction on various moral dilemmas, also all from a Christian perspective. This addition alone makes the book a valuable resource long after the last page is turned.

I read Kyle Butt, Stan Butt Jr., and JD Schwartz's book from the perspective of a Christian parent who is also well versed in the scriptures. I read it with a critical eye, checking to see whether the authors' doctrine was sound. The question in my mind during the entire time was: would I allow my teenager to receive these three men's biblical instruction? The answer is a resounding yes. Kyle Butt, Stan Butt Jr., and JD Schwartz's conversational tone came across to me as a couple of big brothers sitting around the campfire with some young men and 'keeping it real' about girls, life, and God. I would definitely recommend this book to my teenager and to parents and youth leaders looking for ways to approach these delicate subjects with their teenage boys.

-Reader's Favorite review   **www.ReadersFavorite.com**

Also available in E-book form